THE UNDEAD

DA

R. R. Haywood

Disclaimer: This is a work of fiction. All characters and events, unless those clearly in the public domain, are fictitious, and any resemblance to actual persons, living, dead (or undead), is purely coincidental.

It recognises Howie. It knows who this man is. So many hosts have been cut down because of this man. Tens of thousands were sent against him to stop his needless culling but they failed. Darren was allowed to retain intelligence and still he failed. Everything the infection has done to take Howie has failed.

All over the world the infection mutates, evolves, turns and changes. With every passing day it accelerates in its understanding of the human mind, body and ultimately the brain; the muscle that is so incredibly powerful. More so than any other life form ever known.

The capabilities of the human brain are staggering. This species are barely out of infant steps in terms of what they would progress too. But that would take thousands of years and the infection doesn't have thousands of years.

All it has is now. Time does not exist to the infection. Time is a thing used by mankind as a measuring gauge against the history of their race and a way to divide the day and night into zones. The infection understands what time is. From the collective intelligence taken from the hosts it understands the concept of time, and then discounts it.

All that is. All that has been. All that ever will be.

Is now.

The infection knows without conscious thought, that there are many potential hosts left. It also knows that of those left, very few are the same as Howie. Only a handful of the potential hosts have his ability, but those few cause untold damage to the survivability of the infection.

The other survivors flock to them. They gather round them and fight back with such passion. They die for those few; laying down their lives in great numbers just so those few can stay alive.

As with time, the infection understands the concept of sacrifice. It sacrifices uncountable numbers of hosts to keep progressing.

But what the infection does not know, is what makes those few so different. Despite the billions of lives it has taken, it has yet to take one that has the ability of Howie.

There are men and women who are faster and stronger than those special few. Intelligence is not the factor as host bodies with incredible high levels of intelligence have been taken, but they lack what Howie and his type have.

All the infection knows is what happens when it sends the hosts against them. The hosts feel fear. No matter what chemicals are pumped through the host systems. Regardless of how violent or deranged it makes those hosts they still have fear.

Why?

What does Howie and his kind have that makes the hosts react like this? Where does that power come from?

It isn't something born from gender or race. The infection knows that those few are men and women of all races.

Without being inside them, without examining the cell structure, the DNA, the gene pool, without surging through the brain it cannot comprehend why they are different.

Force failed, but now there is another way and one of those special few is about to be taken. No violence will be used. No damage will be inflicted on the body or brain, because it will be done willingly.

The infection grew in cunning and stealth, allowing Marcy to act as she wished with barely a hint of control.

The infection had learnt what chemicals to pump into the host body to drive it faster and heighten their levels of aggression and violence. But there are other chemicals. Chemicals that work just as strong but in different ways.

Pheromones. The scent secreted by the body so subtly they are not noticed but the effect can be far stronger than anything else. The infection knows organisms such as Ants use trails of pheromones to communicate. Female animals produce scent when in season which drives the male animal crazy with lust.

Ultimately the human is just another animal, a far more complex being but still an animal. And the male of the species will react the same as the rest.

Howie and his group will be taken. Without injury. Without pain. They will be taken and examined.

Tonight.

One

Day Thirteen

Wednesday

My head spins with a dull ache that pounds through my skull. I can’t think straight. Words become meaningless. Lust so powerful I want to tear her clothes off right now.

My thumb in the corner of her mouth slides in. She licks the end, flicking her hot wet tongue over the end of my digit. Low groans escape from my throat as I start to swell. Her hand grips my thigh, kneading and rubbing, slowly getting higher.

So beautiful, so perfectly beautiful. She is the one for me. Above all else she is the one I have to be with. I’m drawn to her stronger than anything else in my entire life. Nothing in my head apart from right now and feeling her so close.

Our cheeks rub, gently she nuzzles and nips my ear lobe, sending electric currents rippling down my spine.

Never in my life have I felt so turned on. The charged hot air, the sultry night, waves gently lapping at the shore, moonlight framing her perfect face. Lips so full and ready to be kissed. The sweep of her neck, long and elegant. The shape of her slender shoulders. My hands move down her face, feeling the majesty of her body. Down her arms I brush my fingertips lightly.

She shivers with pleasure, a low quavering sound that excites me.

My breathing increases, heart hammering in my chest. Mouth dry with desire. I push into her, a rough movement that takes her from the sitting to lying position. On top of her I let my hands run all over her body. Moaning she starts to writhe, wrapping her arms round my back to pull me in closer. Face to face and staring down, her legs open and I move into position. Still fully clothed but the pain of denial just increases the tension.

Grinding against each other, groins connected. If we were naked I would be inside her right now and I know that will happen. I want that to happen more than anything. To take her would be certain death but I don’t care. It doesn't matter. We’ll be together and that’s all that counts.

She grabs one of my hands and forces it to her breasts, pushing my grip so I knead and rub the soft mound. I start to lift her top, sliding my hand under the thin material of her t-shirt and pushing it up over her tanned stomach.

Arching her back she moans again as my hands touch her naked skin. She lifts slightly and helps me pull the top off. I drop down, our lips so close. We writhe and grind. Passion building with every passing second. We roll across the narrow beach, limbs entwining, hands grasping and holding each other. Her mouth finds my neck and starts kissing, licking and gently nipping. I am helpless. Unable to stop. The force of my lust is so incredible. I would kill to be with her. I would kill anything to be able to keep going.

April watches Cookey through half closed eyes. The heavy hoods hanging low as she watches the young man take a swig from his bottle of beer. Slowly she crosses the ground towards him, swaying her hips suggestively. He watches her closely, half drunk and full of lust. He takes in her form, watching the coy smile spread across her face. Never has he seen such a beautiful woman. Never before has someone so perfect shown an interest in him.

A dull ache pounds through his head, heart rate increasing. Flushing from intention he waits for her to get to him and wraps an arm round her waist, marvelling at her slender body and feeling the push of her breasts against his chest. She sways to the side, a slow dance starts. Legs become close, hips swing slowly. Groins pushing against each other. Everything else ceases to exist. Something about her is driving him wild with passion. His normally jovial face becomes serious, his cheeks flush, eyes narrowed and pupils dilated. She runs a hand up his arm, feeling the tight muscles across his shoulders. Gently raking her fingernails across the skin. He shivers with excitement, feeling himself grow. April feels it too and pushes harder against him.

Blowers and Nick watch the girls moving towards them. The most beautiful, devastatingly attractive women they have ever seen. The joking banter has ended. The atmosphere becomes charged with eroticism. The girls move slowly, swinging their hips, lips parting gently to lick at their full lips.

Both of them become flushed in the face. Not noticing as their breathing becomes faster. Eyes fixed on the women. Overwhelming lust building in both of them. The girls move slowly round the lads, draping hands across the defined chests of the young men. Fingers brush against buttocks. Nick and Blowers stand stock still. Letting themselves be touched by many hands.

Slender and voluptuous bodies move in close. Nick widens his stance, feeling the dull ache in his head as soft lips find his neck and start kissing gently. Another hand moves to his groin, rubbing as he grows.

Panting from the build-up of tension, Blowers feels the hands move across his wide shoulders and down to his narrow waist. Fingers running up the muscles of his stomach. The girls guide him away, gently drawing him from Nick. They coax and tease, touch and squeeze. He shakes his head at the fog descending. Something in him telling him this isn't right. This shouldn't be happening but powerless to stop it. They are so beautiful and so perfect. They want him. They all want him. Nothing can stop this happening.

Clarence sits with his back slumped against the wall, his long legs stretched out in front of him. Reggie was here a minute ago. Where did he go?

'Reggie?' Clarence bawls. He must have gone to get more booze. Yeah, that was it. But this bottle is still full. Clarence holds the bottle up to the soft flickering lights and looks at the level of liquid inside. Soon be gone so yeah*, we need more booze*.

That Reggie is a great bloke and funny. Clarence smiles broadly as he thinks fondly of his new friend.

'Took your time,' Clarence feels the body drop down next to him, turning to chastise Reggie for taking so long.

'Oh...sorry...' Clarence blanches at the beautiful young woman sitting next to him. He can't help but look down at the cleavage presented on display. Grimacing from the ache starting in the back of his skull he widens his eyes and tries to focus. She smiles at him, perfectly even white teeth and she looks gentle and loving too. She tilts her head to one side with a sad look. That look says it all. She knows. She is a woman and she knows the pain in his heart from losing Chris. She can understand the way only a woman can. Sarah too. Howie's sister so lovely and...

A thick tear rolls down his cheek. She reaches out and touches his shoulder. A caring gesture that he understands. She can give comfort where no other can. The huge warrior feels broken inside and at times like this it's only that soft womanly, maternal love that can heal.

She shuffles in closer, moving her hand up to stroke his bald head. Another tear falls as he wraps a muscled arm round her waist drawing her closer. She comes willingly, letting him rest his big head on her chest as he cries. But being so close to her invokes a different response within him.

He senses his passion growing. Drunk and full of pain he looks up at the girl who moves to straddle his lap. She smiles softly. He blinks hard, feeling the fug coming over him. Lust builds. His hands move to her thighs, she rises gently from the touch, giving a low moan and letting him know the pleasure she feels.

Gently she shifts her weight on him, giving him space to grow. She feels the pressure beneath her and starts to move back and forth. Tiny movements that make him close his eyes. His cheeks become flushed, his breathing harder. Her hands reach up to feel his thick neck, rubbing her thumbs across his ears.

'Good girl,' Dave fills the bowl with water and steps back, watching as Meredith starts lapping at the cool liquid. He watches the dog drinking. Taking satisfaction from the simplicity of her; eat, drink and protect the pack. That's it. No confusion. No strange ways that he cannot understand. Riddled comments that confuse him, things said or not said, hidden meanings that make him feel stupid and dumb.

Using his torch he inspects the wounds on her flanks, nodding at the clean cuts. Healing quickly but then dogs always do. They have to heal quickly or they would die in the wild. He knows she has a natural antiseptic in her saliva that will keep the wounds clear. With good food and clean water she'll be back to normal in no time.

Both of them tense at the movement behind. The dog turning round to stare into the shadows. Dave watches with a deadpan expression as a female undead walks towards him. She is very pretty with long hair but she is walking weirdly, moving her hips more than she needs to. Her top is pulled down too, showing the tops of her breasts off.

She keeps coming, her eyes fixed on Dave. He doesn't speak, he has nothing to say. Meredith watches her with interest, her head cocked to one side as though confused at something.

Dave watches the woman. She smiles at him, a big broad grin. Dave tries smiling back but it doesn't work and he stops doing it, reverting to his usual expressionless face instead.

The woman slows as she gets close, moving gracefully over the last few feet. Dave detects no threat so stands his ground, content to see what she wants. She keeps smiling which is weird as Dave hasn’t done anything to make her smile. She stops within arms-reach and stands there, staring deep into his eyes.

Dave stares back. Wondering what it is she wants. He doesn't blink or move. She sighs deeply and stretches her neck up, showing how slender it is as she pushes her chest out. Dave looks down at the dog and shrugs. The dog keeps her head cocked and sniffs the air in front of the woman. A scent. A distinct scent coming from her.

Meredith takes a step forward, sniffing harder. That scent is like the one she has when blood comes from her. The scent used to attract the males. This woman wants to mate with the man. The scent becomes stronger but the man doesn't react. He just stares at the woman.

The dog watches as the woman moves her hands over the front of her, the outer layer she wears falls away showing her naked body underneath.

Meredith looks up at Dave. Dave looks down at Meredith. The scent becomes stronger. This isn’t right. The scent is wrong. The scent is too much. Meredith understands this without knowing.

Dave stares at the woman, wishing Mr Howie was here to ask this woman to get dressed. The hairs on the back of his neck stand up. Danger close.

Danger close.

Danger close.

Something bad.

One hand already grips the handle of the knife at his back. He stares at the woman. She steps closer and smiles again. Meredith growls and shows teeth. The growl gets louder, fiercer.

Dave gets it. Realisation hits him.

Danger close.

With one step he has passed the woman, letting the blade of his knife whisper across her neck, opening her jugular and hears the slump of her body as he starts running.

A decision must be made. Go for the lads or go for Mr Howie. The lads are closer and there are more of them. But Mr Howie must survive above all else. So it has to be Mr Howie.

A furry black Exocet missile launches past him as Meredith opens her stride, galloping flat out towards the rear of the fort.

Trusting his instinct, Dave veers off, heading towards the lads. Meredith will get to Mr Howie faster than he can.

As he runs he pulls both knives and holds them flat against his forearms, he takes a deep breath, deeper than normal and roars his loudest yet, 'TO ARMS...AMBUSH....STAND TO...'

Dave bellowing from somewhere in the fort. I hear the words but I don't care about anything other than Marcy being on top of me, straddling my lap. Sitting up she pulls her t-shirt off and unclasps her bra. I groan audibly at the sight of her breasts. My greedy hands already kneading and squeezing. She grinds into me, moaning and rubbing. Gripping the bottom of my top she starts tugging it free. I try to help and lift my upper body free of the ground. The top becomes free and is cast aside. Soft hands rub and feel across my chest and stomach.

Marcy stands and fumbles with frantic movements to undo her belt and button of her jeans. Pulling them down she yanks one leg free and lowers herself back down. The jeans still attached to her leg.

Lowering herself down her hands start working on my belt and trousers. I try to help but we get in each-others way. She growls at me, animalistic and guttural, telling me to let her do it. Her face is inches from mine. I lay back and watch as she sinks closer and closer, lifting her naked arse up to start tugging my trousers down.

Still we haven't kissed. But we will. We will kiss as I enter her. That almighty pleasure will be doubled by the sense of both intimate acts happening at once.

Her hand grips my erection as she starts lowering herself down. Her mouth coming closer and closer, inch by inch. Lips parting, tongue flicking out. The tension is so powerful. A dull roar behind my ears. I feel aggressive and angry. I want her now. No more fucking about and teasing.

'Do it,' I growl at her. She grips harder, squeezing me as she guides my member. Must be close now, so close. Her lips are right by mine. This is it. I want this woman more than anything.

Closing my eyes I feel an explosive shock as we are both ripped clean from the ground and tumbled over the edge into the water. The cold shocking my system, making me gasp and thrash about.

Water sucked into my lungs. Panic sets in as I start to try and retch the salty liquid out. Kicking out I break the surface. Hampered by my trousers round my ankles. Pumping my arms as instinct takes over. A stubborn refusal to die. Breaking the surface I try to take air in, and feel the water surging up from my stomach

My vision is blurred, hearing gone as I retch and lash out. Sinking back under I kick again and break the surface. Stretching out, I feel the bank and start trying to grip it. Sliding off but I kick and get closer, using both hands to grip and start levering myself up. Puking sea water as I clumsily get my upper body out and start rolling across the bank, retching over and again. Eyes burning as the water ejects from my stomach and lungs. Coughing, gasping for breath. Something hot touches my face, lashing out I feel the wet fur of Meredith as she licks at my cheeks and eyes. I try to push her away but she gets her head under mine and pushes up.

'What?' I gasp, my throat burns from acid. My head pounding with pain. She barks at me, a high pitched yelp that keeps coming.

Staggering to my feet I get to the edge and look out. The water is still again now, barely a ripple on the surface.

What happened? The lust has gone. Instantly gone. What the fuck was I doing? I was about the have sex with her. Did I enter her? I shake my head trying to remember. A thick cloudy fog in my head. The whole thing like a dream. Did I kiss her? No, no I didn't. I was about to though. I was about to penetrate and kiss her.

The dog. Looking down she spins round barking at me, running back and forth to the gate. Where's Marcy? We both went into the water...

'STAND TO...AMBUSH...' Dave's voice roars across the night air snapping my senses back.

'Shit,' I try to move across the beach to reach my assault rifle and trip from my trousers still wrapped round my ankles. Cursing foully I pull them up, no time for boots or a top. Assault rifle in hand I make towards the gate. Meredith gives one last bark and shoots off, bounding through and into the fort.

Is Marcy dead? Did Meredith kill her? Maybe she drowned. Either way with her gone the hold she had over the others will be finished.

A thousand undead rising up and the lads are drunk.

Not good.

Two

She stands at the end of the street waiting for night to fall. Ahead of her is the long wide road stretching off into the distance. High walls on both sides. Behind her is another high solid wall with a single door wedged open.

She sips from a bottle of water, forcing herself to keep drinking. The heat is intense. It would be energy sapping but she hasn't allowed that to happen. She's worked all day getting this ready and defied the heat, refusing to succumb to the humidity. Drinking sugary drinks, taking water on and eating whenever she could.

And now it's ready. They'll come for her soon. The same as the last few nights. They'll gather whatever numbers they have left and come for her. They'll see her stood at the end of the road and think they've got her trapped. A single gate leading into the building behind her. No other way out.

A smile twitches at the corners of her mouth but the eyes are humourless.

So much has changed in just eleven days. That's all it is; eleven days since it began. It feels like a lifetime ago. She was a different person then.

The last tendrils of light fade from the surface of the road, bathing the area into deep shadows. Won't be long now.

She can feel the drying sweat on her skin, pulling it tight. Too much sugar today, too much crap food too. She drops down to open a rucksack, pulling out a toothbrush and toothpaste held in a clear plastic bag. After wetting the end of the brush from her bottle she applies a thick tube of paste and starts brushing her teeth. Relishing the instant clean taste.

She stops, holding her head to one side, listening intently before shrugging and carrying on. Working the brush into her mouth, scrubbing her teeth thoroughly. She spits the remnants of the saliva mixed paste onto the street. Taking a gulp of water she swills it round before jetting that out too.

The toothbrush and paste go back into the plastic bag. From the rucksack she takes her last clean top. Laying it on the bag she strips her filthy pale blue t shirt off and unclasps her bra to crouch topless in the darkening street.

Using wet wipes and water she scrubs at her body. Removing the stale odour of sweat from under her arms. Working methodically she pulls the bra back on takes a can of deodorant from the bag. She smiles at the colourful pattern on the front of the can. Remembering her previous life that was surrounded by things like this. She sprays each armpit, sniffing at the pleasant smell from the can. She knows they'll be able to smell her. She hopes they do, it'll make them charge harder.

She listens for a second, opening her mouth and staying perfectly still. Nothing. She stands up and unclasps the belt from her black cargo trousers, unfastens the button and pulls them down. Again using the wet wipes, she cleans herself, wiping sweat away from the creases of her body. With her trousers and knickers down she hobbles forward a few steps, squats down and pisses on the road, knowing she has to go now because there won't be time later, and no way she's going to piss herself. Not after the last time; that stank and caused a rash.

Finished, she wipes clean and dresses.

The last thing she does is pull her hair free from the tight bands, shaking it loose and running her fingers through the long brown locks. A hairbrush from the bag and she works the knots and tangles out, grimacing at the pull. She sweeps it back, re-fastening the tight bands to secure the locks into a bun, tight against her head.

The bag is re-packed and sealed. Finally she stands up, stretching the tight muscles in her legs. They feel taut and strong. Far stronger than ever before. Despite the tiredness and fatigue, she feels strong and fit, lithe and capable.

She checks the knives are still there, both of them attached to her belt, one on either hip, handles ready to be pulled. The pistol comes next, drawing it out, ejecting the magazine, checking the rounds. The top is pulled back, the first bullet engaged. The pistol is pushed back into the holster and made ready. She checks the straps on the black sub machine gun, ensuring they're fixed securely, the magazine is full and the safety is on. She props the MP5 police issue single shot weapon next to her bag then checks her pockets for the spare ammunition clips.

That's it. She's ready. All done.

Seconds go by. Minutes tick along. She taps her foot, pursing her mouth then checking her nails, wincing at the dirt under them.

Full night now. No doubt about it. Not dusk or evening, but proper night.

So where are they? They must be far off if she hasn't heard the howling by now. Not a single howl. Unless they've changed tactic and decided not to howl anymore. It's possible. They seem to be getting weirder every day. Moving fast in the day, working together, and the last few nights she's definitely noticed an increase in aggression.

'Come on,' she mutters, checking her watch. Listening intently, still nothing.

Sighing she drops back down and pulls a tube of Pringles from the side of her bag. She flips the lid off and grabs one out. Crunching it noisily. Sour cream, she shrugs. She would have preferred barbeque but those were eaten yesterday.

She crunches away. Pausing every now and then mid bite as she listens. Rolling her eyes before carrying on.

'Just brushed my teeth too,' she tuts. She grows fed up with the Pringles and puts them back, Once more using the water to swill her mouth out.

She checks her watch again, huffing with impatience. She hates tardiness. A sure sign of a general lack of respect and a poor work ethic. No wonder they're losing every night if they can't even be bothered to turn up on time.

A far off howl. A faint sound carrying on the warm still air. She looks up, smiling with satisfaction. She pulls the bag on, adjusting the straps and securing the waist band. She jump tests on the spot, checking everything is secure.

Yep.

This is it.

A glint in her eye from another far off howl. Wolves circling in the urban forest. She doesn't feel scared. She feels excited.

More howls. Louder. Closer. They're coming. Loads of them too judging by the noise. She detects the sound of drumming, of feet pounding the ground. Distinct in the quietness but still out of sight.

She nods with respect, hearing them but not seeing them means they've brought a lot. Good, it's about time they took her seriously. She's killed enough of them to earn it.

She shrugs at her own thoughts. At least this promotion to being taken seriously is quicker than the last one. Oh wait...yes that's right, the last one never came did it. No, she wasn't promoted but left on the office floor.

Still, where are they all now? Dead, that's where. Dead or quite possibly in that giant horde that's going to charge into view any second. Either way they are not here. But she is. Alive and doing rather well, even if she does say so herself.

Self-respect should be given. It's as important to know when you've done a good job as it is to identify areas of improvement. Yes, she can feel good about this. After all, that giant horde are coming for her, not anyone else. So that means she's pissed them off enough to get their full attention.

And if she can kill this lot too, then maybe they'll take her even more seriously. No, not if...the outcome is certain. She will survive. She will kill them.

Seven P's. The effort has been taken, the time invested, the work completed so there is no reason why it shouldn't work. Seven P's.

'Proper pre-planning prevents piss poor performance,' she recites to herself, smiling at the memory of the office manager who would say at least once every day.

And that idiot Clarke who tried to copy him. Her mood plummets at the memory of Clarke. The first death she saw. Eleven days ago, when she was a different person.

Three

'Are you sure you can't come?'

'I'd love to but I've got to get this done.'

'Oh come on! It's a beautiful summer evening and the place is crawling with wealthy men.'

'Don't tempt me...I would like nothing better than being there but I can't, I just can't.'

'Well what's so important that it keeps you in the office on a Friday night?'

'Contract for a new client...'

'Stuff the new client! Do it Monday.'

'It's got to be ready by Monday.'

'When did they give it to you?'

'Today at four-thirty.'

'Bastards...there's no way you could get that done in time...'

'Unless I stay on and work...Yes I know but look, this client is a big fish so if I get this done properly then...'

'Then what? Then you can spend more time at work and be even busier than you are now!' Just go in on Sunday and do it...come here and help me find a rich man, you should find one too then tell that firm to piss off...'

'I don't need a rich man, if I want something I'll do it myself, I'm not going to be some trophy wife to be shown off at the golf club every Sunday...'

'Yeah yeah...heard it all before....boring! I'm going to mingle and find me a hedge banker.'

'You mean a hedge fund...'

'Who cares! Stop being a boring accountant...As long as he's rich he can do what he wants with his hedges, call me.'

'I will, have fun.'

'You too!'

Paula takes the mobile phone away from her ear and presses the red button, ending the call. Friday night and here she is, doing a contract for another new *big fish* client. How many Friday's was this now? Too many. Far too many, and while everyone else was out enjoying themselves she was here, putting the hours in.

She grimaces at the cold bitter coffee sipped from her mug. The plain white mug that sat on her plain desk.

If a woman wants to succeed in a man's world she has to think like a man. Do not be seen as the soft maternal figure in the office and that means clearing your desk of all the photographs and items of sentiment. Work is a place for work. The desk is not an extension of your social life. If you want to be taken seriously then look serious.

Right now she could *seriously* murder that woman. She'd paid for the *Workplace Empowerment* course herself, and used her own annual leave to attend. The self-righteous tutor made it clear how she felt women should promote themselves. Not by slinky outfits and putting up with the arse slapping, but by hard work and a ruthless determination. Don't make the tea, don't tidy everyone else's desks, don't listen to poor old Donald talking about the problems with his wife, work. Work and work hard and be utterly ruthless.

Paula looked down at her pencil skirt, the perfect length of being just below the knee. The plain white shirt made her feel harsh but she also knew it made her look professional. No necklaces or heavy make-up, subtle earrings and her long brown hair was tied back and fixed up.

She knew she looked the part. She also knew she was highly capable with the highest work-rate in the office. Her clients were all more than satisfied with her performance and month on month she was well above target.

So why was she the only left in the office on a Friday night? Why were all the other staff, *all the male staff*, out having fun and doing whatever normal people do on Friday nights? That was it. She wasn't male. She lacked the necessary appendage between her legs and didn't play golf or squash. Maybe that was what she should do; start playing golf and squash. But no, that would just give them idea's and it was hard enough getting them to keep their bloody hands to themselves as it was without turning up at the local sports club and getting sweaty with them.

She noticed the photocopier and stationary cabinet had been moved to the far end of the office after just a month of working here. It was placed in the very centre of the far wall; in full view of the entire office and it was amazing how often it ran out of paper, meaning she would have to bend down and open a new box, remove the protective paper before re-filling the drawers. Knowing full well that over a dozen men were staring straight at her backside. The silence that came over the office floor whenever she did it gave it away, then the sniggers that always followed.

Funny but they never did it when Dominic was here. The regional manager worked from another office but he came in several times during the week. Tall with dark hair and a serious face but he was different to them and spoke to her like she was a person and always took the time to check she was okay. The office staff never did anything when Dominic was around but she also knew that to survive in the office she shouldn't rely on other men to save her.

It was a fine line between becoming ultra-feminist and challenging every bloke who even glanced at her chest or letting everything go and being seen as a soft touch that would just put up with it.

She'd learnt various tricks, like asking if there was something stuck to the front of her shirt when they kept staring, and making a point of politely asking what they were staring at, always with a smile of course. Then she'd learnt how to crouch down when filling the photocopier instead of bending over. Turn slightly sideways, legs together and reduce any kind of sexual profile they might have.

Her perfume was always carefully chosen as she knew they loved to use her scent as an excuse to lean in too close. So it was subtle and sparingly applied.

The raucous banter was mostly ignored and never joined in with. Normal office jokes were one thing but when it came to the sexual comments she simply moved away and carried on working. Of course she could always take it to the office manager or even Dominic. They'd deal with it, they'd have to, but that would be her finished and destined to a career on the main floor.

She looks over at the side offices, at the row of doors that marked the boundary from the main office to those private areas used by the Account Managers. That was her first goal. Become an Account Manager.

She should have got the last position that came up but it was given to Tim instead. Nice man and competent enough but his figures and targets were nowhere near hers.

You need more experience. Maybe next time.

So here she was. Friday night and she was getting that experience now. She could feel the unfairness of it starting to niggle her but she had to channel it, make it work for her. Once she was an Account Manager she would then be in charge of the office and things would be different. The photocopier would go back to where it was for a start.

Damn it was hot. The air conditioning was automatically switched off at five-thirty and with no air flow it soon warmed up.

She'd already undone the two top buttons of her shirt and now she reached for the next one, knowing that this button would expose some cleavage. But then she was the only one here so she was safe, safe to show some skin without being stared at.

That felt better, she wafted the shirt away from her body, feeling the flow of air circulate down the sleeves. She longed to release her hair from the tight bun but even though the office was empty it somehow felt wrong, that she should maintain that professional image.

She worked on, writing the contract manually. Importing the sections that applied to every client and working out the specialised terms as agreed. Everything was checked, then checked again and then checked more. To make a mistake would be awful. The office manager wouldn't hesitate to walk through the main office and inform her of what had been done wrong.

It wasn't that Paula minded being corrected, she knew that learning from mistakes was an integral part of self-development. It was when he walked through the main office and told her in front of everyone else, that was the bit she didn't like, especially when the room went silent and she knew they were all listening.

'Section one, parties to this agreement…' Paula paces the main floor holding the completed contract in her hand while reading it aloud, something she'd learnt from a writer friend who said he always read his stuff out loud.

With another button undone and her hair now pulled free from the bun she kicks her shoes off and feels the pleasure of her feet being free. The heat was awful, oppressive even.

'The client in order to properly conduct its business…' she went on. Feeling the hard worn carpet under her feet as she moved between the desks.

'…during the length of this contract, the accountant shall serve the client and perform any and all services,' she passes her desk and grabs her coffee mug, grimacing again at the cold contents. She drinks it anyway, knowing the caffeine will keep her going.

She slips into a broad Scottish accent as she reads the next section, mimicking the tones of Bill who normally occupies the desk next to her, 'och aye…I dunnae know mooch aboot ya businezz but ah dooo know aboot numbers,' she rolls her eyes at the speech he gives every client on the phone. She had no Ill-feeling towards the Scottish, just Bill. The way he made the accent stronger on the phone so he appeared more "real" as he put it.

'Och my wee lassie, why dunnae you fill up the photocopier and give us a wee flash o'ya arse.' She tuts with distaste and walks on, reciting the sections and sub-sections.

At the photocopier she rests the sheaf of papers on the top and glances back to the empty room before dramatically bending over to the bottom draw. Wiggling her arse that pokes out behind her she turns and presses one finger to her mouth, giving the imaginary work-force a nice show.

'I'm going mad,' she mutters to herself as she takes the contract up, about turns and starts heading back down.

Loud banging stops her mid-stride. She cranes her neck to listen. There it is again, a solid banging noise.

She drops the contract on her desk and heads back down the office into the hallway. She listens at the top of the stairs, waiting until she hears the banging noise again.

At the top floor of a four storey office block she knows the noise must be coming from downstairs. She starts to descend, using the moonlight shining through the large windows to guide her way.

Past the third floor architects offices, then past the financial advisors second floor and onto the first floor where the communal meeting and conference rooms were held.

The banging gets louder as she drops down. Firm and sustained. She heads towards the secure front door, seeing the silhouette through the frosted security glass.

'Who is it?' She calls out. The office was close to the town centre and on a Friday night she was always worried about passing drunks and teenage revellers.

'Paula?' A familiar voice calls. She smiles and opens the door, grinning at the young man stood there holding the pizza box. 'Working late again then?' He smiles, passing the warm box over.

'Yep,' she takes the box and slips the bank note from the top pocket of her shirt, 'Friday night pizza in the office...my favourite,' she jokes.

'You're here every Friday,' the lad comments, 'you must be earning a fortune.'

'You'd think so wouldn't you,' she replies with a roll of her eyes, 'trust me, I'm not.' She looks past him to the battered red coloured motor-scooter propped up with the engine noisily ticking over, the white top box still open with more pizza boxes inside.

'Ha, gotta be better than my job,' he grins, 'that thing's a bloody death-trap, indicators packed up last week and he still ain't got 'em fixed.'

'Ooh, well you be careful,' she says as he sorts her change out, 'just give me a fiver back,' she adds quickly as he fumbles with the coins.

'You sure? Thanks Paula,' he face splits apart from the enormous grin. She might not earn much but it was a lot better than he made, so a few quid tip was deserved, and besides, he always made sure the food was delivered quick while it was still hot.

'See you next week,' she smiles.

'You should get out more,' he replies pulling his crash helmet on.

'I will...one day,' she closes the door, shaking her head that life has got so bad she's taking social advice from a pizza delivery kid.

She stares at the lift, then at the pizza box and sighs. Trudging up the dark steps she wishes she had more time for the gym, these stairs were about the only exercise she got these days, and this pizza isn't going to help. Still, it is Friday and she would never dream of eating food like this in front of the other staff. Their greedy dirty nose-picking fingers would be straight in the box.

Back in the office she leaves the box on her desk, takes a thick slice of the pizza and once more resumes her pacing, taking care to hold the coveted contract away from the slice for fear of getting greasy melted cheese on it.

The shame of it was that Paula knew that by the time she'd walked to the end of the room, paused and walked back the first slice would be gone, enabling her to scoop the second slice on the way past.

She examines the contract, trying to read the sections with mouthfuls of pizza. Step, step, turn, pause, step and step, grab slice and keep going. Work, exercise and dinner all rolled into one.

On the third slice she pauses, standing slumped and wondering what Karen was doing right now. Probably outside a lovely wine-bar, cold drink in hand and laughing. Oh laughing. She missed laughing. She could do without the men, that sacrifice had been made over a year ago, she could do without the social life but the laughing. She missed that more than anything.

She stares at the greasy pizza in her hand, the slice hanging limp and looking distinctly unappetising. Then round at the office, at all the other desks covered with pictures of wives, girlfriends, children, football mementoes. She compares her sterile desk, functional and bland. Her eyes track across the room to the account managers offices. Getting there will take a long time, and even when she gains it that's still only the first rung in the very long corporate ladder.

It didn't seem worth it. A sudden realisation that she was missing out on life. Even the pizza guy knew her first name, that's how bad things had become. There had to be more to it than this. All those hours, all that time staying on and working extra, none of the guys did it; they concentrated more on getting on with each other than getting work done.

That was it. Sod this. It couldn't be a test because she'd stayed on every Friday for as long as she could remember and there were people in the office newer than her that weren't being asked to stay on.

No. This wasn't on. She being taken advantage of and she knew it. At the desk she dumps the pizza slice back into the box and picks her mobile phone up.

This was discrimination. It wasn't just about having your arse slapped or the blokes staring at your chest. Singling her out to constantly do the extra hours; that was discrimination. First thing Monday she will make an appointment to speak with Dominic and ask to be moved to another office, and sod the contract, let the manager explain to Dominic why it wasn't done, right after she's had her appointment with him.

She thumbs the screen of her phone to life, selects Karen from the contacts and pushes the green call button. Smiling she pushes the phone to her ear as she commences tidying her desk.

Tutting she pulls the phone away at the sound of the constant beeping sound, ends the call and tries again. Modern phones, too full of software and she knew this happened sometimes. She waits for the call to connect, frowning at the beeping noise when it comes again.

This time she looks at the screen, signal bar is full. She tries again and carries on pushing the sheets of the contract back together.

'Come on Karen,' she tuts again at the beeping noise. Why wasn't it going to answer-phone? Must be a mast down.

Sod it, she knows where Karen is and will grab a taxi from the minicab office down the road. She smiles for the first time in days as a feeling of naughtiness comes over her. Bunking off and ditching the work to go and do something fun.

Shoes on and she grabs her bag, pulling the strap over her shoulder as she picks the pizza box up and heads towards the door. She fumbles for the light switch and starts heading down the stairwell with a definite bounce in her step.

On the last flight down she pauses, hearing the beeping sound of the numbered key pad at the main door. Who would be coming here? It was unheard of for any of the other floors to have people working late. Unless it was the manager coming to check on her. A sudden feeling of guilt floods through her body, cursing that she'll be caught skipping out before the work is done. Then she remembers her earlier thought process and stiffens her resolve. If it is the manager she'll tell him straight and honest.

The door comes into view as she reaches the ground floor. The distinctive longer beep of the reset button being pressed, which is only done when someone gets the combination wrong. The sound of the reset button makes her pause again.

Who is that? Maybe she needs to wait before she goes out there. Could be a drunk or someone trying to break in.

Keeping to the shadows she tiptoes towards the door, watching the silhouetted figure through the glass, she holds her breath and stares with wide eyes at the longer beep emitted from the correct entry code being entered.

The front door bursts open, a violent jarring action followed by a gasping figure stumbling through. The figure grabs at the door and slams it shut, using both hands in an almost over exaggerated motion to force it closed. As the locks clicks home the figure sags against the door. Deep ragged breaths coming fast and shallow with low murmurs.

Paula stays quiet, not recognising the person and feeling a sense of fear at revealing her position stood a few feet back in the deep shadows.

Another sound reaches, something else above the noise of the course breathing of the figure. Something getting closer, running. That was it, the distinct sound of footsteps, of flat soled shoes slapping against the concrete surface of the car park outside.

'No,' the figure whispers and jumps back from the door as something impacts from the outside. A deep thud that vibrates against the frame making Paula jolt with fright and drop the pizza box. A shadowy form presses against the glass. Arms outstretched as it clings to the door, a low groaning sound that builds to a throaty growl as the figure inside starts back-stepping.

The person inside is male, big and tall with short hair. That much is obvious as he fumbles through his pockets with shaky hands. He pulls his mobile out and activates the screen, frantically pressing buttons.

'Clarke?' The name comes out of her mouth before she can stop it, the light from the screen illuminating the man's face. He yelps and spins round, dropping the phone and backing away towards the door.

'Who is that?' He asks in a terrified voice.

'Clarke...it's Paula,' she answers quickly at hearing his tone, 'what's happened?'

'Paula? Oh fuck...I...shit, oh my god,' his hands clutch at his head, pushing his hair back as he stammers in panic.

'Clarke what is it? What's happened? Who is that outside?'

'Call the police...do it...quickly,' he hisses. Still holding her phone she slides her thumb and looks at the numbered keypad.

'Okay...what's happened?'

'Just call the fucking police,' he whispers hoarsely.

'Clarke, they'll need to know why I'm calling...shit, hang on something wrong with my phone...where's yours?'

'Oh fuck...what...what's wrong with it?'

'Won't connect, it did it a minute ago...must be a mast down or something, what network are you on?'

'Oh god...' he rushes down the hall, pushing past her and into the main conference room. Paula follows, watching his shadowy form as he crosses to the big round table and grabs the receiver from the landline.

'Come on...come on,' he whispers with impatience as he pushes the buttons on the set, 'oh fuck...no...please no.' He pushes the lever down to end the call, then tries again, cursing with increased fear.

'Clarke? What the hell is going on?' Paula asks from the doorway. She tries her phone again, dialling three nines and listening to the beep coming back from the speaker.

'The fucking phones are all down,' he slams the handset down and moves to the end of the room, grabbing the second set and trying again, 'oh shit...this isn't happening...'

'Clarke! What isn't happening?' Paula asks again.

He slams the receiver down and again pushes past her, heading further down the hall to the staff lounge at the end. He pushes the door open and fumbles round for the television remote control, pressing it firmly while he points it at the flat screen mounted to the wall.

'Clarke...what is going on?' Paula demands.

'Outside,' Clarke barely looks at her, 'outside...everyone is going fucking nuts...like attacking each other...'

'What? Like a fight?'

'No!...Yes...not a fight but...' his voice trails off as the screen comes to life. The room fills with the sound of a news reporter speaking directly to the camera. Paula moves closer, drawn by the sound of the anchors voice.

'...Once again we have lost all contact with our reporters, the satellite feeds are down and it appears both landlines and mobile phones are now in-active. We do not even know for sure if we are still broadcasting....'

'What's he going on about?' Paula stares at the screen, looking the news anchor, at his tie pulled down from his neck, the top two buttons of his shirt undone, sleeves rolled up and a coffee mug on the desk. Even his hair was sticking up a bit.

'...There has been no update from the government, we are not aware of the military mobilising...the only advice we can offer is that you stay in your homes and away from public places, don't answer your door to anyone and do not go outside under any circumstances...'

'Clarke...what is this?' Paula demands, 'why is he saying that? Clarke!'

'Ssshh,' he responds abruptly, eyes fixed on the screen.

'...we know the event started in Europe with outbreaks of violence that have spread across every town and city within a matter of hours. London is exploding in violence that we have never seen before. Bodies litter the streets, the police ceased functioning hours ago, murder after murder is being reported...stay in your homes.'

'Murder? What like riots? Are there riots going on?' Paula shakes her head, confused and feeling that she's missing something.

'No,' Clarke whispers.

'...I cannot believe I am saying this,' the news anchor shakes his patriarchal head, *'but all we know are the facts as reported to us...people are biting each other, those persons who are bit then appear to die or become unresponsive within a very short space of time, those victims then re-animate and commence trying to bite more people...'*

'What the fuck did he just say?' Paula spits, she stares at Clarke, refusing to believe what she just heard.

'...do not let anyone with blood on them near you, friends, associates, even family members...if they do not respond in a normal way then get away from them as fast as possible and take all measures to stay away...'

'Oh,' Paula shakes her head as a slow smile forms, 'you bastard,' she chuckles, 'you knew I was working late...nicely done Clarke...'

'What?' He looks at her with a puzzled expression

'Running in here like this, oh no the zombies have risen,' she waves her free hand about jokingly, 'no offence but I've had a long day and I'm going...'

'This isn't a fucking joke,' Clarke shouts, 'what...how the hell....you think this is a joke?'

She shakes her head again, rubbing her forehead with the edge of her phone and sighing, 'look Clarke, this isn't funny okay...I'm tired and I'm going home.'

'He's a fucking news reporter,' Clarke shouts, 'how the hell would I make this up? Look...' He switches channel to show the standard technical error message displayed across the screen when broadcasting is interrupted. 'See...' He flicks again, showing more technical error messages, then more with just blank screens, then another news channel with the camera facing an empty chair behind an equally empty desk. That channel cuts out as they watch, the screen simply going black.

Clarke operates the remote control, navigating back to the original news channel. The screen activates just in time to see the anchor removing his microphone and throwing it on the floor before walking off.

'It's everywhere…I saw it…I saw what he just said, they're eating each other,' the words spill from Clarke, rambling and fast.

'What? Hang on,' Paula waves her phone at him.

'Fucking eating each other…oh my god,' Clarke pushes his hands through his hair again, 'the whole town just went fucking crazy…people dying and…and…then…oh fuck they chased me here…'

'Clarke just slow down, something chased you here?'

He nods, his head illuminated by the screen of the television.

'Who chased you?' Paula asks, still trying to comprehend what was going on.

'Ssshh, they'll hear us,' Clarke whispers.

'Who will?' Paula whispers back, 'who will hear us? Who is outside?'

'Not here,' Clarke pushes past her again, walking into the dark hallway where he stops and stares at the front door, he waves his hand back at Paula, motioning for her to be quiet before he starts easing himself onto the stairs and climbing up gently.

Paula follows, walking into the hall and looking down at the front door. Several distinct shapes move around outside. Figures blurred by the opaque glass but clearly distinct human form. Fear builds inside her, coupled with confusion and a feeling that she's missed something vital, like trying to watch a movie after missing the first half hour.

At the top of the stairs, Clarke heads into their offices and heads straight for the water cooler, grabbing a paper cup and filling before downing the liquid quickly.

'Don't turn the lights on,' he whispers as Paula walks in.

She stops with her hand stretched towards the row of switches, staring at his shadowy bulk as he takes another drink.

'Who are those people outside?' Paula asks after giving him a chance to drink. He's still breathing hard but that could also be from the exertion of the stairs and having to carry his fat gut up four flights. In his early forties, Clarke was one of the longest serving main office accountants with the firm, and also one of the sleaziest. Paula knew it was him that arranged for the photocopier to be moved and his desk was one of the closest to the front. He was also the one that reduced her spray of perfume as he was always leaning in to *get a whiff* as he called it. Yeah right, get a whiff while trying to stick your tongue in my ear and look down my top.

'They're not people,' Clarke replies dramatically, he glances back at her and breathes out. A long unhealthy sound that wheezes from his chest.

'Okay,' Paula says slowly, 'then what are they?'

'Ha, what are they she asks,' Clarke shakes his head, giving a humourless chuckle, 'you been in here all night?'

'Yes Clarke...you know I have, I was given the new contract to do...'

'Lucky you,' he cuts her words off, 'safe and secure in here.'

'Clarke please...please tell me what's going on, what did he mean about people biting and dying or...'

'Exactly what he said...'

'Clarke!' She snaps and takes a breath, 'please...just tell me what you saw happening outside and who was chasing you?'

'You wanna know?' He asks in the same dramatic way, 'okay...we were sat in the pub having a few drinks, this bloke runs in covered in blood and collapses on the floor. Everyone screams and we all rush over to help him...someone starts doing CPR as he stops breathing then he jumps up and bites the woman doing mouth to mouth...'

'Oh my god.'

'You wanted to hear it,' he says in a surly tone, 'so yeah this bird gets bitten and she runs off, her husband or boyfriend or whatever, well he punches the bloke in the face but the bloke just jumps on him and starts biting him too,' Clarke reels it off quickly, like it's a chore to explain, 'and it just went off, birds screaming and this bloke biting everyone...we all tried getting away and got outside but it was worse out there...'

'Worse? How?'

'Let me explain then,' he snaps, rolling his eyes, 'everyone was going nuts, like blokes biting birds and birds doing it to other birds...whole street was going...Jason got bit.'

'Jason? You mean our Jason?' Paula looks over at Jason's desk, thinking of the quietly spoken man.

'Yeah,' Clarke nods, 'on his cheek, tore a bloody great chunk away...We tried running but Jason went down after a couple of minutes, he was like rolling about holding his stomach and screaming...I told him to shut up cos he was making so much noise and people were running towards us, then he went quiet like he was unconscious.'

'What did you do?' Paula asks in horror, staring wide eyed.

'Fucking legged it, what'd'ya think I did? I tried hiding but then Jason got up and he was coming after me with some others...he had blood all over his face...some fella came out of his house and shouted for them to shut up and Jason just went for him...like attacked him and was biting him, they were all biting him...'

'Jesus Clarke,' Paula gasps.

He shrugs, shaking his head again, 'so I ran...but then they came after me again and I got to here, figured I could get in before they saw where I went but I couldn't get the fucking code in quick enough.'

'Oh my god,' Paula slumps against the edge of a desk, still holding her pizza box and phone.

'Kept trying to phone triple nine but it didn't work, just wouldn't connect...but that bloke on telly said all the phones were down.'

'Try these,' Paula shifts round to dump her pizza box and grab the phone receiver, she lifts it to her ear expecting to hear the normal solid tone. Instead a constant interrupted bleep come back. She dials nine for an outside line then keys nine three times. Nothing, just the same incessant bleep.

Activating her phone she opens her contact list and starts to dial the number for her friend, nothing happens, just the bleeping noise. She tries her mobile, pressing the call symbol next to names from her contact list. She watches each one as it tries to connect then cuts off.

Opening a text box she keys in *call me* and sends it out to everyone on her contact list. She navigates back to the messages and watches as each one is headed by the word *sending.*

'Anything?' Clarke asks after finishing his third cup of water.

'No, signal bar is gone now...landline isn't working either.'

'Told ya,' his tone snaps her head up, almost like he's glad to be proved right. In the hot confines of the office she can smell the beer and tobacco coming from his breath and clothes. The same office clothes he wore at work today. He must have gone straight to the pub and sat there drinking for hours.

'I need to think,' Paula replaces the handset and stares down at the desk.

'About what? We're fucked love,' Clarke replies with a belch.

'We can go out the back, the fire exit...'

He shakes his head again, wobbling his double chin, 'no chance...those things are everywhere and they're fast as fuck too.'

Fast for you with your fat gut, Paula thinks quickly. She crosses to the window at the end of the room and tries looking down. Tutting in frustration at the sealed frame and being unable to open one of them. Grabbing an office chair she wheels it over and clambers up, gaining height to look down.

The car park below is dark, with just a few street lights casting soft orange glows and making the shadows deeper and darker. Her eyes fix on a huddled mass by the edge, just on the cusp of the shadows. It looks like a pile of rubbish has been dumped there. A solid back mass of something.

Paula's heart rate ramps up as the mass starts moving. Human figures standing up and moving away, shuffling and staggering on stiff legs. Several get up and break off leaving the distinct shape of a person lying with their arms and legs splayed out.

Her breathing comes hard as she watches the figures start heading across towards the building. More come into view, crossing into the pools of lights as they too head shuffle towards the building.

Movement catches her eye. The body that was lying down sits up. A clear movement even from this distance. It slowly gets to its feet and stands swaying for a second before staggering out of sight as it follows the others.

She drops down and slumps in the chair, trying to make sense of what she just saw. Looking up she spots Clarke stood at the front next to the open pizza box. A half-eaten slice in his hand being stuffed into his mouth.

'How can you eat now?' She asks as she pulls her seat out from her desk.

'Cos I'm pissed, that's why,' he answers with a mouthful, 'what you doing?'

'Checking online.'

'Yeah great...email the police and tell 'em where we are, they won't do anything anyway the lazy fuckers.'

Ignoring the caustic comment, Paula presses the screen to life and adjusts her keyboard. An unconscious act done every time she sits down. Pull it back, then push it forward. Using the mouse she double clicks to access the internet, going straight to the accountancy firm homepage. Paula keys in Google and waits for the search screen to come up, tutting when she gets a message saying the network is not currently connected. She checks the internet access signal bar at the bottom right and finds it empty.

'Internet's down,' she informs Clarke.

'No it's not,' he swallows the mouthful of food, 'internet can't go down, it's like a worldwide thing...the phones are down so the internet isn't working.'

'Either way it's not working,' she adds, 'what do we do?'

'Do?' He laughs, spraying food over the desk in front of him, 'we can't do anything, we're fucking trapped and stuck here.'

'Is there another way out?'

'Nope, front door and the rear fire exit,' he replies, pushing the last of the slice into his mouth.

Paula watches him lick his greasy fingers while he sways gently on the spot. With the initial fear and adrenalin easing off he's left in a normal drunk state, slurring his words and swearing coarsely.

Panic threatens to grip her stomach. A deep feeling that bubbles and churns inside. A sense of sudden helplessness but also that she should be doing something, calling someone, telling someone. How did this happen without her noticing it? Why didn't anyone call and tell her? But then with her career dominating her life so much she had very few friends left and her mother would be out playing bingo.

Oh god. The thought of her mother sends her stomach plummeting to the ground. The bingo hall was in the centre of town. Clarke said it was everywhere, her mother would be out tonight, she was out nearly every night enjoying her life, which is something she kept telling Paula she should be doing.

'Oh god,' Paula feels vomit rising in her throat, her eyes sting with tears.

'What?' Clarke asks.

'My mother was out tonight...playing bingo...'

'In town?'

'Yeah at the Commodore.'

He doesn't reply but just stands there chewing on the next slice of pizza, noisily working his jaws, squelches and chomps sounding into the quiet of the dark office. He swallows the mouthful, another noisy action that sends a feeling of repulsion through Paula.

'You gonna say something?' Clarke asks at hearing Paula starting to speak then stopping.

'No, well yeah I was going to ask about your wife but I forgot...sorry.'

'That bitch, ha! Fuck her...stupid slag.'

'Clarke!'

'What?! I'm only pointing a fact out, I hope she got bitten on her saggy fucking tits.'

'Don't say that,' Paula replies in a soft tone, feeling a growing sense of unease at his drunken shouting.

'Can say what I like,' he slurs, 'bitch left me didn't she...fucked off with that...that...cunt,' he sounds the final word, emphasising every letter with a voice getting louder by the second.

'Okay I'm sorry Clarke, I shouldn't have mentioned it,' Paula says softly, trying to placate the angry man.

Paula winces as he lurches to his desk and grabs at the photograph of his children, holding it close to look through blurred eyes.

'And the fucking CSA take a fortune off me every month too, don't even get to see 'em,' he casts the frame down with a heavy clunk as it hits the desk.

'Maybe we should have a look at the rear door, it might be clear,' she offers gently.

'Yeah, yeah whatever...' he turns round to follow her. Paula moves into the darkness of the hallway, away from the big windows of the main office. Clarke shuffles behind her, belching and exhaling stale beer breath into her face.

They move down the stairs, pausing before the final flight and listening for any noises. Just the odd soft thump from the front door. Paula winces from the noise of his heavy feet and wheezing chest as they descend the final few stairs.

'Ssshh,' she whispers softly. He ignores her and pushes past, turning at the bottom and heading straight down the hall to the staff room they were in just minutes before.

She follows him in, holding her head aside from having to be in the wake of dirty fumes he trails behind him.

They stop close to the windowless rear fire exit door. With no other windows giving a view onto the back they have to make do with listening and the sounds coming through indicate the route is blocked. Groans, thumps and feet shuffling. Different voices making distinct noises, all of them low but varying in pitch.

'S'blocked,' Clarke tries to whisper but ends up speaking in a normal voice. The response is instant with an increased noise from outside. More determined thumps against the door, the growls throatier and closer.

Paula backs away, moving silently across the room. Clarke shrugs and walks behind her. Using the moonlight to stare at her backside as they ascend the stairs and head back towards their office.

Back in the office, Paula heads to the small cubicle used to make hot drinks, taking the kettle into the toilet to fill from the tap. Get him some coffee, that's the first thing. He needs to sober up and think straight.

She turns from switching the kettle on to see the main office is empty. A loud thump followed by a curse coming from the manager's office.

'What are you doing?' She asks, looking through the door at Clarke bent over as he rummages through the desk drawers.

'Ha! Fucking yes!' He stands up grinning, clutching a three quarters full bottle of whiskey, 'knew he kept it here.'

'How about some coffee instead? I've just put the kettle on.'

'Coffee? Fuck off love, this is the end of the world...I'm going out pissed.'

'It's not the end of the world,' she replies, still keeping to the gentle tone for fear of provoking him, 'we just need to wait a few hours until they can get a grip on it.'

'Listen to it,' he barks with laughter, 'get a grip on it she says...you heard the news, government ain't doing nothing, the fucking pigs have lost control...'

'Don't call them pigs,' she tries to soothe him.

'They're fucking pigs,' he bellows, his face flushing with anger, 'all of 'em...dirty fucking pigs...she can keep her new pig boyfriend and they can both have my money every month...'

'Okay...okay that's fine,' Paula backs down, moving away from the door.

'Did you know he was a pig?' He shouts as he stumbles from the office, 'a fucking pig driving a pig car...she left me for a pig...'

'Er...yeah I think you mentioned it once or twice.'

'Yeah well, they're all bent anyway...I got a fucking speeding ticket cos of him.'

No, you went through a fixed camera and then blamed him, I've heard this so many times now. She stays quiet, slowly making coffee. Going through deliberate actions of spooning the granules into the mug, then adding milk before pouring the hot water in.

She turns holding the mug. He takes a big pull from the bottle, gulping the fiery contents neat into his stomach before wiping his mouth with the back of his meaty hand.

Lowering the bottle he sighs, a long drawn out wet sound that pushes the air from his lungs, making him wheeze. A rattling coughing fit follows. 'End of the world,' he slurs after recovering from the chesty phlegm coated hacking, he lifts the bottle and takes another swig.

Paula looks away, disgusted at the sight. Her hands tremble as they clutch the hot mug, her heart racing inside her chest. Her mother, all her friends, everyone. The news man said it was everywhere, that it spread across Europe within hours. Every town and city was affected. Now she's stuck here with a fat aggressive slob drinking neat whiskey.

When he doesn't speak for a few minutes she glances up, seeing his face swathed in moonlight. Watching his greedy eyes fixed on her, he takes another swig from the bottle, keeping his gaze fixed on her body. His eyes visibly moving up and down to take her in.

Her shirt is undone. The top few buttons and her hair loose around her shoulders. Without taking her eyes off him she suddenly becomes aware of her own appearance. The air becomes charged as she imagines the view through his eyes. The reveal of cleavage, the shirt hanging out from her pencil skirt, the long flowing hair. Like something from a cheap porn movie. That's how he would see her.

'Where you going?' He sneers as she turns to walk off.

'Toilet, I need the toilet.'

'Shout if you need a hand,' he laughs.

'Yeah thanks,' she crosses in front of him, knowing he'll be staring straight at her backside. Out the door and into the hallway. She pushes the toilet door open and closes it firmly behind her, putting the lock over before feeling for the light switch.

The sudden glare burns her eyes, causing her to squint and squeeze them shut. They slowly adjust until she can view herself in the mirror. Nodding with disappointment that she was right. She does look like someone from a cheap porn movie.

Paula knew she was attractive and worked hard to avoid using her looks to gain approval. Relying on hard work and sheer determination, but now, with the top buttons undone and her hair cascading down her shoulders she looks the very opposite of the professional accountant.

Working quickly, she deftly pushes her hair into a bun and fixes it in place before tucking her shirt in and doing the button back up. Adjusting her skirt and smoothing herself down she nods and takes a deep breath, staring into her own hazel eyes.

Too many thoughts whirling in her mind. Everything that Clarke said about outside, about the fights and attacks, people biting each other, Jason attacking another man. Then the news reporter with his tie pulled down and walking off the set. Her mother being at risk, her friends she couldn't get hold off.

Clarke now getting drunk and becoming nastier by the second, and more than anything she was worried about the way he was looking at her, the leer on his face.

Keep him calm and keep your distance. Don't do anything to wind him up or set him off. She nods at her own thoughts, wishing she'd just left an hour ago. But then she'd have been outside and in danger, maybe that was better than being stuck in here with him.

Outside she crosses the hallway, forcing herself to adopt her normal work manner. Head upright, face passive and look professional.

'What the hell are you doing?' She stops dead at the sight of him stood at the back of the room. A pile of files emptied and dumped on the floor at his feet, his hands clutching at his groin as he pisses a jet of urine over them.

'Having a piss,' he hiccups, 'I've always hated these fucking files...that alright with you is it?' His voice becomes barbed with a hidden edge. 'Paula,' he adds slowly, swaying side to side as he directs the piss over the pile, 'Paula the accountant,' he sniggers, finding something funny with the words.

She moves to the cubicle and takes her mug, sipping at the still warm contents as she listens in disgust at the stream of liquid hitting the thin cardboard covers with a dull sound. He finishes up, grunting with effort as he spurts the last few drops out, making them spatter onto the covers.

'That's fucking better,' he heads back towards Paula, fumbling with his flies that are thankfully hidden in the shadows of the office. 'Have a nice piss did ya? You were gone long enough.'

'Yes thank you,' she replies dully, keeping her eyes fixed on the ground. He stops a few feet away, breathing heavily. Making her only too aware of his presence. The stench of booze, smoke and now piss mix in with the scent of the greasy pizza and the hot air of the office.

'You got changed,' he says in a suspicious voice, 'why d'you get changed?'

'I didn't, I just tucked myself in...' she speaks softly, trying to keep her voice as neutral as possible.

'Why?' He demands.

How do I answer that? 'Er...just felt like it,' she shrugs.

'Felt like it? Why...the fucking world is ending and you rush off to make yourself look tidy...what's all that about?'

'I don't know, I just...'

'I know why,' he states, 'you think you're better than me don't you...'

'No Clarke, really nothing like that, I just...'

'Yes you do,' he waves a dismissive hand at her, 'you've always thought it, we all see what you're like...all prim and proper...oooh don't look at my arse...oooh don't look at my tits,' he mocks her voice, speaking high pitched as he waves his arms in the air.

'Clarke I don't think like that,' she says quietly. Just the words *tits* and *arse* being mentioned by him set alarm bells ringing in her mind. A threshold passed. A step taken.

'I'm Paula and I'm better than all you fat old men...you can look at my arse...at my perfect arse but you'll never have it...'

'Clarke please stop...'

'Only Dominic can tap this arse.'

'What?'

'You and Dominic, everyone seen you together, fucking in the toilet and sucking him off in the office...'

'Clarke that's enough,' she snaps, making her voice hard and hoping he'll stop.

'Ha! You don't deny it though do you...you wait till I tell everyone...oh,' his voice falls flat, 'there ain't no one now is there...'

'There will be Clarke,' she replies quickly, 'everyone will be okay, the police and army will get control and this will all be sorted within a couple of days...we'll be back here on Monday laughing about and wondering who pissed on the files,' she jokes feebly.

'No,' he growls, 'there ain't gonna be no Monday morning here no more, s'all gone ain't it...fucked...everyone's fucked...'

'Oh I don't think so,' she smiles keeping her voice light.

'I don't fucking care what you think,' he barks in a sudden angry tone, 'you can stick what you think up your perfect little arse.'

'Okay, I'm sorry...I just meant I'm sure everything will be okay.'

'Perfect little arse,' he repeats in a lower voice, 'does Dominic like your perfect little arse does he?'

'Nothing has ever happened with Dominic,' she replies stiffly.

'I bet he fucks you in the arse doesn't he...you look like the kind of girl that takes in the shitter...all prim and posh in here, bet you're a right dirty slut in the bedroom.'

She grips the mug tighter, feeling trapped and very alone. Her senses screaming to run.

'Eh?' He asks. She doesn't reply but stays quiet. Keeping her head lowered and doing nothing to provoke him, 'eh?' he repeats angrier.

'No,' she whispers.

'No what? You don't take it in the arse? Fuck off...I bet you've had more cock up there than I've had...'

'That's enough,' she shouts, 'stop it...get a grip and just stop it.'

'Eh?' He says again, this time his voice is loaded with intent, 'get a grip? You want me to get a grip?'

'No I just meant...'

'She wants a grip does she...all that talk of fucking has turned you on hasn't it...I bet you were in the toilet touching yourself...fingering your wet pu...'

'STOP IT,' Paula shouts, 'that is disgusting...' She realises she's taken a step away from the cubicle and is stood facing him.

He exhales slowly and even in the moonlight she can see him sagging, 'sorry...I'm sorry...I'm pissed and...'

'Okay but please just stop, we'll get through this but...'

'I haven't had a shag for ages...Not since the wife left and that was over a year ago,' he takes a deep breath as her mouth drops open in shock, 'I don't want to go out like this...fat and ugly and no one loving me...' he lets the comments hang in the air.

'You're not fat or ugly Clarke but this isn't the time to...'

'You don't think I'm fat and ugly? Listen...we're fucked...those fucking things will get in here and kill us, we can't get out...'

'We've just got to wait for help.'

'There ain't no help coming...no one is coming...we're here and fucked...so let's go out with a bang eh?'

'I beg your pardon?'

'Come on Paula, me and you, I'm not the best looking bloke in the world but hey,' he grins, holding his hands out to the side, 'it is the end of the world.'

'No, please just stop it...'

'Why? Why not? You just said you didn't think I was ugly or fat.'

'It's got nothing to do with that Clarke, it's just wrong...'

'And you went in the toilet and made yourself look all pretty for me.'

Oh god he's taken it completely the wrong way, 'Please can we just drop it.'

'I've always like you Paula, you know that...your perfume you wear and those tight skirts, always bending over the copier and wiggling it about eh?' He takes a shuffling step forward. She takes a big step back.

'No Clarke, I'm sorry but no...'

'Eh?' He whines, 'why not? Fucking hell love I'm only asking for a shag, I'll be in and out quicker than a rat up a drainpipe, you won't even notice.'

'No.'

'Paula, just bend over for me, pull your skirt up and let me have a quickie...I won't grope your tits or anything, not unless you want me to that is,' he adds hopefully.

'No Clarke, stop, just please stop.'

He shuffles closer, his voice low and whining as he starts pleading, 'oh come on, I won't spunk in you or anything like that, I'll jizz in my hand...'

'That's disgusting, stop it...just stop...'

'Just pretend I'm Dominic, ah come on Paula, I haven't shagged anyone for ages, I'll blow my load within minutes...please love, come on just let me shag you.'

'Absolutely not and stop talking about it,' she speaks clearly, keeping her voice neutral.

'What harm will it do?'

'Clarke there are people dying outside, my own mother is out there somewhere...we're trapped and everything is going wrong, please I'm begging you to just stop...'

'And I'm begging you to just let me shag you, fucking hell Paula, just let me stick it in.'

'Please Clarke, please just stop.'

'Okay, no shagging...just a blowjob then...I can give it a clean in the toilet and I won't like you know...do it in your mouth or anything.'

'Oh my god,' she gasps with fear and frustration, 'no...I said no! Get it...no.'

'Paula,' he whines, 'just the tits then…just show me your tits and I'll wank myself off, maybe give one of them a touch…'

'Fucking stop it!' She shouts, surprised at herself for swearing.

'Just the tits, keep your knickers on…just the tits…show me your tits Paula and I'll have a quick wank and we can go out happy. My wife broke my heart when she left, I don't get to see the kids, I lost the house and the car…I can barely afford my rent…we're going to die Paula, I just want to feel like a man.'

'What by standing there in the dark staring at my boobs?' She asks in shock.

'Yes, I'm worthless and fat and ugly, I'll never get promoted or do anything other than sit in this shitty office…I drink myself stupid every day and hate myself so much,' a drunken sob bursts out, quickly cut off with a hard sniff.

'Clarke I'm sorry, I'm sorry but please don't ask me…I can't help you and…'

'You didn't see what I saw Paula, it's everywhere…dead bodies and everyone killing each other…please love, please just let me see a pair of real tits before I die, not just internet tits but real ones.'

'Clarke you're scaring me now, please don't.'

He takes a deliberate step forward, 'show me your tits,' his voice changes, the pleading tone gone, replaced with a firmer edge.

'Stop this,' she snaps but her voice quavers, showing the fear running through her.

'Show me your tits,' he growls, harder this time, demanding.

She puts her hand to her neck as though covering herself, stepping backwards towards the cubicle, 'Clarke...this is wrong, please just stop.'

'NOW,' He shouts, she catches a glimpse of face from the moonlight. The angry expression, set eyebrows and thinly pursed lips. 'Show me your fucking tits.'

She flinches at the sound of his zip being pulled down, with the windows behind him his form is silhouetted, his hands lost in the shadows at the front of his body. Material being moved, he breathes hard as he fumbles to release himself.

'Clarke...please...don't do this.' Too late. It's happening.

'Come on love, just talk to me while I do it...say something nice to me,' his tone softens again, breathing gets faster, in the quietness of the office she can hear the rustle of his shirt sleeve against his belt as he starts stroking himself.

She stays silent, utterly shocked to the core of what's happening. She wants to run and hide from him. But just the thought of doing anything that might set him off, might provoke his anger again. Right now he's masturbating just feet from her, but he's not touching her. Frozen to the spot she listens to his breathing, feeling repulsed and sickened but unable to do anything.

'Say something Paula...'

'I can't...please don't do this Clarke, you're a decent man and this is horrible.'

'Just talk to me, say something nice.'

'No.'

'What bra are you wearing?'

'What?'

'Is it white and lacy or black or see through?' His voice rasps out.

'No, just...no.'

'Tell me,' he whispers, 'come on just tell me...'

'No Clarke, I'm not doing this.'

'I bet it's white and lacy...it is isn't it...all white and lacy and tight.'

'No.'

'What about your knickers? You wearing a thong?'

She closes her eyes, feeling a knot of fear and disgust grip at her stomach.

'It's a thong isn't it...bet it goes right into your arse,' he makes a grunting noise, then snorts to clear his nasal passage. 'I know the window is behind me, you can't see me...but I can see you Paula, please...just undo your blouse for me...just a few buttons.'

'No,' she whimpers, rooted to the spot.

Her eyes fill with tears, trapped, alone and scared. *Get it done, get it done quickly*. She raises a shaking hand to her top button, he gasps with excitement at seeing her move. Her trembling fingers work at the button, she squeezes her eyes closed. Hating herself for doing this, hating him, terrified and praying this isn't really happening.

'Yeah...oh yeah...' he breathes out as the first button comes undone, 'do the next one...the next one.'

She stifles the sob, clenching her jaw and willing herself to just let him get it done, show him something to get him to finish quickly. She works at the next one, using her finger tips to push the material apart, showing him the skin of her chest.

'Oh god Paula, oh my god...keep going...please I'm begging you...do the next one.'

'Promise me you won't touch me,' she says with a shaky voice.

'Just fucking DO IT,' He bellows, his voice cracking with anger. Spittle hits her face. She flinches, jerking her head back. Ice cold fear grips inside.

Tears stream down her cheeks, silently falling from her chin onto the soft material of her shirt. Her lip trembles as she works the next button, praying he'll finish soon. She pushes the material apart knowing her cleavage will be on show now. A strange urge to look down, to see what he can see comes over her, can he see the cleft of the cleavage in the dark.

'I can see your tits...fucking hell...oh keep going, please...' he grunts, his tone back to being softer.

She does the next button quicker, determined to get it done as quick as possible. He hasn't seen a naked woman for a long time. He's drunk and will pass out. *Just get it done quickly*.

She pulls the material of her shirt apart, revealing the front of her bra, the next button and she tugs the material free from the waistband of her skirt. At the same time of feeling utter repulsion she wills him to be turned on so he'll finish.

'Yeah...fuck they're nice...really big too...pull your bra down for me, come on...' He steps forward, a quick deft movement that belies the size of the man. She jolts backwards, her backside hitting the edge of the cubicle counter. He stands close, breathing stale breath into her face.

'Almost....' He grunts, going faster,' his bulk blocks her path. His body shuffles closer. She can feel his erection against his hip, the movement of his hand. The fast breathing and stale air being blown into her face.

A rustling of clothes. She flinches, tenses as the hand gently touches the material of her bra. A testing movement. A probe to see the reaction.

'Stop,' she flinches, pulling away from him.

'Stay there you fucking whore,' he snaps, the anger instantly pouring from him. He stops mid-stroke, pushing her body one handed against the counter. His hand finds her jaw, grabbing it to hold tight, 'don't fucking move.'

She holds her breathe, craning her head away. Forehead knotted in terror she stays stock still as the hand starts probing further. Finger tips groping at her breasts. She feels the hand cup her, squeezing harder as his breathing becomes more laboured. His hand working faster.

'Yeah,' he gasps. One fat greasy finger slips inside the bra, yanking it down to reveal the nipple. He starts tweaking and rubbing it, making it stand up. She can feel the grease from the pizza being smeared over her, feel her nipple start to erect, an internal rage starts to build that her body responds like this. A physical reaction that she has no control over. Disgusted, repulsed with a growing feeling of sick building in her stomach.

'You want it...you're getting' turned on,' he whispers hoarsely.

'No,' she says through gritted teeth. The vomit starts to rise. She bites it down, swallowing hard and breathing heavy to force herself to not puke.

'Fuck yeah...' he keeps working the nipple, taking her heavy breathing as a sign she's enjoying it. Flicking harder, pinching and pulling at the same spot. She winces with the pain, desperate for him to finish. His hand working furiously now, surely he must be close, he must be nearly there.

'Please just stop,' she begs.

'You fucking want me, I'm gonna fuck you...you hear me, I'm gonna fuck you, turn round and pull your panties down.'

'No,' she whimpers, a tiny sound that shakes and cracks with fear. She gasps in terror, trying to push herself back against the cubicle, desperate to be away from him pawing at her.

'I,' he breathes hard between each word, 'am...gonna....fuck....you,' the last word is whispered in her ear followed by his hot, wet tongue darting out to lick her ear lobe. His hand drops to her groin, pushing the material of her skirt between her legs as he fumbles and rubs.

Smothered, trapped and feeling his penis driving into her hip, almost dry humping her. The heat, the stale breath, his foul odour, fear, terror, anger and she snaps. Lashing out with both hands to drive him back. He takes a step back, grinning at the prospect of now being allowed to get rough. He slaps her across the face, once and hard. The noise sounding out like a clap and snapping her head to one side.

'Plenty more where that came from,' he grins, his face sickening in the pale light. She takes a quick step forward and drives her knee into his genitals, feeling the hardness of her knee cap impact against the softness of his testicles.

He bends double, staggering back with his hands clutching at his groin, small gasping noises coming from him.

'Stay away from me,' she whispers, her voice low.

'CUNT,' he screams. She tries to run past him but he grabs out with one big hand, clenching the bun on the back of her hair. He grips and spins her round into the nearest desk. She hits it hard, the solid plinth sending shooting pains through her shin bones.

She feels a blow to the back of her head as he punches out, sprawling her over the top of the desk. He's on top of her, grabbing at her skirt, first trying to pull it down, yanking at the material. She kicks and bucks but his body weight holds her down. Bent over the desk she can hardly move. He gives up trying to force the skirt down and starts pushing it up, grabbing the hem at the bottom and forcing it up over her thighs.

She screams, a long ear piercing noise. He reacts with another punch, smacking her hard on the back of the skull, driving her forehead into the desk.

She can feel her skirt being pushed up, her backside exposed. He grabs at her flimsy knickers, thrusting his fat greasy fingers between her legs.

'You wet yet?' He hisses, his fingers probing violently for the penetration. Paula can hardly breath, the weight of him is immense, his huge gut pressing into her, one heavy arm pinned across the back, his legs pushing into hers, trapping her in place.

She gasps with agony as his finger jabs violently inside her. He pushes harder, driving his hand back and forth. Raping her with his fingers. His thumb angles round, starts groping for her anus. She can feel the fat digit pushing between her cheeks. She tenses with everything she has, clenching her muscles taut. He pushes in, unable to get inside. He hits her again, slamming her head against the desk. Still she tenses, locking her muscles up tight.

'CUNT,' he screams in frustration, not content with raping her vagina but wanting to defile all of her. Drunk on power, crazed with lust. No law, no police, nothing. He can do what he wants and he's dreamt of this for a long time now.

'Okay,' she screams, 'okay…you're hurting me…'

'Fuck you,' he roars down, pressing his mouth next to her ear.

'I'll let you…I will…please…' she sobs, begging him to get off.

He doesn't reply but works his hand harder, sending shooting pain through her whole body.

'Not like this,' she gasps, 'please Clarke…let me turn over, come on…let me turn over.'

'Nah, I'll fuck you like this,' he grunts.

'You can't see my tits,' she calls out, 'don't you want to see my tits Clarke…'

He pauses, his hand going still. 'Yeah, yeah fucking right I do…roll over and if you fucking do anything I'll smash your fucking teeth in, you hear me you little cunt?'

'Yes,' she begs, 'I won't…I'm sorry, I should have let you, you were right.'

Gripping her hair he eases back, sliding his fingers out from inside her. With his weight gone she gasps for breath and pauses then starts to move, rolling onto her side. He glares down at her, sniffing his fingers. She watches as he licks them, sucking on the one that was inside her.

'You taste of spunk,' he grins evilly.

She lashes out, hard and fast. A signal runs from her brain to her hand. Telling her not to use her fist. Telling her not to risk damaging the bones. She opens her hand as she slams the base of her palm into his nose, using the power of her wrist and arm to snap the bone with a dull crack. He reels back, hands clutching at his face, blood pumping out between his fingers. On her back she grips the edge of the desk with her hands and kicks out hard with his legs, driving her feet into his soft stomach.

He falls back with an audible oomph as the air is driven from him. Taking her chance she pulls herself free of the desk and runs for the door. His arm lashes out, catching a glimpse of her movement between his fingers, punching her hard to the side of the head. She spins off, staggering and losing her balance. He takes a step and kicks her stomach, his heavy foot driving into the softness of her stomach.

Rolling with the blow, Paula scrabbles to move as his heavy foot stamps down, narrowly missing her head.

Clambering to her feet she jumps back, moving further into the room, the escape to the door blocked by Clarke standing there.

His breathing comes out hard. With her back to the window she can see his face, the dark patches streaming down from his nose. He wipes the blood away, smearing it along his cheeks. The alcohol anaesthetising the pain.

Cold hard rage settles in her mind. The pain still pulsing from his fingers raping her. Her stomach hurting and tender. But the fear is gone.

'You're fucked,' he wheezes and charges. She doesn't run away this time. She charges at him, hardly believing what she's doing. She launches herself onto him, slamming the palms if her hands into his face again and again. He tries to lash out but she dances, ducks, weaves and moves. Hitting him again and again. He roars with pain and frustration, turning to keep walking at her.

Paula backs away, leading him on. He takes the bait, stalking her with murderous intent. She backs into the cubicle and reaches round to grab the kettle, launching forward and swinging it into his head. He goes down hard. Collapsing on the carpet.

He rolls onto his back in an effort to sit up. She stamps down, driving the heel of her sensible office shoe into his scrotum, rupturing one of his testicles.

Reacting in instinct he rolls away, screaming and gasping from the agony. Her mind feels clear. Clearer than ever before. A glimmer comes into her eyes. A dangerous smile twitches at her lips. She puts the kettle back on the side and turns it on before striding over to the photocopier. She grasps one of the heavy boxes of paper and lifts it above her head. Slamming it down onto the side of his face. Another one gets launched at his fat gut.

He screams and bucks, twisting and writhing as he gets pummelled by the heavy sharp cornered boxes. Clarke rolls and tries to rise, scrabbling with adrenalin to his feet.

She moves to the side of the copier and takes the heavy guillotine, the solid plank of wood with the strip of metal and cutter using for trimming paper. He crabs backwards, his back hitting the front of his own desk. The same desk she was assaulted over just seconds ago.

She swings the hard edge of the guillotine into the side of his knee. He screams and goes down as the edge drives into his flesh, tearing it open. She brings it up, holding it high above her head before driving it down with every ounce of strength she has into his elbow. A loud crack as the bone snaps. He screams with a high pitched wail.

Behind her the kettle clicks off, still warm from the coffee she made a short time ago and taking only minutes to re-boil. She grabs the handle and walks towards Clarke. In the darkness, with agony searing through his body he doesn't see her until the last second but by then it's too late. The boiling hot water is poured over his head, scalding his face.

He screams, thrashing his limbs then screaming as more pain comes from his broken elbow.

'You raped me,' she hisses in a low voice, 'you put yourself inside me.'

'I'm sorry,' he splutters, wailing in pain as he wipes at the peeling skin on his face.

'No,' she shakes her head, 'sorry isn't good enough…I begged you to stop…I pleaded with you Clarke. You *forced* yourself inside me…' she growls, the anger building up. She takes two steps forward, slamming the base of her foot into his face. Smashing his cheek bone in.

He slumps over, knocked out. In a rage like she has never felt before she grabs the guillotine and kick down at it, forcing the plastic guard away. It comes free far easier than she'd have thought.

She drops down beside him, grabbing his hand and splaying the fingers over the edge of the board. Breathing hard she pushes the solid metal cutting handle down, so the sharp blade is resting on the top of his digits. The same digits that forced their way inside her.

Standing up she listens as he starts to murmur, his voice getting stronger by the second. He comes back to consciousness, slowly at first. She waits until he tries opening his burnt eyes, screaming at the sight of his fingers wedged under the blade. She stamps down, driving her foot onto the handle. The blade bites deep, severing his pinky and the next one clean off. He jerks his hand back, tearing the flesh even worse. With two fingers gone and the rest hanging on by mere fleshy strips he stares with an open mouth. Imitating a goldfish as he closes it, then opens it. Shock hitting him. Even the alcohol now unable to blot the pain out.

Slowly he rotates his head, looking away from his ruined hand and up at the woman stood there staring down at him. The moonlight bathing her beautiful face. She stares at him blankly. Not a flicker of emotion. His fingers pump thick blood out that drips down his wrist and along his arm. He stares back at it, unable to move his broken arm to stem the bleeding.

Having already lost a pint of blood from the broken nose, his fat gorged body is unable to cope with the trauma. A tightening grips his chest. His over-worked heart goes into spasm. He gasps for breath. Every other pain forgotten as his chest explodes with agony.

He’s dead within a minute. Blood loss and shock finishing him off.

Paula looks down at his body and slowly turns her head towards the door, listening to the banging coming from the ground floor.

She just killed a man. Caused his death by her own means. His life is gone, just a fat bloated, ruined corpse left leaking juices over the office carpet.

Paula doesn't feel disgust, nor does she feel sorrow. He caused this and made it happen. Of all the choices he could have taken he chose that one. Chose to bully, threaten and force himself on her.

She walks to the window, grimacing at the stench of piss from the files scattered about the floor. Looking down she takes in the pools of light cast from the street lights and the figures staggering from the dark edges through the car park towards her building. In the distance of the town she can see the glow of flames from a burning building.

Paula glances back at the dark form of Clarke. The first dead body. Her first kill.

The first of many.

Four

'TO ARMS....AMBUSH...STAND TO,' Dave bellows at the top of his lungs. A decision made to alert the others. Stealth was contemplated; stay quiet and get to them quickly but by killing that female undead he could have alerted the whole horde that he knew what was happening. So instead he roars. Dave's huge voice bellowing through the fort. As he sprints across the ground he notices the undead silently rising up.

Clarence grips his massive hands round the girls narrow waist, staring up at her through misted eyes. The dull ache in his head is nothing compared to the feeling of lust coursing through his system. She leans in, gradually lowering her face towards his. Her lips open, ready for the kiss. With wet cheeks from the hot tears he cried, he breathes hard, waiting for the contact. Dave's voice booms out. Clarence ignores it, intent only on taking this woman and releasing the tension building so strongly inside him.

Clarence was always big. Even as a boy he was taller and broader than everyone else his age, and often bigger than those a few years older than him. Because of his abnormal size he was targeted by older kids who had something to prove, and he learnt to fight from very young. Either that or be constantly taking beatings. He had a warrior's heart and a deep sense of pride and loyalty. Years spent in the Parachute Regiment had instilled a cast iron discipline within his gut. No matter what happens, you always stand by your men. They protect you, they kill for you and they would die for you. The return had to be the same.

Despite the passion. Despite the lust. Despite the pheromones pumping from the woman which drove all of his subconscious senses crazy, something inside Clarence heard that *call to arms*.

The man ignored it. The man gripped the woman harder. The man wanted nothing more than to take the woman.

But the soldier listened. The soldier heard the call to arms. The soldier heard the order screamed with desperate fury, STAND TO. AMBUSH. Those words resonated with the soldier inside Clarence.

Mr Howie. The lads. Dave. They are the unit now, the platoon and his brothers. His eyes widen, face becomes contorted as the soldier beats the man back down. The soldier screams the orders and forces Clarence to react. The soldier makes Clarence's hands reach up and grab the woman by the head and the soldier makes those strong hands twist the head violently, snapping the spinal column, killing the undead woman instantly.

He launches the body away as he takes to his feet. The blood pumping through his body from the lust is diverted into his muscles. Rage builds. Fury grows as he scoops the corpse up and launches it across the ground into the small group of female undead stood in front of Blowers. The corpse narrowly misses the young lad but takes several of the girls off their feet.

By the time they start getting back up, Clarence has crossed the ground and grabbed at the woman draped over Blowers. The young lad snarls at Clarence for taking his woman away. Clarence simply pushes him away while yanking the woman back. He grabs her head, snapping the neck in the same manner as the previous one. Acting on instinct he powers into the women getting to their feet, punching, kicking and smashing them away.

Dave sprints past the massed undead as they start to stand. Cookey and April stood in front of him, Nick behind with several women on him. Dave veers ever so slightly and reaches out to grab a handful of April's long flowing locks. Turning as he passes he pulls April clean away from Cookey, sending her spinning off to the side where she sprawls onto the floor. A few more paces and he's at Nick, hands spinning as he slices the blades into the necks of the women.

Nick shouts with anger, lashing out towards Dave with fury etched on his face. Dave ducks and spins round to sweep Nick's legs out, taking him to the floor. The change in the women is instant. The gorgeous, sultry perfect women are gone. Replaced by undead with lips pulled back and faces contorted with violence. April on her feet and snarling at Dave as Cookey staggers towards her with a face full of lust.

Dave takes in the positions of the women, knowing both Nick and Cookey are unable to fight and will just hinder his movements. With a graceful movement he reaches Cookey and again sweeps his legs out, taking him to the ground as the women charge.

Nick starts to rise, furious at being denied his women. With one foot, Dave pushes him back down and slices out, ripping a blade through the closest throat. Spinning he kicks the woman away so her pumping blood doesn't go onto the prone lads. Cookey staggers to his feet and turns sluggishly to face two charging women. Dave drops, rolls and comes up in front of Cookey, both arms extended to push a blade deep into each throat. With a deft motion he steps back and again sweeps Cookey's legs out, the two women still pinned and held on the knife blades. He pivots to draw the women round, using them as a blocking shield to end the charge of another undead.

Nick roars defiantly, shaking his head and trying again to get back up. Dave doesn't waste breath in shouting but gently hooks his foot round an ankle and pulls it out, Nick collapses with a foul curse.

April coming in full speed with four behind her, going straight for Cookey. Another two going for Nick, and all of them ignoring Dave almost as if they know he isn't affected.

He yanks the blades free of the throats and with a flick of his wrist he sends a blade spinning across the small gap to drive deep into the skull of the nearest one going for Nick, perfectly judged and the impact sends her reeling into the second one, taking them both down and buying a few seconds to deal with the April and her mini horde.

One knife left. Five women. One drunk lad shouting incoherently as he tries to get back up. Dave takes it all in within a split second, takes two steps and uses Cookey's back as a platform to leap from, both gaining height and pushing Cookey back down. In the air and he again grabs April's long hair, jerking her off her feet as he lands amongst them.

One fist gripping her hair he spins and kicks, using his feet to drive them back away from Cookey. One thrust and one goes down. Wrenching April round to his front he sends her bodily into another one at the same time as stretching out to slice the blade across a soft throat. Knife reversed and he drives the point into the skull of the one April barged into. Knife pulled out just as quickly and he back kicks, slamming his foot into the back of a knee joint. The woman sprawls out just inches from Cookey. Still gripping April, Dave jumps and lands on her back, driving a foot into the spine at the back of her neck and feeling the crack of bone.

The speed of his movements renders April, as infected and driven as she is, unable to do anything other than be ragged about. The four are down and dead, only April left and one more getting up to charge at Nick. Still holding April, Dave throws the last knife and watches as it sticks in the face, the body slumping down beside Nick.

Dave snaps his hand back, forcing April to look at him. He locks eyes on her for long seconds, staring through her, staring deep, staring at the thing inside her.

'Please,' April whimpers in a sudden soft tone. The fury gone, the hunger replaced by a pleading tone, 'don't hurt me.'

Dave stares deep, his face utterly devoid of expression. She begs again, reaching out a hand to touch his arm softly. Tears stream down her cheeks as Dave looks for something, staring hard as though examining her, then he breaks her neck and watches the body slump before retrieving his knives and pulling the lads to their feet.

Running through the gate I stop dead and gawp at the sight. Every undead within the fort is stood upright and staring at me. Over a thousand figures completely still. Nothing moving. No sound coming from them. The flickering light from the flaming torches bathes them in a soft orange glow which just makes it look worse. Red bloodshot eyes, drool hanging from mouths. These are not the same undead that Marcy brought in. These are feral and wild undead. Hungry and about to be unleashed.

As one they lift their faces to the sky and begin howling. Screeching in a primeval roar as whatever hold was on them is broken.

'DAVE?' I scream as loud as I can but the howling drowns me out, my throat hurts from retching up sea water and acidic bile.

The Saxon. It's the only chance we've got. I start running across the ground cursing that I've got only one full magazine in the assault rifle and nothing else.

The second they stop howling is when they'll charge. These are fresh and hardly injured, taken with care by Marcy and her group. They'll be strong, fast and utterly focussed on destroying us. Trying to make the most of it I sprint as hard as I can. My head pounding with pain, stomach churning from the sea water and I feel weak and exhausted. Drained of energy. Making my legs move is so hard. I feel uncoordinated, my breathing is out of whack and my eyes start to water from the effort.

My head spins as I become dizzy and light-headed, my legs buckle and I fall to the floor landing on the hard compacted ground. Refusing to give up I force myself on, making my legs work. Get to the Saxon and the GPMG, that's all I have to do. You weak pathetic little man, get up and run. You've almost destroyed everything now get up.

Growling with self-hatred I plough on, only dimly aware as the howling ends. They'll be coming now. I've fucked up. I've fucked everything up. Manipulated and played like a child. Turned on by some rancid infected thing that lured me into believing I loved her. Lani gone and turned. She was amazing, a warrior but so kind and gentle. She held me close when I cried, she stood at my back when we fought and in the same day she died I tried to get with Marcy.

Absolute rage at myself burns through my soul. The lads getting drunk, Clarence losing Chris and seeing my sister, his love, cut down by Dave. All those people we saved, all those lives we lost to keep this fort, all of it fucked up for getting turned on by some fucking zombie.

I will reach that machine gun. I don't care if I die doing it. I don't care if I get bitten or killed, I deserve it. Everyone trusted me and I let them down. Me. Howie. Son of Howard. A fucking stupid supermarket manager out of his depth and out of control.

The growl becomes a roar as the anger at myself builds and threatens to blow me apart. How could I let this happen? What the hell was I thinking off?

The undead are charging in, moving from my right and heading straight towards me, blocking my path in thick numbers.

Cold rage has taken over. Like a hand gripping my insides and twisting them up. I raise the rifle and fire the magazine into them. Clearing a few away. The rounds do deadly work, dropping many bodies but the gun clicks empty within seconds and that's it. I have no weapons. No axe, no knives. Just a heavy gun I can swing about.

Frustration stops me in my tracks. They aren't running at me but coming slowly. Turning my head I see they are gathering behind me and blocking my escape. Surrounded and alone with no weapons.

Marcy. That fucking bitch. Using me. Tricking me. Luring me. Captivated by her beauty. Lani was perfect in every way and I let her die, and now she's one of them. Everything I ever loved has been taken by these things. We should have stayed in the Saxon and tried to drive out. We should have seen the outflanking manoeuvre they were doing and got the fuck out of the way. But we didn't. My vanity and stupidity made us stay and fight. Grinning like a fucking idiot as we charged into them.

We had everything we needed. Meredith and doctors. We had equipment to test her and find a cure. I should have taken action against Sergeant Hopewell and made sure the fort was secure but I failed at that too.

Stupid.

Pathetic.

Undeserving.

I don't see the undead now. Just a reflection of my own self, mirrored back at me. At what I am, at what I tried to be. *Mr stupid fucking Howie. Leader of the living army. Saviour of mankind. Heroic and strong.*

My face lifts to the sky as I scream in pure frustration, copying the undead in their nightly howl. Every ounce of my being is projected into my rage. Even the thought that I held Marcy in my mind when I was fighting makes me feel sick.

I'm fucked. Surrounded on all sides and they're moving in slowly. They know I can't get away from this one. Without Dave and Clarence, without the lads, without the dog I am nothing. I've blagged and tricked my way this far and finally, finally they have seen through me. Out-played, out-manoeuvred, out-tricked and fucked.

My god I hate them. I hate them more than anyone has ever hated anything. Nothing I have ever felt before comes close to this. It takes over, building with greater pressure. Panting for breath, my eyes fixed open and staring down at the ground. There is no being saved this time.

Fuck it. My fault so take it on the chin and go down fighting. Chris was the proper hero, he kept them back long enough for Meredith to get away and then, when he knew he was beaten, he took his own life. He trusted me to do the right thing and I failed him. He could be watching me now, shaking his bearded face with a look of sadness. *Howie, what did you do? You lost everything. We all trusted you.*

Lifting my head slowly I fix my gaze on the closest undead in front of me. Baleful expressions, low evil sounding groans coming from them. Saliva hanging down from chins, dripping onto their chests. Hands clawed, eyes staring at me unblinking and consumed with hatred.

'The feeling is mutual,' I growl back at them drop the assault rifle and start walking. Fists clenched at my sides. Unblinking and I do not feel fear. I refuse to be scared by these things. They are foul and unclean. I will not fear them. They will take my life but I will not go nicely.

Pure unadulterated loathing, fuelled by an incandescent rage that exudes from every pore of my body. Blood pumps into my muscles. My heart beats fast and strong, thumping through my body. I become aware of everything at once. Of all the faces turned towards me. Of the hundreds of pairs of eyes fixed in my direction.

They part and open a path. Perfectly straight and leading directly to the Saxon. As one they step back and wait. Their eyes are no longer fixed on me but staring up at the top of the wall, at the solitary figure stood there framed by the moonlight. Long hair hanging down and I would know that figure anywhere now.

Marcy holds them back and without hesitation I start jogging down the path. Growls become louder as they shuffle and make small lunging motions. It feels she is barely holding them. The hunger is coming from them in waves. Evil intention pouring from the huge horde. They inch in, desperate to go for me. Glancing up she waves her arm, urging me to go faster, telling me she can't hold them.

I start sprinting, running as they creep in bit by bit. The vehicle is just ahead of me. Marcy drops to her knees, her arms outstretched to the sides, she screams with a long painful sound that rips through the air.

Pumping my legs with everything I've got I reach the side of the vehicle. The undead block my way to the rear and to the front. While Marcy screams I start pushing them out the way, physically shoving and battering them back. God knows how she holds them back but she does. The scream grows weaker as I reach the back doors, clambering in as she cuts off and falls to the floor. The last door is slammed shut as the undead break free from the final hold she had and charge. Thuds and screeches as they impact on the vehicle all around me.

Scrabbling in the dark I fumble my way to the hole and climb up, racking the heavy bolt back and taking hold of the machine gun.

'TAKE COVER....FIRING...' I scream out.

'CLEAR,' Dave roars back, his voice coming from my somewhere to my left. Before I squeeze the trigger I glance up to the top of the wall. Nothing there. Just the smooth unbroken line of the wall.

With a snarl I pull the trigger and commence the slaughter.

Five

They come into view. A large solid wall of writhing figures charging down the street. Funnelled by the high walls and the long lines of flat topped vans parked nose to tail on both sides.

They don't think anything of it. But then they don't think. They just see her, alone and stood there, waiting to be taken.

Paula watches with interest, smiling as they get closer. She picked this road on purpose. It was perfect. High walls and one way in, the only exit is the door behind her.

And now, at night, without the street lights on, it's very dark. Too dark to see the thin ropes extended across the road.

The front of the horde reaches the rope, hardly feeling as they push into it. Held at waist height she knew they'd just charge on, pulling the rope along with them. Two days and several practise runs to get everything set perfectly.

The rope gets pulled along, unlooping as it's spooled out. The ends of the rope are tied onto razor wire, coils and coils of shiny new razor wire.

As the rope gets played out, it pulls the razor wire down from the top of the vehicles into the massed moving horde below. Solid continuous lines of deadly wire that slashes feet and cuts deep into limbs. The writhing mass starts slowing as they get tangled. The fury in them is so much they just push on, tearing themselves to bits in desperation to reach her.

The wire finally pings taut as it runs out, the ends fastened securely to the vehicles tow bars. In the dark, the things are unable to see what is eating them, what the thing is that is tearing them apart.

The front of the horde push on regardless. Mindless to the fact they are dragging the rope and wire further into the horde behind them. They screech in frustration, howling with violent rage. Legs and arms cut deep, veins sliced open. Fingers severed through.

The undead at the front are unaffected and push on. But then they reach the layers of broken glass painstakingly put down. Bare feet get sliced deep. Glass embedding into heels and soles. Blood pours from cuts that are made worse with every step taken.

Paula had planned for this, knowing the outbreak started late at night, when most people were in bed without shoes on. The *things* can withstand the pain but the body can only take so much punishment and blood loss before it starts to succumb.

Several go down from nerves being cut through, rendering the feet useless to the brain. They fall down to be cut even deeper by the glass slicing into their flesh. The ones behind them keep going, trampling their fallen brethren harder onto the shards.

The razor wire tangles huge swathes, rendering the ranks into a tangled mess that just tightens and cuts with every jerk and pull of their undead bodies.

Paula nods in satisfaction at a job well done. But it isn't over yet. The best is yet to come. She pushes her hand into the side pocket of her cargo trousers. Gripping the small plastic handle she pulls the flare gun out and aims it straight at the front ranks still getting cut to bits on the glass.

She pulls the trigger, watching as the flare bursts out the end. Trailing a bright light as it arcs through the air and disappears from view within the horde. She cocks her head to one side, waiting for it.

The woomph of the flames igniting is a solid noise. An instant reaction that bursts the road into light. The petrol poured over the ground from the ruptured fuel tanks of the vehicles may have dried somewhat but there's still enough left to cause a huge fire.

The flames scorch up, bursting high. The brightness so harsh she has to shield her eyes from the glare. The smell of burning flesh reaches her within seconds. The hopeless tangled undead with mashed up feet now being burned alive. Well, not alive, she muses...burnt undead. Who cares, she shrugs.

Paula watches the street, knowing she can reach the safety of the door within seconds. The flames die down as the fuel burns off. Just the clothing on the bodies left alight. A rancid smell of burning meat fills the air, not just meat but foul meat. Meat that has gone off turned green and started to decay.

The seven P's. She had planned for this and fastens the white mask over her mouth, securing the elastic straps behind her head. She also knows the heat and odour could make her eyes water, so she places plastic lensed clear safety glasses on and starts forward.

Not one of the *things* remains alive. All of them either burnt to a crisp or suffocating from the lack of oxygen as they lay writhing on the floor.

Gruesome twisted remains blackened and gnarled. Razor wire biting deep into part cooked limbs and roasted torsos. Bare feet cut to ribbons by the glass, those cuts and wounds then cauterized by the searing heat.

She reaches the front, taking care to watch for any crawlers. The MP5 secured round her neck from the strap and held ready.

If only she'd had the guns that night. How a little object like a pistol could have changed everything. Clarke wouldn't have come near her if she'd been armed. But then she'd never have realised she can fight back. She'd never have discovered her ability to kill without hesitation.

That first night she'd stayed in the offices, quietly hiding and waiting for something, but not knowing what it was. When dawn finally arrived she noticed the change, the sluggish movements of the people outside. Back then, she still thought of them as people. That mind-set had changed within a few hours. They weren't people, they were things.

Paula observed the shuffling walking. She watched the speed they moved at. How the heads rolled and seemed unable to be controlled. There was no cohesion or co-operation between them and no apparent communication either. They bumped and knocked into each other every few seconds. They were listless and ungainly.

Using the first floor windows to lean out and shout, she led them from the front of the building towards the back. The process took ages as they stumbled so slowly. The crowd beneath the window grew larger by the minute, as the things from both the front and back came to stare up at her. In the bright daylight, and only being a few feet above them she could see the injuries clearly. A mass of ragged bite marks. Red, bloodshot eyes. Blood and gore everywhere. Broken limbs, heads split open, large chunks of flesh torn away. Injuries that would kill or incapacitate normal people.

Leaving the office was easy. Running to her car was also easy. By the time the things had seen her break for freedom and turned round, she was already at her mini, climbing in and locking the door.

She aimed the car for the town centre, which again in hindsight wasn't the best thing to do as it put her in danger. But that short drive opened her eyes fully to the devastation. Bodies everywhere. Corpses torn apart. Entrails from stomachs laid drying in the sun. Huge patches of blood. Window fronts smashed in. Cars abandoned in the street and those things everywhere, staggering, shuffling, stumbling in all directions. Groups, couples and single ones.

The bingo hall where her mother had been was in the very centre of town, an area she couldn't reach because of the huge horde gathered in the precinct. Sitting in the car with the engine idling, lips pursed, eyes scanning the crowd she knew, just knew her mother was gone. An instinct made from common sense and what her eyes were telling her.

When her mother shuffled into view, a large wound on her neck and the same distinctive movement as the rest, Paula showed no reaction. Simply absorbing the view and nodding gently to herself.

She drove away feeling numb. The shock of everything happening so quickly was too much. Her own flat was inaccessible. Hordes and groups were everywhere. The sheer numbers of them were staggering. How so many had been taken in such a short space of time was incredible. Still dressed in now filthy, blood-stained office clothes she drove out of town, simply not knowing where to go.

The crying was done that day. Parked up in the country-side she sobbed and wailed. Beating her fists against the car. The unfairness of it all. The loss of life. The shock of Clarke attacking her. The self-pity was poured out and finished.

The woman that sat in the car sobbing slowly began to feel a change from the self-pity as a knot of anger started to build. Anger that her mother who had worked so hard all her life to raise Paula and should now be enjoying her retirement had suffered such degrading pain. Anger at the years of hard work and dedication not getting her anywhere. Anger at not being taken seriously. But one thing was sure, that feeling at beating Clarke was good.

This event was worldwide; the news reporters said that last night. So it wasn't just a case of waiting for help. There was no help coming. The end was here and thrust upon her through no fault of her own, and within hours of it starting she had already been humiliated and abused.

Determination settled within Paula, that she wouldn't allow that to ever happen again, and that feeling of defeating Clarke; it wasn't the thirst for violence but the sense of victory. Defeating a stronger force by using intelligence and cunning. And the violence didn't have the effect she thought it would have. She didn't feel sickened or disgusted by it. It was natural and done from necessity and if she was to survive this, she would have to be prepared to do it again.

One thought evolved into another, processes and images flashing quickly through her mind. An inner strength was forming, one that accepted what had happened and now chose to deal with it.

Her mother was gone, she had seen that first hand. That would also mean the rest of her family was taken too, and probably everyone she had ever known. If any of them were still alive she had no way of contacting them.

Alone she would be vulnerable. Men like Clarke would take whatever opportunity they had to take what they wanted. There was no law anymore, no one to rescue her.

The very thought of being rescued triggered a defiance in her. Why should she need rescuing? She was more than capable of defending herself, not just defending herself but attacking those things and killing them. The more she thought about it the angrier she became. Anger at the years she had spent working so hard and sacrificing so much of her life and for what? So this could happen.

For the next few hours she sat in her car with thoughts pouring through her mind. A realisation formed that was first dismissed as fanciful and stupid; fight back and kill them. It was ridiculous and dangerous. No, what she should do is find somewhere to hide, find other people and have safety in numbers.

But the thought of being with others depressed her soul instantly. What Clarke had done sickened her with disgust. The weeks, months and years being kept on the office floor, the endless comments and being seen as a sexual object, a lesser life form. What Clarke did is the same as what many other men will do given the chance. The feeling of being helpless, the terror that gripped her when Clarke defiled her with his fingers, of being forced to give something that was hers.

The longer she sat there the more she realised she could fight back. She could start killing them. Why run and hide. Be strong and never let anything like that happen again.

In the office her workload was far greater than anyone else's and she had developed methods of managing that workload, strategies of prioritising and developing coping mechanisms.

When faced with multiple projects that required an enhanced focus she used varying techniques to break the tasks down. What was essential? What was secondary? What were the objectives and the aims? What would she need to carry out those objectives? How would they be done?

The task in front of her was the same as any other; something that needed to be accomplished and with the right planning it could be executed the same as any other project.

As with many other times when faced with a complex situation, she reached for her bag to pull out the notepad and pen.

Tapping the pen against the notepad she thought about Maslow's hierarchy of needs theory and the five elements that formed his triangle; each one of the elements needing to be fulfilled in order for a person to feel complete in life.

Thinking of the actualisation of the problem in terms of a problem solving exercise started to settle her mind. Viewing herself as a separate entity, someone looking in from the outside.

The first element was physiological, the basic needs for human survival. Breathing, water, food, sex, shelter. Take any of them away and humans die, but that's as a species and not as an individual. The sex is negated instantly. This plan was not about continuing the species by coupling with the first bloke that came along. This was self-survival so it came down to breathing, water, food and shelter. Breathing was sorted instantly, the contagion didn't appear to be airborne and the air felt clear. Water and food should be easy, with so much of the population decimated and if she moved quick enough she should be able to gather enough supplies to last a while. Shelter, well in this weather it was more about protection from the elements of the hot weather. Clothes, sun cream and staying hydrated would fix that.

Safety was the next one up in the ever decreasing triangle. She was safe right now. Sat in the car with a clear line of sight all around her but that wasn't what it was about. There would be no doctors or hospitals now, no ambulances either. If she gets injured she's on her own. Financial security was out the window so that just left her own *personal* safety. Which would mean taking whatever precautions possible and risk assessing each threat as she went along. Some risks would have to be taken, that was fact. But with awareness and forward planning; those risks could be minimised.

What was next? She tried to picture the diagram in her mind, was it Love and Belonging or Esteem? Frowning she thought back to her empowerment courses and tried to visualise the image on the screen. Did it matter? Love and Belonging were gone. Devoid. Negated. Obsolete. Fucked up and fucked off. Esteem wasn't that far behind Love and Belonging either. The only Esteem that could be garnered was by the *self*; self -esteem and self-respect. She would know if she was failing. Paula's internal observations, only too quick to berate and chastise would see to that. Whatever was to be done now was for herself. Screw everyone else. This was about her, doing what she wanted.

Now the biggie, the grandiose element she knew was coming, a subconscious longing to get to this one quicker. Self-Actualisation.

'The desire to accomplish everything one can...' she intoned the mantra with an ironic smile that it never got her anywhere before. Maybe she was too hungry for success? Too determined to be seen as a human and not just defined as female. If she had relaxed and accepted herself as a woman would that have made a difference? The difficult thoughts were cut off quickly as it promoted an uncomfortable glimpse at her life, that possibly she had taken it too far.

What did she want now? The safety element would have to be taken care off, after that it was down to what she actually *wanted.* And that was to kill as many of those things as possible. Why? Shaking her head she couldn't fathom why she wanted to do this, but it was there, and it was strong. A desire, an urge, a need.

Doodling on the page she ran through the hierarchy of needs in her mind and then thought of essential items only. How and where to get them, priorities were established. While thinking she reverted to doodling the same cobweb into the corner of the page, something she had done since her early school days.

That was better. It was written and laid in a rough but logical format. Presented on a page and therefore a plan. It didn't need an overhead projector or a slideshow. It was basic but it did the job and most importantly, it gave Paula a *thing,* a real tangible *thing* that could be stuck to. A plan that needed action.

With a growing sense of resolve she started the drive back into town, avoiding the centre and heading straight for the retail park on the cheaper land to the outskirts.

She felt like she had an advantage over everyone else. They were either at home or out getting drunk, whereas she had seen the outbreak and already made one kill, and that one kill counted for something; it meant she *could* kill if she had to.

The huge warehouse outlet stores had yet to be looted and the acres of car park were mostly empty. Only one figure moved in the middle of the car park, a shuffling man with blood encrusted round his mouth and open wounds on his bare legs. Slowing down she watched the figure closely; now her decision was made she needed to study the enemy and learn what it was capable off.

The figure had already turned towards her and was now shuffling its way over. The movement was stiff and awkward, the knee joints not bending and forcing the feet to take heavy almost robotic steps. The arms hung loose and the head rolled about almost as if the neck was broken.

Paula waited with the windows closed and the doors locked, her foot down on the clutch, handbrake off, ready to pull away. Her heart rate soared as he staggered closer. She could see the red bloodshot eyes and the drool hanging from his mouth.

What would he do? Would he have a final burst of speed or try and smash the window. Tensed and breathing hard she forced herself to wait, gripping the steering wheel as she held the car on the biting point.

Giving a gasp as it walked into the side of the car she watched the awful face for long seconds as it pressed against the window, smearing blood and filth over the glass. It had no control over his hands and made no attempt to open the door or smash the glass, but instead just kept trying to walk into the side of the car.

She pulled away and turned in a long slow loop to face the thing. It turned and started the slow shuffle. Paula fixed her eyes on it and revved the engine, waiting for a few seconds before forcing her foot to the floor. The car went off like a rocket, gathering speed as she changed up the gears. At the last second an image of a television documentary filled her head, of the crash test dummies being run over and going straight through the windscreen into the driver. With a scream she hit the brakes and jammed the wheel over slewing the car to the side. The passenger wing mirror clipped the man with a loud thunk, smashing the plastic casing apart and sending him spinning off to sprawl on the ground.

Without hesitation she ran it over. Gathering enough speed to force the low car over the obstacle. She expected a feeling of guilt to course through her, that her mind would tell her she had just murdered someone. Instead she felt nothing other than an enhanced feeling of security that it was dead and therefore the threat was negated.

She had to use the mini again, this time to ram the glass doors of outdoor equipment retailer. Reversing out from the wreckage she winced at the alarm wailing into the near silent air, cursing herself for not thinking of it in advance.

It meant she would have to rush now. She burst out of the car and sprinted through the destruction of the doors. Straight to the clothing section she filled her arms with trousers, tops, waterproof jackets, vest tops and socks. Back to the vehicle and she dumped everything into the boot, leaving it open she ran back inside. At the far end she spotted the rugged boots all displayed on little plastic shelves fitted to the display unit. Checking the boxes beneath the boots she grabbed several her size and again ran back to ditch them in the car.

The alarm screamed at her with an indignant and petrified wail. The alarm sent a message to the empty alarm company control room, in turn that activated an automated call to the equally empty police control room but that was it. A noise and a meaningless signal that no one would ever see.

With clothes and boots sorted she darted back in and grabbed a rucksack from the display, working quickly to remove the paper filler she went round the display units, ramming torches, lanterns, flasks, water bottles and multi-tools into the bag. A whole box of high energy chocolate bars on the counter, more multi-tools, more socks. The bag was filled up so she grabbed another larger one and stuffed it with camping stoves, small gas bottles, mini pots and pans.

Like a supermarket dash with the countdown timer on, frantic but focussed and refusing to let the constant warble of the alarm make her panic.

The knife display unit was impressive, a whole range of deadly looking commando style knives, straight edged, curved blades, serrated with camouflage grips and leather scabbards. The locked cabinet was prised open and several knives taken along with sheaths.

Each trip outside she checked the surrounding view, nothing moving, no running figures so she kept going, taking advantage of the lack of response and interest. Slowly the mini was filled with kit, clothing and equipment. After several trips she noticed figures in the distance shuffling across the car park, distinct movement with the same stiff legged walk.

She'd gained enough to fill the mini completely, jamming the boot and the back seat high with goods. From the retail park she went back into the countryside and found another isolated spot to stash the gear before heading back into town.

Having already seen the devastation of the town centre she stuck to the outer ring roads. Signs of looting began to appear, especially the shops near the housing estates. The windows smashed in and doors ripped off, debris everywhere, more disconcerting were the amount of bodies littering the streets and the large pools of blood smeared across parked cars, along garden fences and stark against white UPVC front doors.

The second store she checked was on the far edge of town; one of the small expensive individually owned supermarkets. The front door was smashed open but no sign of movement. She left the car outside, pocketed the key and ran in with one of the sheathed commando knives stuffed into the back of the business pencil skirt she still wore.

Whoever had gained access had gone straight for the booze aisle, large empty sections showing where the spirits bottles once were and the shutters on the cigarette display had been forced open. Crates of beer and cider stacked to the side of the counter were laying on the floor, evidently knocked over by the rushing looters.

Paula moved quickly, taking a small trolley she headed straight into the tinned goods aisle, filling the trolley with everything she could grab.

Outside she worked just as fast, sweat dripping from her brow as she scooped the tins out to be thrown into the back of the car.

Running back inside with the trolley she went back for the tinned foods, then into the toiletries to take shampoo, wet wipes, soap, anti-bacterial gel, toothbrushes and toothpaste, mouthwash. Everything she would need to stay clean and healthy. Packets of multi-vitamins, long life and powdered milk, bags of sugar.

On the third trip she rushed to the chilled section, taking cheeses and bottles of fruit juice. Intent on her work she failed to hear the new arrival until the voice spoke, a quavering fear filled voice of a man.

'Hello,' a simple greeting but it jarred her senses, making her spin round as though expecting an instant attack. Instead there was a young man, early twenties and very thin. He was holding the hand of a young girl with long brown hair. She looked five or six years old and was as terrified as the man.

'Do you know what's happening?' The man asked his eyes were wide and filled with tears, clutching the little girls hand as though to draw strength from her instead of offering her a protective embrace.

Paula examined the two figures, wondering why they were out in this; if it was food they wanted they should get it and go.

'The phones are down, telly ain't working...her mum was working nights in a care home and she ain't come back yet, there's like,' he paused, fighting back tears, 'bodies and stuff everywhere.'

Paula looked down at the trolley, deciding she'd got enough and it was time to leave, 'Didn't you see anything last night?' She asked.

'Last night? No, I put little 'un to bed and played Xbox for a few hours, why? What's happened?'

'Disease, it's worldwide, people are biting each other and...' she looked down at the little girl, re-phrasing what she was about to say, 'well, those that get bit then want to bite other people...it's everywhere.' She started pushing the trolley towards the door, wanting to get away as quick as possible.

'Oh,' the man replied, he looked dumbstruck and confused.

'Get what food you can and find somewhere safe to hide,' Paula pushed the trolley past them, staring ahead to make it clear the conversation was over.

'What about the police?'

'There is no police,' Paula called back, 'no nothing, all gone, you shouldn't be out here with your daughter, find somewhere and hide.'

'She ain't my daughter, I'm going out with her mum…I was babysitting so she could work…who do I call?'

'There isn't anyone to call,' Paula shouted back as she reached the car and started loading the goods into the back, the man followed her out, standing there quietly watching her.

'What…what you doing then?' He said at length.

'Leaving town,' Paula lied.

'Got a car then,' he made the loaded statement while looking at the mini.

Paula glanced at the man and nodded curtly, slamming the boot down and using her foot to push the trolley away.

'You got somewhere safe then?' He asked softly, clearly building up to asking if they could go with her.

'I've got to go,' Paula replied, 'get food and stay off the streets, it isn't safe.' She climbed into the driver's seat and slammed the door closed, starting the engine and pulling away before he could ask.

The man and child stood there watching her go, hand in hand, forlorn and lost. It was heart-breaking to think the girl's mum was gone and she was left alone with a man she might hardly know. She forced herself to push the thoughts away and focussed on the plan.

So far so good, she'd done well with supplies and equipment. That just left two things; vehicle and weapons. Do it now while you've got momentum and everyone is in shock. Strike quickly and get prepared.

She felt exhausted, utterly drained from being up all the previous day and then the night too. The adrenalin had worn off, leaving her feeling weak. It was hot too, sticky with no fresh air.

It didn't take long to find a vehicle. She saw plenty that would do the job but they were parked up locked and secure. She needed one from a driveway but that meant going into the house for the keys, the risk was worth taking if it meant having a robust vehicle capable of carrying everything and big enough to be used as a weapon.

Parked up a few doors down in the quiet residential street she stared at the big black four wheel drive vehicle. A Japanese made thing with a double cab and an enclosed pick-up truck on the back, tinted windows, big solid looking tyres and those oversized bull bars in front of the engine, solid and reliable. This street had clearly seen some action judging by the bodies littering the area and the vehicle was parked on a driveway of a house with the front door hanging open.

No movement anywhere, with the windows down she listened intently; taking a few minutes to relax and get used to the normal background noises which consisted of the odd bird chirp. The air was still and listless, no breeze that rustled the trees, no traffic noise either. Scanning the houses she looked at each window and door in turn trying to detect any movement.

If she was going to do this it had to be quick and ruthless. That meant being prepared to attack and not just defend. If there were survivors inside she would flee and find another one, no conversation, no stalling, just turn and run.

She checked the route to the house; out the mini, down the pavement, into the driveway and up the path to the front door. No apparent obstacles and maybe a ten or fifteen second sprint, twenty at the very most.

Where would the keys be? Biting her bottom lip she tried to figure out a way of finding them. The four wheel drive was shiny and clean, the big alloy wheels gleaming in the sun. The grass of the front garden was cut short and the flower beds well-tended. No rubbish stacked outside either. That all suggested a clean and orderly household, in turn that meant the people living there would have orderly minds. So the keys would be kept in one place, probably on a hook near to the front door, in the hallway or the kitchen. Nodding to herself she thought of how she always went into the kitchen first when she got home to put her mini keys into the bowl and flick the kettle on. Thinking back she remembered her mother doing the same and they were both clean living and orderly people.

Checking the knife was still wedged into the top of her skirt she pursed her lips that she hadn't taken the time to put some better clothes on, instead of running about in her work clothes and flat office shoes.

Out of the car she left the door pushed in but not shut, just in case she needed a quick escape. One final check around, all clear. She sprinted down the pavement and into the driveway, heading up the path and pausing briefly at the front door. Eyes staring into the slight gap, moving side to side to increase her view of the inside.

No noise, no movement. She was committed so no time to dwell now. She pushed the door open and stepped in. A quick scan showed her a minimalistic hallway with wooden floors. One unit to the side with a telephone and some papers. No keys. Down the hallway into the kitchen, the row of hooks were next to the fridge. She grabbed the set with the *Nissan* logo and was back outside within a few seconds, pressing the clicker to unlock the doors.

Inside she didn't wait to adjust the seat or wing mirrors but got the engine running and reversed out, leaning forward and using the steering wheel to hold herself up as the seat was too low.

Driving away she allowed herself a quick grin at a perfectly executed mission, her right hand dropping down to find the lever to jack the seat up higher. Slamming the brakes on her feeling of victory soured instantly as she realised the mini still had all the food and goods from the supermarket in it. All that planning and she messed up, cursing herself, angry that she had failed to account for something and refusing to allow herself room for error, even considering how long she had been awake, the lack of food, the danger and tension she faced. It wasn't good enough.

Turning the vehicle round she went back down the road, crawling along slowly as she again scanned the houses, windows, doors. Pulling up next to the mini she burst out and started transferring all the goods, launching them into the rear seats of the new vehicle.

With a flushed and sweating face, her now filthy blouse clinging to her body and loose strands of hair glued to her forehead she got it finished, remembering to grab her bag before climbing back into the four wheel drive.

Breathing deeply, trying to calm herself down she worked her way out the town back to the stash point. Adrenalin was still high from the action of taking the vehicle, hands trembling and her legs felt rubbery and weak. She needed rest and water, knowing that her senses and intelligence would be slowed if she didn't get it soon.

Suddenly the stash point didn't feel so safe. A gravel car park at the edge of a wooded copse, used by dog walkers in the day and god knows who else at night. It was enclosed and oppressive. Paula grabbed her equipment and stuffed it into the rear enclosed pick-up section of the vehicle, the back door split into two halves with one door rising up and the tail gate dropping down.

Once loaded she again drove on, thinking that she needed high ground where she had a view of all sides, somewhere she could sort through her new supplies and get organised.

She found a field with an open gate, the land rising gently to a crest at the far end. Perfect. The hard backed ground was easy to drive over with the big wheels.

Once stopped she grabbed her list, checking through it and mentally ticking each item off. Food and water done, equipment and clothes done, tin opener done, boots done. Shit, no hair bands! That shouldn't be too difficult to do. The vehicle was good and had nearly a full tank of fuel.

That just left weapons. The knives were good but could only be really used as personal defence and it meant getting close too. She needed guns but this was England and the only people that had guns were the police, the army, farmers and gangsters.

Gangsters were ruled out instantly simply for not knowing where they would be, she didn't even know if her town had gangsters, probably just the cities.

Farmers were an option but they were generally isolated so the chances are they may not be affected by what's happened, which also meant they were unlikely to give up their shotguns.

That left police and army. Paula had no idea where any army bases were or where they kept the guns. But the police, they had guns. Her local station was the divisional headquarters and had the armed response vehicle running from it, everyone knew that as it was a big thing a few years ago when the local force started routinely arming those officers, and the sight of British bobbies walking about with pistols was very strange. But only a few were firearms officers which meant they would only have a few weapons and those officers probably wouldn't want to give their guns up either.

Still, it was the best and most feasible option, other than ram-raiding a gunsmith shop but she figured everyone else would have gone for them as soon as possible.

She needed sleep but there wasn't time. She had to keep the momentum going, get prepared now and sleep later. This might be the only chance before other survivors start coming out and trying to do the same things.

Moving to the back of the vehicle she started going through the clothes to get changed then stopped. That man with the child was happy to speak with her and obviously didn't see her as any kind of threat; the clothing did make her look safe and professional. Even bedraggled like this she looks like anyone should look after going through a night like that. Getting changed into black clothes could make her look aggressive or appear in another light, especially if she was going anywhere near a police station.

Decision made, options weighed and she got back into the vehicle and once more headed into town, again chastising herself for not going straight there and getting it done. All of this messing about just wasted time and slowly lost whatever advantage she felt she had.

The police station was near the centre of town, just enough distance away to be slightly safer than the actual dead centre.

How would she do this? There must be an armoury or something inside the station, but it would be locked with keys, or even a numbered keypad that stored the access times for audit trails. This wouldn't be easy, and that was even considering the fact that the station would be empty. There was every chance they were still inside, fortifying the building. What would she do if they asked her to join them? The answer was instant. No, no way. The thought of being near others, having to rely on other people sent a surge of anger through her.

From the outer roads she worked back towards the centre, trying to use quieter side streets wherever possible and contravening one way restrictions to make the route quicker.

Two streets to go, she turned a corner and immediately cursed audibly at the large group of figures shuffling around in the middle of the road. The route was blocked and the road narrow, cars parked on both sides meant she couldn't mount the pavement.

But she was in a big vehicle now, maybe she could just plough through them. Paula inched closer to the group, examining the numbers and depth of the horde. Too many, she'd get through but at a risk of getting bogged down or causing damage to the vehicle. The risk was calculated, the threat assessed and a decision made that it wouldn't be the right thing to do.

Bringing the vehicle to a stop, she tutted and moved the gear stick into reverse, annoyed at the delay. Something in the crowd caught her eye. The *things* were all in a state of undress, clearly roused from their houses and beds when it all happened, rushing out in night clothes to see what was going on. One of them was fully dressed and that was what caught her eye. A figure dressed all in black, he was tall and well-built too. She paused and stared at the crowd, leaning left and right to try and get a view but too many of the *things* were between her and the figure.

Opening the door she stood on the step, using the roof and door frame to hold herself steady. The horde had already turned and were shuffling towards her, a collection of injuries, wounds, gaping holes, blood stained clothes and bare skin. But there, yes there...deep in the middle it was a policeman dressed in black uniform and he was still wearing the stab vest and belt round his waist.

Paula stretched higher, leaning as she tried to get a better view of him. His face had been bitten away from a savage attack, his nose pretty much removed to leave a ragged wound.

She still couldn't see his waist clearly. Was he a firearms officer? She jumped down and used the front driver's wheel to clamber onto the sun heated black bonnet, then up onto the roof of the vehicle. Shielding her eyes she moved left and right, waiting for him to shuffle into view. A fat old woman was shuffling in front of him, her wide hips and broad back wobbling in the way.

They were getting close, too close for comfort. She would have to go, giving herself one more chance she went to the far right of the roof, straining on her tiptoes to see the copper. The fat woman wobbled to the left, then back to the right. The stiff legged walk making her swollen upper body sway like a pendulum. As she went to the right Paula glimpsed the belt and butt of a handgun poking from a holster on his hip.

She jumped down onto the bonnet and slid to the ground, climbing back into the vehicle and quickly reversing down the street, buying herself time to think. Brilliant fortune at finding an armed police officer, but then they were only a street or two away from the station, but now faced with the difficulty of actually getting to him.

There was no choice, she would have to use the vehicle to shunt them over a few at a time. Selecting first gear she started forward, crawling along until just a few metres away from the front of the horde. At the last second she pushed her foot down, giving the vehicle a burst of speed and stamping on the brake as she hit the small cluster at the front.

The power of the vehicle, the bull bars and the act of braking hard sent them flying backwards, in turn knocking more over. She reversed a few metres then did it again, aiming slightly to the left this time.

Back and forth she went, changing path each time and running them over with loud thunks as they impacted on the front of the vehicle. Some got back up, others tried and some were trampled underfoot by the undead walking over them.

Bit by bit she got the first lot down, using the big wheels to drive over individual bodies and crushing them into the road. The fat lady was next, the copper behind her and then a load behind him.

Paula over-compensated for the size of the woman, going too fast into her. She smacked into the front of the vehicle with a loud bang, the jarring action causing her head to smash down on the bottom, busting her nose open. Braking hard again the fat lady flew backwards, acting like a giant bowling ball and taking out several more behind her. The copper being one of them.

Paula saw the gap created and was out of the vehicle before she had time to think. Pulling the knife free from the sheath she jumped over the fallen writhing bodies and went straight for the policeman. He was flat out, facing down but still moving. Getting to him she started trying to pull the gun free from the holster, tugging at the handle. The safety clip had some kind of sliding action to prevent something like this happening, making it very difficult for anyone to grasp the gun and pull it free.

The policeman groaned louder at the feel of the woman touching him, rolling onto his back and sitting up in one fast movement causing Paula to jump back.

One behind her coming in with lips pulled back showing dirty blood stained teeth. Instinct kicked in and she thrust the knife out, driving the sharp point deep into the stomach. The *thing* didn't flinch but kept coming. She stabbed again and again but no reaction, blood pumping out but he kept coming. She went for the throat, driving the long blade into the soft tissue before ripping the knife out. Blood sprayed out, just missing her as she stepped to the side. It did the trick and within a couple of steps he was stumbling and falling to the floor.

Groans all around her, they were closing in and despite their slow movements it would only take seconds to surround her.

Already, some of the ones she had run down were back in their feet, blocking her way back to the vehicle. Spinning round she saw the policeman was getting to his feet unsteadily, she stabbed out, hacking into his neck, the sharp blade cutting deep and easy. Blood sprayed out as he fell back, arcing the crimson liquid high into the air. She went for the gun again, fumbling with one hand to try and release the clip. It wouldn't budge and she could feel panic rising in her.

Close movement, a loud groan she jumped over the body of the policeman, landing on the other side of him as a woman lunged, tripping over the copper's legs and sprawling out.

Paula cursed angrily that she allowed herself to get caught like this. She tried for the gun again, working the safety clip back and forth while trying to prise it open. It wouldn't budge, the bloody thing refused to yield.

The belt. She looked at the middle of the utility belt, a thick leather belt with a double fastener in the middle. Far easier. Stamping her foot down on the coppers groin for leverage she yanked the end of the belt out and pulled it over, releasing the two metal prongs holding it in place before trying to tug the belt free.

'FUCK OFF,' she yelled at the naked man shuffling up close behind her. With a violent movement she turned and stuck the knife deep into his throat, using her office shoe clad foot to push him away.

Grasping the belt she tried pulling it away, belt clips held it in place. She pulled harder, stamping her foot down on the coppers stab jacket. The clips released and she pulled the belt free, tugging furiously as the hand cuffs and other bits got stuck underneath him.

Another stab out into another throat, another violent tug and finally the belt was in her hands, free from the policeman. Now the path back to the vehicle was blocked the ones behind were closing in.

She ran to the side, clambering over a car bonnet onto the narrow pavement, running down the street and away from her vehicle. As one, the horde shuffled round and started heading towards her. She kept them coming while checking all around for any others that might be lurking about.

It took a few minutes but finally there was enough of a gap for her, taking advantage of it she sprinted up the pavement, the skirt hampering her movements and preventing her stride from opening fully. She tried tugging it up but holding the knife and belt and trying to tug a skirt up while running down a pavement and being chased by flesh eating zombies was all too much for even her advanced multi-tasking skills.

Through the gap between the cars and into her vehicle. Engine on and reversing back and away from the horde. Breathing hard she reached the junction and backed into it, getting ready to turn away.

Lifting the belt from the passenger seat she realised now how heavy it was from all the equipment they had to carry, no wonder they couldn't chase anyone anymore.

A set of keys jangled from a clip to the front of the belt, a big Volvo motif on the front. He must have been an armed response officer, if he has the keys with him then the police car must be nearby. But the station is only down the road so maybe he ran here when he heard the commotion and left the car behind. She scanned the area, searching for a marked police car.

Must be at the station. She drove off, taking a longer route to bypass the blocked street. In the police station road she slowed down, inching along as she again viewed the houses, windows and doors. It was the same here as most other places. Bodies lying about, doors open, some windows smashed and blood everywhere. So close to the station too.

She pulled alongside the entrance to the police station yard, peering through the open metal gates to the interior. Several marked police cars were parked up but no sign of movement. She leant out the window and pressed the clicker on the set of Volvo keys, hearing a clear thunk from inside the yard.

Again, with a snap decision she was out of the vehicle and running inside, pressing the clicker again and again and following the noise and flashes of indicators to the big high performance police car.

There it was, in the middle section of the back seat was a large metal box with an opening flap at the front. The gun box that was used to keep the bigger guns inside. That's what she wanted. Ammunition and bigger guns.

Inside the vehicle she worked the separate keys on the set until finding the right one that opened the gun box. Pulling the metal door up she was faced with the stock of a black coloured police sub machine gun. She'd seen them on television many times, and held by police officers outside courts and at airports too.

She pulled it out and grabbed the magazines of ammunition, holding them in her arms before sprinting back to her own vehicle, dumping them all on the passenger seat and quickly driving off.

Ten minutes later she was back out into the country lanes, hardly believing that she'd done it. She'd got everything she set out for, equipment, food, water, a vehicle and now guns. She had no idea how to use them but she would learn and figure it out, like everyone else she had seen enough action movies and cop drama's to have a basic idea.

She felt satisfied and a rare feeling of pride, that she had formed a daring plan and executed it to almost perfection. And already she had killed several of the *things,* and she'd done it without hesitation, and learnt that stabbing them repeatedly in the stomach didn't work but stabbing them in the neck did work.

Shit. Forgot the bloody hairbands again.

Damn it.

Now, eleven days on and picking her way tentatively through the charred remains she thinks back over those long days and nights. And how now, the plan was almost complete. The town was almost completely rid.

Starting slowly she had picked them off one at a time. Driving round to find single undead shuffling in the hot summer day. The first few had simply been run over. Killed by the big four wheel drive.

At night she drove back out of town, deep into the countryside and slept in the drivers seat, ready to turn the engine on and drive away. The next day she went back into the town. Continuing the hunt. Mowing them down in couples and groups. That progressed to using weapons, finding equipment stores. Bows and arrows were tried and tested, but the skill required was too high. She used crossbows for a day, getting better and better at achieving head shots but she soon tired of the constant strain of drawing the string back.

Firebombs made from bottles and petrol soaked rags were used. They were effective but the numbers were too small.

As the days went on, so she developed, honing skills and getting experienced. She saw the change that came over them at night and made it a priority to be away into the country-side, finding a different place each night to park up and rest.

She also sensed the change as the days went on. How they seemed to be targeting her. Whole groups of them following her every move. When they started chasing her in the daylight she knew she was getting to them. That feeling of being taken seriously was addictive. Staying one step ahead while cutting them down in huge numbers.

They got worse, increasing their level of aggression and violence towards her. She matched them in every way. Using cunning and intelligence to lure them into traps.

And this one. This was the best by far. The razor wire had worked brilliantly, the broken glass was okay but not effective enough, but the fire...the fire was awesome.

He wasn't here though. She hadn't seen him at the front and although they were badly burnt she was sure he wasn't here. A creeping sense comes over here as she makes her way through the bodies, taking care to avoid the lethal wire stretched between them.

He wouldn't stay in the middle. He hadn't before so why now? No, he wasn't here. She'd know it if he was.

She stops and stares down the road. Knowing he's there. Knowing he's watching. Movement in the shadows. Definite movement. A figure walking forwards. More figures behind it.

Him. It was him. He was coming down the road with another horde. He knew there would be a trap and sacrificed the first lot to clear the path.

He couldn't have many left now. The numbers she'd cut down were too vast for him to have many left.

The last four days had seen the greatest game of cat and mouse ever played. An intelligent infected that sent wave after wave of undead after her. Always there, always watching. She'd almost come to respect him. Seeing his familiar form every day gave her a sense of re-assurance.

She'd even worried one of the days when she hadn't seen him until the afternoon. Not worried for him but concerned that something else had taken away her right of victory. He was hers. Hers for defeating.

Trap and counter trap had been left. Fires, explosions, trip wires, shotguns, crossbows, gas canisters. They'd all been deployed with great effect. Nearly every street showed signs of the battles as she took them down again and again.

Hand to hand combat had been avoided where-ever possible.

She knew tonight would be it. One of them was going to lose and she'd planned long and hard for it not to be her.

He was a normal looking guy, apart from the obvious signs of decay and deathly pallor, average height, average build, short brown hair. But he was her nemesis. She dreamt about him. Every minute of every day was taken up with thinking how to end him.

She backs away, lifting her feet high as she goes. He comes in, moving at a steady pace. Getting closer she can make out the horde with him. She was right, not too many of them. But it looked like he had saved the best for last, big strong looking males.

That was alright. The bigger they come and all that. She wasn't going to be cowed by the males of the species anymore. This was a new time with new rules.

'Good work,' he shouts down the road, his voice clear. He seldom spoke and when he did it was only ever to praise her for taking down large numbers.

'Thanks,' she yells back, still stepping high.

'You planned it well.'

'I did,' she agrees with him. At least he gives recognition of a job well done, which is more than any of her other bosses ever did.

He stops walking, holding a respectable distance between them. She stops too, staring over the bodies as he stands there with his arms held casually at his sides.

'You must be proud,' he calls out, 'one woman against so many, you've done well.' His voice isn't goading but respectful and calm.

'Thank you, I would say the same back but...'

'Ha!' He laughs, 'no, I really haven't done so well.'

'No.'

'It's almost a shame this has to end, but...'

'It does have to end,' she finishes his sentence for him.

'What's your name?'

'Paula, and yours?'

'Thomas.'

'What did you do before this?'

'Accountant, what about you?'

'I ran a legal advisory service, for what's it worth...I could have done with someone like you in my company, you would have gone far.'

'Thanks.'

'Listen Paula, we will take you tonight...but...'

'Confident then?' She interrupts him.

He laughs, a nice sound that drifts across the empty air, 'very...we will win Paula, but when we do, know that it's with respect and you'll be alongside me.'

'I would look forward to it...but...you won't be winning.'

'No?'

'No Thomas, not a hope in hell.'

'I love it! I love your confidence...I wish I had known you before all this.'

'Maybe,' she shrugs.

'Were you married?'

'No, single, I worked too much.'

'Ah, let me guess...an all-male office, passed over for promotion...my firm dealt with companies like yours all the time.'

'Something like that.'

'It figures, I wasn't married, never settled down either...what could have been.'

'What could have been,' she repeats.

'Another world.'

'Another time.'

'New rules.'

'New rules,' she nods back.

'Well, I don't suppose I can persuade you to give up?'

'I was going to ask you that, give you a chance to surrender now.'

'And then what?'

'Then I kill you,' she smiles.

'In that case, forgive me if I don't surrender.'

'Okay.'

'I would love to shake your hand before we...'

'Thomas, in truth...I would like that too, but it isn't going to happen.'

'Tom, please...just Tom.'

'Are we on a date now?' Paula laughs.

He chuckles clearly, 'I wish,' he mutters, 'you are very beautiful.'

'Thank you,' she takes the compliment with grace.

'You've still got those guns.'

'I have.'

'Why have you never taken a shot at me? You've had chances.'

'Didn't seem right, not like that...'

'And now? You could take a shot...you never know, you might get me.'

'True, I could...but where would the fun be in that?'

'Ha,' he laughs again, 'so what now?'

'I run, you chase.'

'You like being chased?'

'Are you flirting with me Tom?'

'I hope it's me that gets to turn you.'

'Do you now?'

'One thing before we start, if it happens...no...*when* it happens, don't fight it. It hurts more, just relax and let it take you.'

'What does it feel like?'

'Turning hurts, really hurts...you get a really bad pain in your stomach and the more you tense the worse it gets. Coming back is amazing, I've never felt so...so alive and, I don't know....full of energy and vitality.'

'Something to look forward to then?'

'I know you won't but please Paula, just give up...let me take you easily.'

'No, thank you but no.'

'Okay, but when it happens I will be there, I'll do what I can to ease your turning.'

'I appreciate that, but...I don't want to come back, I don't want to be one of them...if any of this means anything to you...if anything you just said is true then *if* you get me, kill me outright...don't let me come back.'

He pauses, nodding while she speaks, 'okay,' he replies in a serious tone, 'I will honour that.'

'Thank you...I'd best start running then.'

'Yep, I'd best start chasing.'

'Bye Tom.'

'Bye Paula, good luck.'

'You too.'

She steps free of the last body and starts moving backwards, staring at Tom as he gives her a sporting chance, holding back for a few seconds. A tiny flick of his hand and his horde start running. She's off, sprinting towards the door. Howling from behind her as the undead are finally unleashed. They can scent her, smell the perfume on her. They can smell her body and the piss she left on the road, but not fear. This woman doesn't exude fear.

A few go down, tripped and snagged on the razor wire, cutting hands open on the broken glass but none of the injuries are enough to stop them.

Paula reaches the door in plenty of time, pausing to look back and watch as the first undead clear the end of the bodies.

Stepping inside she slams the door closed behind her, working at the bolt locks at the top and bottom. Having already tested them she found they were rusted and sticking. A can of spray lubricant and a hammer fixed that problem.

Bolts rammed home she turns the big key in the middle lock and moves into the wide open space. A warehouse by design, and plans had been submitted for developers to turn the old fashioned brick building into modern mews style up-market apartments that could be sold on to idiots with more money than sense. Idiots who found living in exposed brick former warehouses *exciting* and *edgy.* Taking the thin torch from her pocket she presses the end button to illuminate the ground around her. Treading carefully she steps over the trip wires fixed between the thick wooden support posts and moves towards the stairs in the middle. At the base of the stairs she purposefully kicks one of the buckets over, sending thousands of small steel ball bearings over the ground. The next bucket adds several more thousand. Covering the ground between the stairs in a nice layer of bearings.

She listens to the battering at the door, waiting for the first bolt to break. The wooden door splinters. The sound of wood tearing. On the first step and still she waits. At the last second, as the door gives she pushes the *on* button for the two high powered torches on the second step. Perfectly angled so the bright white beams are focussed at head height. The first undead forces through the broken door. His hands immediately covering his eyes from the harsh light, others push him in, jabbing him out the way. They too get dazzled by the sudden light, looking down but still running forward.

Paula bursts out laughing as the first one goes down, losing traction from the bearings sliding underfoot. He goes over like a comedy performer, windmilling his arms then landing painfully on his face. The next one trips over the downed body, going over in a heap. More run in, slipping and sliding in all directions.

Paula laughs harder, delighted at the impact the bearings are having. The fallen bodies scatter the bearings, clearing a partial route. Undead surge forward, hitting the trip wire that tips the buckets of dirty used engine oil down. The filthy sticky contents shower down onto the heads of the first two, covering their faces and bodies in the slimy foul gunk.

Other veer round them, triggering more trip wires and more buckets of oil that plummet down. Tears of laughter pour down Paula's face from the sight of the undead covered from head to toe in oil. They slip, trip and fall. Staggering all over the floor.

First step, second, third, step over the fourth and onto the fifth. She races up ahead, again holding at the top, unable to stop herself from watching.

The first undead reaches the bottom and starts powering up, howling with ferocious rage. He hits the fourth step, the fourth step that isn't there and is covered in a thin layer of cardboard. His legs plummets into the hole, impaled on the sharpened stakes put underneath it. With his body blocking the stairs the others have to beat him out the way to pass. Using his head as a step.

Paula runs through, onto the first floor and round the corner, heading for the second flight of stairs at the far end. Torch light bobs as she goes, picking out the sharp nail ends hammered through the planks laid down.

At the next flight she again pauses, just long enough for the first one to reach the top of the first stairs and see her torch.

Powering on she races up the second flight, listening to the howls as the undead step onto the nails. Thumps sounding out as they fall down heavily.

At the top she stops, shining her torch at the length of wood propped between the wooden door and the frame, holding the door open. She goes low, crawling very carefully under the piece of wood. On the other side she grasps the string attached to the wood and moves away.

Before the first one reaches the top she shines her torch up, checking the elastic bungee cord attached to the inside of the door and stretched across the top of the stairs to the wall on the other side, is still in place. She'd practised this again and again, winding the bungee tighter and tighter until it slammed the door closed once the wood was removed. Only when she was sure she had the correct *tautness* did she drive the long bladed knives through the door, the sharp points poking several inches clear on the inside.

Holding the string she plays it out as she works her way carefully along the room. Thudding of feet on stairs, she holds the torch up, waiting for the first body to appear. When it does she holds that second longer, waiting for it to take a step towards her. Paula yanks the string, pulling the wood away. The door slams shut as the undead runs through. Instantly impaling the body on the knife points.

'Yes, COME ON,' she screams in triumph. Perfect, bloody perfect. Howls and roars rip through the building, screams of frustration at being slowed down from their prey.

The final flight of stairs and Paula grips the torch between her teeth, placing her feet on the plinths either side of the steps. Using the handrail she quickly climbs up, shuffling her feet along the plinths to avoid using the actual steps. Each one with a nice surprise waiting. The first step covered in grease, making it nice and slippery. The second with broad headed nails upturned. Anything she could find went onto those steps, broken glass, another one covered in the bearings.

At the top she spins round, turning on another two high powered spot lights and waiting for the first to arrive and loving every minute. She grasps the first homemade spear, just a length of round wood with a small sharp knife taped to the end. With a grunt she launches the spear down as the first body comes into view. It hits central mass, just an annoyance more than anything but enough of a distraction for the undead to slip on the first step. It's face landing on the broken glass of the third step.

More behind it, trampling the first one down. She launches spear after spear, stabbing them backwards. A bowling ball gets launched down, heavy rocks, stones and bottles. They slip backwards, cutting themselves to ribbons, slipping on the bearings to tumble back into the press of bodies behind them.

Paula hears Tom roaring from in the building, his voice now very aggressive. More missiles get launched down, house bricks, breeze blocks, then larger items; chairs, tables, tool boxes, step ladders. Anything to slow them down and cause misery.

Everything works perfectly. The stairs become clogged as the undead at the front can't fight their way through the constant barrage, and unable to go back due to the press behind them.

'COME ON,' Paula screams, letting her rage go.

Her efforts slow them down but they don't stop them. Still they come on, utterly fixated with taking her down.

She runs through the top door out onto the flat roof and the sticky hot night air. She slams the door closed and rams the locks home. Knowing the thin door will give easily she moves quickly. Making the final preparations.

At the edge of the building several thick planks stretched across the void to the flat roof of the next building forming a bridge. She looks down at the three storey drop and moves into place.

The door starts being battered from within, when it gives the undead pour through with unfettered rage. Seeing Paula at the far side of the next flat roof they race to the edge and start across the planks. A few topple off and fall, unable to use enough fine motor skills to negotiate the narrow walkway.

Tom runs through the broken door, consumed with the chase. All thoughts of respect gone from watching the last of his horde being ripped to shreds by trap after trap. He'll rip her apart, kill her slowly and enjoy every second of it. There she is, trapped on the other flat roof with no escape route left. The cocky bitch assumed the traps would kill them off.

He reaches the planks, starting across and leaping off. It's only when he takes his first few steps onto the new roof that he realises Paula would have never left the planks there. She would have pushed them away.

He stops dead, spinning round with a roar, bellowing at the last two undead to get back off the planks. They stop mid-way, trying to negotiate the tricky act of turning round.

Tom screams with rage at the sight of Paula running from behind the broken door on the first flat roof. She reaches the planks and heaves the ends. The first plank goes, slipping from the edge to tumble down, clattering to the ground. The two undead balance precariously on the remaining planks. Paula heaves on them as they start back across towards her. She pushes with every ounce of strength, another one slips from the edge just as the first one leaps onto the roof. The second undead tries to leap but finds the plank he's standing on is no longer there, he plummets down with a long howl that only ends when his body impacts on the ground.

Paula spins round, drawing the pistol as she goes. The undead has gained his feet and is coming at her with a snarl. She fires, repeatedly pulling the trigger. The loud cracks sounding out clearly in the still air. The undead gets driven backwards from the power of the rounds. Paula runs at him, screaming with fury. She pushes the end of the gun under his chin and pulls the trigger one last time, blowing the back of his skull off.

As the body slumps down she spins to face the other roof, at the remaining horde now stood at the edge watching her. The mannequin dressed in similar clothes and left at the far end now kicked over in anger.

Breathing heavily, chest heaving and a determined glint in her eye she stares across at the horde. At Tom as he glances down at his feet. He lifts a foot up and looks down, sniffing and casting about.

Realisation hits him as Paula uses a lighter to ignite the material poking out the top of the bottle of petrol.

She pauses, just long enough for the wick to flame up. Without a word she launches the bottle high, watching as it sails through the air, coming down on the other side with a smash. The wick ignites the fuel, the fuel ignites the other fuel. The other fuel that was poured across the roof.

'I WIN,' Paula bellows across the gap as the flames take hold, spreading quickly across the entire flat roof.

The undead move about, unable to go anywhere. They start attacking the door, trying to fight their way through and away from the flames.

Seven P's. Paula had already chained the door closed, using big padlocks and thick chains. It would several men with sledgehammers over ten minutes to beat that door down.

She lights another bottle and sends it over, then another. Each one sailing through the air to smash on the ground. The contents just add to already high blaze taking hold.

Paula looks down at the remaining bottles. She didn't know how much of the fuel would dry and evaporate in the hot weather so compensated with plenty of Molotov cocktails.

She watches in satisfaction as the bodies burn. Tom screams out in terror and pain, yelling for Paula to save him. The repartee they exchanged earlier was pleasant but Paula was under no illusion of how dangerous he was. Wave after wave of undead had been sent against her over the last eleven days. With one she destroyed he took more. Finding survivors and turning them, just to send against her.

Paula destroyed every single one of them. Thousands of undead killed not just by her hands but by her intelligence and cunning, by her ability to forward plan.

An undead crawls out of the door behind her. This was planned for too. Knowing some would be left crawling about.

She moves over to the side, picking the sledgehammer up she left there. She waits for the crawler to get closer, letting him waste his energy before she uses hers. The heavy end of the hammer implodes the skull on first strike.

At the door she listens, hearing more scrapes and groans as they keep pushing on, crawling and dragging themselves to her.

Thick smoke drifts over from the now high flames across the gap, with a final glance she smiles and nods before moving back into the darkness of the stairwell.

A few minutes later she emerges from the door at the bottom. The bloodied end of the sledgehammer drips as she casts the thing aside. Every single one of the remaining undead had been killed on the way back down. All of them apart from the one impaled and stuck to the back of the door. How he was still alive she didn't know, but he was stuck fast, so she left him there to think about the consequences of his actions and made her way outside.

The street stinks of death, of burnt flesh and sickening odours that fill her nasal cavity, forcing her to put the white mask back on. The stronger smell of smoke wafting down from the burning building also reaches her. The fire will take hold in this dry heat, with no services racing to the scene to extinguish the blaze it will probably take most of these old buildings out. That'll be nice for the impaled undead. First being stuck to the back of a door and then roasted slowly alive.

Paula threads her way through the charred bodies, using her torch to shine down and avoid the razor wire. She pauses every few metres, scanning round and listening in case of traps or surprises. No noise, no movement, nothing.

She knows she's won. The sense of victory is there and has been hard earned. Once free of the foot traps she picks her pace up. Switching the torch off and using the moonlight to make her way out of the street. Pistol in hand she moves quietly, nothing on her rattles or squeaks, just the soft tread of her shoes on the surface of the road.

The four wheel drive was left several streets away, parked and locked in amongst a row of other untouched vehicles. As she gets closer she presses the clicker in her hand and waits in the shadows. The vehicle clicks audibly and flashes the indicators just once. An annoyance that was now very dangerous, but not knowing how to disable it she had to plan around it. Unlocking the vehicle and waiting to see if it attracted unwanted attention.

When nothing happens she moves down, feeling a greater sense of relief with each step. The secure rear section of the four wheel drive pick-up is stacked full of food, water, first aids kits, weapons and clothes.

Drive out of the town, find a country spot, get washed and changed then sleep. That's the plan and right now it feels lovely, knowing the task she set out to do has been accomplished. This town is rid of undead. There might be the odd one or two, but for the most part, they're gone, dead, killed, cut down by one former twenty-six year old accountant.

She opens the driver's door and shines the torch onto the back seats, checking nothing has crawled in while she's been gone. Unlikely with the vehicle being locked but the seven P's apply to everything.

Satisfied, she slips the rucksack off and clambers in, feeling the relief of sitting in the big leather seat. Paula yawns and stretches, feeling a general ache in her limbs, a heaviness that comes from solid exertion day after day. The key is pushed into the ignition as she notices the piece of paper stuck under one of the windscreen wipers. Not a piece of litter, not debris blown up, but a folded sheet held firmly in place. The tiredness is gone instantly, fully alert now. Her mind works the problem. Someone has put that note there. That means someone could be nearby, watching her now. She'd be expected to clamber back out and take the note, that would expose her.

Instead she starts the engine and pulls quickly out of the space, accelerating down the road. Using the back streets she knows are unobstructed she makes her way out of the town, her eyes constantly flicking down to that damned bit of paper.

No headlights are used, the bright clear sky illuminates the ground enough to see by. Headlights from a vehicle like this will be seen for miles.

Once out of the town she pushes on, taking lefts and rights, driving straight for long minutes before taking more turns. Into the country lanes and she drives on for miles, knowing the town behind her is now probably as safe as can be. But the method has worked so far. Find a rural spot with a good view, park up and feel safe.

At the entrance to a field she stops the vehicle and quickly runs out to open the gate before running back to drive the vehicle through.

The field inclines up a gradual hill. She pushes forward, driving slowly until she reaches near the top. The very top won't do, it would cause an outline of the vehicle to anyone below, so she stops just below and switches the engine off. Windows down and listen. She settles her mind and breathes slowly. Absorbing the normal sounds of the night. Insects buzzing. A far off cry of a fox. Normal. Natural.

Only when fully satisfied does she climb down and retrieve the note. Taking it back to the cab she opens the folded piece of A4 paper, just standard plain white printer paper with a hand-written message.

To the woman that kills everything,

My name is Thomas, I am the one that has been chasing you.

If you are reading this note, then it means you have either won or escaped again.

Something tells me that tonight will be our final dance, and by reading this now it

means you have been victorious

If this is the case, I applaud you. You have been a worthy opponent who is both beautiful

and highly intelligent.

My guess is that you wish to rid this town of my kind. There are very few of us left now, if

you have succeeded in killing me then the town is yours, and I congratulate your victory.

Take that victory and live peacefully for you have earned it. I suspect that you will now

consider moving on and starting again. I would urge you to consider your options carefully.

I am not the only one of my kind. There will be others, others who are stronger, faster and

with greater numbers. Do not devote your life to this cause. You have proved yourself strong

and capable. To continue will see you being either killed or taken as one of us.

However, I also suspect that you are a very strong willed person and will decide

for yourself. But know there will be other survivors, other people who could

use someone like you.

Don't be alone in this. Find more of your own kind and live.

Whatever you do, I wish you luck, and as for tonight, may the best one win.

Thomas

A single tear falls onto the page, soaking into the crisp material. A lump in her throat. She blinks rapidly as a muted laugh escapes from her lips. The sadness of it plucks at her heart. She thinks back to their conversation before the final dance as he called it. She laughs again at the words, a dry chuckle and a shake of her head.

He was right. That was the plan. It was never to re-claim the town. That place is now dead to her. Too many memories, too much painful history. Her intention all along was to move on, find the next town and start again. Using the skills she's learnt she can only get better and find ways to kill larger numbers.

Maybe he's right though. There will be other survivors out there. Others like her.

Paula had seen the other survivors in her town but had actively avoided them, and on one occasion had threated two men with her pistol for trying to follow her. They were just after food and company, there was nothing threatening about them. But after what Clarke did she refuses to trust anyone. At twenty-five years old, slim and attractive she knows she'll be a target and after that night, no man will touch her like that again.

But it has been lonely. Despite trying to convince herself this was the right course, she misses the company of others. Just to talk and discuss things, talk this through.

In her dream she would meet another person or group that were as dedicated as she was to killing them. They would team up and work together. A loyal team that co-existed with loyalty and bravery, a team that supported and fought as one.

Just a dream though. In reality the survivors are going to be scared and fearful hiding and running. There might be little pockets but they'll be dominated by greedy powerful figures that control everyone else. The Clarke's of this world.

She folds the note and places it carefully on the passenger seat before moving to the back of the vehicle. She strips off, cleaning herself again using wet wipes and water. Scrubbed and dried she changes into clean clothes and starts eating cold beans from a tin. At least she can fart out here on her own without anyone judging her.

Head south, find the coast and work along it. She longs to be near the sea. The wide open sea that would be warm and inviting. She could find a boat and use it as a place to sleep every night.

That's it. Head south and carry on. Plan formed she climbs into the back seats and stretches out after locking the doors. The pistol placed on the floor next to her body.

Her final thought as her eyes grow heavy is that she's better on her own.

Far safer.

Six

A thick carpet of mangled bodies stretch across the fort. The tents ripped apart, flattened and torn to pieces. The visitor centre pockmarked where the machine gun rounds thundered through. Some of the hastily erected wooden structures the engineers put up are now hanging in bits with blood and gore everywhere.

My hands gripped the triggers so hard I have to consciously think to unclasp them. Ears ringing from the constant thud of the GPMG. Cordite hangs in the air. Away to my left the lads unfurl from their tight circle they formed to fend the undead off while I made use of the gun. Dave breaks away and attacks the last small group that Meredith is already going for. Between them they slaughter them with ease and as the last one falls I exhale a long exhausted breath.

Dropping down into the Saxon I push the rear doors open and jump down. Finding the weapons that were left stacked there. A fresh magazine goes into my assault rifle. A pistol is checked and loaded with a new clip before being pushed into the empty holster on my belt. Picking my axe up I examine the shaft, thinking of a way to attach a strap so it can be with me all the time.

My eyes keep flicking to the top of the wall but there is no sign of her. It's taken long minutes to kill the horde off. She could be one off the bodies buried amongst the masses. Mixed emotions course through me. Hatred for her, for the way she lured us in, but also a part of me thinks that maybe she wasn't in control of what was happening. That the disease was doing it, making her act in a way she didn't realise.

The desire I had for her was so strong. I couldn't think of anything else and I would have both penetrated and kissed her if Meredith hadn't taken her off me. There is no doubt in my mind I would have done it. There was absolutely no element of hesitation or second thought. Whatever she did to me effectively rendered me helpless. What scares me the most is that I don't think I would have stopped if she had asked me to. I was too far gone. The aggression in me right at that point was frightening. If she had of said no I would have just taken it.

That thought sickens me, for no matter what she is, it makes me realise what I would have done and what I would have become. Never in all my life have I felt like before and I hope to god it never happens again.

'Mr Howie, you okay?' Nick makes his way quickly towards me, taking care to not to trip over the squelchy bodies underfoot.

Nodding back I hand him a fresh clip of ammunition and another pistol I just checked. He takes them both, fixing the magazine into his assault rifle and quickly checking the pistol for himself. Good skills taught by Dave and now ingrained.

The rest follow behind him, going straight for the weapons to repeat the actions of Nick.

Cookey looks at me as he shoves a pistol into his belt, 'what happened?' he asks weakly, shaking his head. He looks young and innocent, the natural inclination to ask the leader for guidance and answers.

'You first,' I reply, 'what happened here?'

'I was about the get shagged by a load of fit women until Clarence knocked them over like bowling pins,' Blowers explains.

'That's nothing,' Cookey groans, 'April was going for me...I knew she fancied me.'

'Enough of the fucking jokes,' I snap and stares across at all three of them. They look at me with surprise, 'they weren't women, they were undead...filthy diseased undead. This was the only way they could get to us and it almost worked.'

'Eh?' Nick asks quietly with a confused expression.

'Everything they've thrown at us has failed...Darren...the Isle of Wight...they took the fort and sent everyone out for us but we walked away each and every time without a fucking mark on us...I'm not boasting but there can't be many groups like us that have killed so many and got away with it...'

'Mr Howie,' Dave nods as he steps towards the back of the Saxon, nodding like normal, like nothing has happened, like we just bumped into each other in the corridor at work. The dog sniffs about, panting hard and wagging her tail as she moves between the lads. Clarence stands quietly, resting his back against the wall; even he now holds his axe in one hand and the rifle in the other.

'When we first saw Marcy out there,' I nod towards the front of the fort, 'it felt like...I don't know...Like I had fallen in love at first sight, this overwhelming feeling of...of...something...it was incredible. She was all I could think about, when we were fighting, after the battle, in here, when we were eating...I couldn't take my eyes off her. We went out the back and the next thing I knew she was naked and sitting on top of me...'

'Did you have a headache?' Clarence asks quietly.

'Yeah, pounding, but it was more than that...I was obsessed with having her, I don't mean to be graphic but all I could think about was...well...you know.'

'Fucking her?' Cookey asks.

'Cookey, for fucks sake,' Blowers chastises him.

'Yeah pretty much,' I nod, feeling ashamed but knowing this has to be discussed.

'Same here, I was talking to April...she looked fucking lovely but then she looked lovely anyway...but...' Cookey trails off, looking at the floor, 'I don't know, she started coming onto me and even though I knew she was infected and I would catch zombie from her...'

'Dick,' Blowers mutters.

'Fuck you, I would have caught zombie from her but I didn't care.'

'Same,' Clarence cuts in, 'but I heard Dave shouting and somehow managed to get her off me.'

'Yeah by throwing her at me,' Blowers says.

'Sorry mate, she didn't hit you though.'

'No fair one, glad you did it...cheers Clarence.'

'Anytime,' Clarence nods.

Nick draws a pack of smokes from his pocket and hands them round, 'you're all wet boss.'

'Meredith took us both in the sea.'

'Do what?' Cookey asks.

'Marcy was on top of me, both of us had our kit off, Meredith came charging out and must have hit us so hard we all went in the water...'

'Bloody hell,' Cookey looks down at the dog, 'yeah she's still wet, good girl...who's a good girl?' He rubs her head as she snakes round his legs wagging her tail, 'you saved Mr Howie from shagging the zombie didn't you...yes you did! Who's a good girl?'

A snort of laughter bursts from my mouth, 'was Mr Howie about to catch zombie? But you saved him didn't you...yes you did,' he carries on with the baby talk, knowing he's getting a few chuckles from the rest of us.

'I think,' he says standing up with a big grin, 'that despite April being a dirty infected zombie that is now dead from being killed by Dave...she is still the fittest girl that I have ever seen and I will hold a special place for her in my heart.'

'She was trying to kill you you fucking moron,' Nick laughs.

'With love...killing me with love,' Cookey replies seriously, 'we would have got married and had little zombie babies and lived happily ever after.'

'How did they do it?' Blowers asks me.

'Pheromones,' Dave replies without looking up from checking the weapons, 'one of them came to me while I was giving the dog some water, took her top off and stood there like I should be doing something...the dog either sensed it or smelled it and reacted. Must have been pheromones, pumped out to make you all get weird.'

'Shit,' Cookey exclaims.

'Fucking hang on,' I step forward, 'she did what?'

'What?' He looks at me.

'Say that again, what did she do?'

'Which bit?'

'All of it.'

'I said she came over to me, she was walking strange and swaying her hips and making her breasts jiggle about, she stopped in front of me and when I didn't do anything she took her top off....then just stood there...what?' He asks, looking at us pissing ourselves laughing at the thought of some poor zombie woman stood there confused wondering why he wasn't responding. 'What? What's so funny?'

'Did she say anything?' Cookey asks between laughs.

'No,' Dave shakes his head, 'just stood there topless...Why is that funny?' He looks round at Clarence braying like a donkey against the wall then down at Cookey kneeling on the ground clutching his sides. 'Mr Howie?' He asks me. I'm sat on the back step of the Saxon leaning forward as tears fall down my face.

'Poor girl,' I try to mutter, 'what did you do?'

'Killed her,' he replies flatly with just a hint of huffiness at all of us laughing. His answer sets us off again.

'You cold bastard...' I gasp between breaths, 'you could have at least taken her out to dinner first.' That's it. We're off. All of us letting the tension go by pissing ourselves laughing at the thought of it. Dave stood there in front of a topless zombie girl, both of them wondering what to do next so he does what he always does and chops her head off.

'Did...oh god,' Cookey moans, 'did she have nice boobs?'

'I don't know,' Dave replies stiffly, 'I didn't look.'

'Why not?' I ask.

'Would have been rude,' he mutters quietly, looking away as Nick and Blowers sink to the floor.

It takes minutes to compose ourselves. Each time we gather our senses one of us looks at the other and starts off again. All of us crying and moaning at the pains in our stomachs. Dave stands with his back to the wall and folds his arms, a posture I have never seen him do and which makes him look positively sulky.

'This is childish,' he mutters, which just sets us off again, 'call me when you've finished, I'm going to check for crawlers, come on,' he clicks at the dog, taking her away with him.

'Don't look at any boobs,' I call out.

'Okay Mr Howie...Ah...very funny.'

Pulling a case of water from the back of the vehicle I throw the bottles out at the lads, trying to do something with my hands so I stop laughing so much. The laughing dies down to random giggles as we drink water and smoke cigarettes. A deep chuckle emitting from Clarence every few minutes.

'Finished?' Dave walks back into our circle.

'Sorry Dave, no offence mate,' I say between a fresh burst of chuckling, 'why didn't they work on you?'

'What?'

'The pheromones?' I ask.

'The boobs?' Cookey quips which just sets us off again.

'Take your time....whenever you're ready,' Dave stands there watching us.

'Sorry, that was it mate...no more I promise.'

'I don't know why they didn't work, I'm different to all of you.'

'How?'

'I can't read social situations or people, I don't understand the meanings within what people say...I don't have sympathy or empathy, I can't relate someone else's situation to my own experiences...' His words cease the laughing quickly, a sudden thought they we could be offending him deeply, 'I have Autism and Asperger's syndrome...I was tested in the services.'

'Shit...sorry Dave...we weren't laughing at you, it was just a funny concept,' I say softly.

'I understand that,' he smiles, quick and natural which changes his face instantly, 'I can see *why* you would find it funny but I don't relate to it...'

'But you know everything,' Cookey says quickly and with real meaning.

'No,' he shakes his head, 'Mr Howie does, I don't...Clarence knows more about life than I do...all of you know more about girls...and movies...and things like that...'

'Dave, can I ask something mate? Do you ever find things funny? You know...like what makes you laugh?'

He thinks for a second before replying, 'I don't really laugh, I do on the inside sometimes, Laurel and Hardy and Charlie Chaplin...they are good, but I don't show emotion...that's the Asperger's...do you remember Morcambe and Wise?'

'Yeah course,' I reply.

'Who are they?' Nick asks.

'Old comedy act, my Granddad loved them,' Blowers replies.

'They did a sketch when they were cooking breakfast to music...'

'I remember it,' Clarence cuts in, 'in dressing gowns and they had the sausage strings pulled from the fridge.'

'That made me laugh,' Dave says proudly.

The biggest speech he has ever made to us, and he's let us know him as a person. Something passes between us. A bond that strengthens. Surrounded by death and killing every day since this began. Watching our loved ones getting cut down but right now, we all feel it. That even if Dave opens up to us there is something special.

'Pheromones then?' I say before the silence gets uncomfortable, 'makes sense...bloody frightening though...'

'Very,' Clarence offers, 'how did you get to the Saxon?'

'Marcy,' I reply, 'I was surrounded at the top by the gate, things were coming in on all sides. Then they just parted and let me through...Marcy was stood on the wall, I got to the Saxon and she'd gone.'

'Not all bad then,' Clarence says with a tilt of his head.

'She couldn't hold them back though, like she was losing her control over them...was Reggie with you?'

Head shaking as they look at each other. 'Dave? Did you see him?'

'No,' he replies bluntly.

'Him and Marcy must have got away, or they're still here,' Clarence adds.

'They could be in that lot I shot down.'

'Unlikely, are we going after them?'

I look at Clarence, then at the lads and then at the mess of the fort all around us, 'not now, we need coffee and rest.'

'Police dogs can track people, we could get Meredith to find them,' Nick says.

'They're trained to do that mate, she's good but we wouldn't know where to start or how to make her know what to look for, we'll rest and figure out what to do when the sun comes up…I need coffee, lots of coffee.'

I head across to the old police office, getting an instant reminder of everyone we lost as I walk in. The rooms are tidy and put back to order. Marcy must have had her lot working hard while we slept.

Marcy.

Something tells me this isn't over yet, not by a long way.

Seven

'Urgh,' Paula groans as she sits up, sweat dripping from her face, clothes sodden from sleeping in the cramped back seats. The morning sun burning through the windows, slowly heating the inside of the vehicle. Feeling groggy she moves quickly, pushing the door open to dash outside, grimacing at the wall of heat hitting her.

She licks her dry lips and pushes her tongue out of her mouth, yacking at the foul taste. Hair plastered across her forehead, red faced and with a full bladder she moves away from the vehicle and quickly pulls her trousers down, squatting on the grass and groaning with pleasure at the relief of urinating.

Taking her time she scans the view. At the top of a hill she can see down into a valley, across meadows and fields, forested copses and the roofs of cottages and farmhouses dotting the landscape. Rural England, beautiful and shimmering in the high summer heat. Rabbits further down the field, moving slowly through the long grass. Movement catches her eye, a burnt orange colour slinking along the hedgerow. Standing up she pulls her trousers up and moves to the vehicle, grabbing the binoculars from the rear. Focussing on the hedgerow she moves her view along. There, a flash of orange. A fox creeping through the undergrowth, gradually working its way to the rabbits.

Paula feels a sense of trepidation at the sight. Wanting to shout a warning but then realising the fox needs to eat, it might have cubs and be starving for food. Mind you, it doesn't look starving. Nicely shaped with a bushy tail it looks anything but starving. With the instant demise of man, animals like this will fare much better. Just the reduction in road kill will boost the numbers.

The fox stays low, creeping forward as it slinks between the thickets. Pausing every few feet before darting on with a quick burst of speed. Pulling the glasses away she looks with naked eye to the rabbits, still happily moving about without a care in the world.

Watching this, knowing their main predators is stalking closer and closer invokes a feeling of helplessness. Mankind is being pretty much obliterated from the planet but they are just one species. Just one of countless life forms trying to survive. Rabbits have suffered disease and pulled through, they even suffered man made disease used to cull their numbers. Myxomatosis was brought in to try and ease the numbers and ended up wiping out nearly all the wild rabbit population. Maybe that's all this is. A manmade disease sent out by a group of scientists intent on cutting the numbers back and taking the world back to a base state of being.

Twelve days ago that would have sounded absurd. But now it is one of a number of highly probable reasons of how this all started. It must have come from somewhere. Something this virulent couldn't have always been in existence. This is made by man, Paula is sure of it. It has to be. But those rabbits, they just carry on the same as before. The fox gets closer and closer, the rabbits keep eating. Their demise is right there. All they have to do is look, but they don't. They enjoy life and take what happiness they can. They know the fox can't catch all of them.

The fox bursts from the hedge into the open ground, a split second later the rabbits starburst. White tails bobbing up and down with incredible speed and agility. The fox fixes sight on one and gives chase. The rabbit heads straight, then turns instantly to the left, then to right, jigging back and forth. The fox right behind it, turning with every twist, neither gaining nor falling away.

The explosion of energy must be huge, both animals running for everything they are worth. The rabbit bucks and leaps mounds, scattering in a haphazard manner of running. No set pattern that the fox can fix on. Paula smiles as the rabbit finds a hole and drops out of sight, the fox stopping dead with its snout buried into the hole. It scrabbles at the ground for a few seconds before giving up and slinking away.

A mixture of emotions greets Paula as she pushes the binoculars back. Stripping off she stands in bra and knickers, washing with lovely cold water and wet wipes, sluicing the sweat away from her armpits. She tries running a hand through her hair, yelping at the knots that catch on her fingers. Greasy and tangled, she sniffs the end, pursing her mouth at the stench of the fires from last night. Remembering the fire she quickly looks about, scanning the skyline. She spots the smudge in the distance, just a thin plume of smoke wafting high into the air. It doesn't look too bad.

Pulling a large bottle of water from the back she manages to get her head under the lip and start pouring it over her hair, shivering with pleasure as it splashes down her neck and back. Awkward and difficult, using one hand to get her hair soaked and one hand to hold the bottle. She pulls the toiletries bag out and selects a shampoo, squeezing the thick liquid directly onto her head she starts massaging it into her scalp, working it through the strands. An idea strikes her, a pleasant day, washing her hair in the great outdoors, but something is missing.

She moves to the front of the vehicle, leaning into the passenger door to push the radio on. Static fills the car until she presses the play button on the CD player. She waits a few seconds and winces audibly at the Spice Girls booming out that they really really wanna do something.

Still, at least it's upbeat and cheerful. Dancing her way to the back of the car she starts rinsing the shampoo out, smiling to herself as the bubbled water pools round her bare feet.

Paula works the brush through her wet hair, ridding the tangles and still singing along to the music. Cheesy songs but a positive feeling inside her. She won. She actually won. Killed nearly every one of those things and walked away.

A whole town rid and cleansed of the things, and all of it done by her, alone and without help. The loneliness she felt last night still tugs deep inside, but she can cope with it. Better that than being stuck with the Clarke's of this world.

Finished with the hair, feeling clean and dressed in fresh clothes she pulls the small camping stove out and starts heating water. Humming along to the music she prepares a mug with coffee and powdered milk. The water boils quickly, the perfect amount measured out from the many times she has done this.

Within a couple of days she had started this ritual, standing at the back of the vehicle, eating food while brewing up. The normal actions of making coffee soothed her. Something about boiling the water and doing the same thing she had done every morning for as long as she could remember.

With fresh coffee she stares at the bag, knowing she'll do what she shouldn't do it but enjoying the pause to see if she can resist temptation this morning.

Nope. No can do. She slides the packet out and draws one of the white cigarettes out. One a day, sometimes two if she felt like it. No one to judge her, no one to moan or say how bad it was. She hadn't smoked for years but had a sudden craving a few days ago and had enjoyed the hit of caffeine and nicotine while standing in the glorious morning sun.

She lights up and cups the mug in one hand before shuffling her backside onto the rear of the vehicle. Coffee and a cigarette. She settles in for a few minutes, gazing out across the panoramic view. The deep blue sky with not a cloud in sight. Lush green fields stretching out for miles.

With a sigh she takes a sip of coffee then a pull of the cigarette, enjoying the sensation of blowing the smoke away.

Where now? That was the question. That note she read suggested she find her *own kind.* Which meant find other survivors and stay safe. Or, she could find another town and start all over again. She examines her responses inside. The thought of finding others doesn't fill her with any sense of want or need, but the very second she thinks of taking more of those things out and she feels a tingle of excitement.

Nodding her head she makes her mind up. Decision made. Head south and do it all again, and kill as many of them as possible on the way.

How long do they last for? It's been twelve days today since it began and they were going strong last night. Do they eat or drink, do they sleep? At least she knows some of them can talk and think normally. That was strange, very strange. He was stalking her for days, intent on killing her but had the ability to write a letter. Which meant he would have looked for a pen and notepad and then found her vehicle to leave it under the wiper. He could have just staked her car out and waited, trapped her someway. That speaks of vanity which is a weakness she can exploit. If others are like that she can goad them and use that vanity to lure them harder.

The razor wire worked well. The broken glass was okay and felled a few but nothing brilliant. As part of an overall strategy with other tactics it was valued but broken glass on its own wasn't good enough.

Fire was good, very good. Not only burning them but starving them of oxygen too. What else explodes? Anything that is pressurised and contains a flammable liquid or gas. She leans round and grabs her toiletries bag, pulling the can of deodorant free and looking at the flammable sign on the back.

With a mind full of plans she pulls out the ordnance survey map and folds it flat, working her finger along the roads. She finds her town and using a marker pen she puts a bold cross through it. Tracing along she works out her rough position and then moves south to the next settlement.

A wry smile tugs at her mouth as she realises the word she used, *settlement.* Not a town or a village but a *settlement.* Like olden times when people would gather together to have safety in numbers against the beasts and bandits.

'Pretty much like now then,' she mutters. A small town like that is hardly going to have a large enough DIY store to get all the things she needs. Maybe a hardware store but after twelve days the chance of finding one that hasn't been looted will be quite low.

But then a small town or a village won't need the big plans, the numbers should be smaller and therefore easier to cull.

Paula nods, thinking this will be a good test. Drive into the village and use whatever she can find on the spot to do the culling. It will be good experience in case she ever gets caught on the run and has to improvise. Can you have planned improvisation?

'The seven p's,' she mutters quietly, 'proper pre planning prevents piss poor performance, but on this occasion we shall plan not to plan.' Paula's decisive mind works quickly, weighing up the positives, negatives, variables and accounting for unknown eventualities that might arise. After this evaluation of the plan she comes to the conclusion it will be worth it.

The four wheel drive is packed away. Everything stowed where it should be, secured and made safe. She checks her boot laces, making sure the laces are tight and the ends tucked away. Trousers clean and dry, belt secure. Pistol in holster with a full clip of ammunition. MP5 on the passenger seat with a full clip of ammunition and spares for both in her pocket. Flare gun with a fresh flare loaded in. Large bladed knife in the scabbard attached to her belt. Vest top dry and tight to prevent snagging. Hair tied back and free from her eyes. The last two items are put on, a pair of sunglasses, carefully chosen with non-reflective lenses that allow her to see in the day without worrying about glare but not so tinted she would lose vision if running into somewhere darker. Finally a black baseball cap, cotton material and perfect for preventing the sweat rolling down her forehead into her eyes. And if she loses the glasses then the hat will protect her vision.

With the map folded to show the route and placed on the passenger seat she drives back down the field, a full bottle of water between her legs to sip from and stay hydrated. She tuts at the fuel gauge showing less than a quarter of a tank. That will mean either a re-fill or finding another vehicle. No matter, that is to be expected.

At the gate she keeps the engine running while she yanks it open. Driving through she doesn't bother closing it, knowing it will be there and open if she needs to use it again.

On the lane she keeps the window down and one arm rested on the sill, enjoying the blast of hot air rushing past her head. The lane ends at a T junction with another five bar gate leading into a field ahead of her. A brown horse with a thick mane stands with its head hanging over the gate. Paula holds at the junction, staring at the animal as it cranes its neck down to try and reach the juicy grass. The animal's ribs are showing clear along the flank, its head low with huge sad looking eyes. She switches the engine off and drops out, heading across the road. The horse watches her coming and gives a tiny toss of its head. At the gate

Paula looks into the field at the bone dry water trough a few metres along.

Reaching over she pushes the handle down and swings the gate open. The horse moves straight to Paula, rubbing its nose against her shoulder. She pats and rubs the hot muzzle before moving down to look at the waterless container and the tap fixed to a pipe above it.

The sadness of it strikes her hard, that the water is right there but completely inaccessible to the horse. She twists the tap on, water gushes from the end, thundering into the container beneath. The horse is there within seconds, dropping its head down to start licking at the rapidly pooling liquid.

Standing back she spots the brown mound further down the field. She walks closer slowly recognising the form to be another horse, laid flat on the ground and hardly breathing. Like the other one, the ribs are showing along the side. Dying from thirst, in this heat with no shelter it must be only a matter of time before the farm animals start perishing.

Feeling a sense of anger that the owners probably didn't spare a second thought for the poor creatures and were simply occupied with their own survival. But that's not fair; it's human nature to protect yourself. But the sight of the suffering creature still fills her with a sense of unfairness. They relied on humans for everything. Held in captivity, forced to remain within the boundaries of fields and stables. Unable to find food or water.

The horse lifts its head and snorts, letting her know it's not quite dead yet. She rushes back to the vehicle and drags a water bottle out from the back. Running into the field she spots the other horse still stood at the trough drinking deeply as the water pours out.

She scoots round and drops to her knees in front of the prone horse. Unscrewing the cap she gently lifts the horses head and shuffles her legs underneath. With the head raised she tries pressing the bottle to the horse's mouth, pouring a gentle stream of water into it. The horse responds immediately, its large tongue darting out. Remembering from the films or a documentary that water must be given slowly if a person has suffered serious dehydration. Is that the same for horses?

She has no idea but it can't hurt to take it slow and let the water trickle in gently. Paula feels the animal's throat working as it takes the water down. The relief must be immense, to have cool refreshing liquid after such a long hot dry period. How have they lasted this long? But it rained a few days ago, that sudden heavy downpour. That must have given them enough to last a few more days. But the parched ground and hot weather would have sucked the moisture away quickly.

She pulls the bottle away and waits for a few seconds, stroking the animal's long face. The horse looks up at her and snorts again, sending a blast of hot air onto her arm. She shuffles to ease the cramp, not realising how heavy the head would be rested on her lap. The horse snorts again, seemingly demanding more water. She presses the bottle to the mouth and starts pouring the water in again. It splashes down and soaks her lap but the horse drinks and takes what it can. Lips pulling back to show a row of even stained teeth.

A shadow looms over her, making her drop the bottle and reach for the pistol before feeling the warm muzzle of the other horse on her shoulder. Grinning foolishly she carries on, holding the bottle with one hand while rubbing the other ones nose. It moves round and lowers its head to the prone horse. Sniffing at its face before pawing the ground with one front leg and snorting loudly. *Get up. Get up and drink.*

The message is clear and repeated several times. The upright horse even starts nuzzling the downed one, pushing its nose against the neck. Paula watches with interest, realising the intelligence of the animals, the attempts at communication and the clear show of concern.

Not knowing if she is helping or hurting, Paula squeezes out from under the horse and rushes back to the vehicle, mooching through the back and finding the box of sugar cubes. Will this hurt them? The horse is huge so one or two shouldn't hurt and maybe it will give it enough energy to get up. She runs back, hoping she isn't doing more harm than good.

She starts with the horse on its feet, breaking the seal on the box and laughing as the horse smells the contents and starts pushing the box with the end of its nose, eager to get the contents out. The cube looks tiny compared to the horse but then she guesses they don't have a great amount of sugar in their food so it might be quite a strong effect. She holds it flat in her hand and grins again as the horse rubs its lips over and snatches the thing away, within a second it's nuzzling her open hand, asking for more. She gives another two and watches, worried in case it will do something bad but not sure what the bad thing would be. Maybe get hyperactive like a child and start running round in circles. But it doesn't do anything but keeps pushing at her hand, demanding more sugar. She feeds another two and then goes back to the one lying down.

'Hey,' she rubs the nose, smiling in relief that the horse is now holding its own head up. Still lying down but at least it's not sparked out now. She takes a cube and presses it to the horse's mouth, letting the animal sniff it before taking the cube. The other one comes back and keeps nuzzling her, pushing her harder and harder until she relents and feeds it another two cubes.

The lying down horse hasn't died so she gives it another cube, watching carefully in case it starts reacting. Within a couple of minutes the upright horse is showing signs of a sugar rush, pawing the ground and tossing its mane. It becomes more demanding, pushing her roughly for more cubes. The eyes look quite wild now, big and staring. Too much sugar. She tries to ignore it but it persists, nuzzling her shoulder and then taking a nip at her collar bone. With a yelp she relents and feeds two more cubes before going back to the one of the ground.

It too shows signs of reaction. Snorting more and kicking out with its legs, the eyes look sharper too, more focussed and animated.

She feeds another few cubes and moves back just in time as the animal starts moving to get up. A slow action at first and unsteady on its legs, but it does it and gains its feet.

Paula stands back grinning proudly as the horses rub necks and push against each other, both of them now appearing to be full of energy. They trot side by side to the water trough and start drinking, taking huge noisy sucks of water, tails swishing the flies away, flank muscles shuddering with tension and nerves.

Something good just happened. Take the positive and feel good about it, she may have just saved the animals life. Paula strolls slowly towards the gate, watching the horses as they drink. As she passes they both lift their heads and start moving after her. She laughs at the sight or her two new friends coming to say goodbye. The big animals move in and start nuzzling her, pushing her about as they sniff for the sugar cubes. Taking a step back Paula tries telling them no, like a mother would tell a naughty child. But the horses are not children, they're big powerful creatures that want more sugar and they know she has the sugar, so hand it over, give us the sugar now.

Noses push against her, mouths grope and snort down her arms trying to push her hands up. She yelps in alarm as a big shoulder barges her back. The horses are suddenly not so nice, but very big and very strong. They push harder, demanding the sugar be handed over. One goes round behind her, pushing at her back. She tries side stepping but they don't want her to go, not until she hands the sugar over. Pushed, shoved and barged. Lips pulled back to show dirty strong teeth that want to nip and bite until she understands that she will be giving that sugar over.

'Bloody hell,' Paula jumps back, one of the horses snorts louder and paws the ground. This time an aggressive act or one that Paula perceives to be an aggressive act. Being mugged by horses. The oldest trick in the book. Pretend you're injured and when she comes over to help we'll steal her sugar.

She eyes the gate and accepts defeat, they know they can outrun her with ease so she upends the box and sends a little rainfall of glistening white sugar cubes falling to the ground. One of the horses sees the box and goes for it, knocking it out of her hand and sending her flying back. The other one moves in, scooping the cubes up. The box splits, showering Paula in the cubes as she falls to the floor. The second horse moves in, looking with delight at the little white squares distinct against Paula's black clothing.

Paula scrabbles back as the horse comes in for the bite, nipping at the cubes. She rolls away and gets to her feet, running for the gate while drawing her pistol. She runs into the lane, straight to the vehicle and glances back, convinced the horses are chasing her. What she sees are two majestic and gentle creatures grazing contentedly at the ground.

She looks at the pistol and shakes her head, knowing she wouldn't have shot them no matter what, but still impressed that she had the gumption to at least draw the weapon.

'Bloody countryside is more dangerous than those things,' she mutters, climbing back into the vehicle half expecting a herd of cows waiting to carjack her.

Eight

'That's a lot of bodies.'

'It is Mr Howie.'

'Going to be a hot day again.'

'It will be.'

'How the hell we going to get rid of them all?'

'Use a digger.'

'What just scoop them away.'

'Yes Mr Howie, we've got the fuel now...'

'Dirty job though.'

'It is.'

'Too much for just us I think Dave.'

'We can do it, Clarence can drive the digger, we can pile the bodies into a truck and drive them to the estate.'

'Hmmm, still a lot of bloody work though, and all those tents will have to be taken out, they're covered in blood and bits of body.'

'You have a plan.'

'Do I?'

'You do Mr Howie.'

'What's my plan then?'

'To get extra help.'

'That's my plan is it?'

'Yes Mr Howie.'

'Great plan Dave.'

'And you'll be asking Maddox and his group to move here.'

'How the fuck did you know I was thinking of that?'

'It's obvious Mr Howie, we need help and they are the only other group we know.'

'I thought you said you couldn't understand people.'

'This is different, it's tactic and strategy.'

'So what do you think then?'

'What about?'

'Fucking hell Dave...about the moon...what do you think about the moon?'

'It's held in place by the earth's gravitational pull.'

'Very funny.'

'About Maddox you mean?'

'Yes Dave, about Maddox.'

'There are pros and cons, advantages and disadvantages. They are young, untrained, no discipline but also clearly very loyal and brave.'

'True, lads, you alright?'

'Morning Mr Howie, shit...that's a lot of bodies.'

'It is Cookey, we were just saying that.'

'How we gonna get rid of them?' Blowers asks.

'I was thinking of getting some help.'

'Who from?' Clarence asks, then, 'oh...them,' as he makes the same connection as Dave.

'Who?' Cookey asks.

'Who do you think?' Blowers replies.

'I dunno, who?'

'Fucking hell Cookey, even I can work that one out,' Nick sighs.

'Work what one out? Who we asking...?'

'Your mum,' Blowers shakes his head.

'My mum? She won't clear bodies away, she never did the housework at home...who we asking?'

'Jesus mate, are you still pissed?' Nick asks.

'Fucking wish I was,' Cookey grumbles, 'pissed with April and finishing what we started before Dave chopped her head off.'

'I didn't chop her head off,' Dave adds.

'If we find a tattooist I'm gonna get her name done.'

'Cookey you dick, she was a fucking zombie.'

'Fuck you Blowers, she loved me...Anyway, who we asking?'

'Oh my fucking days, have you still not worked it out?' Nick gasps.

'No, who?'

'Who else do we know?' Nick asks him.

'Nobody, they're all dead or zombies...or dead zombies.'

'So we don't know anyone else that's alive?'

'No.'

'Living near here.'

'No,' he shakes his head with a look of concentration.

'Living in a secure compound with big fences...' Nick continues as we all stare at Cookey.

'Big fences? What big fences?'

'Young...'

'Young?'

'Fuck me...this is like pulling teeth...young and living on a fucking housing estate, guns and speaking like chav's.'

'Oh,' Cookey grins, 'them! Why didn't you just say, yeah I get it now...sorry about that.'

'Unbefuckinglievable,' Blowers sighs again, 'Mr Howie, I apologise on behalf of Cookey and his half a brain cell that is still in April's knickers.'

'Oh April,' Cookey adds wistfully, 'she loved me. So we gonna get Maddox then?'

'Worth a go,' I add with a smile, 'there's enough of them, and we got to get this mess cleared up somehow.'

'So we are going to ask a bunch of children to clear away a thousand dead and mangled bodies?' Clarence asks.

'Pretty much mate.'

'Fair enough,' he nods, 'just checking.'

'But they're chav's, they'll steal everything,' Nick says.

'What is there to steal?' I ask him.

'The stores will be emptied, the booze'll be shoplifted, they'll be hanging about on the corners with their hoods up and spitting everywhere.'

'That's racist,' Cookey adds.

'Fucking idiot, it's not racism it's stereotyping,' Blowers replies.

'You're a racialist,' Cookey nods at Nick.

'You're a twat,' Nick promptly replies.

'I don't think we got much choice really, we can't clear this away and manage it on our own. There's only six of us plus the dog.'

'How we going to do it then?' Clarence asks.

'We'll have to go and see them, ask them nicely…that woman, what was her name?'

'Er…Lenski or something like that,' Cookey gives a serious answer for once.

'Yeah Lenski, she was switched on…we'll have to go together, I'm not splitting our team again so we'll have to risk leaving this place empty.'

'What if someone else comes while we're away?' Nick asks.

'They'll find a big empty fort with lots of dead bodies mate,' I smile.

'Okay.'

'Stupid question,' Cookey tuts.

'Fuck you.'

'Fuck your back.'

'Fuck my back?' Nick laughs.

'Fuck it...I meant fuck *you* back.'

'You want to fuck my back?'

'I bet he does,' Blowers adds with a grin.

'Christ,' Clarence shakes his head.

'We might as well go now, nothing else to do,' I say.

'Can you give me ten minutes Mr Howie,' Cookey asks quickly, 'I think that food last night is making a big poo in my tummy.'

'Urgh you fucking dirty bastard,' Blowers grimaces.

'I need a dump too,' Nick rubs his stomach.

'Thinking about it,' Clarence shifts position, 'that's not a bad idea.'

'I might as well go now too then,' Blowers nods.

'How many toilets are in that visitor centre?' I ask, already starting to move away. The others clock my movement and start shifting position.

'I said it first,' Cookey starts running. We all do, flat out sprinting towards the centre, leaving Dave stood there shaking his head. Meredith bounds along barking in a high pitched tone at the sudden excitement.

Cookey takes the lead but the rest of us are right behind him. Even Clarence keeping up as we spring along holding axes and assault rifles.

Yelling and shouting at each other we watch Cookey turn and grin as he keeps the lead position. With a few metres to go he raises an arm in victory, just as Dave runs past him, goes through the open door and sprints down the short corridor to the toilets, scooting through and out of sight.

Cookey yells out and runs through with the rest of us hot on his trail, he gets to the toilet door and bursts in, turning to stick one finger up at Blowers and Nick before disappearing out of view.

'There's only two cubicles in there,' Blowers moans, 'where you going?' He adds as Nick jogs past, heading for the ladies.

'Using the girl's toilet, they're always cleaner anyway,' he shouts and pushes the door open.

Blowers, Clarence and I all look at each other and start running for the last remaining cubicle in the girl's toilet.

'CONTACT,' Nick bellows from inside. We rush through the door to see Nick inside stood a couple of feet back from one the closed door of a cubicle. 'In there,' he nods, holding his rifle up and ready, 'the doors locked, must be someone inside.'

'What is it?' Dave bursts in, pistol in hand, followed by Cookey holding his trousers up with one hand and clutching his rifle with the other.

'Someone in that cubicle,' I motion with my head to the closed door. Dave drops down, looking through the few inches of gap at the bottom of the door; he looks up nodding and holds one finger up.

Blowers creeps into the open cubicle and steps onto the rim of the toilet, lifting himself up to see over the wall. The rest of us stand back, weapons aimed and ready. Blowers peers over and quickly looks back at me, then down again before hopping off and standing there with a worried look on his face.

'Who is it?' Clarence asks after a few seconds pause, but judging from his face I can take a guess who is in there.

'Lani,' Blowers replies quietly.

'Fuck,' Cookey exclaims.

'She's taped up.'

'What?' I ask him.

'Taped up,' he repeats. He steps out of the cubicle so I can squeeze in behind him, passing him my rifle so I can lift up. Taking care not to grip the top of the plinth wall I lean over and look down.

Lani sat on the closed toilet seat with thick tape wrapped round her ankles and knees. Her hands bound behind her back and more tape wrapped round her mouth and a blindfold tied round her head.

'He's bloody right,' her head is already tilted up and cocked to one side as though listening intently and at the sound of my voice so close to her she starts murmuring being the gag.

'What she doing in there?' Clarence asks, 'can I pop this door open?'

'Yes mate, she's wrapped up tight.'

'Sure?'

'Go for it, she's sat down with tape round her legs, gagged and blindfolded.'

Clarence leans his bulk on the flimsy door and gives it a tiny shove, popping the plastic lock off with ease. Stepping back he uses his foot to push the door open. The rest of them all try to peer in at the same time, leaning round the sides of the door at Lani sat there, completely immobile. Muffled sounds come from her as she rocks her body side to side then back and forth.

'Ah fuck it, she's gone,' Clarence mutters with a sad tone, 'look at her, poor thing.'

'What we gonna do?' Cookey asks as we all stand back from the cubicle and stare in at the writhing figure.

'Kill her,' Dave suggests in his usual flat tone.

'We can't kill Lani,' Nick replies.

Looking at her squirming now I can just imagine her getting free of the bonds and attacking us, launching like the others outside. Even so, it's horrible to see and without the danger of an imminent threat it's hard to make the decision to kill her, 'it's not Lani though is it,' I say after a pause, 'it's one of them, same as Marcy and the rest, fucking diseased.'

'Kill her then,' Dave suggests again, 'one to the forehead, quick and painless.'

'She's going nuts to get at us, look at her,' Blowers shakes his head as Lani gets more animated, the sound of our voices must be driving her mad with hunger and I can just imagine the saliva building up behind that gag.

'Why did they put her in here?' Cookey asks.

'Keep her away from us I guess, maybe Marcy thought I wouldn't fall for her if I had Lani in view.'

'Ah yeah, that makes sense,' Nick nods, 'bloody hell she's gonna bust that tape in a minute, she's going crazy.'

'Infection must be driving her mad, telling her to get us, maybe it can hear us?' Clarence says with his eyes locked on the cubicle.

'What the infection can hear us?' Cookey asks, 'how would that work?'

'It seems fucking clever enough and its latest master plan just went tits up.' I add.

‘I couldn’t kill her,’ Nick shakes his head, ‘not like this.’

‘Me neither mate, if she was attacking us I could but not in cold blood...not Lani,’ I reply.

‘Dave then,’ Clarence states, ‘or the dog.’

‘You can’t set Meredith on her,’ I look up at him.

‘Why not,’ he shrugs, ‘the dog doesn't care who it is...or rather who it was...she’d go for any of us if we turned.’

In a sick way it makes sense, Meredith wouldn’t hesitate and isn’t hindered by emotions the same way we are and we all saw what she did to Paco that night.

‘Maybe it’s best then...fuck,’ we all jump back as she kicks out, slamming her feet into the door, balancing her backside on the toilet seat she thrashes out again and again with her legs bound at the knees and ankles.

‘Where is she?’ I ask looking round. Nick goes to the door and calls for Meredith, whistling loudly.

‘Nick hurry up mate she’s going nuts,’ Cookey calls out. Lani gets to her feet and bounces side to side against the cubicle walls, shuddering the thin ply-board with her lithe but powerful body. The growling gets louder, fiercer as she jumps and hops towards the opening and out into the toilet. We dart away keeping our distance.

‘Nick for fuck’s sake get the dog,’ Cookey shouts.

‘I’ll do it,’ Dave draws a knife as Lani drops to the floor and starts rolling back and forth across the floor. Yelling in alarm we have to jump over her body as she rolls into our feet, sensing the contact with us just makes it harder.

‘Hang on,’ Nick shouts and runs down the corridor.

'I can't watch,' Cookey bleats heading for the door with Blowers right behind him.

'Boss,' Clarence shouts in alarm as Lani rolls into my feet. I try leaping over her but get tangled and fall down in a heap, scrabbling away as she writhes and squirms, kicking her legs out and bucking her body violently. She must be screaming with hunger behind that gag, the veins in her neck bulge out with effort and her muscles stand taut against her frame.

Dave pulls me away, dragging me to my feet as we hear Nick shouting in the corridor, 'She's coming, she found a crawler on the other side.'

'I thought you got them all,' I look at Dave who suddenly looks aghast that he missed one.

'Sorry, I thought I did, I'm really sorry Mr Howie, I promise it won't happen again.'

'Fuck!' We leap over Lani rolling across the floor at us, clearly following the sound of our voices, 'don't worry mate, it happens.'

'She's here,' the door bursts open as Meredith runs in, tail wagging and giving a high pitched bark at finding us hiding. Lani rolls harder, slamming her body into the frame of the cubicle. Meredith looks down at her, head cocked to one side. I twist away, unable to watch and catch a glimpse of Clarence doing the same thing. Lani keeps rolling, crashing into the wall then into the frame. Her legs kicking out as she growls and howls behind the gag.

Meredith yelps with another high pitched bark as Lani crashes into the side of the room. I look round to see the dog watching Lani intently, her upper body down low to the ground but her arse in the air with her tail going crazy. Lani rolls again, a fast motion that shoots her body over the floor. Meredith barks and leaps over her, landing the other side to spin round on the spot then drop down again.

'What the fuck?' Cookey calls out from the door.

Meredith creeps forward towards Lani, nose stretched out and her tail still going nuts. As Lani starts the roll she jumps back playfully then shoots forward again to push her nose at Lani's head. Lani squirms and sits up in a fluid motion, Meredith bounds round her barking with excitement. I look at Clarence who just stares at me and shrugs.

'Is she...?' I start to stutter then watch amazed as Meredith gets close to Lani and sniffs her face, I hold my breath thinking this is it, this is the point that the dog realises Lani is one of them and goes for her. Squeezing my eyes closed again I feel a tugging on my arm and see Dave stood there pointing at the dog gently leaning in to nip at the gag in Lani's mouth, her tail still wagging like mad like it's a game. She pulls backwards and shakes her head gently pulling Lani with her who keeps murmuring with increasing volume.

Dave darts in with knife in hand, his movement so quick that for a split second it looks like he's going to cut her throat. Instead he deftly swipes at the material of the gag tied at the back of her head. With Meredith still pulling it, the gag comes away. Meredith drops it instantly and starts licking Lani round her face, tail still going.

'Don't let Dave kill me,' she blurts out, her voice hoarse and rough.

'Shit,' I rush in and grab the blindfold, working at the knot to pull it free. Cookey and the lads pile in as Meredith keeps licking at her face.

'Aah,' Lani spits, 'her tongue went in my mouth.'

'Come here,' Nick pulls the dog away.

'Dave, cut her wrists,' I say as I struggle with the knot tangled in her hair.

'No! Don't cut my bloody wrists,' Lani yells with panic.

'The tape, not your wrists...Dave cut the tape.'

'She might go for us,' Dave says.

'I think we'll be alright mate, there's bloody six of us plus the dog.' He drops down and pushes his blade through the tape between her arms. They pull away quickly and immediately she lifts her hands to the blindfold, pulling it roughly up over her forehead.

'Get off, let me do it,' she snaps, 'you've got my hair caught.' Grimacing she tugs it free, pulling several long black hairs from her head at the same time. Dropping the blindfold she starts rubbing her eyes, groaning in pain or pleasure, or quite possibly a mixture of both.

'You were going to let the dog eat me,' she shouts suddenly with anger.

'You're one of them, we thought you were trying to get us,' I say.

'How would I do that exactly, taped up and stuck in a toilet, you're bloody idiots...all of you damned bloody idiots.' Taking her hands away she stares down at the ground, stretching the muscles of her face, opening her mouth wide, 'oh that's better, it's really bright in here.'

'You've been blindfolded for ages,' Clarence points out.

'Really? Was I?' Lani snaps back at him, 'give me a minute, my eyes hurt.'

'How come you can speak?' I ask, 'you couldn't speak before...'

'I don't bloody know, can you give me a minute please,' she snaps again.

'Take your time,' I reply softly.

'I will, after you tried setting the dog on me.'

'We didn't want to kill you,' I reply.

'Dave did, he kept bloody offering...' Lani retorts.

'Well...shit I don't know...we thought...holy fuck!'

'What?' She stares up at me.

'Your eyes!'

'What?'

'Fuck...fuck...'

'WHAT?!' She looks up at the lads who blanch at the sight of her, mouths dropping open, 'oh...are they that bad?'

'Fuck,' I repeat again, 'fuck...'

'Stop saying fuck,' Lani snaps, 'you must have seen thousands of them by now.'

'Lani,' Clarence stares down with a stony face, 'come here,' he bends over and lifts her easily to her feet.

'What?'

'Fuck...' I repeat again.

'Stop saying fuck!' She wails.

'Look,' Clarence steers her to the smudged mirror on the wall above the hand wash basins, Lani squints at the light then leans forward, with her legs still bound Clarence holds her steady.

'Fuck,' she mutters at the sight of herself, 'oh fuck...' She turns away blinking and rubbing at her eyes before going back and checking again, 'fuck...' she uses her fingers to stretch the eyelids away, rotating her pupils left, right then up and down.

'They're normal,' she gasps, 'they're normal…white and brown and….fuck!'

Nine

One main road through the middle. An old fashioned shop with a red awning over the door on the right side. Smaller roads leading off to side streets with stone built cottages and pretty front gardens. An average village centre in an average part of southern England.

And no sign of the things. Not one. Not anywhere. Paula purses her lips and leans forward resting both her hands on the top of the steering wheel. Where is everyone? Having driven through once she saw front doors hanging open, some dried stains on the ground presumably from pools of blood. But nothing other than that. Cars still parked on driveways and everything looks pretty normal. Even the shop doesn't look smashed up or damaged.

Several minutes go by and still no sign of anything. Eventually she presses the horn, sending a loud honk into the perfectly still air. With a good line of sight to the front and rear she waits, expecting to see them stumbling from somewhere, but nothing. Not a thing. No movement.

She presses the horn again, longer this time. A determined honk sounding out, *I'm here...come and get me...I'm fresh and juicy and nice to eat.*

This doesn't feel right. The village is small but the doors to the houses have been opened and with the blood stains it means people have been taken here. So where are they? Paula starts the engine and crawls along at a slow speed. Watching either side, bending down to look out the passenger window trying to detect any movement. She keeps pressing the horn, giving regular honks to draw them out.

Biting her bottom lip she stops the vehicle and climbs out, wincing at the heat. Standing at the side of the open car door she looks up and down the deserted street. She switches the engine off and listens intently, turning her head to stare up and down the street, scanning the houses. Nothing. Nothing at all.

Her eyes fall on a blue van parked on a driveway, vans run on diesel, so does her vehicle. She scans about again checking the area. Might as well take advantage of the quiet, she gets back in and drives to the house, parking alongside the van. The house looks empty, the front door ajar and presenting the dark hallway inside.

Pistol in hand she stalks towards it, moving with fast determined steps. No point in messing about, get in, find the keys and get back out. Pushing the door open she holds for a second, listening and staring at the tidy clean interior. No nasty smells, no flies buzzing everywhere, no sign of death or those things.

Moving through the rooms she works her way to the kitchen, finding a row of metal hoops fashioned from a wrought iron decoration fastened to the wall and each one with a set of keys hanging down. She takes the set with the biggest black plastic fobbed key and heads outside, pressing the key clicker and nodding as the van doors click unlocked.

Paula had no idea how you got fuel from a vehicle, and with the internet down she had to rely on finding an old book from an abandoned house and reading the section carefully.

Now, with the length of hose pushed into the van fuel opening she makes sure the tube is long enough to be below the level of the fuel tank and gets the container ready. Lips wrapped round the end and she starts sucking, drawing the air from the tube while watching as the fuel starts to rise in the opaque tubing. She drops down, keeping as low as possible, the fuel hits her mouth with a bitter acrid taste. Wrenching her head away she spits it out, holding her thumb over the end of the hose to prevent it going everywhere.

It tastes awful, really awful. She pushes the hose to the plastic container and removes her thumb, listening as the fuel starts to pour inside. Leaving it there she goes back to her vehicle, retching and gagging on the way. Yaks coming from her stomach at the taste of the fuel in her mouth. Ignoring the bottles of water she grabs a warm can of coke, pouring the sickly sweet content and swilling it round her mouth before spitting it out.

With the fuel can filling up she pulls the hose free and uses a funnel to pour the diesel into the fuel tank of her own vehicle. Smiling with satisfaction of planning ahead and making sure she had the right equipment to do the job.

Paula repeats the action until no more fuel comes out the hose, draining the van fuel tank and replenishing her own. Back in her car she turns the ignition on and grins broadly as the fuel gauge rises to almost full.

'Yes!' Slapping the top of the steering wheel from the joy of doing it herself. It was easy and now she's got almost a full tank of fuel.

'Couldn't get bloody promoted though, oh no...not good enough for promotion Paula, not ready for it yet...maybe next time eh?' Shaking her head she drives away, feeling a sense of purpose and pride.

Out the village and back into the long twisting country lanes, arm on the window sill and once again enjoying the breeze blasting by. Looking at the map, the next village is a quite a few miles away and looks about the same size as the one she just left. Just another ornate selection of country cottages looking all picturesque and homely. The sort of place anyone would want to live, especially city fold who've worked hard for long years and grown sick of the traffic and constant noise.

Coming out of a long sweeping bend she spots something on the road ahead of her. Something low down and moving along. As she gets closer she makes out the form of the woman, dressed in a nightshirt ripped, torn and filthy. The thing crawls along, using just her arms to drag her onwards, the legs feeble and unmoving suggesting a spinal injury.

Paula holds behind it, driving slowly along as she watches it keeps going, the skin on her legs is scraped off, bright red glistening wounds that crawl with maggots and flies landing to feast and lay more eggs. The thing pays no heed, simply dragging along, cutting her flesh to pieces on the rough surface of the road.

The vehicle bounces as she drives over the body, looking through the rear view mirror at the now inert corpse. With barely a glance back she pushes on trying to work out where it was going.

Something about the crawler makes her think. It was so intent on getting somewhere. They always just stood about at the last place they saw a survivor, or gathered in large numbers in the centre. They only kept going when there was something to head towards.

Paying more attention to the immediate area she notices the verges look trampled, the grass flattened and branches sticking out from the hedgerow are snapped or bent. They must have come this way, it's only a narrow lane but there must have been a lot of them if they had to use the sides in addition to the road.

What made them all come this way? For a second she considers if they were coming after her, but the thought is dismissed as quickly as it forms. Her town is back the other way, north not south. Something else is making them head this direction.

The next village comes into view. The standard main road through the middle with a small collection of shops in the centre, the shops are larger with a butchers and mini-market. It still looks pretty with the stone walls and flower beds bursting with colour, although on closer inspection she notices the flowers are now wilting from the heat and the colours not so vibrant. Another few days and they'll have dried up and died, just like everything else.

No movement though. No things staggering or shuffling about. The same as the previous village, devoid of life, empty and eerie with silence.

Paula goes slow, taking time to look at the sides of the road and spotting signs of heavy foot traffic. Trampled flowers and a blood stained solitary shoe left in the middle of the road.

She drives through to the other side, turns and heads back. Examining every window and door, looking at the cars and front gardens. The same as before, doors opened, blood stains here and there. One of the houses has a corpse across the threshold of the door but even from a few metres she can see it's rotting and decomposing.

Stopping the vehicle at the shops she waits for a few minutes, listening quietly and scanning the area. So quiet she can hear her own breathing and feel the beat of her heart. With one hand on the pistol grip and the other on the hilt of the knife she makes her way slowly across the road towards the mini-market. The door has been forced open, smashed in with shards of glass littering the ground. The windows are still intact and displaying faded sun bleached signs. Dark patches on the ground indicate blood loss here. She draws the pistol keeping it low as she crunches over the broken glass.

Holding at the door she peers inside, listening and looking, waiting for anything to move. Nothing, no noise, no sounds, no movement. She steps into the looted interior, looking at the empty shelves. Every food item has been taken, all the toiletries and cleaning products gone. Just magazines and newspapers left

Out the village and back into the country lanes. She follows the route on her map, taking bends and junctions until she reaches a much wider main road. A signpost points to Bereford in one direction or her town the other way.

Bereford. That was quite big. Not anywhere near the size of her own town but big enough. She takes the turning and heads on, still watching the sides for signs of foot traffic. The verges look intact but then the road is much wider here, plenty of room for a large group to walk down without the need to go on the verges.

Taking it easy, Paula drives the route, slowing to look at the houses and buildings at the side of the road. Another corpse lying forlorn and forgotten at the side of the road. Rancid and decaying with the skin eaten away by creatures and birds.

The buildings become more frequent as she gets closer to the town. The spread from the urbanisation spilling out over many years of growth. A mile out from the town she spots a group of them in the distance. Their movements and manner signalling exactly what they are.

Slowing down she drives up slowly behind them, a large group spread across the road. Maybe fifty or sixty and all of them moving towards the town. Keeping her distance she watches them for a few minutes. They're walking faster than normal for the day, a clear and determined pace. Not fast, but certainly quicker than normal. She drives closer, watching them to see for any reaction. They don't turn or glance back but keep on towards the town.

Closer now, just a few metres away from the stragglers and still no reaction. She pushes her foot down on the clutch and revs the engine; making noise to alert them she is there.

They keep on so she eases forward and bumps into one of them, thudding him down to the ground. She brakes hard and quickly reverses away, convinced they will now turn and start attacking her.

The rest keep going, the one on the floor just rolls over and starts getting to his feet, not bothering to look in her direction. With a frown she accelerates and runs him over, feeling a slight jolt as both front and rear wheels crush him into the road. Again they just keep going, ignoring her completely.

Paula takes another one down, shunting it hard then braking and watching as the body flies forward into more of the things, knocking them to the ground. The rest of the group push on, leaving the others writhing on the ground. Paula drives over them, veering and turning the wheel to get as many as possible and then reversing to get the ones she missed.

The numbers get reduced as she picks them off, using the big chrome bull bars at the front of the four wheel drive to smash into them and crush them under-wheel.

With only a handful left they reach the edge of town, the fields giving way to rows of houses, street lights, roofs, line markings, sign posts and urbanisation everywhere.

They get taken down too, run over and killed. An easy fifty count done without the need to get out of the vehicle. It was good but time consuming and lacked the finesse of some of the other big kills she'd done.

Leaving the broken bodies behind she drives through the main road, looking at the desperate signs of fighting and suffering.

Bereford obviously saw some hard action when the event happened. A large population all living in a relatively small area.

Within a minute Paula notices the next horde staggering ahead of her. A huge group that clog the road, hundreds of them all walking through the town away from her. On the flat road she can't see the head of the horde.

This must be all the things from the villages, all pressed together and going the same way. What's drawing them? What is so important they have to be gathered in such large numbers?

She can't get through, there are too many of them. She could plough into the back of the horde but the risk of getting bogged in is too great. She could pick them off but the numbers are too vast.

There must be a way of getting round them to see how many there are and where the front is and then work out where they're going. The ordnance survey map shows the side roads loop into each other, forming a network of estates, avenues and through-roads. Taking a random side junction she curses within two minutes as she reaches the end of the cul-de-sac, chastising herself for not looking at the road sign. Something like that could be a potentially fatal mistake if she was being chased. It would mean giving the vehicle up and having to run on foot.

Vowing to stay vigilant she heads back out and stays behind the horde, waiting as they pass the next junction. Turning in she accelerates the four wheel drive, bouncing over the speed humps as she navigates the smaller side roads. The signs of devastation are much worse here, nearly every house looks damaged and bodies litter the pavements and gardens. Rotting corpses and mutilated cadavers festering in the heat and providing a food source for countless disease spreading bacteria that will be ingested by the maggots.

At each point where the side roads link back to the main road she pauses to gain a view, looking at the constant stream of the things walking past. Not one of them looks in her direction, not a flicker or a sign that they've seen her. The size of the marching column surprises her, stretching on and on. There must be hundreds and hundreds all contained together and keeping to an orderly rhythm.

She has to take the vehicle deeper into the winding estates, searching for a way to get ahead of them. Reading the map as she coasts along she works a route out, turning up a road that leads to a tributary carriageway that eventually feeds into the town's main thoroughfare.

Driving faster now, pushing to find out where they're going and desperate to know why they don't react to her presence or try and take her.

She pulls up short of the junction, mouth hanging open as she looks at the things traipsing past. No way, they can't be this far ahead. There must be a shortcut somewhere. She checks the map, tracing the road they're on back to the town centre then using the top half of her thumb to measure the distance against the scale at the bottom of the map.

'Shit,' she whispers quietly. Over a mile. A mile long column of the things. Not hundreds but thousands and she still hasn't seen where the front is.

They're coming out the town onto this road; she looks at the red line on the map. It snakes through open country for miles, through woods and farm pasture before finally hitting another town, but that one is smaller than Bereford. Why would they be going there? The red line goes straight through the small town and continues back into open land.

She has to know why they're going there. What's in that town? And the thought of so many in one place is a challenge just waiting to be taken up. If she can get ahead of them she could lay traps and ambush sites, maybe get something rigged up to start killing them before they get there.

First thing is to find out why they're heading there. The road marked in red is no good so she works another way round. It'll take her miles out of the way but with a full tank of fuel and empty roads it should be done easy enough.

Decision made. Options weighed. Advantages and disadvantages accounted for. With a resolute nod she backs the vehicle into a driveway and heads back down the road.

Ten

'Stop staring at me.'

'Who?' I ask.

'All of you, you're freaking me out.'

We turn away and stare elsewhere for a few seconds before slowly turning back to look at her again, all of us fixated by her eyes.

In the former police office we sit round the table while Cookey brews up and Meredith lies down by the door.

'Cookey stop it,' Lani exclaims at the lad stood there staring at her holding the jar of coffee with the spoon hovering above it.

'Sorry,' he turns away to keep spooning the granules into the mugs.

'So what happened?' She asks us.

'Fuck,' I say for the hundredth time, my head seemingly unable to keep up.

'Stop saying that,' she gasps, 'what happened? Why haven't I got red eyes?'

'How do you feel?' Clarence asks.

'Normal, hungry...not like that Cookey,' she rolls her eyes as he opens his mouth to say something then promptly closes it again, 'thirsty, tired...normal and my stomach hurts,' she winces and pulls the front of her top up to reveal the puckered wound where she was cut. It was only yesterday but it looks several days old already. The skin knotted together and a large bruise round it. Clarence and Dave both lean in, closely examining the injury.

'No sign of infection,' Clarence mutters.

'Healed quick too,' Dave adds then looks over at Meredith, 'like a dog heals, faster than us.'

'Did you just call me a dog?' Lani asks.

'No,' Dave replies seriously, 'I said the wound is healing faster, like a dog heals faster than us...the infection has accelerated your ability to heal.'

'How?' Lani asks staring down at her stomach.

'I don't know,' Dave replies, 'can I touch it please?'

'Aren't you worried about catching it?' She asks him with a serious expression which he returns as only Dave can.

'It's a sealed wound, how would I catch it?'

'There might be bacteria on my skin or something.'

'If that was the case we'd all be infected by now, it's transmitted by fluids.'

Dave uses the back of his hand to touch the wound, feeling along it gently, 'no sign of heat,' he says, 'does it hurt?'

'Yeah but not that much, not like it should if it was only yesterday.'

'What's the pain like inside?'

She shrugs and stares back at him for a second, 'it aches when I move but nothing that bad.'

'It was a deep wound, the pain should be a lot greater than that. Do you have a high pain threshold?'

'I'm a woman aren't I?' She replies with one eyebrow raised.

'I don't understand,' Dave replies in his flat tone.

'Forget it,' she says laconically, 'er...not really, I don't know if my pain threshold is any different to anyone else's?'

'May I try something?' Dave asks.

'Yeah,' she looks up at him puzzled, then flinches as his hand shoots out to grab her ear lobe, giving it a nasty little twist. 'Ow!' She yells and pulls away, 'what the hell Dave,' she stares back with a flash of anger, 'that really bloody hurt.'

'Pain threshold normal then,' Clarence mutters having watched with great interest.

'Yes,' Dave replies turning away.

'You could have asked first,' Lani moans rubbing her ear.

'I did.'

'Jesus, it felt like you pulled it off, so what does that mean then?'

'Your pain receptors are normal now, unless you're faking it but judging at the angry flush in your face I would say not,' Dave explains, 'but, a wound like that should see you in agony for days, so whatever infection was in you, it caused you to heal faster and dulled the pain.'

'So it's still in me then?' She asks.

'I don't know... we don't know how fast the rate of healing is, it could be that the wound is healed the same way someone else would be in a week or two weeks, but it only happened yesterday. We don't know if you're still healing faster than normal or if you're now back to normal,' a long explanation for Dave and he trails off as though suddenly aware of himself.

'Do you remember it?' I ask her.

'Sort of,' she feels the wound with her finger tips, pressing lightly, 'like a dream or something, all hazy but with clear bits...I know I could talk but Marcy was stopping me,' the others all glance at me quickly, 'what was that?' Lani asks.

'What?'

'That look, what was that about?'

'Later, go on keep going,' I wave her on desperate to avoid that conversation.

'I didn't feel any pain or anything else but Marcy made me go straight in that toilet, they taped me up and left me there...'

'And you just let them?' Nick asks.

'Yeah,' Lani nods, 'it was the most normal thing in the world, like someone else was completely in control and I just had to do what I was being told.'

'That's fucked up,' Blowers remarks.

'Completely,' she agrees, 'I couldn't hear her voice or anything but like...I could feel her will and knew it was her but it was so natural and...well I guess organic,' she shrugs struggling to find the words, 'I take it you killed her?'

'Who Marcy?' I ask with a guilty start.

'No the wicked witch of the west,' she snaps, 'yes Marcy...how did you kill her? What happened?'

'I don't think she's dead,' I explain slowly.

'Right,' Lani looks at me, stretching the word out, 'thanks Cookey,' she smiles as he places the mug in front of her.

'I put sugar in it, do you still take sugar?' He asks softly.

'Yes, I still take sugar,' she replies with forced patience.

'So, Marcy then? Not dead?' She looks back at me.

'Don't think so, er...hang on, when did you stop feeling like...er...well like you just said and then normal like now?'

She shrugs and thinks, shaking her head, 'It was weird, I was out of it but I didn't come back like instantly, it was slow, like sobering up from being drunk or...or coming round from anaesthetic...like bit by bit I could feel more of my body and my mind was swimming in and out. Then gradually I just sort of became aware of where I was, the more my mind came back the more things started to hurt, like my wrists and my stomach and I got cramp from being stuck in the same position too.

'I heard the shooting and that snapped me back to full...er...alertness? Is that the word? Yeah, alertness...I recognised the sound of the GPMG and the assault rifles then later I heard you all running in and then saying how to kill me,' she lifts one eyebrow at Dave.

'Sorry Lani,' he says.

'The dog? Really?' She asks, 'you were going to get Meredith to eat me...that's awful.'

'We didn't know,' I reply.

'I'm glad you didn't, but just let Dave shoot me in the head next time, don't use the dog, that's awful.'

'Okay.'

'But check my eyes first,' she adds quickly.

'Okay,' I reply again sheepishly, 'I don't get it...are you immune then?'

'I don't know,' she replies quickly, 'probably not, maybe I carry it without it showing or doing anything...'

'But it healed you quickly, like it does with the other ones,' Clarence points out, 'and we saw you being the same as them....and Marcy controlled you...'

'I don't know,' she repeats.

'Which means that either your body has found a way to fend it off or stop it,' I lean forward, 'or you're still infected and one of them and this is another trick.'

'Another trick?' She asks.

'Yeah like Marcy did with Mr Howie,' Cookey cuts in. I close my eyes quickly, grimacing as he realises what he just said.

'Why? What did Marcy do with Mr Howie?' She asks with a sidelong glance at me.

'Er...you know...like tricking us into thinking she was er...like helping us,' Nick adds quickly.

'Yeah that's what I meant,' Cookey nods, 'that...what Nick just said...'

'Cookey?' Lani asks.

'Like Nick just said,' he says too high pitched, 'she tricked us like she was helping us...'

'So where is she then?'

'Who?'

'Cookey you are a crap liar, what's going on?'

'Oh fuck,' he mutters, 'Nick have you got any smokes?'

'Yes mate, we going out for one?'

'Yeah,'

'I'll come,' Blowers adds standing up.

'No,' Lani cuts in, 'smoke in here.'

'Dave said were not allowed,' Cookey adds with a frantic look.

'Did I?' Dave asks.

'Er...no?' Cookey replies.

'What,' Lani snaps, 'is going on? Where is Marcy? Howie...' she looks at me.

'Fuck I'm out of here,' Nick walks quickly to the door with the two lads, leaving the rest of us sat there in silence.

'So you could be immune then?' I ask with a faint hope at changing the subject.

'Where's Marcy?'

'Which would be good news of course,' I nod.

'Where's Marcy?'

'And could mean we found a cure...yay,' I smile and nod again.

'Howie,' she looks at me, 'where is Marcy?'

'Oh she's gone,' I wave my hand, 'just went off I think...'

'Right, you leave me no choice,' she turns to face Dave, 'Dave, where is Marcy and what happened?'

'Marcy and some of the other girls were giving pheromones off, making the men get all...er...' he shrugs, 'er...horny I think Alex called it, and they lured the men into almost getting with them...Marcy went for Mr Howie out the back but the others...'

'Sorry what?' Lani leans forward, 'Marcy did what?'

'Went for Mr Howie,' Dave repeats, 'but the others were down here and...'

'Went for Mr Howie? Like how? Attacked him or...'

'No, turning him on...' Dave explains in his flat voice, 'like I said, we think they were putting pheromones out and it made everyone get horny so Mr Howie went out the back with Marcy and they were getting naked when...

'Dave,' I shout in alarm.

'What?' Lani shouts at the same time.

'Dave,' Clarence shakes his head with a groan.

'What?' Dave asks innocently.

'They were doing what?' Lani shouts, 'you were doing what?' She repeats looking at me.

'Right hang on, let me explain…'

'I think you should,' she sits back glaring at me, 'you were getting naked with Marcy while I was tied up in a toilet?'

'Hang on,' I wail, 'just wait…she was like…er…in my head or something, I couldn't stop thinking of her…'

'I beg your pardon,' speaking softly she drops her head and lifts both eyebrows.

'Ah, fucking hell, she was like in my head since we first met yesterday…I just couldn't stop thinking about her…'

'Yesterday? When I was alive and stood next to you? That yesterday yes?'

'Yes,' I groan, 'that yesterday, I don't know what happened, like Dave said it was pheromones or something, whatever it was it worked…'

'Just on you?' She asks me, 'not the others…Clarence did you have the same thing with Marcy?'

'Er…no not really,' he rumbles nervously, 'I got lured later by another one though, we all did apart from Dave.'

'So, keep going,' she looks back at me with a glare.

'Right well yes, er…so we had the fight and she saved us, and then you were down and er…'

'Get to the point,' she growls folding her arms.'

'I am,' I whine, 'then we were like fucked, completely fucked, everyone had died, Sarah and you and Chris and we just went to our rooms and slept, then when we woke up they had cleaned up and…'

'Cleaned up? She didn't do a very good did she? Have you seen the mess out there?'

'Listen,' I wave my hand at her, 'it was all clean and with lights on, they made food for us and we er...well we had the food.'

'Oh very nice, a romantic meal,' she says slowly.

'Then er...the lads were drinking and getting pissed, I was annoyed and feeling like manipulated like it was all contrived so I went out the back and Marcy came with me and then er...well I don't know.'

'Don't know what?'

'I don't know,' I say weakly, 'oh fuck it,' I sigh and rub my head. She deserves the truth so I spit it out quickly, 'she was coming onto me, and I responded but I was aggressive with it, it wasn't romantic or loving or anything else...it felt like that at the time but it wasn't...it was lust, pure lust...and the most terrible thing is if she hadn't of given it I would have taken it...'

'My god?' Lani looks at me in shock.

'Yeah,' I nod, 'that's how bad it was, we didn't do anything...we didn't kiss, we didn't have sex...almost but not quite...but I was so turned on and so...I don't know...aggressive and...'

'I felt the same,' Clarence cuts in, 'and even one of the lads went for me when I tried getting the girls off them.'

'Same here,' Dave adds, 'I had to trip Nick up as he was trying to fight me.'

'Seriously?' Lani asks.

'Yeah, it was that bad,' I reply.

'I'm not talking to you,' she snaps, 'fair enough I get it, not your fault but I was tied up in a toilet and had only just been taken and you were trying to shag Marcy…so forgive me but you can fuck off for a bit.'

'What? Hang on.'

'No, fuck off,' She snaps without looking at me, 'just don't speak to me for a minute.'

'Lani,' I plead.

'Remember that bloke in the back of Saxon? The one who had his head cut off?'

'Fine,' I sit back quietly.

Lani shakes her head with a look of anger mixed in with hurt and confusion. She masks it well, keeping her face mostly impassive.

'So where is she?'

Clarence explains the last bit, where Meredith pushed us both into the water, then the fight in the fort and Marcy on the top of the wall. Lani listens intently, nodding her head to show understanding. 'So you don't know where she's gone?'

'No,' I reply and earn a filthy look from Lani in the process.

'What about you?' Clarence asks gently.

'What about me? You've already asked me that and I told you, I don't know…I could be infected, or it could be dormant in me…I don't know.'

'Meredith didn't show any reaction to her,' Dave says, 'and her eyes are clear, either way she is now the important asset we have.'

'Asset?' Lani baulks, 'I'm not an asset.'

'Can we come back in yet?' Nick calls out.

'Of course you can,' Lani replies, 'it's only Mr Howie I want to throttle, not you.'

'Oh…er…that's good then,' Cookey says quietly as they file back in.

'Lani, I guess the boss told you but we all had it,' Blowers explains, 'Dave was the only one not bothered by it.'

'I had April,' Cookey states proudly.

'That's not a good thing Cookey,' Lani replies.

'What? Did you see her? She was gorgeous, well, until Dave chopped her head off.'

'I didn't cut her head off,' Dave replies.

'Is that how you feel?' She looks at me, 'Marcy was gorgeous,' she adds icily.

'Eh? That's not fair.'

'Oh Mr Howie gets the best zombie girl yeah?'

'Lani stop it,' I sigh.

'I will stop it,' she adds softly, 'but only because we're in front of other people, but the minute we're alone you'd better get ready.'

'I will.'

'I mean it.'

'Okay,' I hold my hands up.

'Are you going to attack Mr Howie?' Dave asks with alarm.

'No Dave, not like that but I will be having a bloody good go at him...and it will be going on for a very long time.'

'Okay,' Dave says seemingly satisfied that my life isn't being put in immediate danger.

'So,' she looks back at me, 'Mr Howie, what's the plan?'

'Plan? I don't bloody know!'

'You always know,' Cookey adds.

'Well, we're going to have to find a doctor for Lani and the dog... I don't get it,' I add suddenly, 'why us?

How come we find the dog and one of ours ends up being immune?'

'We don't know if I am immune,' Lani replies.

'So we work on the assumption that you are infected right?' I ask her.

'Probably should yes,' she replies.

'So that means we can't give you weapons,' Dave adds, 'if you turn quickly you could kill everyone...well apart from me that is.'

'Modest Dave,' I add.

'No,' he shakes his head firmly, 'realistic.'

'Okay, no weapons then and I'll stay close to the dog to save you having to set her on me if I do turn,' she says archly.

'Huh, that's funny,' Cookey snorts, 'what? Well it was funny...I'm really glad you're back Lani,' he gives a huge grin with genuine feeling and rushes over to her. She stands up laughing as he grabs and hugs her, holding her tight.

'Me too Cookey,' she laughs again, 'don't squeeze too hard my stomach hurts.'

'Sorry Lani,' he grins and hugs her again, gently this time.

'Me too,' Nick grins as Cookey lets her go, 'fucking good to see you again.'

'You too Nick,' she gives him a hug and quickly rubs his back.

Blowers goes next and not one of the lads show the slightest bit of embarrassment at showing affection for her.

'Come here,' Clarence rumbles and gives Lani a hug, taking extra care from the weight of his arms round her back.

'I don't do hugging,' Dave says quickly as she turns to him, 'glad to have you back but no hugging.'

'I understand,' she replies with a smile, 'and Mr Howie doesn't get a hug either until I know he's washed that whores smell off him,' she smiles sweetly without looking at me, 'and if we find her...I will be having a weapon and she will be mine, is that clear?' She beams round the room, everyone nodding meekly.

'So,' she sits down, 'the plan?'

'The plan,' I sigh, 'was to go and get Maddox and see if he wants to move in here, but now...'

'You say it like we're moving house,' Lani says, 'it's a good idea though...shouldn't we get those bodies cleared away first?'

'That's why I was going to ask him, get his help with clearing up.'

'That's not fair,' she replies, 'it's our mess, we should clear it up and how are you going to get him without splitting the team? You can't leave this place empty with the armoury so full up.'

'Okay, you being here changes things...we need to be uber bloody careful from now on, we don't engage unless we have to, we don't get into a scrap unless we're cornered or threatened...and we keep them as far away from us as possible, Lani and Meredith have to be protected at all costs. Dave, I want you with Lani at all times and Lani, I want you with the dog at all times...understood?'

They nod back, which gives me some relief that at least she's still willing to take orders from me.

'And I mean it, the dog goes on a lead and Lani you hold that lead all the time, she doesn't go anywhere without you holding that lead.'

'Do you want Dave to put a lead on me too?'

'Don't be funny.'

'Sorry, er…am I with the dog so she can protect you if I turn or…'

'Both,' I cut her off, 'to protect you as much as possible and to protect the dog…and us,' I add quietly. 'Clarence, can you drive the plant machinery we got between the walls?'

'Probably,' he nods, 'shouldn't be too hard.'

'Nick, find a truck or a lorry, something old that we can burn. Clarence will scoop the bodies up and get them in the truck, we take them out to the estate and burn them…I want everyone in face masks and safety glasses too. I know we've got some here somewhere.'

'In the stores,' Lani adds quickly making me realise how valued she is, not just as a fighter but someone we all respect and admire.

'Long day but we'll get it done. The back gate stays locked and bolted and I want one person on the top wall at all times, we take it in turns…actually we can park the Saxon up there again.'

'Got it,' Blowers nods, 'I'll get it up there.'

'Does that include me?' Lani asks.

'When Dave takes his turn yes,' I nod back, 'and Meredith too.'

'Once that's done we'll re-assess and figure out what we do from there. Nick will drive the truck out to the estate with Clarence in the fuel tanker, Blowers and Cookey will go too and Dave will stay here with Lani and Meredith.'

The lads stand up and start heading outside, Blowers saying he will get the Saxon up top and Nick saying he will get the stuff from the stores. Cookey files out with them, then Clarence realises Lani is holding back and subtly suggests to Dave that they go outside.

'But Mr Howie said I had to stay with Lani,' he replies.

'Yeah in a minute Dave,' Clarence nods for him to leave, motioning with his head. Dave finally gets the hint after looking at me, then at Lani then back at Clarence.

Alone and we stare at each other in silence for a few minutes, 'so you can have a go now,' I say quietly.

'Not now,' she replies quickly, 'I get it Howie, I get what she did...but it hurts like hell.'

'I'm sorry, I just couldn't think straight.'

'Why me Howie?' She looks at me intent, 'why am I immune or different? I don't get it.'

'I don't know,' I reply, 'We'll have to figure it out and like I said, this changes everything now. I am glad though Lani...seeing you...well normal...it's...'

'Let's get through today,' she starts walking off.

'Lani,' I call out, she stops a few feet from me, 'I am glad you're okay.'

'I might not be,' she shrugs, 'we don't know anything yet.'

'But I thought I lost you, I thought you were gone.' She locks eyes with me for a long second. I don't know if I should move forward to hold her or what. She seems to sense my uncertainty and steps in, quickly wrapping her arms round my chest and pulling me in.

'Shit that feels nice,' I exhale deeply and hold her close.

'Don't get used to it,' she pushes me away with a hard look, 'you hurt me.'

'I'm sorry.'

'We'll talk later, I've got Mr Howie's orders to do now.'

'You'd best get on then,' I smile, 'I hear he can be a right nasty bastard.'

She cuts me off with a hard look, 'more than you'll ever know,' she says before walking out.

Eleven

Another small market town in the south of England, further south than Bereford and further still from her town.

The map shows one main road leading into the town from Bereford, a thick red line indicating the route across the paper. By taking a long detour, Paula comes back onto that main road several miles away from Bereford.

At the junction on the quiet country road she looks to the empty road at the right, wondering how far back towards Bereford they are. She turns left and within a few hundred metres she can see signs of passage along this road too. Verges trampled down and some smeared blood stains along the road. They're dried and dark but clearly blood stains and they indicate the *things* have come this was. It can't be the same horde she saw in Bereford, it's not possible for them to get this far that quickly. With a jolt she realises these tracks must be from the ones that were already in Bereford. The *things* she saw were others passing through.

What was drawing them? Picking up speed she accelerates down the road. High hedges on either side that wound along with the twists and gentle bends, fields, pastures and meadows dotted with copses here and there, overhanging trees dappling the surface of the road, giving a slight strobe effect on the windscreen as she drives along.

The heat is oppressive, even with the windows fully open she still sweats from the hot air buffeted past her.

Another crawler round the corner, this one crawling up the centre of the road. One leg seems to be working as it uses it to push along. Scrapes and flesh cut away, the tight drawn skin red and damaged from the abrasion.

She doesn't hesitate but goes straight over it, feeling a slight bump and a popping sounds as the skull is crushed.

A country pub stands proud before the start of the town. White walled with a thatched roof, black window frames and sills, a sturdy black double front door propped open. Manicured grounds with a big pond to one side, ducks, geese and swans swimming about between the floating corpses. One duck stands on the back of a body, using the few inches of height to give it an advantage over the rest.

Bodies everywhere. Spread over the patio tables and chairs, lying in amongst the reeds at the side of the pond, children bitten and mauled at the multi-coloured playground. Friday night at the local boozer and the event swept through here the same as everywhere else.

She snorts with irony at the name of the pub, *The Dead Duck.* The ducks are doing fine, she thinks. Just everything else is dead.

Speeding up and the hedgerow gives way to cottages, then short rows of terraced houses and then into the town.

Same as before. Same as every market town in this area. Pretty cottages, pretty walls, pretty flowers, and the same formulaic methodology. Everyone moans when the local pub gets taken over by a corporate chain but yet they fail to see their little kingdoms are the same, town after town, village after village.

It jars her senses and makes her feel on edge. If someone dropped her into one of these blindfolded she would never be able to tell which one it is. A main road going through the middle, a post office with faded posters, a convenience store owned by one of the chains, maybe a unique village square with some benches or a café.

Oh and don't forget the church and the village hall. Used for everything from the local school play to election polling stations, village meetings, weddings, funerals and everything in between.

The pleasant surrounding should be soothing and nice but they aren't, they are the same again and again and every one of them will be full of those *things.*

Except, like the first villages she went to, this one is empty too. The ones coming from Bereford are yet to arrive but the rest here have already shipped out, gone, vacated, rats deserting a sinking ship. But no, something else. Not deserting but flocking somewhere. Going to another place for another reason.

As she drives down the main road, once more looking at cottage after cottage she realises the same as before, that most of the doors are propped open, windows smashed and the odd body lying here and there.

Food. It must be food. They've run out of new people to eat or chomp on or whatever they do...*infect* she guesses is the right word. These small villages only hold finite residents and once they're taken there isn't much else to hang around for.

She pulls into the village square and gets down stretching her legs, still stiff from the previous night's exertions. Pushing her hands high into the air she groans with pleasure as her back muscles stretch out, a very slight and nice feeling of being light-headed for a minute. The Bereford *things* will be a way off yet, time for a brew and think about what's going on.

Paula pushes the top half of the back door up and drops the tailgate, pulling the gas stove out and going through the motions as she thinks.

With the stove on and heating a small pan of water she unwraps a health food nutty chocolate chip bar and chews slowly, eyes narrowed and staring off into the distance as she lets her mind relax.

Are they simply spreading out to find more people? No is the answer to that one. They are moving together and with purpose. If they were just after new people to turn they would have tried to take her.

So that's not it, and in the absence of any other logical reasoning it suggests they are going somewhere to do something. Marching together in the same direction.

But if not here then where? She makes the coffee and pulls the map free, first of all finding her own town, then working along through the villages she went through until Bereford, then further along the red line to this place. Glancing up she scans round and checks the view before continuing. The red line of the road goes straight into her, then out the other side into more countryside and then more shitty little villages.

Maybe they're working the route as they go, sweeping through to check every house on every street on the way. But no, that would be too much wouldn't it? Every street on the way?

Thomas displayed intelligence, especially towards the end with leaving the note and the conversation he had. They definitely changed too over the last god knows how many days. Moving faster in the daytime, getting more aggressive and quicker too.

But what would the ultimate goal be? London is back the other way; if they were massing they should be heading towards the biggest city and not the coast. What's on the coast that they could want so much?

'Come on Paula,' she mutters then takes a sip of the coffee, 'think like them...you are being cut down by one woman in one town so maybe they're leaving to escape me,' she shakes her head, 'no, as much as I'd love to take the credit that isn't it...' frowning she continues, 'so not running away but running to something? But why? If they're struggling for food now why get so many together when surely getting food will be harder in one place,' not that, definitely not that, every strategic plan in the world means you don't put all your resources in one place, unless you want to gather a large force for a specific purpose, 'aah, that's better, a large force for a specific purpose...like an invasion or something,' she nods, feeling she's on the right track this time.

'What's the purpose?' She muses to herself, 'they show intelligence and cunning, they work together too, using large numbers controlled by one at the top...hang on,' she sinks back into internal thoughts now, her mind running too fast to give voice to her processes. She reaches round to pull the carefully folded letter from her back pocket, using one hand to flick it open. She scans reads the note, eyes flicking over the sentences...

... ***I am not the only one of my kind. There will be others, others who are stronger, faster and***

with greater numbers…

That's it. Thomas knew he wasn't the only one of his kind, and he must have meant that he was intelligent and able to think. *There will be others, others who are stronger, faster and with greater numbers.*

Was he trying to warn her? She smiles suddenly, a broad grin that lights her face up. He wasn't *trying* to warn her, he *was* warning her outright. Don't go after them. Stay away.

Why? What were they doing?

The question burned inside. She had to know the reasons. She had got the head-start in this event; she had killed thousands so she had the right to be in the middle of whatever it was.

Pushing the stove away she takes the mug of coffee into the front and pushes on, determined to know where they are heading.

Twelve

He rolls over, the bed creaking under his broad frame. Eyes snap open, instantly alert. He doesn't smoke or drink and rarely takes caffeine so when he wakes up, his head is instantly clear and ready for the day.

Glancing up at the window he can see the sun is already up with the promise of another scorching day. Standing up he flexes and stretches his long muscular legs and pushes his arms out to the side, feeling a slight increase in his heart rate as the blood is pumped quicker.

Before doing anything else he stares at the calendar on the wall and counts the days off. Thirteen today. Thirteen days since this began. Not even two weeks yet and everything has changed so much, and it's about to change again.

He sniffs the air, detecting the scent of her deodorant. He vaguely remembers her getting out of bed before him and feels a slight pang of guilt that he slept longer than her. That's not fair; he should be up with her, working to get everything done.

But then the last two days have been non-stop; every minute of every hour filled with something to do.

He picks the water bottle up and takes a long swig of the warm liquid, it isn't pleasant but he knows the importance of staying hydrated, especially in this weather. Something he needs to enforce with the others too.

Dressed quickly with a clean plain white t shirt pulled over his head he moves to the door, pushing the pistol into the makeshift holster made for him a couple of days ago. It still feels weird putting the gun on his belt but he knows that within a few minutes he will have forgotten it's there.

Ready for the day he pulls the door open and steps out with the tiniest of reactions at the hive of activity going on. People everywhere, already up and moving about. Laughing and joking with each other, animated conversations going on. The smell of cooking wafts through on the hot air. Faces turn to look at him as he emerges; smiling in greeting at their leader.

'You get up then,' Lenski smiles, her clipboard already glued to one hand and holding a mug of coffee with the other. Maddox smiles back at her, a genuine smile full of admiration for the woman he now shares a bed with.

'Mornin' bruv,' Darius shouts from the other end of the unit. Now cleared of cannabis plants and given over to chairs and tables, used as a central eating place and somewhere for them all to meet and talk, out of the sun and heat. The smell of the plants still linger and it was a hard sell convincing everyone they didn't need the weed anymore, but eventually, with bribery of music, video games and a very small amount of alcohol the plants were taken out and burnt on the fire pit.

The effect was that everyone got more stoned than ever before from the fumes billowing across the compound but Maddox knew it was the last time, an almost sacrificial act and one that marked a turning point.

Without the weed he could get clean water and food into the youths, plus the daily ritual of everyone taking their multi-vitamin pill too. They were already looking better, in just the few days since the bossman was killed they had been working solidly, moving heavy stuff, knocking walls down and carrying load after load of items back to the compound. Regular patrols were still done and the constant exercise had sparked their natural appetites to kick in.

They almost looked like normal kids now. Well, as normal as they could be given the circumstances, but things had yet to change even more.

That night after Howie had left saw the biggest change. Maddox spoke to Darius, Sierra and Lenski at length, opening up to them in a way he had never done before. They all shared that night, talking of their lives before the event and the people they missed. Maddox made it clear he was not the bossman and that if he made a mistake or a bad call they had to tell him, this would only work if they did it together.

They accepted it readily enough and promised, and to a certain extent both Sierra and Darius stepped up to their new roles and the kids looked to them with almost the same level of respect they gave Maddox. Lenski was a special case and different. A naturally stern woman that spoke her mind and could multi-task unlike anyone they knew. Nothing escaped her and nothing got past her.

As for Maddox. He was still the number one, feared respected and loved in equal measure. He had proven himself time and again for the youths and had worked and sweated alongside all of them. His natural aloofness gave him an air of authority, his broad muscular frame coupled with his passive face and deeply intelligent eyes all worked in his favour to create an air of a natural leader.

He didn't flap or panic and remembered the names of every youth in the compound, taking time to talk with all of them in turn.

Letting Howie go wasn't seen as an act of weakness, in fact it worked the opposite and showed the youths they had a leader who was prepared to make decisions. The fact that he went after them showed how brave and tough he was, the way he faced Howie down but then later changed his mind only added to the mystique and regard he was held in.

'How long you been up?' Maddox asks Lenski as he walks closer.

She smiles and lifts one eyebrow, pursing her lips as though to suggest she's been awake for hours while he slept like the lazy dog he was, 'not long, maybe the half hour,' she replies with a wink.

'You should have woke me,' he grumbles looking round at the youths who have now gone back to the far more interesting concept of eating breakfast.

'Why? We can feed everyone without the great and powerful Maddox no?' Lenski teases softly, taking care to keep her voice low, knowing he felt uncomfortable with open displays of affection, not through arrogance but simply because of who he was. She'd change him slowly, she knew that.

'You eaten yet?' He asks, making his way to the table put in place to serve the food from, the girls behind smiled as he approaches and spoon porridge into a bowl for him.

'Of course,' Lenski replies, 'there is much to do yes? We have busy day today.'

'The day of days,' he replies with a frown.

'You ready then bruv?' Darius booms across the room with a huge grin.

'Yeah I'm ready,' Maddox replies. Taking his bowl across the room he sits down at the end table, the one specially reserved for the top four. A conscious act taken to give a line of separation to the youths.

'Sierra comin'?' Maddox asks as Darius takes a seat.

'Dunno bruv, she should be here.'

'She come in minute yes? We wait for her,' Lenski plonks the clipboard and coffee down before taking a seat with a sigh, blowing a strand of hair away from her forehead, 'is hot already.'

'Damn hot,' Darius replies in a deep gravelly voice.

'Hotter than hot,' Maddox mimics the same.

'Stop,' Lenski groans, 'not the voices, too early for the voices.'

'Hey, what's up?' Sierra joins them, pulling a chair away with quick movements belying her already frantic morning.

'Nuffin, you?' Maddox gives the standard reply.

'Nuffin, we ready then?'

'Guess so,' Maddox spoons a mouthful of porridge in and nods, 'anything in the night?'

'Nah,' Sierra shakes her head, 'Jagger had his crew on duty, he didn't say anything when he went to bed.'

'Bed? He ain't got time for bed,' Maddox says with forced harshness.

'You leave him, he tired and I say he have some hours yet.'

'They all up then?' Maddox asks taking another spoonful.

'Yep, all up and going at it,' Darius replies, 'you's the only one having a lie in bruv.'

'A lie in?' Maddox snorts, 'didn't get to sleep until…' he looks at Lenski for confirmation.

'I not know this, I was sleep when you came in,' she shrugs.

'Well it was late anyway, spent some time with the crews, they's worried, which is fair enough,' he accepts with a tilt of his head.

'They buzzin' this morning,' Sierra smiles, 'never seen 'em like it, they look like proper kids all runnin' about.'

'Good, that's the weed,' Maddox says pointing his spoon at Sierra, 'no weed for what, two days now? So we ready then? You sure about this?'

'It's your idea bruv,' Darius spreads his hands open.

'My idea but we gotta agree,' Maddox replies.

'We been through this, we agree, we say we agree…we all agree and we double the agree so now is too late to not have the agree yes?'

Maddox pauses mid munch to look over at Lenski, she rolls her eyes but smiles straight after, showing she is half joking, but as always with her, the hard tone suggests it is only a half-joke.

'It's the right thing to do,' Maddox continues his eating, tucking in with gusto, 'if Howie hadn't come when he did we'd be fucked, they'd have got through here in minutes. I like this place but it's not safe enough and we can't make it safer.'

'So we go,' Lenski shrugs, 'he offered the fort and said we can go, is done now, we go.'

'Yeah,' Maddox says quietly as though unsure, 'shame though, I like it here.'

'So do we,' Sierra replies seriously with a look at Darius, 'but you's right Maddox, this place ain't big enough and we alright now but the kids'll get bigger and want more space...'

'More food...more drink...more women and more boys and more showers and more clothes...' Lenski adds quickly to a grin from Sierra, 'it is good idea, best idea...'

'So we still planning on just turning up?' Darius asks, 'I still think we should send someone first.'

'No,' Maddox shakes his head, 'we been through this, we turn up together, all of us...all our food, stocks, supplies, vehicles...everything, we show them we ain't coming on our knees and begging, we joining forces...we got stuff here, loads of stuff...and our crews are young but they're good fighters.'

'I don't know,' Lenski cuts in, 'I think same as Darius, we send someone first.'

'Nah, I'm with Maddox,' Sierra shakes her head, 'if we send someone it looks weak and we ain't weak, Maddox is right, we show them we coming to join them, not run away from what we got here.'

'But we do run away from here, you say this place not safe now.'

'Yeah we know that, but we don't want them to know that,' Maddox explains with a wave of his spoon, 'and we ain't running away, we're re-locating,' he adds with a flash of white teeth.

'Upgrading,' Darius grins.

'How many survivors we got out there now?' Maddox asks, watching as both the girls start flicking through sheets on their clipboards.

'Twenty eight,' Sierra replies. Maddox nods and thinks of the new families now living in the houses closest to the compound. After the big fight, those that didn't get involved in the planned take-over were approached and offered the chance to move closer to the compound where it was safer, and in exchange for helping dig the school playing fields for crops and fishing from the shore. But that was before Maddox made the final decision to leave and head for the fort.

The night of the attack had played on his mind constantly, knowing they were one step away from being wiped out. He didn't like the thought of relying on someone else but the initial few days were over, they'd survived and now it was about getting somewhere proper where they could live and not just get by.

Besides, Sierra and Lenski were right, the kids would need more space and even having some adults might not be such a bad thing. He only hoped they would be put together in the fort so he could keep them safe until they were ready to start mingling with the other survivors.

Maddox had spoken to each crew at length and had spent the last two days going round all the youths, explaining why they were moving, pointing out all the benefits but also warning them strongly that he was still in charge of them and if they fucked about he'd be on them instantly. They represented him and the compound now so they better show some pride.

They took the news badly at first, fearing change simply for the unknown factor. But these kids were strong and resilient, from broken homes and backgrounds that would make most social workers weep.

They knew they were going together and that's what mattered. Maddox was still leading them and

Lenski, Darius and Sierra were still the leaders too. The comfort and structure they'd missed out on before now was still there.

So the excitement grew, rumours spread at how they would get to use the big guns that Howie and his men had, and be part of the guards that kept the fort safe. How they would all be together somewhere inside and still stay in the crews they were in.

Even the huge explosion yesterday didn't faze them. Word soon spread it was probably the refinery going up from the heat, then it was explained what a refinery was and then where it was. Most of them stood looking in awe at the huge smoke clouds in the distance and they all felt the rumble through the ground that rattled the old windows in their wooden frames.

'They all coming with us then?' Maddox asked about the survivors, having explained to them the plan and offered the opportunity to travel with them.

'Most yes,' Lenski replies, 'some they stay here, they say they lived here many years and they don't want to leave so,' she shrugs, 'I tell them where we go so they come later, it's up to them I think.'

'Yeah right, vehicles?' Maddox looks at Darius.

'All done,' Darius grins, 'they in the street now getting loaded up, I got the crews doing their stuff first and then we got the stuff from the store room to go out, all the food...'

With the morning meeting finished they separate with each one of the four heading off to deal with the many tasks that lay ahead. Once the decision had been made, Maddox had applied his mind to the fullest and planned with his usual intense focus, making sure everything was thought out and prepared.

As he walked through the units he mulled it over again, was this the right thing to do? He knew he could change the plan and stay here and it would be accepted it readily enough. It was the right thing. The high front gates looked good but they were structurally weak and a concerted effort would see them either pulled down or pushed open. They had weapons but only shotguns and some rifles, which all took time to reload and expended vast amounts of ammunition for relatively little damage inflicted.

If that horde had reached the gates they would have been lost, same with the estate survivors. They would have got kills, and probably quite a few of them. But it was also only a matter of time until someone, or *something* worked out a way of going through the houses that bordered the compound. If they did that *and* attacked the gates it would be over in minutes.

They needed walls, big walls that couldn't be breached or climbed and that meant going somewhere else. The seed had been planted by Howie and it quickly out down roots to spread through Maddox's conscience.

The crews living area at the rear of the compound looked barren now, the tents taken down and stacked ready to be loaded up, bags of clothes and personal effects were being carried out with each crew taking responsibility for their own, and the chiefs overseeing the whole operation.

The solar panels were being stacked up, they were bulky and heavy but the Bossman had made sure he got the best equipment to grow his beloved plants and they were too good to be left behind. Same with the grow lights and wiring loops. They were all being loaded into vehicles sourced and brought back from the estate.

Driving wasn't an issue as nearly all the youths had at one time or another, driven cars and motorbikes illegally through the estate. Maddox and Lenski were probably the only ones with proper driving licenses and Maddox knew that even Darius had owned several vehicles before the event happened.

Round the other side and he watches the girls from the units bringing the piles of food out from the stores, stacking them by the gates ready to be loaded up. It was important they appeared on mass with all their equipment, and Maddox knew they had to arrive looking clean and disciplined too, that creating the first impression was more than important, it was essential if they were to be taken seriously and not seen as another bunch of desperate refugees.

Maddox knew how the kids would be perceived with their street language, constant swearing and reverting to putting their hoods up at the first sign of trouble. An instinctive reaction done to cover their faces so they couldn't be recognised and arrested later.

They must have thousands of people in the fort already, so finding space might be hard. But then they only needed a small area, maybe in a corner or something. Somewhere they could stay together. Maddox had thought ahead and understood he would have to see how the ground lay before making the decision to hand over all their stock, food and equipment or whether it formed part of the negotiation for extra space inside, and he'd even planned for making sure crews were assigned tasks otherwise they'd quickly get bored and cause trouble.

Howie and the fort leaders needed to understand they might look like kids, but they were hardened and would kill without hesitation. They only had loyalty to each other and didn't have the same moral base that others did. That meant discipline and punishment had to be hard, they had to be given respect and freedom, with time to unwind but if they fucked up, the resulting action had to be swift and brutal, and more importantly it had to come from Maddox and not someone else.

He felt an almost overwhelming sense of devotion to the kids that made up the crews, and he knew first-hand the lives they had before all this happened, and how in many respects, their life was now better than it was before.

There is a time for thinking and a time for doing. The thinking was done, the plans laid down and put in place. Now was the time for doing and Maddox jumped straight in. Smiling and laughing with the crews as he manhandled the heavier items up to the vehicles and made sure they were being loaded properly.

The girls from the unit brought regular supplies of water out, ensuring the youths drank often and regular. The heat was intense, scorching in the sun with high humidity that had them all soaked with sweat within minutes of working.

They didn't complain but stuck at it, moving and carrying, lifting and stacking, crew chiefs nipping between their groups shouting and calling instructions out. The boys soon had their tops off, showing off their lean underdeveloped physiques as they tried to impress the girls, making jokes about the gun shows and puffing their chests out.

Hard physical graft, harder work than any of the youths had done before but with over a hundred of them, it was done quickly with a methodical approach overseen by the clipboard wielding Lenski and Sierra.

Pausing to take a drink of water, Maddox looked at the two women stood next to each other. One tall and Polish with a stern countenance, the other black and much younger but they had taken to each other and developed a strong relationship. Both of them holding their clipboards and pens, comparing notes and lists, talking quietly and smiling often. Sierra seemed much older than her years but girls on the estate always grew up faster, they had to. It was a brutal life and full of predators that preyed on the young and naïve, especially if they were pretty and innocent.

With the two women checking everything that passed them, and with Maddox and Darius on the ground it was done with relative ease and far quicker than they had given themselves credit for in the planning phase.

By late morning they were ready. Loaded up and walking through a now stripped out and emptied set of units. The tables and chairs in the central area looked forlorn and sad, a space used for large groups to gather and meet, now empty and their footsteps ringing out on the concrete floor.

The rear area looked even worse, now littered with rubbish and debris. Items dumped and left and the grass flattened and dead were the tents had been up for almost two weeks. It looked so big now without the life inside it. Vast and empty without the colours and noises, and the kids running about or sat talking.

It served a purpose and got them through the first stage of the disaster but it was time to move on, and if the fort refused them they could just come back, or find somewhere else.

They walked round to the front and up the walkway towards the now open gates. The houses they had worked so hard to claim now emptied and open.

The long line of vehicles stretched down the road, the crews stood in their units near their assigned vehicles talking nervously, smiling with excitement while looking back at the compound with a sense of regret and longing.

The estate survivors coming with them were ready, the families stood separate and away from the crews, keeping that respectable distance.

Maddox led his small group past the vehicles, checking each one was ready to go and who was driving, and did they have the keys, and did the vehicle have fuel.

As each vehicle was checked he gave the order to load up, walking on to the next one while the kids started clambering inside behind him.

He'd even planned the convoy placement. He would have to go in the front with Lenski, and he wanted Darius and Sierra close to him. But that meant a huge long line of vehicles stretched out behind him. Mohammed was spoken to, being one of the more serious and switched on crew chiefs he was picked to bring up the rear and made sure his radio was working with fresh batteries.

And now it was done. The estate exodus was underway. A way of life was being left behind with the promise of something better ahead of them. A safe place with other people. It would be hard to start with, but Maddox knew deep inside this was the best course of action.

He climbs into the driver's seat of the first van, getting a thumbs up from Darius behind him in the second vehicle. Switching the engine on he grins and shakes his head, smiling at Lenski sat next to him still hugging her clipboard.

'Why you smile? This is stressful and hard,' she says with a groan.

'Done now,' he remarks casually, 'all done.' Easing the handbrake off he selects first gear and pulls away, using the mirrors to watch behind as the vehicles pull out one by one.

Thirteen

'Holy fuck,' Paula whispers with a very rare use of swearing. High above the town on the crest of the rolling downs she looks down to the coastal town and the deep blue shimmering sea stretching off to the horizon.

Late afternoon and after hours of solid driving, heading through village after village and following the trails of crawlers and trampled verges she reached this point.

Two things draw her attention and cause a quickening of her heart rate. Far in the distance, off to the right she takes in the huge plume of smoke billowing from something. So far she can't see the land it comes from but big enough to still be visible.

The second thing that draws her attention, and the cause of the profanity is the town resting between her and the sea. An average coastal town tucked into the base of the rolling hills. Picturesque and scenic. White washed houses dotted amongst the open playing fields, stone built cottages forming quaint and narrow streets, spiralling round in a haphazard way to the town centre. Large and urbanised. With the binoculars she can see the long straight central High Street, set back from the shore and running adjacent to the beachside.

She sweeps across the town, taking in the cricket pitch, the football grounds, the open air swimming pools, the large gardens of the big houses and the postage stamp gardens of the inner town cottages.

Paula lowers the binoculars and rubs her eyes, hardly believing what she's seeing; convincing herself it must be a mirage, the heat playing tricks with her mind. She squeezes her eyes shut and counts to thirty. Opening them gradually and taking in the immediate surroundings, the grass field sloping down away from her. The hedgerow bordering the field. The tyre tracks across the grass where she drove through. The trees nearby, the bushes and rocks.

Nodding her head she accepts what she is seeing, everything as it should be, no leprechauns or fairies flying about. So her eyes are seeing normal images that her brain is processing.

Satisfied, she pushes the rubber skirt of the lenses to her eyes and looks again. Purposefully starting to the far right at the brown smudge. Yep, that's still there. Gradually she works back along to the town beneath her. Taking in the long lines of *things* working their way in. The streets clogged with motion of bodies slowly working their way into the centre.

The playing fields covered in shuffling figures, long lines of bodies strung out on the feeder roads that lead into the town. The winding cottage lined streets filled with *things.* Every street, every spare bit of land, every road covered in *things.*

Thousands upon thousands of them. More than that, countless numbers bunched together. The High Street is jammed full and still more of them moving in towards it. Like the crowd of a festival undulating, or the busiest of city centres with everyone moving at exactly the same pace.

Paula had followed them to here, working through the villages and towns until reaching the coast. As she worked along she realised the roads were full of them so she worked inland, aiming for the downs and using the four wheel vehicle to cross open country. Stopping at the top of the sweeping field to look down.

'Holy fuck,' she repeats, the looking glasses glued to her eyes. Must be hundreds of thousands here and more heading in. The immediate roads are full; the outer roads still show long lines. Why? Why here?

Paula forces herself to examine the town, what is here that makes them want it so badly. An ordinary coastal town, nothing special or unique about it. It could be anyone of a hundred towns like it. Golden beaches that sweep along the gentle curvature of the land, small piers and jetties, a harbour full of white masts and pleasure cruisers, car parks, streets, roads, houses, shops. And everywhere full of the *things.*

Leaning her back against the side of the truck she kept looking, sweeping left to right and taking in every street.

A dull pain flashes across her forehead, warning her that she's been staring now for a long time, straining to watch and utterly absorbed in the slow shuffling movements of the figures drifting in towards the town. Lowering the glasses she lifts her eyebrows high to stretch the muscles of her forehead out.

Sighing deeply she checks her immediate surroundings and moves to the back of the truck, dropping the tailgate to once more pull the camping stove out. Maybe too much coffee? Her hand hovers over the jar, trying to decide if she should have herbal tea this time.

Options weighed, advantages and disadvantages calculated, a decision reached. More coffee is called for. This is an extreme time of extreme actions and it needs caffeine and quite possibly a cigarette.

They haven't showed any reaction to her presence. Can they see her from that distance? Without binoculars she'd just be a dark speck on the side of the hill. Mind you, best not hang around too long just in case they decide to come this way.

Sitting on the tailgate she stares down at the town with the naked eye, holding the coffee mug in one hand and a lit cigarette in the other. The pain in her forehead eases while she tries to work out the significance of this place.

Paula leans her back against the side of the vehicle and draws her knees up, the feeling of isolation hits her more than ever but still, the sense of challenge is there. A whole town rammed to the rafters full of them. She looks at the feeder roads planning traps to lay there and a town this size would have a decent DIY store too. She frowns with the realisation it could have the best stocked and biggest DIY store in the country but with that many *things* down there it might as well be on the moon. No way she could get to it without clearing a decent path first, but with so many they would just keep pouring in.

This needs a plan. A decent well thought out plan. She stares idly out to sea, smiling at the thought of a big navy ship with big navy guns that would just flatten the town within minutes. Or a tank, that would be good. But no tanks and no navy ships. No anything other than what she can make or find.

Cigarette stubbed out she once more lifts the glasses and starts re-examining the town. One coastal road in from the right side or the west, and another in from the east. One more coming into from the north and that's it.

The section closest to the shore looks the oldest, with smaller cottages built close together. Must have been a fishing village once and then just grew as the populations increased. Not even a rail line though which meant it would have only grown once the advent of cars became popular.

What does that matter? Who cares how old the place is? But all information is good information she reminds herself.

About to lower the glasses she snatches them back up. Her eyes taking in an image that her brain takes longer to process. Longer than it took for the hands to receive the signal to take the binoculars away. Pressed against her eyes she leans forward and looks again. Rapid movement caught her eye. Movement that was faster than anything else and therefore stood out.

Somewhere near that field there, the big buildings bordering it. The municipal layout suggests a school or college. Figures darting along the edge of the field. Two large and several smaller ones. Must be adults with children. She watches one of the adults move ahead to the edge of a building. They all wait and then run forward to join the first figure. The second adult in the rear.

A road next to the school holds hundreds of shuffling *things* all heading past just metres from the people. They must be able to see them.

The figures drop down at the back of the building and wait. Paula scans the area, seeing every road filled with shuffling bodies. Trapped in every direction, they should stay quiet within the buildings and hide. But then it will be dark in a few hours and being in a town jammed full of those *things* at night isn't an option.

How have they survived this long? Especially with children that make noise and cry, let alone the smell they would create.

Paula stiffens, sitting up straight as she notices an escape route for them. If they cross the fields keeping to one side behind the row of trees they could make the far end and the copse of trees. Through the small housing estate and then just one road to cross before they're out into the fields. The road has the shuffling bodies at both ends but if they move one at a time and quickly they'd make it, or stand the best chance.

They can't see it from their position, but being on high ground Paula can see the route easily. Her mind whirls trying to think of a way to communicate with them but there isn't anything. Even if she flashed a mirror against the sun she'd only give her position away and not be able to tell them anything.

But she has the pistol and the machine gun, she could get to them just as they could get out. The thought of being with others is outweighed by the fact that she can't just leave children trapped in that town if she can see a way out.

And only two adults with them. What are they doing there? Why didn't they get out before?

There's no choice, she has to act and do it now. She knows it and throws the last dregs of her coffee from the mug before packing everything away.

She can't just drive down, she'd been seen easily. Work away to the west and then come back in from ground level, use that field and hide the vehicle before going the rest on foot. In the driver's seat she turns the vehicle slowly round and heads back along to the gate, then through and steadily getting lower until the town falls from view.

Once satisfied she's clear from sight she drives straight down the hillside and works her away back along towards the outer edge using fields and narrow farm tracks.

Finding a five bar gate that leads into the fields that border the small estate she stops the vehicle and gets the gate open. Closing it behind her once the vehicle is through. She parks up close to the hedge in amongst a copse of trees with low branches.

Making herself ready she checks her pockets for the facemask, eye glasses, ammunition, flare gun and then the police rifle and pistol. Knife tucked on the back of her belt and no bag this time so she can stay light and move quickly.

With the vehicle keys safely in her pocket she moves along the hedge in a steady crouch, finding a sty she pauses, listens and only goes over once satisfied there are no odd noises.

The sty leads to a narrow track with fences on both sides. Twisting round she looks up the hill at where she was parked and works out her location. These fences must be the gardens of the houses on the small estate.

Paula moves swiftly down the footpath, pausing at the end to peer out and check both sides. At the ends of the street she can see a steady flow of *things* walking past and heading into the town. Hunkering down for a few minutes she takes turns to watch both ends of the street, taking in their motion and the way they keep their heads forward. Not one glance to the side and no heads turning to look down the street.

She looks ahead and picks out the route; across the pavements and get between the parked cars, then across the road to the rows of the parked vehicles on that side. No footpath on the other side so it will have to be through the gardens. She spots a low fence leading into the rear garden of a detached bungalow and picks out the features that will provide cover; that low wall, then those bushes. Once she's in the driveway she'll be blocked from view.

Now or never. The risk has been weighed and calculated and determined that the odds are in her favour.

Staying low she moves out and makes it to the parked vehicles, dropping down between two hatchbacks and looking through the windows to the ends of the street. Perfect, no indication of being seen.

Again she gets across the road and between the next row of vehicles. Still no reaction. She waits for a full minute this time, making sure there isn't any kind of delayed reaction.

Then across the pavement to the low wall, check, clear to the bushes, check, clear and into the driveway up the path and over the fence.

Dropping to the ground on the other side she grins stupidly, feeling like a commando from a low budget movie and wishing she'd put some black stripes across her nose and maybe had a big tattoo done on her upper arm, something black and tribal, and a change of name of course, Paula doesn't sound very macho or tough.

Paula the secret ninja commando runs across the garden, making little huh huh huh noises in her mind, only stopping when a fit of giggles threatens to come out audibly. Bloody hell, she shakes her head thinking maybe she's spent too much time alone.

At the rear fence she climbs up in the corner and peers over into the next garden. That house must face onto the playing fields. She clambers over and drops down into the flower beds, holding steady while she stares at the windows and back doors.

No movement, no noise so she creeps on with a strange urge to try a commando roll across the floor but dismissing it just as quickly. *Grow up for god's sake, this is serious stuff.*

Down the side of the house and she drops down, smiling at the road ahead of her and the edge of the playing fields on the other side.

Perfect. Bloody perfect. All she has to do now is get across here, stick to the edge and find those people then lead them back out. Tea and medals all round.

She waits at the side of the house, staring across the fields to the building line trying to see the figure again. No sign of them. They must have gone back round to the other side thinking they were trapped.

The ends of this road bend away from view and with no foot traffic in sight she bursts out from the house and sprints across the road, up the slight bank and down onto the fields, immediately going left to the tree line.

This time she doesn't stop, realising she is now committed and speed is the key. She moves fast, going at a steady jog and controlling her breathing, pleased that nothing on her person makes noise.

With a hundred metres to go she stops and waits, getting her heart rate and breathing fully controlled before the final sprint to the back of the building.

Examining the structure she remembers what she saw from the hillside and that the closest line of the walkers was to her left, so she needs to go round the building to the right. This is the back of a set of classrooms by the looks of it, so those people could be at the side, round the front or somewhere inside one of them.

Why couldn't they just stay there and bloody wait? She runs the hundred metres flat out and makes the back of the building, amazed at her level of fitness and how much easier she finds running now.

Without pausing she moves down the line to the edge of the building and peer rounds, frowning at the empty ground.

Ducking round she works along to the front, the rifle held ready with her finger pressed against the trigger guard, something she'd seen on movies and figured it must be the right way of doing it and prevents accidentally firing the weapon and giving your position away, or shooting yourself for that matter.

A scream splits the air, coming from the front of the building. Paula drops to her knee with the rifle up and aimed. Eyes fixed on the corner. Another scream, then more. The unmistakable sound of terrified children being hurt. Instinct kicks in and she moves forward taking long steps with the gun aimed and ready and her finger now holding the trigger.

The screams and wails fill the air, blood-curdling and full of pain and agony. She moves faster, heart hammering in her chest. Movement as someone bursts round the edge of the building sprinting towards her. The suddenness of the action sends a tiny jolt through Paula, she squeezes the trigger sending a round into the forehead of the little girl running with her tiny hand clamped to the wound on her neck.

The child is blown back from the force of the round, her skull flying off in chunks to spatter the ground in a wide arc behind her. The sharp crack of the gun sounds out louder than the screams. Paula freezes her mind unable to compute what she just did. Undead surge round the corner, drawn by the sound of the shot. She fires again; pressing the trigger at the oncoming bodies and watching them spin away. The sub machine gun is well built with little recoil and she plants the shots easily. The bodies drop as she starts backing away, more children screaming out in agony then appearing at the corner running amongst the undead. Blood and injuries everywhere.

She fires again, dropping another undead and wincing at the repeated loud cracks of each gun shot. Too late, nothing she can do now. She turns and starts sprinting away across the field cursing with anger at the sight of the figures coming in from the other end.

She keeps running, judging the distance and gaps between them. No, too many coming now. She veers away from the tree line, the only way to go now. Howls rip the air behind her, roars from the undead as they charge in her wake. The screams of the children still ripe on the air as she runs faster and faster.

She can hear them charging behind and see the others coming in from the bottom of the field. With her legs pumping away she plans her route. The field leads into more houses of the estate, but they are small and no good for hiding. They will see where she goes and simply follow her path.

She needs to avoid the centre and work away to the outer edge where the numbers are fewer and the streets less clogged.

Glancing round she picks her pace up at the sight of the thick crowd charging after her. Pouring through the gaps between the school buildings into the field.

At the edge of the field she runs across the road and clambers over a high garden fence, dropping down before going garden to garden. Out of sight she takes side and rear fences, zig zagging away and deeper into the small estate.

Trying to picture the layout of the town in her mind she uses to the high hills of the downs to keep her bearings. She needs a distraction, something to re-focus them but there's nothing usable here.

In a garden she spots an open back door and runs into the house, going straight for the kitchen to examine the cooker hoping to get some gas pumping out. Electric hobs and electric oven.

She runs into the lounge and pulls her lighter out, breathing hard as she holds the tiny flame to the bottom of the curtain, praying it's old and not a modern fire proof material.

Small tendrils of black smoke start to wisp off the curtain, she mutters quietly, urging the flame to take hold. It does, just small but it soon spreads and she makes for the front door, unlocking it to race outside and down the street.

At the end she hunkers down, looking in every direction. She can hear them but not see them. Sounds of crashing, fences being trampled, smashing glass and roars as they keep charging after her. Within a minute she spots black smoke coming from the open front door of the house. It will serve to show where she had just been but it might also draw them there instead of after her.

Checking her position against the high hills she works down the street away from the centre of town, trying to hold the layout of the town in her mind. The image of the child flits through her head with the knowledge that she fired on impulse and didn't see the wound until after, or maybe she did see it first and her brain moved quicker than actual thought could take place. The thought of firing at an uninjured child sickens and repulses her, but it wasn't uninjured. The child had been bitten which means it would turn.

A knot of tension grows in her stomach as the images replay in her mind. She's killed thousands and seen the human body dissected and blown apart many times over, even children that had been turned had been slaughtered in droves by Paula. But a child that hadn't turned and the sounds of them screaming in agony permeate her mind. If only she'd been five minutes faster, if only she'd flashed a mirror or sent a signal, done something and done it faster.

She knew those children would now be coming back and would be joining in the chase after her.

Just keep going, get out the town and work back to the vehicle then drive off and work a plan out. She reaches the end of the road and takes a swift right into a junction and away from the oncoming *things* charging at her from the left.

The houses here are older brick built cottages with wooden framed windows and wooden front doors with faded and peeling paint. Old and cheap looking, indicating she must be on the outskirts now. A high wall takes over from the end of the terraced houses, she keeps going looking ahead to examine the layout and plan a route.

She veers towards a wide entrance further up on the left. She can hear them behind her, the footsteps as they pound the ground and the odd howl and groans as they press on.

Breathing hard she reaches the entrance, catching a glimpse of the large sign on the wall welcoming her to something or other industrial estate with the signature logos of the businesses next to a row of unit numbers.

Casting about she heads down the main road of the industrial unit, flanked by large dome and flat roofed buildings. Breakdown vehicles parked up, delivery trucks and white vans left abandoned.

The units look untouched, secure and locked up tight. But that's all they are, just squat buildings with open land round them and nowhere to hide or create a zig zag trail. The deeper she goes the more frantic she becomes, fearing she will get trapped or run out of energy before something presents itself.

Up ahead, just after the slight bend; a quick view of a chain link fence. That must mean a compound or secure inner area. Paula grits her teeth and ignores the pain in her side flaring up from the stitch. Shouldn't have had that coffee, stick to water next time.

The bend opens up, revealing the long fence separated into sections with thick concrete posts embedded into the ground and razor wire coiled at the top. Perfect, she just needs to find a way in now. Double gates closed and locked but no razor wire on the top, just sharp spikes. It'll have to do, she goes for them and leaps high at the last second. Grasping the bars to pull herself up, thanking her forethought of leaving the bag in the vehicle.

Carefully she braces one foot on the top of the gate and steps over the sharp spikes, twisting round to draw her trailing leg over.

The horde are in view, eyes fixed on her. She knows the spikes won't stop them but it will delay them. Sliding down she drops to the ground and starts off, running towards the much larger buildings within the secure area. Some have rear loading bays with bakery trucks backed up to them.

She heads that way, knowing bakeries work during the night and hoping either one of the trucks will be left with the keys in or there is something else she can use.

A flash of blue and red objects in the distance catch her eye, familiar shades that stop her dead in her tracks then running back to peer through the gap in the buildings. A huge smile splits her face apart and she charges towards the new sight.

Two big units side by side with a narrow alley down the middle, she takes the alley, stepping, jumping and tripping over the piles of litter and broken up wooden pallets left there.

At the end she pushes a big wheelie bin away and takes a second to stare in wonder at the sight. Perfect, absolutely perfect but she'll have to move quick if she can make it work.

Taking a breath she runs for the new fence, this one higher and far more solid. Gasping from the exertion she reaches the top and climbs over, no razor wire this time but plenty of big signs and warnings of CCTV security systems and uniformed patrol guards.

Onto the ground and she glances back, nodding that the mouth of the alley is still clear. The nearest truck is across the yard. She sprints over and hoists herself up onto the tailgate and onto the back of the flatbed lorry.

Must be just twist and release, please let it just be twist and release. It is!

'Yes!' she grips the first nozzle and starts turning it, listening as the jet of gas starts escaping. Leaving that one she moves on, grasping and turning another and then another.

She works her way through the truck, twisting the valves on the gas bottles one by one. She doesn't do all of them on the truck, there must be over thirty on this one alone and not all will be needed.

She glances round at the row of flatbed lorries all loaded with gas bottles, offering a quick prayer to whoever or whatever led here to this place.

Down from the first truck and onto the next one, valves twisted and the air fills with the solid noise of gas escaping. She makes sure to turn some fully and others only half so the gas doesn't just escape into the atmosphere and dissipate.

Leaving the next truck she moves round and goes to the one after, increasing the chances of igniting more of them. Quick glance round and the first are out of the alley, tripping and stumbling to fall against the wheelie bin, sprawling out but quickly getting back up.

The alley disgorges *thing* after *thing,* spewing them out so they can pick up speed again. It takes a few minutes for them to realise where she is, standing round and running in different directions.

She almost laughs at the sight of the stupid creatures until she jumps down and heads for another truck. They spot the movement and start charging towards the fence. Looking over at them she spots the thick pipe running to the huge tank at the end. That must be the main supply where they fill the bottles up.

Knowing she has but minutes, Paula flat out sprints towards the huge tank emblazoned with signs warning of *no smoking* and *no naked flames.*

She curses at the sight of the electronic display, wishing it was old fashioned with a big wheel she could turn that would dump loads of gas out. She grabs dials and starts turning them but the display board is void of life, inert and dull.

Forcing herself to think rationally she realises they must have a way of operating in the event of a mains power outage. They're at the fences now, the masses increasing with every passing second as they throw themselves at it.

Tracing the pipes she finds a fitment that must connect to the bottles and working back she finds the release lever, pulling it over she listens at the end of the pipe but nothing is coming out. The gas must only come out when something is pressed into it.

Too late, time to go and she can already smell the heady scent of gas filling the air. If that fence goes down and causes a spark they will all be blown to bits.

This is the back of the gas compound so the front must be round the other side of the building. She sets off, jogging now instead of all out sprinting, knowing she has one flare left for the flare gun.

How far should she go? What's the range on the flare gun? And will it ignite the gas in the air or does it need to impact on something?

Halfway towards the entrance she stops and about turns, breathing hard with sweat pouring down her face but the baseball cap does the job in keeping the sweat from her eyes.

Paula holds her ground and waits for the first fence to get pushed down. It won't take long. Sniffing the air she can't make out the smell of gas from here, but the force of the explosion will still be dangerously close. She gauges the distance to the front gates and calculating how long it will take to sprint that way. The gas bottle lorries are behind the building, which means the solid structure will take some of the energy from the explosion and give her a few more seconds to get away.

If she goes any further she will lose line of the sight with the trucks, no it has to be here. Right here. She draws the flare gun out and breaks the barrel open, checking the flesh flare is loaded and ready.

With the sound of metal being twisted the fence starts to buckle inwards from the sheer press of bodies forcing themselves against it. She takes aim, holding the flare gun out in front of her towards the row of lorries.

The fence falls down with a whump, bodies sprawling out from the sudden loss of resistance and getting trampled by the immediate surge that follows. A loud howl goes up at the same time as the *things* realise their prey is now but seconds away from being taken.

Here goes, she pulls the trigger and watches the trail of the flare as it scorches across the air and straight over the top of the trucks to sail off into the distance.

Missed. She missed the only shot. With a determined growl she yanks the rifle round and starts firing at the gas bottles on the truck. The sharp crack of the rifle sounds out, followed instantly by the pinging of the low calibre bullets bouncing off the side of the hardened gas bottles.

She aims lower for the fuel tank of the vehicle, grimacing with horror at the sight of the huge horde now pouring across the ground towards her.

Shot after shot goes into the lorry, she strikes a tyre blowing it out. The lorry sags which causes the bottles to lurch over, they start to fall from the back banging noisily to the ground and rolling across the concrete base.

Paula twists round and starts firing at the big tank in the corner, repeatedly pulling the trigger. A gas canister falls from the truck and hits hard against the ground causing a single solitary spark. One spark that ignites the gas in the air turning it into an instant fireball that blows out sideways straight into the horde.

Paula’s blanches at the sight, unaware of the spark from the falling canister but taking full advantage of the distraction to start running like crazy towards the gate.

The fire roars across the ground as it ignites more gas escaping from bottles. The first one goes up with a dull thud which sends it soaring high into the air like a missile.

Paula hears it go but doesn't waste time in looking but is head down and sprinting with everything she’s got.

More canisters start going up, some with dull thuds as the valve ignites and forces the bottle away like a rapidly deflating balloon. Others explode like giant grenades that send super-hot chunks of ragged metal deep into the horde.

Like a pressure wave hitting them they go down, the force of the explosion and ragged metal ripping them to pieces.

Reaching the gates Paula grabs the bars and starts pulling hand over hand, cursing loudly when the gate swings out with her still trying to climb it.

Check the bloody thing is closed next time, she berates herself inwardly and keeps running, heading deeper into the units of the estate.

Turning back after a full two minutes of running round and between the commercial buildings she almost feels disappointed at the lack of anything to see. The gas burns itself out cleanly and doesn't create any smoke. The flames are forced out along the ground so don't go high into the air.

But the heat builds and the pressure builds with it. The gas ignited from the opened canisters heats the air well beyond the safe operating temperature of the bottles.

The remaining bottles explode, the rapidly heating gas expanding inside the pressurised containers and literally forcing the metal to shred apart. Bang after bang sounds out as they go, mini fireballs scorch up with each one. Paula nods, satisfied that she at least got a visual aid that something is happening.

It won't take them long to find a way round it so she moves off, running further into the estate and again clocking the position of the downs to guide her away from the town centre.

Hundreds dead already and she only just arrived.

A thought hits her, that the power and might of an exploding gas facility is great, but it will still only kill a set amount. If she could have used those bottles to plant and prepare she could have caused much worse damage. But on the run like that, she only got a few in relation to the overall size.

Suddenly the task seems so much harder, something she maybe shouldn't be taking on. The children already paid with their lives and in a truly awful way. A glimpse of movement and she ducks left, heading down the side of another unit to crouch and listen. The sound of footsteps grow louder, feet drumming on the ground as more of the *things* flood past heading for the fire, cutting her route off and forcing her to remain still.

Working quietly down the side of the unit she reaches the rear and drops down, trapped in a courtyard with a high wall running round the end, sheer sided with broken glass embedded on the top. No way over it. The only way out is back up the side and out the front, which is now crawling with undead moving towards the fire.

They seem different, more organised and cohesive. If there is another Thomas here he must have a tight grip on them. Paula berates herself instantly for assuming it would be a male undead, why not a female?

If just one of them comes down here she'll be spotted. The ground is clear and open with nothing she can hide behind or under.

She looks at the rear of the building, the door is secure and fastened shut. The only way in would be the window but that would mean breaking it and causing noise.

Trapped. Failing to save the children and trapped in a stinking industrial estate. She rests her head against the pane of glass cursing her misfortune and listening to the gas bottles still exploding in the near distance.

They're exploding properly now, not just thudding off but detonating like bombs. Without pausing to think she twists the rifle round and taps the butt against the pane, waiting for another loud bang of an exploding gas bottle. As one goes up she taps the glass and winces. Not hard enough so she waits again, holding the butt inches away from the glass pane. Now, she hits the glass immediately after another quick explosion, the glass fractures, seemingly noisy from being stood right next to it.

With the rifle reversed and held ready she waits for them to come thundering down the side of the unit. Nothing. Going low she peers round and finds it clear. Back at the window she waits for more explosion before raking the rifle round the glass and out the frame.

Before climbing in she shoes the broken glass away from underneath the window, scattering it further down and into the gap between the door and the ground. Satisfied she climbs up onto the windowsill and crabs through the hole, dropping down and holding in a crouch.

The room looks like a staff room, except it's a filthy staff room. Old blue cushioned chairs covered in oil stains, the table littered with salt and pepper pots, tomato ketchup bottles and everything covered in grimy oil smears.

Even the once white sink is mostly black from grime and an industrial size tub of abrasive hand wash rests by the sink.

Dirty coveralls hang from hooks by the door, posters of topless models adorn the walls. Without going any further Paula knows the place is a garage, an old style back street dirty garage with hairy men with fat stomachs and tattoo's staring hungrily at every woman that dares walk in.

A foreign environment and one that sent shudders through her. Simply because the people here knew more about cars than she would ever know, which meant she had to rely on them and take their word for whatever was wrong, which is something she had grown to hate over the years.

Scanning round she looks for something to prop in the broken window, anything will do, even if it just blocks the eye from registering a freshly broken pane of glass.

In the end she settles for the large side of a cardboard box, using her knife to cut it down to size and pushing it hard against the gap. Using the tub of hand-wash to hold it in place she rushes out of the room into the large main workshop, several vehicles sit high on ramps or jacked up with bonnets open and mechanical entrails littering about.

Going from workstation to workstation she finds what she's looking for and heads back into the staff room, using the sticky tape to secure the cardboard to the window, then changing her mind she pulls it off and finds a marker pen, scrawling *this building is alarmed* on the side before sticking it back up, then she pulls it off again and smears from oily dirt over the edges to make it look old, her art project finished she sticks it back up and stands wondering what to do now, biting her bottom lip as she looks round.

Thirsty, it's hot and she's sweating profusely, replenish the fluids and find some food. The tap still runs so she leaves it on for a minute to draw any stagnant water out and starts looking through the mugs. All of them filthy and tea stained.

Using a scouring pad and a new bottle of washing up liquid that looks like it has never been touched, she scrubs a mug clean, rubbing the brown stains away until it gleams in the original ceramic white colour with a picture emblazoned on one side.

'You are shitting me,' she shakes her head at the cover image for the movie *28 days later* on the side of the mug. You couldn't make it up she muses, filling the now clean mug and drinking deeply.

She searches the room for food, finding a couple of chocolate bars in the rancid fridge, her fingers squish the melted chocolate as soon as she touches it. Discarding the ruined bar she keeps looking but finds only pasta pots and noodles which require hot water.

Sounds of feet scuffing from outside, she freezes and listens intently. Footsteps getting closer, coming down the side. Backing away from the staff room she moves into the workshop, scanning round for somewhere to hide.

A small customer office over the other side near the front, she gets inside but other than under the desk there's nowhere to tuck away.

Back into the workshop and she spots a single wooden door on a partitioned section in the corner. Pulling the door open she winces at the rancid smell of stale urine and human waste, grimacing at the sight of the filthy toilet bowl. No air flow in here, just stale air mixed with the waste of all the mechanics using it every day.

Holding at the door she looks round for somewhere else, anywhere else but this is the only place. She drags a stack of old tyres over and places them in a pile by the door, making sure she's got just enough to squeeze inside. Again it's not perfect but it might draw the eye away from the door.

The scrapes and knocks sound from the rear double doors, just feet from her position. Low groaning noises and scuffs as feet are dragged and placed noisily.

Taking a big breath of semi clean air she heads into the toilet and quietly pushes the door closed before slumping down in the pitch dark with her back to it, staying as far away as possible from the filthy toilet bowl.

Fourteen

With Dave and Lani on the top wall looking out I take the opportunity to speak with Clarence while the lads piss about moving the vehicles to get to an old lorry. We both stare up at the two slight figures standing with their backs to us, the smaller shape of Meredith lying down next to Lani.

'So?' He says at length, 'what do you think?'

'Dunno mate, I want to believe it but what are the chances?'

'You think it's another trick?' he speaks quietly, voice low and muted. I don't know what to think so I don't answer for a minute, 'Boss?' He prompts.

Shrugging I try and find a clear thought process in my head, 'Why Lani? Why not you or one of the lads? Why her? Of all the thousands and thousands of undead we've killed, every one of them being a person before they were infected...why Lani?'

'There's always the chance that I am immune, or Dave or any of us...we won't know unless we get infected...'

'Nah, you think so?' I look up at him.

'Not really,' he shrugs, 'just thinking it through.'

'Right,' I start off with my hand in front, palm turned up, 'we find each other right, I was going into London and we meet you and Chris, then we get down here and get the fort...now there can't be many places like this so that's makes us kind of unique, plus we've killed so many, which again makes us unique...then we not only hear about Meredith but we find her too, again that makes us unique...and now with Lani? It just seems...I don't know...'

'There'll be hundreds of communes and places like this,' Clarence says inclining his head behind us and clearly meaning the fort even though we're stood in it, 'plus other survivors could have killed as many as us and we still don't know if it is just Meredith or all that breed...we might not be as unique as you think.'

'So if we look at it like that,' I pick up on his train of thought, 'then Lani being immune or repressing it or whatever she's doing, then it could genuinely be that she's the one in a million...or billion....or whatever comes after billion.'

'Trillion.'

'One in a trillion then...but we only had about fifty million in this country so...maybe one in fifty million...but like you just said we don't know that, there could be loads of people the same as her, we just haven't met them.'

'Sorry to bring her up, but Marcy was different, she had a chance to infect you and she didn't, she had time to take all of us but she didn't.'

'Why not? If the plan was to pump out pheromones so we all get turned then why not do it when the battle was on, or when we were sleeping?'

He shrugs and shakes his head, exhaling a long breath at the same time, 'I get the impression that Marcy meant what she said when she first turned up and the pheromone thing came later.'

'Yeah I did think that,' I agree glumly, 'fuck this is hard, the end of days should be easy and running about killing zombies not wondering about this kind of shit.'

He laughs and looks round at the sea of bodies stretched out in every direction, 'we not killing enough for you then?'

'Well,' I exclaim loudly, 'we can only do what's in front of us, we get this place sorted and worry about it after...'

'I'll get the digger and see what the lads are doing,' he strides off towards the gate leaving me alone and thinking hard. Glancing up I see Lani turned and staring down at me. I wave and she just stares back before turning away.

I remember at work, in the supermarket that when I felt stressed or worried I'd go onto the shop floor for a bit and stock some shelves. The repetitious work somehow soothed my mind and enabled me to think a lot clearer. Looking round at the bodies I wonder if clearing these away will be the same thing.

Shuffling over I get to the closest one and look down at the decaying mess of what was once human flesh and is now just a bloodied, barely recognisable corpse. Red eyes stare up at me lifelessly, the mouth hangs open with flies buzzing in and out of the cavity. Bending closer I see fat white maggots writhing inside against the swollen tongue. Somehow, it just doesn't look the same as a crate of baked beans in tomato sauce that needs opening and putting on the shelf.

The heat is already decaying them, the flesh will tear easily now and will be a bloody nightmare trying to clear them by hand. I snort to myself at thinking of it as a bloody nightmare, *bloody* in more ways than one.

This fort was thriving just yesterday. Thousands of people feeling maybe that first stab of hope that they can get through it. Who was to blame? Sergeant Hopewell for not getting the security done faster? Or whoever messed up and let them get inside?

Not that it matters now. A loud diesel engine chugs to life somewhere between the two gates, followed by another one a few seconds later, this one much louder. Staring at the gate I watch as first Clarence drives a big yellow digger through with a massive metal scoop on the end of the extending arm, then Nick behind the wheel of a tatty old flat bed lorry.

They park up and clamber down to start putting the protective gear on, glasses, thick gloves and face masks.

Why Lani?

It doesn't make any sense. I want to believe in it, I truly do. But after Marcy and all the other things it just seems too good to be true. If she is immune, or has a way of fighting it then we need to do something. We don’t even know for sure if she died before she came back, she might have just got infected and not actually died. Either way her eyes are clear, she’s speaking normally and seems in full possession of her own mind. Nothing about her seems different apart from the wound that’s healed much faster.

She could be the hybrid that Marcy said was possible, all of the good but none of the bad. Not likely though.

‘Here boss,’ Clarence walks over holding a pair of glasses along with the other gear. Taking them I get dressed slowly, still deep in thought as the lads stroll over with freshly lit cigarettes.

‘Ready,’ with the glasses and face mask on I turn round to and sigh again at the sheer number of bodies, then another sigh as I glance up into the clear sky and the heat coming down.

It's gruesome work, disgusting and filthy but after all the fights we've been in I guess we've become desensitised to it by now. Clarence gets to work trying to figure out how to use the digger and operate the scoop. Going too high with the scoop and too fast with the speed he ploughs into the bodies squashing them under the big wheels and driving the metal prongs of the digger through the corpses instead of under them.

The lads burst away from the shower of guts and body parts that get thrown up, yelling in disgust as Clarence grins and stops the digger. Pulling levers about he smashes the scoop down, flattening more bodies, then up too high and going forward, driving yet more of them into the ground.

'I'll get it,' he shouts above the noise of the engine. Concentrating hard he lowers the scoop bit by bit until Nick shouts for him to stop, then he inches forward again guided by Nick until the scoop is full of bodies. With a yell and a thumbs up Nick steps back, watching as Clarence pulls more levers to lift the scoop up.

He starts turning in a wide circle, flattening and popping more bodies as he goes round. Facing the right way he jolts the digger forward and presses something that makes the scoop tilt forward dropping all the bodies back onto the ground.

The lads all cheer and clap as Clarence goes red in the face and backs up, re-adjusting the scoop and trying again. Each time he does it the bodies get mangled more and more, becoming a heap of limbs and torsos instead of whole corpses.

Finally he gets one in the scoop and lifts it up, the lads cheering as he starts inching forward towards the lorry. The single mangled body has one leg hanging out, threatening to pull the rest of the body down.

Clarence stares at the dangling limb, sending thought waves of exactly what he'll do if it dares fall out. Which then causes a problem as he's watching the leg and not where's he's going and drives into the side of the lorry with a loud bang. Amazingly, the body stays in the scoop and the big man doesn't even glance at the lorry but operates the scoop to drop the body into the flat bed.

'YES! GET IN!' He bellows with a roar, standing up with his arms in the air. The lads cheer and applaud, we hear a whistle and look up to see Lani with her fingers in her mouth and waving down.

'That's one,' I shout over, 'nine hundred and ninety nine to go...'

'On it,' he shouts back buoyed up at his success. We watch as he goes back and attacks them again, causing more damage and just making it harder to get the flattened bodies up. He drives the scoop too low and grinds a huge divot of earth up. Cursing as he operates the scoop to drop the earth and change direction, going for another pile further on.

In the end we pile in, the lads and I grabbing bodies to stack them into little piles for Clarence to get at. It works better and before long we've almost forgotten what we're doing and shouting to each other as we work. Or clothes get covered in gore and we slip and slide through the mess, chatting away as we bend down to scoop bits of bodies up.

At one point I look up to see Cookey a few metres away holding an arm as she explains something to Blowers who just nods back as though it's completely natural. Cookey even uses the arm to emphasise whatever point he's making before glancing at the limb and throwing it onto the pile.

Clarence does get the hang of it, eventually. The lorry gets filled up with bodies and then Clarence has the bright idea of using the scoop to pat them down and make more room. We all see what he's planning and we all try to shout, but he does it anyway and it does work to a certain extent but also reminds me of squashing your hand down on a sponge cake and watching the jam in the middle ooze out the sides.

The scoop bounces down, rocking the lorry on its suspension, the hydraulic arm whirring as it lifts and drops with a squelchy thud. Bloodied things get popped and drop out and he goes back for another scoop.

Nick gets into the lorry, Clarence swaps to the fuel tanker and we clamber in, driving out through the gates to the flatlands, leaving Dave and Lani on the top wall. We go slow as the unmade road bounces the lorry about, threatening to spill the bodies out.

We head into the estate, or what was the estate and pull up next to the already huge pile of bodies. Even with the face masks on the smell makes us want to gag. Putrid foul eggs mixed with sulphur and rancid meat. Insects buzzing everywhere and the cadavers almost writhe from the maggots living within them. There were bodies here since the first attack by Darren, and Marcy stacked the people from the fort here too after the big fight yesterday.

The sight is indescribable, just solid mounds of bodies in varying states of decay. None of us look too hard for fear of seeing faces and features we'd recognise.

Nick operates the back of the lorry, holding a button down that pushes the hydraulic arm up to lift the flat bed. It grinds noisily, threatening to give out and I notice Clarence innocently looking away and pretending not to notice.

It does lift and the bodies slide down to land in a wet heap on the scorched ground.

'We burning these now or all in one go?' Nick shouts out.

Looking about I can see we've got enough space to make more piles and burn these now, but that would mean coming back up here with the bodies on fire.

'We'll do them all when we've finished,' I shout back which means there was no need to bring the fuel tanker up here.

Driving both back we head back inside the fort and park up in the same positions and take five minutes to get water and have a smoke.

'DO YOU WANT TO SWAP?' Dave bellows down.

'Cookey, Blowers you go up and get out the sun for a bit.'

'You sure Mr Howie, don't seem right getting Dave to shift bodies like this.'

'Ah get on,' Clarence shouts, 'what you on about? He'll love it.'

'Can I do the digger this time?' Nick asks quickly.

'Fill your boots mate,' I nod and laugh as he runs off, clambering up the side. Clarence strolls after him shaking his head, 'hang on Nick, let me show you...'

'I'll figure it out,' Nick shouts back and starts the ignition. Clarence stands back watching as he does the thing with his hands hovering over each stick, lever and button while murmuring to himself. He grabs levers and starts pushing and pulling, watching the hydraulic arm lift, drop and the scoop tilt up and down.

'Clever fucker,' Clarence looks at me with a shocked expression. Nick powers forward and aims the scoop perfectly. Slicing the pronged bottom lip under a pile of corpses and shovelling them into the bowl with his forward momentum. He judges it right and lifts the arm while tilting the scoop up, securing the bodies safely within.

'I hate him,' Clarence mutters, stomping over to start throwing bodies into a pile. The other two lads get up the top and stand talking to Dave and Lani for a minute before heading towards the Saxon.

Within a couple of minutes they're both down the bottom with us, pulling gloves, masks and glasses on.

'I said Meredith should stay on a lead,' I approach Lani as the dog scampers about sniffing the ground with her tail going crazy.

'You did,' she replies flatly, 'but how do I do that and shift bodies?'

'Well you don't, you stand back and hold the dog.'

'Here,' she throws the lead at me as she walks past, 'you hold her.' I turn to watch her stride off, waving at Clarence who nods back as he throws another body with ease.

She gets stuck in, heaving at a corpse to drag it over. I watch her for a minute, and she knows I watch as she point blank refuses to look back in my direction but starts making conversation with Clarence.

'Mr Howie,' Dave nods in greeting as he walks past, heading over to them both, but I notice he stays quite close to Lani and despite being seemingly focussed on the task at hand I know he'll have one eye on her.

'Just me and you then,' I look down at Meredith. She stares up at me grinning with her tongue hanging out. But clearly I'm not as interesting as Dave and Lani as she trots off to join them and within minutes she gets the idea and starts digging into the corpses with her front paws, splattering the ground behind her with sodden bits of body. She doesn't so much as help as cause an almighty mess but she seems quite happy so she gets left alone.

Nick operates the digger with far greater finesse than Clarence, scooping bodies up to drop them into the lorry, and this time he uses the heavy scoop to flatten them down before loading them up. Which also doesn't work either as it just creates more of a mess.

The second load is done and this time just Nick and I head out with the lorry, leaving the others in the fort getting the bodies ready.

I drive while Nick gets the smokes out, both of us sweating heavily but maybe there was something in my earlier thought process as the work has cleared my mind and I feel a great deal more settled.

'You think she is immune boss?' Nick asks, clearly thinking the same thing.

'I hope so mate,' I reply, 'time will tell.'

'I think she is,' Nick says confidently.

'What makes you say that?' I ask with a laugh, then curse as we hit a pothole and a body drops from the back.

'Dunno,' he grins, 'just do, why not? Lani is fucking awesome so why not her?'

'Yep,' I nod back, 'she is that mate.'

We get into the estate and back the lorry up to the fresh pile. Nick jumps out to press the button and we stand there watching as it slowly tilts up and the bodies slide out into another wet sticky pile.

'What's that?' Nick asks, turning to face away from the flatlands.

'What?' I spin round but don't see anything. Nick releases the button and quickly shuts the engine off. We stand in silence for a second but then he starts nodding and looking at me.

'Engines?' I ask him quietly at the distant rumble.

'Definitely,' he replies.

'Get the rifles ready,' I press the button in to raise the back, watching as the last of the bodies fall out, then push it back in again and stand tapping my foot as it slowly lowers back down.

'Nick, did you bring a radio?'

'No, did you?'

'Bollocks, we'll drive back...get in mate,' I leave the back raised slightly and get in the driver's seat. Nick stares at the entrance to the estate. As soon as we start the lorry the sounds of the oncoming vehicles are drowned out.

Getting back onto the unmade road I get the speed up, bouncing over the potholes and rough surface that shakes and vibrates the old lorry, and us within in.

Nick leans out the window, staring back along the track until he shouts they are in sight, then more of them.

'Bloody loads Mr Howie,' he shouts, 'all vans and trucks,' he slumps back into his seat and stares forward, then thinks better of it and leans back out to wave his arms at the fort.

The silhouette of the Saxon stands alone on the top wall, then movement as one of the lads pops up in the middle.

Clarence runs out the front and grabs the gate, planting his legs wide as he heaves it closed; normally a two man job that he does with apparent ease. The others must be inside closing the inner gate.

He disappears inside as we pull up, parking the blood smeared lorry to the side we jump out with our rifles and run for the gate.

Aiming for the single walk through gate I meet Clarence coming the other way and find myself on the floor after bouncing off his massive chest.

'Sorry,' he picks me up, virtually lifting me from feet, 'who are they?'

'No idea, but they've slowed down,' I remark spotting the now slow moving convoy heading down the road.

'You got a radio?'

'No boss,' he replies shaking his head, 'Blowers is grabbing them from the Saxon, Cookey's on the machine gun.'

'Dave and Lani?'

'Getting the inner gate closed, Dave has given Lani an assault rifle but the magazine is empty.'

'Was she alright with that?' I ask with a worried frown.

'Not really, but she sees knows we'll all look the part.'

'You on about my empty gun?' She asks stepping out.

'Yeah...er...sorry.'

'Not your fault,' she says stiffly, 'I can always throw it at them.'

'I got the radios,' Blowers runs out breathing hard as he hands them round.

'Cookey, you hearing me?'

'Yeah loud and clear, who are they?'

'No idea, how far back do you need them to stop with the angle of fire.'

'Walk forward and I'll tell you...bit more....bit more....yeah that's fine...'

'You got the binoculars up there?' Nick asks through the radio.

'Fuck yeah...hang on...'

'Don't swear on the radio Alex.'

'Sorry Dave...er...wait a minute....it looks like Maddox in the front one,' he adds after a spell.

'Really?' I ask.

'Looks like him, yeah and that girl too, definitely them.'

Exchanging glances we walk a bit more down the road, Meredith back on her lead held by Lani. We spread out into a line, Dave standing next to Lani. The first long van slows down and comes to a stop several metres back from us but with the sun glinting off the windscreen I can't see who is inside.

The doors open and Maddox jumps down from the driver's side, closely followed by Lenski out the other.

'Mr Howie,' he calls out with one hand up in greeting, 'alright to come up?'

'Yes mate, of course,' I stride towards him with a big grin, letting them know we're happy to see them.

'Darius, tell 'em to stay in the vehicles for now,' Maddox calls back as another thick set youth walks up from the second vehicle. We hear a muted radio transmission as Darius speaks into a black handset, pausing briefly to make sure the order is being followed before walking down.

'Bloody hell mate, what's going on?' I stick my hand out which he takes with a firm grasp.

'We thought about what you said,' he answers with a smile.

'Lenski isn't it?' I offer her my hand, 'nice to see you again.'

'You too,' she gives a quick shake. Clarence and the lads all say hello, exchanging quick handshakes which takes a few minutes as Darius and another girl come forward and join in with the greetings.

'So what you doing here then?' I finally ask.

The smile fades slightly from his face, a serious expression replacing it as he looks back with his deeply intelligent eyes, 'like I said, we thought about your offer.'

'You brought everyone with you?' I step out to look down the road at the vehicles stretched out.

'Yeah, but I wanted to talk to you before we agree if we coming in or not.'

'Right?' I look to each of them noticing the resolute looks on their faces, something planned and prepared.

'I don't want you to think we're coming with our tail between our legs, we ain't running scared,' he says firmly, 'we got supplies, loads of food and other equipment, we got weapons and the crews might be young but they're disciplined and I wanted to agree terms before we do anything...'

'Hang on a minute mate,' I put my hand up cutting him off, 'we we're going to come and see you later anyway and ask you to join us...'

He stares back at me with interest, 'we er...' I hesitate, not sure exactly what to say or where to start, 'they got inside yesterday and turned everyone.' I blurt out.

'What?' Lenski steps forward staring at the fort with a look of horror, 'is this why you outside?'

'Eh? No! We killed them all and well...other things happened too...' My voice trails off as I glance at Lani, who ignores me with one eyebrow arched, telling me exactly what she thinks.

'But yeah, everyone's dead,' I shrug, my voice drops low as a sudden stab of hurt goes through me at the thought of Sarah and everyone else.

'Jesus,' Maddox sweeps his gaze across us, 'you killed them all? You said you had thousands.'

'We did,' I nod back wincing at the memory of Sarah running towards me with her lips pulled back.

'Listen,' Lani steps forward, taking over from me as I struggle to compose myself for a second, 'it's been bloody terrible, everyone got killed and the fort is covered in bodies. We've started clearing them out but, well you're welcome here, all of you,' she speaks clearly with a strong voice, 'we've still got loads of food and everything but adding your stuff will be good. We were going to come and ask you to move here with us, the fort is too big for us to defend so we need more people and Mr Howie said you were the obvious choice, seeing that your crews are disciplined and organised.'

They stay quiet for a second, shock etched into their faces as the realisation hits them.

'The fort is safe,' Lani stresses, 'we weren't here when they got inside so we don't know how it happened but we had problems with some other people, so we think they just didn't guard the gates properly...did you see the refinery go up yesterday?'

They nod back, looking at each other again, 'it was the refinery then?' Maddox asks.

'That was us,' Lani continues, 'we were getting fuel when it happened here, we've lost everyone...our families, friends...the doctors and well...everyone,' she adds quietly.

'Oh,' Lenski says quietly with a pained look, 'that is bad, so for you...I...' she pauses as she thinks of the right words, 'we are so sorry this happen, we did not know this.'

'How would you,' I shrug, 'but as Lani said, the fort is empty now, just us left...so you're welcome to join us.'

'Got some clearing up to do first,' Clarence adds.

'We can help,' Maddox states, his voice quiet and low as he absorbs the information, 'we got plenty of people and my crews will...'

'Our crews please,' Lenski corrects him.

He smiles with good humour, 'our crews will get them cleared away...I'm really sorry for all your loss,' he adds seriously, showing a respectful nature that belies his appearance.

'We get people turning up every day,' Lani replies, 'so we need to get it done as quickly as possible, plus we'll need guards on the gate at the front and back and on the walls...inside is a real mess...'

Clarence and I glance at each other as Lani lists the immediate tasks that need to be done.

'...You can stop staring at me now,' she says for our benefit which earns some confused looks from Maddox and the others, 'come inside and we'll show you what we mean,' she adds.

Lenski steps forward quickly, walking beside Lani as the rest of us follow them through the gates.

'These gates open up to let vehicles in and we keep them all in here between the walls...those tents were our medical assessment points, anyone coming back in had to be checked fully before they were admitted,' Lani gives a running commentary as we walk across and into the fort proper, carrying her empty rifle across her chest in the relaxed position.

'Fuck me,' Darius states slowly as they step inside. Maddox, to his credit, remains mostly expressionless but just stares across at the thick layer of mangled bodies that look even worse now from lying in several hours of heat and having been run over and squashed by the digger.

'See what we mean?' I ask as they stand in silence taking the view in.

'All these...people, they lived here?' Maddox asks slowly.

I hesitate just long enough for him to shoot me a hard look, caught out and there's no point starting off on deceit. 'It's a long story that you can either hear now or later.'

'This is big place yes?' Lenski looks up from the bodies and takes in the size of the interior, her head turning as she follows the wall all the way round, 'the doors, what they for?' She points to the recessed and wooden doors along the walls.

'Stores, offices, armoury, engineering rooms...all sort of stuff. Most of the people lived here in tents, a few of us had rooms, ours are at the back and we used the police offices to organise everything as they're most central.'

'Police offices?' Maddox queries.

'We had police here until yesterday, we had doctors, engineers and even a vet...gone now, all gone.'

The four of them look at me, reading the hurt expression on my face. In a way I feel better that I am feeling the pain of loss. That there is a burning jolt inside me every time I think of Sarah and the others. Something I haven't felt before, no guilt or remorse or pain, just numb. Even now the feeling isn't strong like it should be, but buried deep and easily swallowed down.

'Whole place was thriving, thousands of people, families, children...what a fucking waste,' I shake my head sadly, 'an absolute fucking waste.'

'How did they get in?' Maddox asks, watching me closely.

'Don't know,' I say quietly, 'they can talk now so maybe they just walked up to the gate or something, we had issues about the interior defence and security but it wasn't taken seriously and they paid for it. A few people at the top who couldn't make their minds up and were too twisted with grief and power to see what should be done.' I look back at Maddox, then at all of them, 'but that won't happen again...not ever.'

'I understand,' he nods holding my gaze.

'If you are going to stay here then we get the basics sorted before anything else, that means...as Lani said, security round the clock on the gates and we get a vetting process set up for new people arriving.'

'You gonna let new people in then?' He asks.

'Definitely, that's the most important thing...the most important thing,' I emphasise, 'it has to be safe and we have to learn from someone else's fuck up and make sure it doesn't happen again. We got better guns here than you have, assault rifles and stuff. Your lads can use them but only if you agree to take instruction from my lot first.'

'Agreed,' Maddox nods.

'The food will be split evenly and shared out with someone guarding it all the time.'

'Agreed,' he replies again.

'We keep the police office as the central point and *we...as in us'* I motion to all of us stood there, 'run things from there, there will be a running order here and that means I am in overall charge but you run your crews. My team stay together all the time so if we go out or something, then you are in charge.'

'Agreed.'

'Your crews are your responsibility and we won't interfere unless absolutely necessary.'

'That is my main condition,' he cuts in, 'they will listen to you, I'll make sure of that but they take time to respect new people especially anyone they see as authority...they look rough but they'll get better. As for discipline you have no concerns.'

'Agreed,' I smile at him, 'anything else?'

'There will be,' he looks away, 'but not right now, you understand that we're not running to you yeah?'

'I get it mate, we're joining forces. We need someone to run the fort while we're not here, someone who can make decisions quickly for the benefit of everyone and someone who won't become a fucking dick about it too.'

'I make sure of this yes?' Lenski adds with a quick smile, 'what is first to be done?'

'Bodies need removing,' Maddox replies then looks at me, 'you alright if I get my crews on security now at the front and back?'

'Please do, we've got a couple up there keeping look out with heavy weapons,' I point to the Saxon.

'And the vehicles? Do you want them inside here?' He asks.

'How many crews you got?' Lani asks quickly.

'We have plenty, we get crew to front yes? And crew to back and two more to take the things from the vehicles and the rest they help you in here yes?' Lenski replies.

'Sounds good, let them all come in and have a look first if they want. I don't think we'll have enough rooms for everyone so some might have to stay in the open but most of these tents are ruined,' I explain.

'We got our own stuff and all the crews will be together outside, if it's alright with you it'll only be me and Lenski and Darius and Sierra that need rooms, but we can stay outside too if...'

'No we got enough for you.'

'Are you both couples?' Lani asks.

'Yeah,' they nod with looks at each other.

'You two are the couple yes?' Lenski asks Lani with a glance to me which causes Nick and Blowers to look away, Clarence to look up at the sky and Lani to glare at me.

'Not our business,' Maddox senses the glaringly obvious atmosphere that suddenly descends.

'You look like the couple before,' Lenski shrugs.

'Yeah I thought so too,' Lani replies sweetly.

'On that note,' I cut in with a low voice, 'we got a lot to do.'

Fifteen

Did she fall asleep? There is no difference between eyes open and eyes closed but her memory has a fuzzy gap. Fully awake now, heart hammering as she remembers where she is, a flood of adrenalin surges through her system. Her body getting ready to fight or flee but she has to stay here until she knows they are gone.

How will she know they are gone? She shifts position and wipes the sweat pouring from her forehead. The stink in here is awful, truly terrible. No air vents and no window so the stench just builds up. Pitch black too, she waves her hand in front of her face but can't see it. The door she rests against is well made and flush to the floor, no light coming through.

Groping at her watch she presses the small button to illuminate the screen, early evening but still plenty of hours of daylight left. She must have been in here for a couple of hours already.

Thirsty now she has woken up but nothing to drink other than the filth that would be in the toilet bowl. Why did she come in here? The darkness pervades her mind, lulling her into a false sense of security.

There were noises outside, that was it. She got in here and hid, listening to the scrapes as they moved round the outside of the building, but the heat and after effects of the adrenalin made her sleepy, probably light headed from the stench in here too. But at least it should mask her own smell.

Are they clever enough to start searching buildings? Would they do that? They must have seen the direction she ran in.

Time passes slowly. She counts seconds into minutes and checks her watch to test her accuracy, but counting in her head like that makes it feel so slow.

Should she go now or wait longer? Her instinct is telling to wait for darkness. They're faster and meaner at night but she stands a better chance of moving through the shadows and getting back to her vehicle at night. What if they've found it and set up a trap? That needs to be factored in and assessed. She did lock it so they can't get inside and wait for her. It can't be that far away, maybe a mile at the most and with all the street lights out this place will be very dark. She knows which direction the hills are so just aim for them and she'll find her way back. After that? Well, the town is too full for her to attack them without a serious plan in place. Withdraw and think it through, that's the best option. Find DIY stores in other places and set traps up on the roads.

But then why are they all here? This town is isolated, only a few roads in and the hills on one side and the sea on the other. No reason to come here unless it is for something specific. Out of sight too. Maybe just a safe place for them to stay, but that doesn't make sense. Stay here for what reason? Just for sake of staying here? No. Something else. Something nearby that they want and they need large numbers for.

What was that? A noise inside her small room, a faint scuffing sound. Listening intently she convinces herself it as her imagination before it happens again. A noise like paper rustling. Rats maybe? Coming silently out of the toilet bowl to lurk and scurry about. Rats don't bother Paula, but the thought of the room slowly filling up with them sends a shiver down her spine.

Slowly she feels for her lighter and draws it out of her pocket, feeling for the serrated wheel to push down on. The small flame flickers brightly, illuminated the tiny room. She casts about but nothing there. A rat would be seen instantly in here.

Outside, another noise. Something scuffing against the back of building. Then the rustling from inside the room comes again, faint but quick. Worried that the lighter make noise she feels for the small pen torch in her pockets. Groping about and gently prising it free from the depths of her cargo trousers. The end twists on, no buttons to press that make noise.

She holds the torch ready, intently listening for it to happen again. Outside, more scuffing and then a low groan. They must be at the back, right by the rear doors. A dull thud then another followed by something crashing to the floor in the staff room. Stock still she remains, her hand gripping the torch, eyes wide and mouth open slightly.

It has to be the cardboard she put across the window, they've pushed it in and knocked something from the counter top.

The rustling from inside again. She twists the end of the torch, the powerful beam of light sweeps over the room picking out the bit of crumpled paper in the corner. Keeping the torch on it she watches as it twitches and moves. Staring with interest as it jerks with tiny movements.

Another bang as something else falls from the counter in the staff room. Faint groans and louder scuffing noises. They have to be climbing through the window.

The bit of paper twitches again as she both watches while listening to the noises coming from outside.

No. Please not that. Anything but that. Give me rats or a mouse, anything but that. She holds the torch on the ball of paper watching as the legs start to appear, one then two, three...more come into sight as they grip and pull the huge hairy body up onto the paper. The weight of it flattens the magazine sheet as it sits on top. Eight thick legs branching off from a thick body.

Revulsion grips her as tight as the knot of fear inside her gut. Not here, not now. Anything but that. But the spider doesn't care. It senses the change in the air and feels something else is in here. This place is quiet and dark and lately there have been plenty of flies to eat and now something bigger has come in. Something bigger that needs investigating.

Paula listens in abject terror as the first of the undead falls from the counter to land on the floor with a loud thump and a groan. Then another one. The spider lifts front legs to hold them in the air as though waving at her.

It’s big, bigger than anything she has seen before. Like a mini tarantula with thick legs and solid body. The glossy magazine ball rustles again as it moves. The spider has actual weight that can impact on something else. It moves forward and starts to drop down from the ball, front legs on the floor with the body extended back over the crumpled material.

Sweat pours from her face and drips down her neck. Skin crawling and a feeling of being sick threatens to take over. Since a young child her phobia of spiders has terrified her and many times sent her running and screaming from her room to find her mother and tell her about the eight legged monster on the wall.

Evil malevolent things not from this world. Oozing predator and the way they scurry then stop, and dangle from invisible thread. Lifting their feet up and down gently, twitching and bursting away with a speed that frightens her even more.

This one goes slow, painfully and dreadfully slow which is all the worst for it. She knows she could extend a foot and crush it instantly but the thought of it roots her to the spot. That she would miss and it would jump onto her leg and run up to her waist and over her clothes to get her face. An image of the thing climbing into her mouth, feeling as the teeth or the pincers start taking bites.

Gritting her teeth she suppresses the whimper threatening to spill out and slowly draws her legs in, pulling her knees to her chest. Behind her, the sound of feet scuffing across the floor get closer.

Unable to move now, completely frozen to the spot she keeps her eyes fixed on the eight legged freak as it climbs down deftly from the ball of paper to sit low and squat on the ground. It looks even worse now with those legs splayed out, the classic perfect shape of an enormous house spider. Pure evil radiates from its thick body sending pulsing waves of terror flooding through Paula. She clamps a hand over her mouth, squeezing tight to stop any sound coming out. Her hand holding the torch starts to shake, tiny trembling motions that flicker the beam of light and make the spider dart forward an inch closer to her.

Groans come from outside as the undead shuffle about, sensing her closeness, smelling her trail but unable to see her.

The spider darts another inch. Paula screws her face up and fights the urge to scream with every ounce of strength she has.

Rooted, frozen, trapped and utterly terrified she watches as it remains still. Testing the air and she imagines it sniffing and detecting her fear which must be coming off her in buckets.

The *things* outside become animated, knowing she must be somewhere, knowing she was in that room. They can smell her, they *know* she was here.

The spider watches through many eyes and slowly lifts one leg, then another...then another and takes a few tentative steps forward. Slow and careful, watchful as it stalks the prey.

With her feet drawn in the spider has maybe just a few feet before it gets to her, and it would take a second or less if it ran flat out.

She wills herself to think that the creature is small and she is big. It cannot harm her and the bite would be far less than a wasp or bee, no worse than nettle rash. But the thought of one of those legs touching her body, even her clothing or boot is too much to take.

They're closer now, shuffling towards the door. Groaning with hunger as they move and look and search. The spider twitches and takes another step, the legs rippling with hateful coordination. Stopping after every movement to sense and sniff and taste the air.

So close now she can pick out the stubby hairs on its body and the joints of the legs. Thick straight line of the first section, then a joint and another straight bit, then another joint. Too many joints like knees, too many straight lines that make it look made instead of created by nature. Two stubby pincers stick out from the front, extended eyes like mini legs that waver and move about.

One front legs lifts high and then back down. She can't look away, she can't move or do anything but sit here trying to squeeze herself against the door while sending mental orders begging and pleading for it to just go back. *Have your end of the room, stay there and I'll stay here. We don't have to touch each other. Please just go back. I won't stay, I promise I will go as soon as I can.*

But the spider doesn't think like that. It detects her presence and wants to know what it is that disturbs its lair. What is this thing that comes in here after so much time of darkness and quiet. Curiosity and an ever growing need to eat pushes the spider on. One step, then two. Getting closer each time.

Inside her mind she screams and wails. Her hand now pushing so hard against her mouth she can hardly breathe. Forcing herself to take short soft breaths through her nose instead. Aware of every inch of her own body, of the hard floor underneath her, the hard door pressed against her back. The foul air within this tiny room that chokes and makes her want to gag. Sweat dripping freely down her face, sliding in warm salty rivers over her fingers.

Shit, right at the door now. They must be just steps away. She can hear the ragged breaths they take, inhale and exhale. Another low groan that sounds just inches away. The rustle of clothing as one of them moves.

The spider darts an inch and stops perfectly still. Less than twelve inches from the tips of her boots now. The torch light wavers for a split second then steadies again. The fear ramps up another notch. The things outside brush against the tyres she stacked up, knocking one of them off which bounces against the door. She feels the vibration through her back.

Move your foot and crush it. That's all you have to do, just step down and kill it. But what if it darts or jumps and lands on her. What if the feet touch her skin?

It knows it is close now, the heat coming from the new arrival is strong. Something with that much heat must have food. Flies, maggots and prey love heat, the spider knows this and takes another step towards her foot.

Paula stares down with wide eyes, the body of the creature is so big, so squat and heavy. Just one step to go and it will touch her.

Vibration against the door and she feels something brush against it. Chesty breathing just the other side. A long inhalation like it's smelling the air. It thumps against the door, not an attack but a clumsy motion as it navigates the littered floor.

The spider makes the final move and steps to the front of her boot. Lifting one foot it taps the outer edge of her boot. Too light and she can't feel it, but her imagination runs wild with sensation. Vomit threatening to purge up from her stomach.

Eyes watering from not blinking. The torch light wavers, dims and comes back to full strength. She wills it to stay on, she wills the spider to go away, she wills the things outside to give up and leave.

But today her will is ignored. The gods do not cast favourably upon Paula this day, for as the light grows weaker so the spider uses those strong legs to embed the claws into her boot and start to climb up, the motion is smooth and controlled and it sits on the front of her boot, mere millimetres above her toes. It claims the victory and knows it has almost defeated the invader for she will die from a heart attack any second. The life giving organ in her chest booms so fast her head spins. Terror like no other grips her. A primeval urge to kick out and stamp and stamp while screaming. Move fast, clench your eyes and stamp while beating your hands against your body. Do that and kill it but scream so you don't know you kill it. Scream and panic so you don't feel the thick body slowly crushing under hand or under-foot.

They can smell the fear. The stench of the toilet masked her odour, stale and old and they knew it wasn't the fresh scent of a host waiting to be taken. But now, now there is fear and fresh sweat and it's right here. Right behind this door.

Bumps and bangs as they move against the wooden door, scuffing and shuffling, feet gliding over the concrete floor. Hard breaths getting faster as they sense the proximity of her.

Torch light dims, slowly fading to a dull glow that weakly illuminates the spider. She shakes her hand, desperately trying to get battery juice to make the bloody light work. The brave torch rallies and fights her corner, pushing a bright light out for a few seconds. But the power drains and no matter how hard the little torch fights it cannot hold on and the beam weakens and fades once more.

The motion of her shake vibrates her body, the sensitive feet of the spider feels the movement and darts an inch, then another. Reaching her laces and starting the slow steady climb towards her leg.

Every muscle is tensed and straining sending waves of energy that pulse from her body. The spider detects the energy and the pheromones she emits, the slight quaver of the tensed contracted muscle.

Cramp starts to grow in the back of her thigh. A tightness that pulls at her hamstring. Searing pain shoots out. Her body urging her to release the muscle and stretch the leg out before injury is sustained.

Another bang against the door. The spider moves. The torch grows weaker still. Tears fall from her eyes as the pain grows and cramps the muscle up, sending shooting barbs of agony into the cheeks of her backside and down the length of her thigh.

The torch dies.

She breathes out in panic.

The spider goes for her leg, the weight of it plucking at the material which she feels.

The things drive harder against the door.

Instinct takes over. Intelligence is gone now. The spider will kill her, it will devour her slowly and lay spider eggs in her mouth that will hatch and thousands of the creatures will climb down her throat to eat her insides and drink from the tears pooling in her eyes.

The cramped leg shoots out, thudding her backwards against the door. She's on her feet less than a second later. Stamping. Stamping. Hitting at her own body. Clenched fists beating at every inch of her legs. Forgetting the things on the other side of the door she yanks the handle down bursts out, slamming the door into the nearest one. She runs flat into the next one but the power of her panic is so great she sends it sprawling.

The spider had already dropped off and scampered across the toilet back to its corner, but convinced the creature is still on her she beats and hits and stamps down. Vaguely aware of the thing coming at her she lashes out, punching it hard in the side of the head and driving it down to the floor. The only thing she doesn't do is scream. Some intrinsic part of her brain prevents that so she fights quietly. Killing the hundreds of spiders that must now be crawling up her legs and stomach while stamping down on the undead at her feet. Breaking fingers, arms, legs and then beating the skull to a pulp.

The second one rallies and surges in. She doesn't realise or plan the move but the simple explosion of her panic reigns blow after blow into it, driving it down where her feet keep stomping and stamping.

She backs away from the area and scrabbles at her clothes. Convinced the spider has got inside her top she rips it off and stands there in her bra shaking it hard, then throwing it down to stamp on that too.

No, it got inside her trousers. Definitely inside her trousers. She beats every inch of her legs. Sitting down on the ground to press the backs of her legs into the ground while she pummels the front and sides.

Not the legs, her hair. It must have gone for the hair. The baseball cap is thrown down and stamped on, then open hands beat her head all over. But that hurts so she grabs handfuls of hair and clenches her fists, intending to crush and kill any giant evil spiders lurking there.

Topless, bruised, with a painful arse cheek and hair disarrayed she slows down and starts to come back to earth. Breathing hard and the panic abates, easing back gently as common sense screams that the two inch spider must have been killed a hundred times over by now.

Her top is on the floor, her hat further away. The rifle is still in the toilet, left there when she burst out. Two dead bodies lie bleeding with broken bones and crushed skulls. Did she do that? Bloody hell.

She checks the top for any spider corpses and pulls it on, then her hat, beating it against her leg and checking the inch of folded material round the sweat band. Smoothing her hair down she walks quickly to the toilet, peering in and checking the spider hasn't booby trapped the rifle. All clear so she leans in to grasp the barrel, glancing up to see the fucking thing sat back on top of the paper ball.

It sticks one finger up as she backs away, taunting her and daring to come and try again. sod that, she pushes the door closed and moves well away, almost convinced it will batter the door down to try and attack her again.

She shudders with the after-effects, legs shaking from adrenalin burning off. Standing quietly in the middle of the room she gets her breathing back under control and holds steady until her heart rate goes back to normal. No more noises from outside. No sounds at all. No steps or scuffs.

Another hour to wait then it will be dusk, just hang on till then and get ready to run.

Sixteen

He kicks the door hard, cursing as it refuses to yield. He kicks again harder this time and the door bursts open. Oh yes, there they are; laid out and safe inside the stock room. A feeling of relief floods through him.

Turning round he glances to the front of the shop, checking for movement or sound. He doesn't care if the zombies come here. They can be killed and dealt with. They are visible and real and actual foes that can be chopped, sliced, shot, stabbed or run away from. No, they don't bother him one little bit.

The butts of two sawn off shotguns poke from the top of his rucksack, in easy reach and ready to be pulled out and used. A heavy bladed sword hangs between his back and the bag, the hilt sticking up behind his shoulder, also ready to be pulled out and used.

Knives on his belt, one on either side. Shotgun shells in the side pockets of his trousers. Food and water in his bag but this, this in here is what he needs.

He ventures inside and starts examining the arrays of bottles and medicines, all of them sealed into plastic cases ready to be opened and put on display on the shelves of the chemist shop.

Yes, new toothbrushes. He needs a new toothbrush desperately, he only brushed his teeth eight times yesterday and then convinced himself the brush would be infected somehow and once that thought was there he couldn't use it anymore so it was discarded.

Grabbing the case he rips the plastic outer layer away and grabs a hard bristled brush, breaking the cardboard to yank it free. Toothpaste. He scans the shelves and finds a box, breaking it open to pull a fresh tube out.

Easing his bag off he draws a bottle of water out and wets the end of the brush before squeezing a nice thick layer of paste on the end. Then he brushes, and brushes, and keeps on brushing.

The gums are irritated and just the tiniest bit sore. Most likely it's from the constant brushing but to him, they are growing deadly tumours and diseases that will grow and spread throughout his whole body.

So he brushes. And then he brushes again just to be sure they're clean. But that isn't enough, the brushing will only do so much so he scans the shelf for the most important ingredient of the mouth procedure.

'Come on,' he mutters. They have bottles of Listerine which is okay, nice and strong. Colgate and other ones, and that stuff that makes the green bits come out. No...where is it?

With a yelp of triumph he grabs the case of Corsodyl mouth wash and starts shredding the packaging. Clinically proven to stop bleeding gums, that's what he wants. Something that is clinically proven. Not something marketed and sold to idiots with funky adverts. Clinically proven meant something. It meant smart people in white lab coats did tests and stuff.

Twisting the lid off he takes a swig and groans with pleasure at the familiar taste. His last bottle ran out two days ago, which just created a sense of rising panic that if he didn't get the Corsodyl soon he would develop mouth tumours which would spread. Probably too late, two days without it and they would have started by now. It was only twelve days since this all began and already he had run out of something vital and lifesaving.

He swills the liquid round his mouth, blowing his cheeks out and in to force it into all the nooks and crannies.

Finally he spits it out onto the floor, feeling a sense of relief that he now has a whole six bottles to last him. Maybe he could mix it with water to make it last longer?

He shoves the bottles into his bag and start scouring the shelves again. Remembering the funny sensation he felt in his armpit he looks for wet wipes, specifically antiseptic wipes.

Maybe a slight chaffing from the high temperatures, sweating and clothes rubbing or the crease of his skin. But there was definitely a sensation there, not pain, just a very mild discomfort. Had to be a tumour, they grew in armpits. They grew and spread and that was it; you died.

A groan from the front of the store. He turns round to see a zombie staggering in through the smashed door. Old by the looks of it. Wispy grey hair and skinny limbs attached to a fat body. Turned a few days ago too. Dried blood on its face and down its front.

Why do the things come in here when he had serious stuff to contemplate and deal with? He's not wasting a shotgun shell on this one, oh no. This one can get stabbed in the face for the sheer impudence of disturbing him. This should be like sacred ground, like a church or something. Just wait outside for him and then they can have a scrap.

Using the sword he plunges the sharp pointy end deep into the face, through the eye socket and into the brain. Then with a kick he sends it backwards and sliding off the sword to land in a heap.

He looks at the sticky goo on the end of his clean sword and frowns before using the corpse to wipe it clean.

Back in the store room he grins with excitement at finding the antiseptic wet wipes and pulls his top off to start cleaning both pits thoroughly. Then for good measure he does his chest and sides, then the arms too. With a thought he undoes his belt and button, opening the front of his trousers to push another wet wipe down to clean his groin.

'Fuck's sake,' he mutters as another zombie shuffles inside. The bloody things can't just piss off for five minutes can they? Oh no, they got to keep pestering and annoying, drooling everywhere and groaning like idiots.

'I'm bloody cleaning myself,' he shouts but the zombie ignores his protests and comes on.

With that one stabbed through the face too he goes back to the cleaning ritual, forgetting what he's done so far so starting again from the beginning and finishing off with shoving all the packs into his bag.

'Hmmm,' he muses, got three packs of multi-vitamins but will that be enough? One a day and sixty in each so that's what? One hundred and eighty days. What if he loses one or all of them? Yeah, best chuck another one in just in case.

'What else,' he asks himself. Sun cream, that was it. It was so hot outside and with an almost bald head he worried about getting burnt which would make tumours grow from his skull which would spread and then you die.

The chemist had loads of different sun creams, too many to choose from which just irritated him. Why didn't they just have one? How can they all claim to be the best?

'Bollocks,' he grabs a factor fifty and squeezes a big dollop of the thick cream into his hands before rubbing it into his head, then down his arms. The only problem with sun cream is that it made the sweat full of chemicals which stung his eyes. He hates baseball caps as the peak cuts down your vision which isn't good.

So instead he sticks with a floppy brimmed sun hat, the old fashioned type but in an urban camouflage pattern. That wasn't chosen from choice but just grabbed out of necessity. He would have worn a pink Barbie one if it was the first to hand.

Painkillers and anti-inflammatories get put into the bag. Then the stronger prescription only painkillers. Then some big packets of anti-biotics get shoved in too. All different types and he knew he could use the chemist book to look up what each one did. They were rarely used as he knew the body built up a resistance to them, but they were kept *just in case.*

Same with the first aid kit, the sticking plasters, bandages, eye wash and everything else he carried.

'Feet,' he remembers and scans the shelves once again for the anti-fungal powder. It was hot and feet got moist which harboured bacteria which developed and became skin infections.

Unlacing his boots he shrugs them off and uses the bottle of water to clean the sweat off before rubbing them dry with paper towel. Then a liberal sprinkling of powder which was carefully rubbed in.

Powder was tapped into his socks then everything put back on. *Anything else?* Nope, that was all he needed.

He shrugs the bag back on and keeps the sword to hand. Fastening the chest and waist strap of the bag he heads outside with the sword held in his right hand.

Sunglasses on and he steps out into the street, rolling his eyes at the sight of the three decrepit zombies shuffling towards him.

They were back to being slow today. Not fast and nasty like they have been sometimes. Why's that then? Why couldn't they maintain a constant speed? Too slow in the day and stupidly fast in the night. He'd already figured out they were doing it to conserve energy, *that was obvious.* So why didn't they just choose a speed in between the two and stick at that? That would make more sense.

But oh no, it wasn't like he had enough to contend with, dealing with his immense health problems but he also had to do battle with hordes of screaming zombies every bleeding day.

Stress. That would kill you too. Too much stress would make tumours grow and then you die, or lead to a heart attack, or raised blood pressure.

On that thought he went back inside the chemist, heading for the stock room to find a blood pressure machine. What if he became diabetic? He should check blood sugar too, in fact, come to think about it he was quite thirsty today and that was sign of diabetes. Thirsty and pissing a lot. He suddenly needs a piss, like an urgent pressure on his bladder.

Diabetes. He knew it. He knew something like this would happen. Diabetes and tumours. Shit. Probably one day left to live at the most, that and the high blood pressure.

He finds a blood pressure kit and takes it out the box, reading the instructions while wrapping the thick black sleeve round his arm. *Batteries included.* That was nice. It was always nice when they put batteries in ready for you. Even if they were the cheap shit ones that ran out really quickly.

Remarkably simply to use so he turns it one and feels the sleeve tighten on his arm. The machine whirred while he read the accompanying booklet. Systolic, oh that didn't that sound good. He's definitely got Systolicism and the other one too, oh my...Diastolic. That sounds like a killer. Oh wait, they're the words for the measuring chart. So Systolic is the heart when it pumps and Diastolic is when it rests between the pumps, so those numbers they always say on the medical programmes when the handsome doctor shouted it was one hundred and eighty over seventy, that's what it meant.

Nodding with understanding he waits for the machine to calculate his, knowing it will be really high. Probably up there at the top; one hundred and ninety. Easily one hundred and ninety. All this stress and what with the diabetes too. The machine bleeps with flashing numbers.

'Systolic is one hundred and ten...it's too low, oh...no that's perfect...hmmmm. Diastolic is seventy,' checking the chart he reads that is in the ideal range too. Perfect blood pressure. That can't be right so he shakes the machine, switches it off, shakes it again and switches it back on.

'Fucking hell,' he whines as the next zombie gets to the doorway. He presses the button and waits, feeling the sleeve tighten again. This time will be the proper reading.

'Just fucking wait,' he shouts at the shuffler heading across the shop floor. One hundred and ten over seventy again.

'Fuck it,' he shouts, so why did he feel so ill if his blood pressure was perfectly okay. The machine beeps with a change as his blood pressure rises another ten to hundred and twenty.

Heart attack. Got to be a heart attack. The zombie groans, making him roll his eyes. Grabbing the sword he walks out and shoves it through the eye, holding the hilt which holds the zombie up while also holding the blood pressure machine in his hand. One hundred and thirty now. Shit, this is it. The final end. He takes a deep breath and waits for the burst of pain to explode in his chest. The machine bleeps again. One hundred and twenty, now one hundred and fifteen and dropping.

It was the zombie that made it rise. He kicks the thing away, pulling his sword free as he stares at the screen.

So his blood pressure was okay. Just the diabetes to worry about now. How would he control that? Insulin, yeah that was it. People took insulin every day.

Back in the store room he finds the stock of blood sugar testing machines, and goes through the same motions; stripping it free from the box and getting it rigged up and ready.

The machine comes with a device to prick the end of his finger, the blood goes on that strip which goes in the machine. He does it quickly, knowing he will have to find the insulin quickly.

'em em oh el stroke el….what does that stand for?' He looks again at the letters; mmol/l. Millimoles per litre. What the hell was a mini mole? An image of a burrowing animal with thick glasses swimming through his veins comes into his mind.

'Five point five,' he nods at the numbers on the screen. Six must be the limit, so he's got point five until he dies. Reading the chart he narrows his eyes that the figure is the perfect range between meals.

When did he last eat? Two, maybe two and half hours ago. He had that tinned fruit and some Shredded Wheat.

Not diabetes then. That settles it, it's gonna be the big one. The big C. Or it could still be the big heart attack waiting to happen.

Outside again he walks towards the last zombie still making its way towards him. Where had all the rest gone? This area was crawling with them yesterday. Just these few left and they looked fit to drop any second. This one could hardly walk and was trailing a leg with the ankle broken at a right angle. How was it still walking? It was limping down and putting its weight on the broken ankle.

He winces with the thought of the pain that must cause. Swinging the sword left and right in a casual manner he walks towards it and side steps at the last second, sweeping the sword through the things neck. The blade bites deep, severing the arteries which spray blood out across the pavement as it slumps down.

Walking on he wonders what to do for the rest of the day. His mouth felt better already, that was for sure. And his armpits too and come to think of it he didn't feel thirsty or need to urinate anymore now either.

Back to the base for a cup of tea and some reading. Sounds perfect. He'd have to stay in the shade though, this sun was dangerous.

He reaches the car and gets in, a small sporty hatchback; perfect for nipping in and around town and ideal for cornering and accelerating on the short roads. He drives the hatchback out of town and parks in a layby. Leaving it there he climbs out and walks the few paces to the big four wheel drive Volvo. Perfect for the country lanes, holding the road and with great power.

Driving the Volvo he navigates the country lanes driving into a field in a small valley. With higher open ground in every direction he could see everything. Parking the Volvo he walks into the field and across the short grass to the extra-long wheel base high top van left there. The thing was huge, the sort of vehicle the motorbike racing teams use and it was a perfect find.

Clicking the doors he grasps the big sliding door and pulls it back, looking in at his home from home. He draws the folding chair out and opens it on the grass. The sun is on the other side of the van now so this side is in the shade. Still stupidly hot but at least he will be out of the sun.

He places the sword propped against the van and the bag nearby with the butts poking up ready to be grabbed. He pulls out a long barrelled shotgun and rests that next to the sword before climbing in. The van is high enough to stand upright with a long bench down one side split into hinged doors that prop open with storage space within.

Truck and caravan batteries stacked at one end, several deep and secured against the bulkhead of the van. Crates of bottled water, cases of tinned food, dried pasta, rice and noodles.

A folding camp bed and stacks of smaller batteries, first aid kits and everything imaginable tidily stowed away.

Paper and hardback books rest on a shelf, all of them relating to survival, electrics, hunting and gathering but the majority of the well-thumbed books are medical encyclopaedias.

One battery is separated from the rest, set aside with a multitude of wires coming from the two metal prongs. One set lead to the split relay which charges the battery from the engine. The other wires lead to an inverter fitted with a household plug receptor, enabling him to plug household objects in.

He picks the item currently connected to the inverter and checks the battery level, fully charged. Detaching the charger from the e-reader he drops it into the seat of the chair outside an plugs a small travel kettle into the inverter. Once filled with water he gets a mug ready, choosing a teabag from the many boxes stacked neatly under a bench.

'Earl grey, a perfect afternoon pick me up and full of anti-oxidants too,' muttering away to himself he gets the cup ready and waits while the kettle slowly boils the water. Going to the back of the van he drops down to check the fuel containers and still there, wedged out of sight safe and away from the sun. He did have them inside but the smell was too strong so they were removed and put under the vehicle.

With the e-reader charged up he settles down and activates the home page. The Kindle was a great device and when he saw the outbreak starting, and how quickly it spread he correctly sensed what was coming so quickly went online and downloaded every single book relating to survival he could find, then cooking, butchery, health and fitness, mental stimulation exercises, *how to* books of every description, ranging from *How to Succeed In the Workplace* to *The Art of War*. He downloaded tongue in cheek zombie survival guides and then the more serious post apocalypse accounts. In addition to the hundreds of instruction books, he also downloaded as many fiction books as possible. Everything he could find from every genre. The retailer had made it easy with *one click purchase.* His credit card was already linked in and with the balance being very low he was able to keep going.

Then, while everyone else was fighting for the tins of beans in the supermarket aisles, he was going for the vehicle auto shops to get batteries, inverters, leads, wires and travel accessories. He then went for the local Cash and Carry, getting there before the masses had time to stop and think about safe refuges with good supplies. He set the alarms off but he was in and out within minutes. Going for bulk supplies of essentials that he would need to survive.

A loner anyway, the sudden loss of mankind, civilisation and the fall of society hardly bothered him. What he did miss however, more than anything and what he would give his right arm for, was a doctor. Even one on a phone that he could talk too and relay all the weird symptoms as they arise.

He was forever in the local surgery and on first name terms with the nurses and reception staff. He was almost banned from attending due to the sheer number of emergency appointments he made. But the last doctor to see him understood and humoured the appointments. Knowing the simple act of laying hands on whatever part of his body was complaining now, and then saying "nothing wrong, you're fine" would see him through for another couple of weeks.

But now there were no doctors and the pressure was building. He had no recourse to medical expertise and had to rely on self-diagnoses from the books, but that just scared him even more.

Fit and healthy, he exercised every day without fail. Going through a varying mixture of cardio and resistance training. He wasn't huge with bulging muscles but he was strong and lithe. He ate carefully and paid attention to the ratio of proteins to carbs to fats, essential fats and avoiding fatty acids like the plague.

Not just five a day, but most times he was ten fruit and veg a day. His meat had been organic, his food was GM free. Eggs came from free range hens and he avoided processed food like the devil had made it himself.

Now he had a simple life, and one that hadn't changed that much. Apart from now living out of a van in a field and making the odd trip into the towns and villages to find the bits and pieces he needed.

The shotguns had been sourced from farms and he read about the advantages and disadvantages of sawn off versus long barrel. In the end he opted for both.

Keeping the big one at the van and the two sawn off's in his bag for ease of carriage.

The sword had been taken from an antique shop. It was strong with a long blade and decent handle. The balance and weight were perfect and after finding a grindstone and then reading how to put a new edge on he was away; learning how to cut and thrust. Practising for many hours in his field to build his strength up. And it was a good weapon too. The sharp point easily penetrated the sternum to pierce the heart or if they were slow enough he went for the eye socket and the brain.

Cornered or fighting hard and he used the weight and long cutting edge to slash and hack. He had body armour found in the back of an abandoned police car and had taken the small round riot shield too, adding it to his supplies.

It was hot and he didn't feel like studying right now. The pressure of the day had been hard and finding out he almost had Diabetes and incredibly high blood pressure had worried him immensely. He needed distraction and humour. So navigating the menu he flicked between the Flashman series by George Macdonald Fraser or maybe some Discworld fun instead, Terry Pratchett always made him feel better, and that crazy wizard *Rincewind* always brings a smile to his face.

Discworld it is so he settles back into his luxury executive folding chair, makes sure his mug of Earl Grey tea is within reach and extends his legs to rest his feet on the edge of the van step.

A few pages in and the ambience starts working; the heat of the day, the stillness of the air, the soothing quality of the tea, the background noise of birds chirping and singing and his eyes are closing. Lids blinking slower and slower and with each drop of the lids, they find it increasingly hard to lift back up.

He lets it take him, sinking deeper into the chair as his head falls down, chin resting low. Eyes closed.

Eyes awake and open. Bathed in sweat and going from sitting to standing and holding both shotguns ready within a split second. Dusk and the heavy curtain of night is coming down quickly. He slept too long and came awake too quickly. Heart racing as he stares around, slowly lowering the shotguns and taking a deep steadying breath.

The Kindle is on the floor having slipped from his lap while he slept. He feels sticky and uncomfortable and his shirt clings to his body. Head fuggy and slow, brain working to catch up.

There's just no air here, it feels stagnant and oppressive. Putting the sawn off's down he reaches into the van and pulls out a bottle of water, taking a long drink to re-hydrate from the liquid lost while he slept. The remainder of the bottle is poured over his head, soaking the sweat away and sending a pleasant shiver down his spine.

He stretches, pushing his arms out and arching his torso, wincing at the pain in his lower back from staying in the same position for too long. Twisting side to side he tries to stretch it out but it doesn't go.

It's just muscle pain from sleeping he tells himself but the seed was planted as soon as he felt it, not only planted but watered and harvested too. It might not be muscle pain, it could be a growth, something spreading towards his kidneys and liver.

His heart flutters in panic as he feels the icy grip of fear clutch and twist his stomach. This is it. It's starting and it will be incurable. Even if a team of doctors walked in this field right now with all the equipment they would ever need, it would be too late. The tumours are growing so fast they are attacking all of his organs at the same time.

'Stop it,' he says firmly, shaking his head. He stands in a relaxed manner and draws a long breath in through his nose inflating his stomach in an exaggerated manner. Then he releases and exhales slowly from his mouth, sucking his stomach in and exhaling as far as he can.

He repeats the relaxation technique several times, flooding his system with oxygen which resets the nitrogen levels and helps balance the brain chemistry.

Opening his eyes after several minutes of breathing he feels calmer, his vision sharper and everything suddenly not so bad.

A quick fix that doesn't make it go away but it helps, and right now, he'll take all the help he can get.

But that pain is still there, nagging away. He tries feeling his own back, groping his hands round to run over his skin, expecting to find a huge lump. Nothing there so he tries looking round, like a dog chasing its tail which is fruitless and has him chastising himself within a few seconds.

Must be a rash there, some tell-tale sign of a horrendous illness starting to develop. But he feels fine other than the back ache, a tiny dull headache from sleeping during the day but nothing else.

'Shit,' he knows what's coming as the nagging starts, telling him the tumours have spread up his spine and into his brain already. They're growing now and will cause his head to cease functioning.

Should he take the painkillers now or later? But taking painkillers just masks the pain, it doesn't fix the problem. And it's dangerous taking painkillers, they can rot your stomach lining and make you ill.

No, better to monitor the rate of spreading so he can chart whatever disease he is developing. Checking his watch he realises he slept too long and is behind on time. Mind you, not that it really mattered, but then those self-help books all said that the key to success was self-discipline and maintaining a strict regime.

He wasn't sure he *actually* believed in a lot of the stuff within those books. Yes it was important to stay focussed and keep the mind active but surely those books were written for morons who couldn't otherwise think their way out of a paper bag.

No real person in their right mind would actually read a self-help book would they? Mind you, the sales ranking on the sites were high so the market was obviously a big one.

Stripping his t shirt off he grabs the long sleeve black wicking top and shrugs it on. The material clings to his body like a second skin, tight and specially designed to draw the sweat away and remain breathable. Modern materials like this were a god send for his night time activities.

He takes the sawn off's from his day bag and places them next to the night bag. Many hours had been spent getting the night bag just right, stitching compartments and making adjustments so everything would fit and be readily accessible.

Two long hand stitched sections in the main compartment that held the shotguns barrel down with the butts poking out and easy to grab. They didn't rattle or sway and were held snug but without the risk of snagging when drawn quickly.

Inside the main compartment were black latex medical gloves, first aids kits, bottles of water and high energy snack bars. Plus painkillers and now a bottle of Corsodyl mouthwash with a spare toothbrush and paste. Can never be too careful when it comes to mouth hygiene.

Antiseptic wipes, anti-bacterial gel and then the specially designed back quiver that had been stitched in. He had tried a leg quiver, and undoubtedly the leg quiver made it easier to draw the arrows and was perfect for timed competition shoots, but it impeded movement especially when it was full.

The back quiver was the only alternative but he also had to carry the bag with the shotguns and other things he needed, so the quiver was incorporated into the bag, and then tested, adjusted, tested again and re-adjusted until it was just right.

He checks each arrow as it goes in. The carbon fibre hunting arrows were barbed with screw tips and specially designed for penetration but not to travel through the target. Each one was thirty inches long and he examined the straightness of the shaft, felt the weight and examined each fletch before placing it point first into the quiver. With the quiver full he takes the spare arrow heads and pushes them into a side pocket along with the shotgun cartridges.

In the van he stares at the side wall with the range of bows hanging from hooks. Definitely the compound bow. He'd used the recurve and straight bows several times, just to keep his hand in and have the novelty factor. But the compound was by far the best.

Eighty pound draw weight reduced to just fifteen pound pull weight, and holding fifteen pound on your fingertips was far easier than eighty pounds. He checked the pulley cam wheels at the ends for sign of corrosion or resistance. The bow was well cared for and in perfect working order.

About to leave the van he stares for a second at the wooden shafted long bow, considering if he should take that one for tonight. But the heavy draw weight would just aggravate the giant tumours growing in his back, best to stick with the compound.

He liked the name of manufacturer had given the bow too; The Black Knight. It resonated with him, the play on words with knight and night, blackness, dark, saviour and righteous but with a hint of a dark side, and he had a sword too, like a proper knight would have. Only he wasn't a knight, he was a normal bloke with extreme anxiety and a propensity to get obsessed with his own health. He knew that and was under no pretensions and no illusions either.

The last thing to be taken before he locked the van up were the night vision goggles. They were tugged on to his head and held in place by thick elastic straps. Almost night now so he pulls them down, staring at everything bathed in differing shades of green. Pushed back up onto his forehead he pulls the bag on, double checks the van is locked, grabs the bow and starts off. Then walks back and checks the van is really locked.

Across the field and he stops at the gate, worried that maybe he didn't lock the van properly. Better to be safe so he trots back and goes round tugging each handle several times before setting off again.

Back at the gate he has to force himself to keep going, knowing the van is locked and secure and ignoring that nagging urge telling him to go check again.

Into the Volvo and back to the layby, swap over and into the hatchback, then drive towards town. Once at the outside of the town he first switches the headlights off then pulls the night vision goggles down. The moon is bright so the ambient light is perfect for the night vision aid.

Selecting a quiet side street he parks up and checks the vehicle is locked before leaving the key on top of the front driver side tyre. That saved having to dig into pockets if he was moving in a hurry.

Chest strap securely fastened, waist strap likewise, arrow drawn and placed on the arrow rest, nock the groove of the arrow into the string and he walks on. His left hand holding the frame with his right hand holding the undrawn arrow in the string.

Archery had always made him feel better. It was the only time he didn't worry about lumps, tumours, growths, rashes, illnesses, sore throats or what disease and illness he has today. On the range, whether it was practise or competition he felt at peace and soothed. The constant action of taking the arrow and checking it over. An arrow had no internal parts, it was smooth and straight and exactly what it was. It couldn't develop tumours or growths either. He liked arrows.

He liked the action, the repeating action of arrow rest, nock, loose. Arrow rest, nock, loose. It was soothing. Adjusting for rain or high winds, gauging the distance, selecting what bow to use, what design of arrow and then just firing them.

Highly skilled and an exceptional shot but he only ever went for local competitions and such was his skill level, he purposefully made sure he never won first place. Often adjusting to precisely land the arrow an inch away so he would come second or third. The problem with first place was that everyone wanted to talk to you after, shake your hand, take a photograph maybe and then the awards ceremony too. He hated speaking to groups of people and didn't like unwanted attention. Second or third place meant you kept some dignity but avoided the limelight.

His club had long since put it down to *on-the-day-nerves* as they knew he could shoot better than anyone else. He'd even started to fire badly at the club lately as they were starting to talk about coaching him for nerves to get him ready for bigger competitions, even mentioning the nationals and the England team try outs.

The best days were when it was just him in the field, alone with his bow and the target. Then he could fire properly and land every arrow exactly where he wanted it. If there was risk of anyone else turning up he kept the target at the standard ninety metre range, but on those rare occasions when he knew he would be alone, he would shift it back to one hundred and fifty metres and then all the way to the two hundred metre mark. They were the best shots as he had to take so much into consideration; the weight of the arrow tip, the breeze, humidity and atmospheric conditions. And over time, as with anything done many times, it became second nature. An instinct done without conscious thought. Visualising where he wanted the arrow to be and making it happen.

Along with the trips to the vehicle auto centres he also went to the club and secured the best bows they had, plus every arrow they had in stock too. Strings, arrow heads, lubricants for the cams and wheels, everything was taken and loaded into his van.

Living alone meant he wasn't encumbered by anyone else and he could move quickly to get out of the population density zones, selecting isolated fields with good visual range.

It had worked well and kept him alive for the last twelve days and the step from survivor to hunter had been a natural one. He wanted to survive. They wanted to eat him. The less of them there were meant the greater chance he had of *not* being eaten. Simple, and within a few days of being set up he noticed how hard it was to get into the town to source the things he needed.

He'd hunted them in the day at first as they were slow and easy but once they changed and got faster and meaner he switched to night hunting. Using shadows and stealth to pick them off like an archery sniper, fire a few and run. Fire again and run. It was slow but effective and whittled them down and above all else; it gave his head some peace and quiet and something else to think about other than his impending slow and painful death.

Quiet. Far too quiet. Half an hour of walking the side streets and he'd yet to see a single zombie. Plenty of bodies and quite a lot of them done by him on previous nights. But he knew there were plenty left.

So where were they?

At the end of a residential street he stands contemplating the direction to go. Carry on through the safer residential zones or go into town? His back was aching and he could feel the tumours growing quickly and it was only a matter of time before they burst out and caused him untold pain and agony.

The town. He takes a right turn and walks steadily along, his night vision goggled head turning constantly left and right, and every few steps he did a full turn to check all directions. The clarity of the image was fantastic, the moon providing enough natural light to make the view almost pin sharp.

Nothing in the next street, nor the street after that. Houses silent, dark and empty. The only sound was the tread of his boots on the ground and his low controlled breathing. Sweat was forming on his head, making the elastic band of the goggles itch and worry him. Pausing at a junction he ducks into the deep shadows of a front garden and takes a drink of water while rubbing his head and wiping the straps down with a paper towel.

Pressing on and still nothing. No movement and no sounds. He reaches the edge of the town centre, the top end where all the cheap shops were located. The road was much wider here than the side streets and he took a couple of minutes to look at each premises, the doorways, windows and alleys branching off. Listening intently but still seeing and hearing nothing. Then a bang further down the road out of sight. It sounded like a car door.

Keeping to the edge of the building line he stalks down the street, scanning and watching every entrance, constantly turning to check behind.

The road slopes down on a gentle decline and reaching the crest he holds position and stares down at the small group gathered round a vehicle. Gripping the arrow he pulls it back just an inch and keeping low he starts moving forward. There must be someone in that car. They got in and slammed the door closed to keep the zombies away. But they're not attacking but just stood there, moving round slowly.

One of the car doors opens as someone clambers out to stand talking to the others. The zombies had been changing a lot over the last few days but he'd never seen them getting in and out of cars before.

People. Normal people. Other survivors. Stepping out of the building line he walks into the middle of the road and starts towards them with the bow pointed down.

The people at the car keep turning to look about and spot him within a few seconds. He raises an arm to wave, knowing he can see them much clearer than they can see him.

Their body language changes, becoming worried as they start to load items stacked on the ground into the car and then another one parked in the front.

With just a couple of hundred metres to go he notices them talking and peering at him, the men pointing as though explaining something to the women and children.

'Hi, is it okay to approach?' He calls out at the hundred metre point.

'You the bow and arrow guy?' One of the men shouts back.

'The bow and arrow guy? I've got a bow and some arrows...does that make me the bow and arrow guy?'

'We seen you before, we was watching when you shot the things with the bow, few nights ago on Prince Street.'

'Prince Street? Yes I remember that one, have you seen the zombies? I can't find any.'

'No mate.'

'Can I come over?'

'Er...yeah I guess so,' the spokesman looks to his group for confirmation.

'I don't suppose any of you are doctors are you?' He asks quickly, walking towards them with his bow now held right down.

'Doctor? No mate, you hurt then?'

'Not injured no, no nurses or anything like that? Vet maybe?'

'No mate,' the man repeats, 'sorry.'

'You leaving town then?' He asks the man.

'Yeah, you heard about the fort?'

'The fort? No,' he shakes his head, 'what's that?'

'We met someone yesterday, well Steve did anyway,' the man nods at another man who steps forward, 'said they got a fort down on the coast, thousands living there...'

'Oh right, yes I figured they might get used.'

'So you just go round shooting them with arrows?' The second man asks.

'Yes, I figured the less there were of them, the safer I would be...so...er...yeah.'

'I'm James, this is Steve...'

'Roy,' he says shaking hands after swapping the bow to his left.

'We're going for the fort,' James says, 'this bloke told Steve they got police there, security and some army blokes that go out and keep the things away...Mr Howie? You heard of him?'

'No,' Roy shakes his head, thinking he doesn't like people so the fort holds no appeal to him.

'Ere Steve,' one of the women calls out, 'you said that bloke said they had doctors and all sorts at that fort.'

'Bloody hell, yeah he did say that,' Steve points quickly at Roy, 'sorry mate, got freaked out with you wearing them things on your head.'

'Oh crumbs, sorry,' Roy pushes his goggles up and rubs his eyes, 'forgot I had them on...you said they've got doctors at the fort?'

'Yeah, well this bloke did anyway, he said they had doctors, an hospital, shops and all sorts, like a proper town but in a fort with big walls and...'

'You said doctors?' Roy asks, emphasising the "s", 'as in more than one doctor?'

Steve shrugs as though what does it matter.

'Where is it?' Roy asks quickly.

'Dunno, on the coast before you get to Portsmouth, can't be that hard to find, must be on the tourist maps if we can find one.'

'We will,' James answers confidently, 'is it just you Roy?' He asks.

'What?' Roy replies startled out of his dreaming of having access to doctors, 'er yeah, just me.'

'You can come with us if you want? We got plenty of space.'

'Me?! Gosh no, thank you but I got all my gear to sort out but thanks...I will definitely go but I'll have to sort my stuff out first.'

'Fair enough mate, make sure you pass it on if you see anyone else.'

'Of course, er...this hospital? Does it have equipment like normal hospitals?'

Steve and James exchange a quick puzzled look, both of them shrugging.

'No okay, don't worry...I'll er...get myself ready and see you there I guess...so you don't know where all the zombies have gone?'

Both men shake their heads, 'no, not seen 'em all day, figured they ran out of food or something so buggered off elsewhere,' James replies.

'Yeah right,' Roy nods, 'not likely though is it.'

'Eh?' James blanches at the slightly rude tone.

'Well they don't eat food do they, just people and that's only so they can make them into zombies.'

'Must have run out of people then,' James replies abruptly.

'Hmmm,' Roy stares round, 'but we're still here...'

'Maybe they got pissed off with you shooting them all the time,' Steve suggests helpfully.

'Hmmm, maybe,' Roy nods, 'well, nice meeting you and have a safe journey.' He turns to walk off, striding into the night.

'You just going then?' James calls out.

'Yes, I just said I was didn't I?'

'Okay,' James says slowly, 'you going to the fort then?'

'I already said I was,' Roy calls back then walks off.

'Rude bloke,' James mutters to Steve who nods as they both stare at the shadowy form disappearing from view.

Seventeen

'Listen in, we got a lot to talk about,' Maddox shouts clearly into the air. The youths start gathering in front of him, instantly responding to his voice. Surprisingly they didn't show that much surprise when they walked in and saw the mess. A few raised eyebrows here and there but the young adapt quickly and they've certainly seen enough carnage by now.

'We're gonna get this place cleaned up, Lenski and Sierra will be in those rooms over there, that's where the police worked from and where everything was organised. We gotta get these bodies moved out to where the others were stacked when we first came in, but we also need security at the front and back, outside and on the top wall. Skyla, your crew take the back. Stay at that gate and don't let anyone come in or out. It stays closed all the time. Mohammed, your crew is out front. Liam, you're on the inside here and Ryland, you're up top. Everyone else starts shifting bodies and get this place cleaned up. We'll swap round every hour and make sure you drink water. They got an armoury here with proper weapons,' a few cheers sound out, 'but, we don't use them until we've been shown by Mr Howie and his crew, got it?'

A chorus of "Yes Maddox" sounds out, the youths hang on every word he says.

I step forward to speak while their attention is on us, 'If anyone turns up outside they do not come in until we've got a few things set up. No one comes into the fort unless they are checked over for bites and we can see their eyes. You all know what you are doing, that is very clear, but if something does happen then listen out for my team, the only reason is that we've got very powerful weapons and you might need to get down or move to the side or something. We have got a lot to do but I'm glad you're all here.' It feels hard not to talk down to them and despite the hard faces most of them have, they still look young.

'Mr Howie, he in charge here,' Lenski takes over, 'he agree with Maddox that we still in charge of *you,* but he in charge of here. If he say to do something then you should do it yes?'

Again another wide response of "yes Lenski" and I can see the youths are already stood in set groups gathered round one older youth that must be the crew chiefs as they call them.

Maddox says another few words and then they burst to action. One group going straight to the back, another finding their way to the ramp and up to the wall while yet another group start organising themselves at the main gate.

The remainder walk off towards the bodies, chatting noisily and making jokes amongst themselves.

'There goes the neighbourhood,' Nick mutters to a snort from Cookey and Blowers.

'Nick you take the digger again...'

'Oi,' Clarence says with an offended glance at me.

'No offence mate but...well Nick you take the digger. Cookey and Blowers I want you moving between the two gates and keeping an eye on the front.'

'Who is going up top?' Dave asks.

'None of us.'

'The Saxon has got loads of weapons inside, those kids could get them easily,' he replies.

'They could also get into the armoury easily but we've got to trust them, they came to us...go up there with Lani if it makes you feel better but I wanted Lani to work with Lenski and that other girl...'

'Why?' Lani asks, 'all the girls together doing the paperwork yeah?'

'No,' I sigh, 'but you know the fort and you're switched on so you can guide them as they go and I'll be around too.'

'I was joking,' Lani smiles, 'it does make sense, but that means Dave has to stay with me...and Meredith too.'

'Yes it does. Lads,' I turn to Blowers and Cookey, 'feel free to walk about and stroll up the top, get to know the er...crews I guess we should call them but keep an eye on the front.'

'Got it,' Blowers nods.

We split up, moving off with Nick and Clarence heading for the digger, the lads going for the front and Dave, Lani and me walking over to the offices, stepping in to see the four older leaders chatting quietly.

'Everything alright?' I ask, heading towards the gas stove.

'This place is huge,' Darius grins, 'you got loads of space.'

'It is mate, you all up for a brew?'

'Mr Howie,' Lani gets my attention, 'Sergeant Hopewell had some forms they used when new people arrived, okay if I try and find them to show Lenski and Sierra?'

'Yeah of course.'

'You call him Mr Howie?' Lenski asks, 'he your boyfriend no? Why you call him mister?'

Lani blanches slightly at the direct question, 'er...we just agreed that's what we'd do in front of the others.'

'You can call me Mr Maddox then from now on,' Maddox grins.

'I not call you this,' Lenski replies quickly with a deadpan tone.

'And you can think again,' Sierra cuts Darius down with a glare as goes to say something.

'I never wanted to be called Mr Howie, Dave started that off,' I add.

'It suits you,' Lani replies quickly with a smile, 'and Dave is right, you should be Mr Howie, everyone calls you that. Can I show you what they did when new people arrived?' She turns to Lenski and Sierra. They follow her down to the end of the room where she starts leafing through the sheets re-stacked tidily by Marcy and her horde.

'What do you think then?' I ask Maddox and Darius.

'Like Darius said; it's a big place,' Maddox replies, 'did you say you had people turning up here every day?'

'Yeah we did, bloody queues of them sometimes too, I think word spread that it's here and most of them were turning up expecting shops and hospitals and a proper police force.'

'What you gonna do with all the bodies?' Darius asks.

'Burn them mate, or at least that's what we keep trying to do anyway.'

Coffee is made and I notice Maddox is the only one not to drink it, sticking with water from a bottle. We chat and slowly break the ice as they explain how they were getting things set up at their compound.

Before long we're outside, leaving a disgruntled Dave staying with Lani and the two women while the rest of us start helping to pile the bodies up. Already there is a distinct difference with so many people working hard.

Bodies get stacked ready for Nick to scoop up and dump in the lorry. They work with a determined efficiency and it doesn't take long to spot the crew chiefs, those being the ones who get asked questions and direct the smaller groups. Maddox has an easy air of authority with them, laughing and joking and working alongside them.

The youths are wary of me and Clarence and avoid conversation with us, apart from the odd comment about Clarence being "hench as fuck". His natural strength wins them over as they marvel in awe at the apparent ease he moves the bodies with. Then the braver ones start asking questions, *can you lift a car? Can you push a bus? How much can you bench? What's the heaviest thing you ever lifted?*

He takes it well and in good humour. Standing back for a minute I glance down to see Blowers and Cookey doing what they do best, bantering with the lads at the front, laughing and joking while managing to look like professional soldiers. The way they hold their assault rifles relaxed but ready. The semi wide stance they take on their feet, keen eyes and friendly manners and I can see they're already winning some of the kids over.

They stroll up to the top and do the same with the crew up there, speaking to them individually while making sure they can see out the front.

Once the lorry is emptied and returned we keep going, steadily clearing the bodies away. The ground is covered in blood and bits of gore which is dealt with by Maddox ordering a crew to start picking the bits of *shit* up. And they do it without complaint, just another task that needs to be completed.

I join in helping them, bent over as we scoop brain matter and god knows what else up from the sticky grass. Stiff brushes are found and slowly the area starts getting cleaned.

The digger moves back and forth, scooping and loading. One of the older lads says he would love to have a go and at a nod from me, Nick shows him how to do it. The boy takes a few minutes to get the hang of it which causes some good humoured joking about but like Nick, he takes to it quickly.

The lorry gets loaded and taken out to be emptied. With the ruined tents all pulled down and stacked up it does start looking a hell of a lot better. With all the debris getting cleared away I can see the central cooking area where we had the meal with Marcy last night and it quickly sours the uplifting mood I was beginning to feel.

'Blowers to Mr Howie,' the radio warbles on my belt.

'Go ahead Blowers.'

'Got a van coming down the road towards us, it's going slow.'

'Just one?'

'Yes, just one Mr Howie.'

'Lani did you hear that?'

'Yeah I heard it, do you want us out there recording details?'

'Yes please, I'll see you out there.'

'We'll have to get our radios on the same frequency,' I say to Maddox stood nearby listening.

'Alright if I come down too?' He asks.

'Of course mate, you don't need to ask.'

Clarence puts his radio back on his belt and gives me a thumbs up, checking if I want him to come along. I motion for him to keep an eye open but stay there.

Cookey jogs across the front, heading for the ramp and the Saxon on the top wall.

The small group from the offices are ahead of me, walking in a trio and chatting happily with Dave bringing up the rear. He must be bored stiff but until we know what to do about Lani we can't take any risk with her.

Reaching the front, Maddox and I step through the outer gate to see Blowers stood just slightly ahead of the crew positioned there. The crew chief taking position next to Blowers with the rest staggered out in a line.

With all of Maddox's vehicles still stacked up the van driver clearly doesn't know whether to stop at the end or come round them until Blowers steps out and waves them forward.

'Eyes on,' I call out, 'nice and relaxed, don't point guns at them and if we start shooting then move back quickly so we can use the big gun up there.'

'Lani, me and you will take the lead on this one if that's okay with everyone else?' This diplomacy stuff is quite good fun really. Lenski and Sierra both nod, clearly excited at the formal way things are being done. Maddox stays close and watches intently.

Blowers waves the van down and does us proud by holding back with his rifle at the ready but smiling nicely.

'Hold there please,' he calls out, 'how many you got in there?' Words exchanged before he turns to me. 'They got nine Mr Howie, six adults and three kids, no sign of any weapons in the front.'

'Cheers mate, Hi! Sorry about the security but obviously we have to be careful,' I greet the nervous looking man sat behind the wheel who nods back with very tired looking eyes.

'Do you have any weapons in the vehicle?'

'No guns,' he says quickly, 'knives and things but no guns.'

'Okay that's great and have any of you been bitten or scratched?'

'No Sir,' he replies just as quickly.

'Okay, you can get out and stretch your legs,' the rear doors spring open as soon I finish speaking with a loud groan coming from the back.

'Oh my poor back, cramped up in there for hours and hot too, hotter than hell,' a very large built black woman comes into view and seeing us she smiles a huge grin and walks over, 'so this is the fort is it? Oh my word we're glad to be here, why you got all them children with guns? We thought you had police and army here...'

'And shops and a hospital,' someone else says as they clamber from the back.

'We did have,' I reply seriously, 'not shops but...'I wait until they all walk into view, six adults as Blowers said and three children. Clearly not one family but several different couples or small groups banded together.

'We're glad you're here,' I say looking at each of the adults in turn, 'but we've had some er...issues,' they look back with a mixture of alarm and worry. I go through what happened, the abridged and short version and re-assure them that the place is now secure and safe but is still being cleared up.

The big lady acts as the group spokesperson, nodding her head as she listens intently.

'We can help,' she offers instantly, 'tell us what you need doing young man.'

'Howie, my name is Howie, sorry I should have introduced myself before.'

'Mr Howie?' The woman asks with a broad grin, 'we heard a lot about you young man.'

'Oh god not that again,' I groan as the others start looking at me with renewed interest, then round me to Dave.

'Is that Dave?' One of them asks.

'Yes, yes it is...'

'Well, we're hungry and dirty and we need a wash, and these children need food, and those children look like they could do with a decent meal too,' the big lady interrupts me, speaking very loud she bursts with confidence. 'Do you have food here?'

'Our stores are very well stocked,' Lani steps forward, 'Hi, I'm Lani, this is Lenski and...' Lani gives each name politely.

'Agnes,' the big woman replies, not bothering to introduce her party, 'so where are these stores then?'

'Ah,' Lani says politely, 'thing is Agnes, is that we don't let anyone in unless they've been checked over.'

'So how did they get in yesterday?' One of the men asks.

'We weren't here,' Lani replies quickly with a firm voice, 'trust me, it wouldn't have happened if we had been here,' which is maybe not the most accurate of statements but it does well to give confidence.

'That's fine, we've got nothing to hide,' Agnes more or less shouts, 'have you got a private area? I will not be getting undressed out here, that's for sure,' she laughs with a surprisingly light voice.

'Give me five minutes I'll get something set up,' I say to Lani and start heading back.

'I need to take all your names and what skills you have...' Lani starts explaining. Taking Maddox and Blowers with me we head through the inner gate into the wide alley and stare at the medical tents. Hearing Lani say that about taking names and skills sends a conflicting feeling through me. Sadness that we gave refuge to so many who then lost their lives after trusting us to keep them safe, but also hope, hope that we can start again and build up.

'If we get Lenski, Sierra and Lani to do the women then we can do the men,' Maddox states, 'this one looks alright, we'll just do them one at a time.'

'I didn't really want anyone in until the bodies were gone.'

'Why not?' He asks me, 'everyone has seen bad things by now, they're gonna just have to get used to it and seeing that,' he nods towards the inner gate, 'will remind them how bad things are.'

'Good point,' I concede.

'And I bet she can cook too,' Maddox smiles.

The men are done first with me and Maddox getting them to strip off and going through the same thing Doctor Roberts did with us. Shining torches all over and checking for bites, scratches and broken skin. Other than bruises and dirt they're all fine.

Coming out we give the space over to Lani for the women to be done. The group standing in the alley chatting quietly while waiting. Blowers and Dave stood nearby as watchful as ever.

It gets done and they're admitted, all of them standing inside the inner gate staring in wide eyed wonder at the stacks of the once human corpses piled up and the groups of children moving amongst them laughing and joking, the giant swinging a corpse onto the back of the lorry while a small group of kids cheer, Nick laughing at the wheel of the digger with a cigarette dangling from his lips.

'Nice and big, I like it!' Agnes beams as she steps through, 'this is a good place, I can feel this is a good place,' she smiles across at her group, using her personality and character to beat their hesitancy and fear away. 'We'll leave our things over there at the side and get started, you men get helping with those bodies, children you need a wash and ladies come with me...we'll get these stores checked and something to eat. How many have we got here?' She casts round, picking on Sierra to answer the question.

'Er...about one hundred and twenty...roughly,' she guesses.

'Is that all!?' Agnes laughs, 'a tea party that is, I've fed many more than that in my time,' she laughs again and strides off, the ladies and children following in her wake leaving three quiet brow beaten men standing looking uncomfortable.

'To be honest chaps,' I say to them, 'we pretty much got this under control if you want to…'

'God no,' the driver of the van says quickly, 'if Agnes says to do something, we do it.'

'Fair enough, jump in then,' he motions his head at the other two, leading them towards the activity in the centre.

'More coming down the road Mr Howie,' Blowers calls out.

'See what you mean,' Maddox says, 'busy day huh?'

'Always mate, bloody always.'

Eighteen

Dropping down from the broken window she crouches and waits then sets off to the corner, peering round to view down the side of the industrial unit.

Dark now but the moon is bright and casts just enough light to see shapes and forms. Reaching the end of the building line she again pauses to check the area, staring at the bright glow of the raging fire further in the estate.

The air is thick with the smell of burning chemicals, rubber, wood and metal melting; acidic and pungent. The twisted fragments of super charged gas bottles have flown off in many directions and embedded into structures and wooden pallets. In this immense heat and dry weather the materials have ignited and spread further. Several of the units are now ablaze with sparks leaping high into the air.

Figures silhouetted against the fire move silently in the distance but thankfully not anywhere in line of sight here.

The darker mass of the hills overlooking the town are that way, but that's also the direction of the fire. No choice but to go the opposite direction and work round. Using the same methods practised before, Paula breaks the route down into what she can see immediately and picks out the best options for cover, calculating the distance and time it will take while checking for obstacles and then a fall back route if something happens on the way.

Those up by the fire will find it harder to see her, but any further down could see her form silhouetted against the glow. Stick to the sides and use the deeper shadows. Do not fire the weapon unless absolutely necessary and for god's sake don't scream or yell out.

Mentally prepared she starts off and runs across the front of the garage and over the small car park, dropping by the side of an old car left on bricks. Then on, past the front of the next unit, her eyes scanning ahead picking out the next route. Pausing at intervals to check the area. Stop, drop listen then run.

Slowly she builds distance from the fire, hearing popping and crashing noises as the deadly flames eat away at the structures within the industrial estate. Paula gains the last unit before the junction of the estate service road. Beyond the junction is a normal residential street. From her view point now she can only see a small portion of it, but it looks clear.

Legs pumping she runs into the street and straight over to the left side, heading into the first open gate to drop down behind the low garden wall.

None in this street either. From the position of the hills and the memory of the town layout she judges that the next junction will be a wider main road leading towards the town centre and one of those that was clogged with the *things.*

Twisting round she tries to pick out the hills but the fierce glow of the fire now blocks anything above the building line out of view. Smoke, sparks and flames licking into the air distorting the shadows and making her eyes hurt from the contrast of dark to light.

Damn it, the town must be left. So she needs to go right. But that service road was bending round to the left, so is it still left to the town?

No choice but to work down this road and see what's at the end. Keeping low she heads out the gate and starts working along. Ignoring the signs of destruction all around her she focusses on anything moving or that doesn't belong. Eyes darting left and right, then pausing to watch the road ahead. Dropping down to check behind and then moving off again.

Closer to the junction she creeps. A determined look on her face as she stares into the shadows and plants her feet carefully. One step at a time, shifting her weight and inching forward. Rifle gripped and legs flexed ready to carry her away.

Expecting to see a thick line of them she lifts one eyebrow at the empty road ahead. It is a wider main road with houses lined on both sides. Big terraced houses all painted different colours with a varying mixture of UPVC and wooden framed windows and doors that just serve to make the area look cheap. To the side of the road a row of parked cars sit dark and forlorn, abandoned and left to sit forever until they slowly rust to nothing. Pimped up boy racer cars mixed with people carriers and white vans of the working class man, loaded with tools and ready for a hard day on site.

Other than that there is nothing. No sign of them. She spins round trying to gain a sense of where she is. Left is the town, it has to be.

Following the contour of the road as it eases round she steps just as carefully and makes frequent pauses to check for movement and noise. Staring left to check the gaps between the vehicles and the front gardens beyond them. Then up at the windows and doors, then back across to the right and then behind. So focussed on those points and she fails to spot the figures standing motionless in the road ahead of her. Expecting movement or noise her eyes simply didn't register the perfectly normal shape of the people.

Suppressing the yelp in her throat she finally does see them and freezes. Eyes fixed on the unmoving figures. Several of them. All silent. All staring towards her. They don't move but watch her as though waiting to see what she will do.

What she does do is very slowly starts to back-step, tiny movements that shift her weight. They detect the movement and as one turn their young bodies to face her. The physical rotation of the children send shivers down her spine. Moonlight casting them in silvery light that makes the shadows of their eyes deeper and far worse than they should be.

The small bodies with arms hanging down inert at the sides. Dressed in a collection of pyjamas and night clothes with pictures of teddies and butterflies mixed with deep blood stains. Taking another step back and the image of the child she shot earlier flashes through her mind, the memory causes her to move faster which in turn provokes them into bursting towards her with an instant frantic speed. One second quiet, sullen and watchful and the next charging with lips pulled back to reveal small teeth stained with blood and filth.

Paula runs, sprinting hard and glancing behind her. She curses at the power of their young bodies gaining with every second. She could fire but there's at least five of them which would mean at least five shots, and that would draw every undead for miles.

An open front door ahead, she turns sharply and runs up the path, bursting in to slam the door closed behind her. The ruined lock hanging from one screw wobbles instead of locking so she grabs the thin metal chain and yanks it across.

Down the hallway to the back door, which is locked, bolted and the key removed. Solid wood and no way of smashing it down.

They reach the front door, slamming into it which yanks the chain taut. She runs down the hallway and slams her foot into door. Feeling the impact as the door smacks into the light bodies beyond and sends them flying backwards. They're on their feet and charging back but just the sight of the pale young girl with curly blond hair and a pink nightie now bleeding profusely from the nose brings a choking gasp to her mouth.

Paula backs away to the bottom of the stairs, watching and listening as the door is rammed again and again. The door bursts open with a crash, young undead spill into the hallway falling over from the sudden lack of resistance.

She charges up the stairs, gaining the landing and grabbing a tall thin wooden shelving unit filled with hundreds of music CD's to launch it down at the oncoming snarling bundles of savage fury. The first one gets knocked down, barrelling into the others behind it.

Paula casts round for an escape route and spots the open loft hatch above her, a thin wire hanging down and glinting in the light coming through the window of the bedroom in front of her.

Grasping the wire she heaves and ducks as the hatch drops open and a metal ladder slides down. Grabbing the thin shaking ladder she starts to climb, feeling the rising panic as the first child reaches the top and makes a lunge for her. She lashes out with a foot, kicking it hard to the head.

Another comes just as she heaves up another few rungs, the tiny hands scrabbling to clamber up after her. She stamps down again and again, slamming the bottom of her hard boot onto its face and hands. It screams and howls but clings on, ignoring the broken fingers and facial bones getting mashed and pulped.

She stamps too hard and loses her grip, sliding down to impact on the child with her full weight. Crashing to the ground she punches out with rapid blows and sends a few flying off. Back on the ladder and she moves faster now, gripping the small rungs to pull up as her feet push hard.

Head through the ceiling hatch, pitch black inside and she doesn't think of the multitude of spiders and cobwebs that will be there but heaves hard and gets her upper body through. Yelping loud as hands grip her feet, pulling her back down. Gritting her teeth she pulls and shuffles to get her upper body over the lip. The child dangling from her legs thrashing about. She kicks and bucks, gets one foot free and kicks down, feeling the tug as the child is booted repeatedly but refuses to let go.

The rifle digs into her ribs, wedged underneath her as she levers herself further into the loft inch by inch. Stamping and kicking she feels the child swinging from her leg, sending a shooting pain through her hip and pulling her weight harder into the barrel of the rifle.

Excruciating pain flares into her stomach, sweating hard, red faced she kicks with everything she's got and hears a loud crack and the sudden release of the body dropping from her leg. With an almighty pull she gets her body into loft and twists round to get back to the ladder.

One coming up already, she grabs the rifle and reverses it to slam the butt down hard on the head. This one goes shuddering down from the first blow and any thought of these things being innocent children are gone.

Grabbing a rung of the ladder she pulls it up, working hand over hand to drag it higher and higher off the ground. One of them grabs the ladder but she pulls it harder, wedging her feet into the solid wooden joists to anchor herself in position.

It growls and snarls, thrashing about and threatening to pull the ladder back down. Breathing frantically, she works hand over hand, drawing it up while desperately working out what to do when the child gets closer.

Holding the ladder with one straining arm she leans down to grab at one of the small hands clinging on. Working to pull the fingers off but the child hangs on with a vice like grip. No matter how hard she tugs and works, the fingers remain glued with the child pulling up to take gnashing wild bites at her.

In wild desperation she pulls the large bladed knife from her belt and digs the blade into the fingers of the nearest hand, sawing back and forth and feeling the jolt as the knife digs into the alloyed metal of the ladder rung. One finger is lopped off, then another and the blood streaming out loosens the grip and finally one hand is released.

The child hangs one handed still pulling its own weight up to take biting lunges. Where the child gets the strength from to do one armed pull ups is beyond her. The knife digs into the fingers of the second hand, sawing in to bite through the bone. The pinkie falls off, slapping into the eye of the child beneath it. Blood spurts out, dripping quickly down the ladder and going into the open mouth of the undead as it takes one final huge surge up to bite at her. She lashes out and flicks the blade across its face, scoring a deep cut across the nose and into one eye.

It finally releases, plummeting the short distance to the ground and squashing another child underneath it.

The ladder is drawn up and pushed back, the flap of the loft hatch still hangs down but well out of the reach of the jumping child zombies staring up at her with twisted faces of hunger and hatred.

She pulls her torch out and curses when it doesn't come to life, remembering the batteries went during the attack of the giant spider.

Using her cigarette lighter she crabs round the loft looking for a way out.

'Come on…think,' she mutters. Terraced houses so the roofs will be joined…she spins round and starts towards the wall at one end. A single skin of fire bricks put in place a few years ago when the fire regulations changed.

She thumps them hard, feeling a slight tremor of vibration. They were designed to withstand the spread of fire, but not being kicked and battered.

So kicking and battering she does, grinning with triumph as the first brick falls out. She batters a hole and forces her way through into the next loft. This one older and without the fire brick wall in place, two houses sharing one loft space. She scurries over, balancing on the thick wooden joists with her cigarette lighter held out, the flame flickering as the heated ignition wheel starts to burn her fingers.

Howls and guttural roars sounding out from behind her as the children keep jumping in futile attempts to reach the opening.

Yelping with pain she drops the lighter as her thumb burns from the flame. Plunged into complete darkness she loses balance, toppling off to land heavily. With a wrenching tearing sound she feels herself plunging down as one legs goes through the ceiling into the room below. Grabbing the joists she pulls and kicks her way free. Pulling her leg up and out of the hole.

The lighter is lost, gone in the gloom. She feels round for it, feeling the rough material of the insulation wedged between the wooden posts. Losing sense of direction she starts making her way bent over to keep feeling for the joist in front of her.

Banging her head on the next fire wall she takes a breath of relief and starts kicking it again. With the total darkness she finds it hard to keep balance and has to work to keep herself on the thick wooden strip underfoot.

The wall takes longer to go down, kick after kick and gradually she weakens the mortar and sends the bricks tumbling down the other side. Battering harder now she detects light coming through the hole and peers in to see the next loft is converted with a window fitted into the roof.

The silvery moonlight could be a thousand chandeliers sparkling in a sumptuous ballroom for the effect it has on her. The bricks are pushed and shoved as she gets through and heads over the ply boarded floor to the loft hatch.

'Who the fuck are you?' A dull voice makes her scream with fright and spin round bringing the rifle to bear, 'easy love...don't fucking shoot me...you just broke my fire wall.'

'Who are you?' Paula whispers, her voice low and ragged from hard breathing.

'Nigel, I live here...well I did live here...downstairs that is....what are you doing?'

'Jesus, how...how long you been up here?'

'Since it started, now what the hell are you doing?'

'They chased me into a house, I got up here and...'

'Broke my loft is what you've done, you can't stay here.'

'I don't want to stay here, have you seen the town?'

'Course I have, but they don't know I'm here see...well they didn't till you came blundering through.' Paula watches as a small middle aged man shuffles into the light. Bearded and dressed in a filthy cotton dressing gown and carpet slippers, he looks a mess with wild hair poking up in all directions. 'You can't stay here,' he repeats.

'I don't want to stay here,' Paula hisses.

'Good cos this is my hiding place, piss off and find your own.'

'I just said I don't want to stay here.'

'Keep your bloody voice down before they hear you,' Nigel whispers harshly.

'Where's your hatch?'

'What? You ain't using my hatch love, oh no...oh no oh no...no way...they'll see you going out my house and come looking...'

'Well how do I get out then?' An exasperated Paula asks.

'Back the way you came and I'll stick those bricks back together.'

'What? I'm not going back that way.'

'You bloody are love, you ain't going out my hatch.'

'I am going out your hatch...now get it open.'

'No...piss off back that way and lead them off.'

'Nigel, I'm going out here and you can close the hatch after me.'

'I said no.'

'Nigel.'

'What?'

'I've got two guns and a big bloody knife and I will use one of them if you don't open that sodding hatch, I've been attacked by bloody big spiders and shot a child in the face so don't push me....'

'Christ alright, take it easy,' he holds his hands up as Paula points the rifle at him, 'no need to get all threatening and violent, time of the month is it?'

'Shut up and open that hatch.'

'My wife was always like that when she was on the rag...'

'Say another word and I'll gut you,' Paula hisses moving forward the ram the barrel into his bony chest. He nods quickly, goes to say something, gets prodded and glared at then thinks better of it and nods again. Moving quickly he unlocks the hatch and pulls it open, waving his hand for her to go.

'Where's the ladder?'

'There isn't one,' he whispers sulkily.

'How do you get up and down then?'

'I drop down and stand on the bannister to get back up,' he replies as if the answer is obvious.

'Right, okay,' Paula moves to look down, ' er...have you got any batteries?'

'Er....what size?'

'Double A.'

'Yeah, hang on.' He moves off for a second, rummaging quietly before coming back with a box of four.

'I only need two,' Paula whispers.

'Torch is it?' He asks while tearing the cardboard packaging open.

'Yeah the batteries went,' she twists the end cap off, tapping the two batteries out. He hands her two new ones as she struggles holding the torch and the old batteries. Eventually he takes the old ones and pushes them into his dressing gown pocket. She slides the new batteries in and twists the end cap back on. A strong beam of light shines out as the connection is made.

'Thanks,' she whispers.

'You're welcome,' he replies.

'Sorry for saying I would shoot you.'

'S'okay,' he shrugs.

'I'm off then, I will be quiet and sneak out.'

'Alright, well have a safe trip, nice to meet you,' he nods.

'You too,' she grips the edge of the loft hatch and lowers her body down, dangling for a second before dropping. The loft hatch shuts with a dull thud the second her feet touch the ground.

Glancing up she shakes her head at the weird encounter before gently easing herself down the stairs to the ground floor.

'Oi,' a whispered shout comes from above her. She moves back up to see him leaning out of the loft hole.

'What?'

'Go out the back door, there's loads in the street out the front.'

'Okay,' Paula whispers back, 'which way to the hills?'

'What hills?'

'The big bloody hills that surround the town!'

'They don't surround the town, the sea is on one side.'

'Nigel!'

'That way,' he replies sulkily.

'What way? I can't see which way you're pointing.'

'Oh...yeah course...out the back and...well the back of the house faces the hills.'

'Thanks.'

'You're welcome,' the loft hatch closes again.

'Nigel...Nigel...Nigel,' she whispers urgently.

'What?!' The hatch cracks open.

'Bye then,' she chuckles mischievously.

At the back door she gently steps outside and takes care to close it slowly, wincing when the lock snaps back into place. The fire still rages in the distance casting an orange glow into the sky which settles over the whole town.

Straight line from here then and with a deep breath she sets off, once more clutching the sub machine gun.

It takes time but eventually she reaches the outskirts, snaking through allotments and playing fields as she works back along in the direction of her truck. Coming in from a different angle now and several times she stops with worry, thinking she's overshot the truck and moving back to search again.

Finally reaching it she holds still for long minutes, scanning the area until sure the coast is clear and no traps have been set.

Out the field and once onto the road she accelerates, leaving it several more minutes before switching the headlights on, and even then she only does the first click to put them on low. Paula drives for several miles along the main road, then turns onto country lanes heading away from the town. Lefts and rights, long stretches then more turns. Sweeping through tiny hamlets until she's absolutely sure there is more than enough distance between her and the seaside town.

Only then does she find a field on raised ground and choose her ground for the night. Driving the last few minutes with the lights off, then out the vehicle and onto the roof, scanning and listening for long minutes. With her eyes adjusting to the dark she can make out the hedgerows from the moonlight and satisfied the field is clear she exhales and relaxes.

A few minutes later, with a cup of black tea and munching a few snack bars she goes over everything that happened. A whole town full of them and still no idea why. But they're aggressive and hungry, pumped up and ready for the kill.

She refuses to let the image of the children enter her head, forcibly removing them and applying her mind to the problem at hand.

There is a reason for the massing. That is obvious and what's also obvious is there are too many for her to take on. They're too hungry, too mean and aggressive.

With decent forward planning and time to formulate she knows she could take them. With enough equipment she could attack them bit by bit and reduce their numbers with every night.

But it's late now, and after another frantic night she can feel the tiredness plucking at her eyes. She gets cleaned up, going through the same ritual as before and walking a fair distance away from the vehicle before urinating on the grass then pouring water on her puddle to reduce the smell.

Cleaned, fed and watered she climbs into the back of the vehicle, pistol and rifle both within reach. Doors locked. Windows cracked just enough for air flow.

Plans and ideas thought and realised become visual images mixed with the fleeting touch of a child's hand as it falls away to the darkness of sleep.

Nineteen

Town to layby; hatchback parked and secured. Layby to field; Volvo parked and secured. Van opened, kettle on and he starts de-kitting. The compound bow, unused for the first night in well over a week is placed on the retaining hook on the wall. Arrows carefully removed from the bag and put away into a second quiver hanging from a hook next to the bow.

Night bag placed nearby, long barrelled shotgun propped against the open sliding door. Sword in easy reach. Night vision goggles still stuck on his forehead.

Doctors.

They have doctors.

This is profound, like a calling. Proper doctors that can look at his mouth and the tumours growing up his spine, although admittedly the pain in his back had now completely gone from the long walk about town but nevertheless, it was definitely still some kind of growth or mutating cells infected by a deadly disease.

Not *that* disease. *That* disease didn't bother him. Things that he could see didn't bother him at all. They were zombies, overtly zombies. The undead. The walking dead. The risen. Biters. Crawlers. Feeders. They were overtly, visually infected so that was different. It was the stuff you couldn't see that bothered Roy.

Over the last twelve days he'd got extremely proficient at hitting moving targets. Hunting with bows was illegal in the England, so getting target practise on a moving target was near on impossible. But, if somebody won't go to the big thing then the big thing will have to go to that bloke instead. He scratches his head trying to remember the saying, or did it involve an elephant and that bloke from the A-Team?

Hitting a moving target couldn't be practised, so he did the next best thing and moved himself round the static target. Walking left and right, up and down. Circling, looping and twirling until he got better and better.

Transferring those skills to the zombies was quite hard at first. Roy had got so used to moving himself, that suddenly being static against a moving target scrambled his instincts. So he moved too until he got the groove back.

No, the zombies held no greater fear than having a finger cut off, or breaking a leg. Those things were regrettable but not fear causing. They didn't inspire the terror that internal bodily problems gave him.

And as for the insides of the body, since practising with the sword day after day he'd seen enough of them to become very familiar. Picking out the major organs of the foes he had slain. Discovering just how long entrails were and what eight pints of blood really looked like when it sprayed out.

He'd been lucky as they were so slow for the first few days which meant he got regular practise with the sword.

After smashing in the window of the local Blockbusters he's grabbed every sword fighting film he could find and taken them back to watch on his laptop wired to a big caravan leisure battery. Most of them were useless but the big budget Hollywood ones were okay in the sense the actors had clearly been given training to look authentic.

With practise he became proficient with not only the blade but with the weight and length of the sword, and by the end of the week he realised why this weapon had endured thousands of years. The more he read and studied the more he also realised just how effective a Roman army *testudo* formation would be against a horde of zombies. Shields locked together and a steady *march and thrust*. If it was effective enough against Barbarian armies ten times the size of the Romans then it would surely work against a few ropey old zombie folk.

But, that would mean finding other people to hold shields, and that would mean talking to other people, which was something Roy had never quite gotten the hang of doing. Unless they were doctors of course.

They have doctors. Roy realised his mind was spinning and working too fast from the exciting news. Good lord! Those doctors will be amazed at how he's been able to function with so many deadly diseases and illnesses within his body. They'd probably keep him as a test subject and write papers.

What first? Pack the van up and move out. But it's still night and he doesn't like driving at night so maybe a cup of something soothing. No caffeine of course, that would raise his heart rate and blood pressure this late in the day. Caffeine was for the morning only. This called for Camomile, yes, a nice hot mug of relaxing Camomile tea. Maybe with some boiled rice to give his stomach something to digest. Rice had slow acting carbs so that was okay and it would mean he had greater energy levels in the morning.

The tea doesn't have the effect he was hoping for. That feeling of nerves was starting to build, that fear that he would be seeing a doctor tomorrow and be given the bad news. Maybe a week to live? Two at the very most?

Roy wondered if they had any stocks of the anti-depressant he was prescribed and stopped taking when the outbreak started. Maybe he should have got some from the pharmacy today. But he didn't like taking them, they were just dulling his sense and making him slow witted. He didn't need them, not now. He needed to be alert and switched on and besides, they didn't do anything anyway.

Maybe he was a bit more tense the last day or so, but that was to be expected with giant tumours and growths sprouting out all over his body, and his gums playing up. Thinking of which he automatically moves to his personal bag to grab his toothbrush and paste, commencing his thorough brushing technique while clutching the bottle or Corsodyl like a security blanket. After brushing vigorously he rinsed his mouth with clean water. Clenching his eyes shut as he spits it out onto the grass. Couldn't risk seeing blood in his spit, that would just send him into full meltdown.

The taste of the Corsodyl had an almost immediate effect of making Roy feel better. The familiar minty chemical taste swilling side to side.

Done, finished and still his mind races with the news. He grabs the compound bow, pauses, puts it back and pulls out the longbow instead. It required far greater effort and skill than the compound so the soothing effect would be better too.

With the night vision goggles still planted across his eyes he nocks the first arrow and lifts the bow, feeling the pull of his muscles as he stretches his right arm back. Loose and the arrow flies off, embedding into the post some twenty metres away.

First shot and he took it steady, easing his muscles into work. Second and third shots were the same, letting his body get the feel for the heavy draw of the bow. Slowly he warms up and as he does so, he steps back increasing the distance to the post. The string is pulled back further, the arrows fly faster, the swish of the string followed an instant later by the dull thud of the arrow head striking the thick wooden post.

Further back he goes and now with his muscles warmed up he increases his rate of fire. They say that the English bowmen at the battle of Agincourt could fire ten arrows a minute, which was one arrow every six seconds. But that was mass firing into the air without picking the target. He couldn't hope to match one every six seconds, not at night while aiming for a post now seventy metres away. No, the best he could do was one every ten seconds unless he really got into the groove, then it might drop down to one every eight seconds.

His mind emptied of everything apart from the arrow; that was all that mattered. He switched posts when the first one became too full, picking a thinner one to stick it full of arrows. Working from the top and keeping them in a straight line going down as low as he could see.

Roy couldn't afford many arrows before the outbreak and constantly had to keep stopping during his target practise to collect his arrows. Looting the store at the club house had yielded more arrows than he could ever fire. So he kept going, loosing arrows until his arm ached and his shoulders tired. Depleting the nervous energy, numbing his mind into a state of relaxed bliss.

It did the trick and after collecting his arrows he heads back to his van.

The bed was made up, thick roll mats with a sleeping bag rolled out on the van floor. A small 12 volt oscillating fan wired to a battery kept the air moving when the doors were closed. Lying on his back with the shotguns and the night vision goggles within reach he starts to drift off. Dreaming of doctors in pristine white lab coats holding stethoscopes while nodding at him with a perfect bedside manner.

Twenty

Nausea swims through her head and stomach. Sweating through the night until eventually with the dawn of the new day she relented from the oppressive heat and flopped down onto the grass outside to sleep in the cooler night air. The heat in the vehicle was just too much and she knew that staying in there would mean no sleep, and in turn that meant lack of alertness and general fatigue which wouldn't do.

There was just no air. It felt stifling to the point of being extreme. Paula thinks of the sea, of the cool waters drawing the heat from her body as she plunges in. A swimming pool, a cold shower, a lake, reservoir, bloody hell a big puddle would do it now.

Instead she settles for stripping off and pouring bottles of water over her head and body. The water was warm but at least a couple of degrees cooler than the air so the effect, although only marginal, was still there.

With the stove heating her water for morning coffee she washes her hair, massaging the suds deep into her scalp before rinsing off. Just the act of having freshly washed hair made her feel cleaner all over, the fresh smell gave her a sense of being civilised and human.

Grabbing a small bowl she fills it with more water and a sprinkling of washing powder before dropping two of her black vest tops in to scrub them with her hands. Rubbing the material to scrub the stale sweat and dirt away.

The thought process of the horde within the seaside town being too big had started to wane during the night. There wasn't too many of them, it just seemed that way. But with the right planning they could be taken and the sense of challenge was there. It didn't need a full on attack, the principle of taking smaller bites out of them was still there.

That was the plan for today; go back and start planning the attack. Work out which part to attack first, draw a list of equipment and supplies she would need then head off into the surrounding towns to find them. It could be done, there was no reason to run away and hide. Not now, not ever.

The tops were wrung out and draped over the already hot roof of the vehicle. The thin material would take minutes to dry out in this weather, until then she pottered about, brushing teeth, cleaning nails, drinking coffee and eating tinned food. She checked the weapons as much as she could, wishing she knew how to strip them down and clean them. They couldn't be that hard to figure out but the risk of doing something wrong was too great. The vest tops were turned after ten minutes and after packing the rear of the vehicle up she was ready but the tops were still damp. They would start to smell musty if she put them on now. Instead she wedges them into the top of the rear windows drives off in her bra, knowing the movement of the warm air will finish the drying off.

Out the field and she starts heading back towards the seaside town. Thirteen days today she mused. Tomorrow will be two full weeks since the apocalypse began and how the world had changed in those two weeks. What would it be like in another two weeks, or in two months? Would there be anyone left?

Not a cloud in the sky, just a vast unbroken blueness that seemed to stretch on forever. The heat was like nothing she had experienced, energy sapping and awful, making her want nothing other than to find cool shade and sit down to do nothing.

This time she used the map to find a way onto the downs from the other side, following an unmade track for several miles as it slowly ascended to the peak where she could look down on the breath-taking view of the gorgeous sea glinting in the morning sun.

The ruined smoking mass of the industrial estate drew her eye first, it was hard not too with the still smoking buildings and the blackened ruins of the units. She'd expected to see the a much greater scene of devastation but the fire had been contained to those units closest to the gas bottle plant and they were mostly burnt out.

Then she saw the lines, stretching back along every main road all through the town, and the thick column marching out on one side. Using the binoculars she twists the focus, bringing the front of the column into view then scanning along through the town, along the centre and out towards the eastern side.

Every single one of them was facing west, the direction they were waiting to move off into. The front was several ranks across and evenly spaced, in fact they were all evenly spaced and controlled too. An army. No doubt about it. Masses of infantry all lined up in ranks and about to march off.

The sight of them, of the organised manner in which they waited sent shivers up and down her spine. From her battles with Thomas she knew they could be controlled and directed, but not like this. They were more like rabid dogs that were just unleashed in the general direction of the prey. But this below her was far more organised and controlled than anything she had seen so far.

As the column moved off, the ones waiting held position and moved off together, visually keeping abreast of one another with the same distance between the others in front and the ones behind.

A chilling sight of an invading army. Suddenly not the grotesque monsters charging round at night but an awful, terrible disciplined mass of hungry beasts that wanted nothing more than to kill and feast.

They were heading west towards Portsmouth. Her instincts had been right; they had massed here for a reason. Using an isolated town to build vast numbers in preparation for something, and it was prepared. Prepared, planned and done with purpose for a specific task.

But what was that purpose? Who or what were they after. Unless it was just a general sweep along the coast to clear everything in their path, like a scorched earth policy, street by street, house by house and turn everyone they found along the way.

Using the map she finds the town and moves steadily along the coast, trying to identify what was there they could be after.

Small towns, villages, seaside resorts all dotted about and then the major cities of Portsmouth and Southampton, then more coastal towns and villages.

Google maps would be better, she could zoom in and try to pick out any likely targets. They were heading west so the target was west. Not inland or any other direction but a specific and chosen route.

She drives back down the hill and finds the main road, navigating to work a route that will bring her out in front of them. Then drive on and find whatever is in their path to warn them of the coming army.

Twenty One

A single drop of water can slide from a blade of grass into a puddle that forms a trickle and glides gently towards the stream which cascades over pebbles into the river which surges forward with ever increasing strength to the sea.

As it is with the fort and the sheer number of bloody people turning up. Agnes and her group were simply the spear head of a much large contingent all making their way here. Families and groups from every direction, all of them hearing about the fort and the pissing shops we don't have and turning up with the promise of a safe haven.

Maddox and I make the decision to keep them outside until we've got the rest of the bodies out, simply because to let them in now will create havoc with the clean-up operation. Lenski, Sierra and Lani do wonders outside and with so much going on I keep forgetting she could be infected. Necessity means we have to trust her, and besides, there is a very glum looking Dave following her every move.

Nick is sent to the GPMG up top with a crew so Cookey and Blowers can team up and work outside. Walking up and down the queues and rows of people and vehicles to smile and nod, make conversation and apologise for the delay, while all the time keeping a bloody close eye on everyone.

The crew stationed outside get the idea and soon they split into smaller groups, walking up and down the sides to copy the two older lads.

The piles of bodies in the estate causes some great concern, as does the lorry constantly going out from the fort stacked high with more rotting corpses. Lani and the others deal with it brilliantly; sticking to the basic facts that someone left a gate open but it is now completely secure with extra guards stationed everywhere.

'Getting there,' I remark to Maddox as we walk through the fort side by side, something we've been doing ever since he got here. He doesn't speak much and clearly isn't one for small talk.

He nods, 'the ground is filthy,' he points, 'once the last of the bodies are taken we'll get those hoses out.'

'Agnes,' I call out as the big woman strides away with a crew following in her wake, since setting up she's taken it upon herself to grab small groups one at a time and take them away for "feeding and cleaning" as she puts it with a hearty laugh.

'Have you two had food yet? Don't make me keep asking,' her voice booming across the fort.

'We will,' Maddox replies quickly, 'have you got disinfectant in there?'

'Young man,' she booms, 'my stores have more disinfectant than you will ever need what you want it for?'

'Er...the ground out here...to clean the blood away,' Maddox explains.

'Leave it with me,' she barks with another laugh before striding off to feed the group behind her.

'Did you hear that?' I ask Maddox quietly once she's out of earshot, '*my stores...*she's only been here an hour or two.'

'She reminds me of my Grandmother,' Maddox says, 'she scared the shit out of me.'

'I can see why...'

'Boss,' Clarence walks up clutching a bottle of water, 'how many we got outside now?'

'Loads mate, fuck knows where they're all coming from.'

'Any medical staff yet?'

'Not that I've heard.'

Maddox glances at Clarence then at me, 'you keep asking each other that, why you need medical people so urgently?'

Shrugging I try to pass it off without issue, 'got to be good to have them, so we can do the vetting and checks...or if anyone gets hurt.'

'Nah,' he shakes his head, 'something else, what is it?'

'Nothing mate, just we realise how important it is.'

'Howie, if you got something going on then we should know about it...none of your crew are injured so...'

'Dave to Mr Howie, can you come out the front please. A nurse has arrived.'

'Okay mate, two minutes.'

'A nurse?' Maddox asks. I look to Clarence who stares down at Maddox with a keen gaze then across to me.

'Dog?' I ask Clarence for his opinion.

'Might as well,' Clarence replies, 'I don't think it can do any harm.'

'Dog?' Maddox asks, 'what about it?'

'She's immune...'

'What!?'

'Exactly, she's killed tons of them, ripping their throats out, biting hands and fingers off, swallowing blood and god knows what else but she hasn't turned...'

'*And* they've bitten her several times and she still hasn't turned,' Clarence adds.

Maddox nods with understanding, looking between us, 'why didn't you say that before?'

'Why would we? No offence mate but it's a big thing and we can't risk her.'

'But now we know we can make sure we protect her if anything happens,' Maddox counters, 'so why she out there exposed if she so important.'

'Because she can smell them,' I reply quickly, 'she detects them instantly and starts growling and going mad...'

'And she's psychotic,' Clarence jumps in again, 'she's probably killed as many as Dave.'

'No way,' I retort, 'not possible.'

'Since we got her?' Clarence asks, 'during that fight she didn't stop killing.'

'Yeah,' I say slowly, 'maybe...that would be an interesting one.'

'What Dave against Meredith?' Clarence grins.

'About this dog,' Maddox prompts, 'that's why you want medical staff, but a nurse ain't gonna do it...you need doctors and scientists for that kind of thing.'

'True, but it's a start until we can find one.'

'All dogs or just her?'

'Don't know mate, she's the only one we've seen. We heard about her and went specifically looking for her.'

'Immunity is possible then,' he remarks quietly then senses something else unspoken between Clarence and me, 'what?' he asks quickly.

'Sharp as a bloody knife you are,' Clarence smiles.

'What then?' He shrugs, 'Lani!' He nods with realisation.

'Lani?' I ask trying to hide it.

'Yeah Lani, what's up with her?'

'What?'

'You got Dave following her everywhere and the dog too, you just said how bad they both are, so you got your two hardest shadowing one person everywhere she goes and...' he points at me, 'she ain't holding her rifle round the front either, she got it slung behind her.'

'So?' I shrug feeling like an idiot for giving it away so easily.

'And she keeps touching her stomach like she been hurt.'

'Fucking hell Maddox, you should have been a copper son,' Clarence sighs.

'Me? A fed? No way bruv,' he grins slipping back into street language, 'come on,' he goads us switching back to a refined tone, 'we in this together or what? We keeping secrets then fuck you.'

'Easy mate,' I blanch at the direct manner.

'No,' he shakes his head, 'fuck you if you gonna be doing all secret shit, I don't like it when people think I'm stupid.'

'No one said anything about you being stupid, clearly the opposite...'

'So what then?'

'Okay, but this stays between us and I fucking mean that, you hear me?' The power in my voice snaps his eyes on me, he nods seriously. 'Lani got cut yesterday, really bad wound to the stomach, she was dying so...well we had a way of turning her...'

'Fucking what?' He flares with an instant look of distaste.

'Listen,' Clarence urges him speaking low and fast.

'It's a long story but we got caught out in the fight, we were losing badly and another...er...well load of undead saved us, a woman called Marcy who said she didn't want to be like the others. She could speak and act like normal...just fucking hang on and listen, you wanted to know,' I whisper fiercely as he starts reacting.

'Okay, go on,' he says.

'Long story and I'll fill you in later but we let her turn Lani, she said she could save her and anyway so Lani got turned, she was one of them red eyes... the fucking works...it all went bent and we ended up killing them all...'

'So this lot are from that woman, not the ones that lived here?'

'Yes mate, the ones that lived here were killed out on the flatlands and stacked up yesterday, but we found Lani this morning tied up and gagged in the visitor centre toilets...'

'She doesn't have red eyes,' Maddox cuts in.

'No mate, she doesn't and Meredith isn't reacting to her either, there's no sign of it. The infection makes them heal faster than us, clots the blood quicker which is why it's so fucking hard to kill them, her wound is healed far better than it should be but now, there's no sign of it. We got Dave and the dog with her the whole time in case she turns...we don't know what's going on with her.'

'She seems normal,' Maddox agrees, 'I didn't know her before but yeah, no sign of it.'

'That doesn't mean she isn't infected, it could be a fucking trick or...'

'A trick? How?'

'Mate, we've been non-stop against those fucking things since this started and they're getting more cunning by the day...that Marcy was a trick to get us turned.'

'I can see why you didn't say anything, but how long would you have left it?'

'Moot point,' Clarence says in his deep voice, 'not relevant now, you know and that's it.'

'So she could still infect others, or,' he pauses, 'she could be immune.'

'Yep, which is why we're keeping it schtum mate, if anyone finds out they could just try and kill her, not wanting to take the risk but...if she is immune then we got to protect her.'

'Yeah right, definitely,' Maddox nods, 'I was thinking we should tell some of my lot but no, they shouldn't know, they're good but they're young and will say something. I am going to tell Lenski and the other two though.'

'Darius and Sierra? You sure that's a good idea?' I ask him.

'Yes, I wouldn't have said it otherwise,' he looks at me pointedly, 'we in this together or we two separate groups living in the same place? What if something happens to my lot and I don't tell you about it? We start off like that and it gets fucked up real quick.'

'Fair enough, but let's do it together later, with Lani there too...' I suggest.

'That's fair,' Clarence nods towards Maddox.

'Agreed,' he replies quickly, 'I appreciate you telling me but...is there anything else I should know?'

'Nothing urgent, we'll tell you the full thing later.'

'Maddox,' a voice calls out. We turn round to see the ground now cleared with the last of the bodies on the lorry, 'all done,' the youth adds.

He gives instructions to get the ground hosed and brushed down with disinfectant before following Clarence and I out the front gate to find Dave.

The sight amazes me, long queues of vehicles stacked up and stretching back into the flatlands, people milling about and chatting to each other. Bottles of water being handed around, food shared and children running between the vehicles.

Lani and Lenski turn and walk towards us with a middle aged man following them.

'How many?' I ask with a shocked voice.

'Er, fifty two,' Lenski replies with a glance at her clipboard.

'You got a nurse then?' I ask looking round.

'Yeah,' Lani grins, catching me out, she waits for a second before looking at the man, 'Mr Howie this is Frank, Frank this is Mr Howie.'

'Good to meet you,' he steps forward, thickset with old faded tattoos on his forearms, receding grey hair and an easy smile.

'Hi, you too...oh you're the nurse?' I realise, feeling very sexist for expecting to see a woman.

'Ha don't worry,' he grins, 'I get it all the time, twenty years in Accident and Emergency.'

'Bloody hell mate, sorry about that,' I grin sheepishly, 'we got medical stuff coming out of our ears but no one to use it, plus we want to get everyone checked before they come in, you know for...'

'Bites, scratches, broken skin, funny red eyes...yeah that's not a problem,' he jumps in, 'guess that means I jump the queue then.'

'Oh yes, but,' I add quickly, 'it means you get checked first.'

'Fair enough.'

'Who you with?'

'My wife and daughter, they're back there.'

'Are they medically trained?'

'Not really, my wife worked on reception at the hospital so she's got an idea of what's bad and my daughter was going to start training next year...to be a nurse.'

'How old is she?' Clarence asks.

'Seventeen, she's sensible and knows a fair bit.'

'Can we use her and your wife to help check the women and kids that come through? If you tell them what to look for?' Lani asks.

'Yeah, yeah of course,' he nods.

'Get them through and set up, Clarence you alright checking Frank?'

'On it.'

I wait a second until they stroll off then get the others gathered in a group around Maddox and I. Darius and Sierra standing next to Lenski, Blowers and Cookey with Lani, 'right we've got the bodies cleared away, last load is going out now...'

'Crews are gonna hose down and clean the ground then we gotta get everyone inside,' Maddox takes over with a seamless transition, everyone looking from me to him.

'But we need to work out where they are going to go first, do we allocate a space or let them go for it?'

'I think,' Lenski replies, 'we get the space for crews yes? Then after this the people they find own space.'

'Or we give them a defined area to use, so they don't just end up anywhere, otherwise they'll be all over the place,' I say.

'Is good point,' Lenski concedes, 'the crews I think go at the back so they have the space...'

'I was thinking of putting them at the front,' I add quickly, 'so we got a sort of fighting force ready to react and closest to the main gates.'

'Definitely,' Maddox nods, 'crews at the front between the gates and the ramp to the wall, a clear line of space then everyone else behind them.'

'That's that sorted, how we going to implement it?'

'Simple,' Lani looks at me, 'we'll just lead them in one set at a time and show them where to pitch.'

'What if they don't have tents?' Cookey asks, 'have we got spare stuff?'

'Work it out as we go, I think we should do the same as before and ask them to give over their supplies but don't force them...'

'We do this already,' Lenski, 'and I sorry but I tell them they not coming in here unless they give it to us.'

'Oh right, okay,' I nod, 'I just don't want people to think we're dictating to them.'

'But there has to be the rules yes? The food it have to be shared so they share it or go somewhere different.'

'I agree,' Lani adds, 'we're doing it nicely so don't worry and everyone seems to understand. We're not taking it off them, we're just saying they have to take it to the stores when they get in.'

'Fair enough, vehicles?'

'Same thing,' Lani replies, 'we're listing who has what vehicle, they get parked with the others and all the keys held somewhere and if they want to leave they can take the vehicle they came in.'

'Sounds good,' Maddox says, 'but we're gonna run out of space, just take the best vehicles and the rest will have to be put somewhere else.'

'Where?' Lenski asks.

'Like the boss said,' Maddox grins, 'we'll work that out as we go.' I pick up on him calling me the boss but don't show a reaction.

'Okay, so we do crews first...Darius and Sierra you do this yes?' Lenski asks, 'once the ground is cleaned we unload and get ready before we get these people inside.'

The group drifts apart, Maddox walking off with Lenski, Darius and Sierra heading inside and the two lads resuming their patrol.

'You alright?' I ask Lani and Dave.

'Fine,' Lani nods.

'Dave?'

'Good Mr Howie.'

'Er...any sign of anything?'

'Nothing,' Lani shakes her head, 'my stomach hurts a bit but I took some painkillers to ease it off, other than that I feel completely normal.'

'Dave, you seen anything?'

'No, she would be dead if I did,' he replies matter of fact.

'Nice,' Lani scoffs.

'I told Maddox,' I say quietly, 'he'd sort of worked out something was going on.'

'Was he okay?' Lani asks.

'Yeah, shocked like we were but I promised to tell him the full story later when we can all sit down, if you're okay with that.'

'We should be honest,' Lani nods, 'I keep wanting to tell Lenski but...we don't get five minutes.'

'We'll do it later. Right...what a fucking day again.'

'Telling me,' Lani says walking off with Dave stepping silently behind her.

Twenty Two

There they are, the front of the horde marching at her. Rank and file holding space beating an even step. The ragged wounds and injuries made all the worse by the organised controlled manner of their march.

Getting onto the coastal road had been easy enough but heading back towards the town had been nerve shredding. Thinking that round every corner would be the horde who would surge and engulf the vehicle. Catching sight of them in the distance was lucky.

The ground was flat so she couldn't see beyond the first few ranks, just a solid wall of undead that blocked the width of the road and stretched back. Terrible and awesome all at the same time.

Dead bodies that were inhabited and controlled by something unseen and evil, an entity that possessed them and made them do things like this. Something so powerful it could control thousands of bodies at the same time, making them march in perfect timing.

They could see her, there was no doubt about it. But they didn't show any reaction but maintained the same pace. She left it until the inner voice was screaming to go, move now before they burst into a sprint. Still they didn't react and held that awful steady clumping pace.

With just metres to go she floored the pedal and felt the surge of the vehicle pulling away. All she had to do now was keep going and find what they were going after.

The coastal road wound inland through hamlets and small holdings before drifting lazily back to the coast, often going close to the shore line with solid views of the blue sea stretching out to the horizon. If it wasn't for the deadly army behind her, the view would be breath-taking and make her want to stop and soak it in. Maybe park up and find an isolated beach for a swim.

At every point of interest she slowed down, examining remote farms in the distance or rows of rural cottages set back behind pretty gardens. Isolated country pubs smashed and looted or boarded up with thick sheets of ply hastily pilfered from the local timber yard.

Nothing stood out, nothing that would warrant a horde that size. The next town was a big one, substantial enough to have a seaside promenade, a town centre and its own commercial, industrial and sprawling residential zones.

The road sweeping in to the town went straight from rural country to urban with no steady transition. Fields then buildings. An abrupt change that jarred the senses and should have had the town planners taken round the back to be beaten with hoses. A heavy sudden vibration of the vehicle catches her unawares, not noticing the cattle grid until going over it. The four wheel drive absorbed the impact with ease but it still jolted her senses and made her realise why the sudden change. The fields here must be owned and used as grazing land for cattle and with an obstinate farmer in possession the town planners could plan all they wanted, but unless they took out a compulsory purchase order their town simply could not extend in that direction.

The cattle grid was an interesting feature, a long metal structure that broke the surface of the road for several metres. High barb wire fences on both sides so it was the only way through. If they could be wired up to mains electric they would set a wonderful trap and slow the horde down. However, the mains were now off so that idea was negated instantly.

No. No it wasn't. Batteries contained electricity and if several of those were wired up they would still provide a nasty shock. She'd used car batteries before in her old town, wiring them to door handles to give the zombies a nice jolt.

Scanning the area she searched for any premises that might sell or use them, there were enough vehicles left on the roadside to use but that would take too much time unbolting them and then she'd still need the connecting wires. Checking the map she makes a quick calculation; they were at least six miles behind her and travelling at no more than four miles an hour, that gave her an hour and a half at the very most. That was enough time to get something rigged up and the cattle grid was a natural funnel that was just too good an opportunity to miss.

She finds a large garage well before going into the town centre. A quiet side street with an old fashioned workshop and costly petrol prices with old style fuel pumps and a faded sign stating *attendance service.* Quaint and a throw-back to a period now never to be repeated. It doesn't take long to smash the window pane of the door, then reach through to unlock and gain entry. Once inside she hurries through the reception area into the workshop and straight to the back where the spare tyres, wheels and other parts are stored.

A stack of batteries under a branded sign informing of deep cycle designed for leisure caravanning. Big batteries and they're bloody heavy too. She starts carrying them out one at a time, staggering under the heavy weight and dumping them in the back of her open boot. Sweating heavily from the rushed exertion she piles them in then hunts along the display stand grabbing plastic bags containing the thick red and black wires with the big crocodile clips.

Back at the cattle grid and she unloads the batteries, stacking them on the ground to one side. Each time she bends over to drop one down, a stream of sweat drips from her nose to soak instantly into the scorched ground. The heat saps at her energy, she breathes faster and harder, knowing that every minute that passes brings them closer.

Red to positive and black to negative, she clips the leads on and connects the batteries to each other. Seven of them lined up and the last set of leads are stretched to the cattle grid.

'Shit,' she spits with anger at the leads not being long enough. Seven weighty batteries are shifted along inches at a time so the wires don't unclip. Back to the last one and she curses again at the crocodile clip being too small to bite onto any of the thick metal bars of the grid.

The bolts on the frame are the only bits small enough to stretch the mouth of the crocodile clip on and again that means shifting every single battery. Rushing like a competitor from a strong man competition she runs between the batteries heaving them along until the last wires will reach the bolts.

Once on the grid will be live. Now does she attach the black first or the red? With the heat, the rushing and the growing sense of pressure she forgets which goes on first. Has to the red positive lead.

Biting her bottom lip she leans in and hovers the red wire above the bolt, grimacing she sticks it on and exhales when nothing happens.

Now the black, if this is wrong she will either be sent flying off or the muscles in her hand will clamp down and hold onto the surge of electricity. No time to waste so with another grimace she sticks the black clip to the next bolt and jumps back.

No sign that the grid is live, no arcing sparks or hum of electricity. The batteries could be dead for all she knows. A sudden desire to test the grid comes into her head, but how? Pretty short of stepping on the thing there is no way of knowing. The live rail on at train stations doesn't look any different to the others. It must be live.

Seven big leisure batteries all in a line, the combined voltage or wattage or amps, or whatever they use to calculate it will be pumping into the grid. The second anyone touches it and the connection is made, they get zapped. The grid is long so it will slow them down for a few minutes at the very least, and if the ones behind push the front ranks forward then a few will get zapped to death too.

What else? This road is prime for traps to be set. How long has she taken to get the batteries rigged up? Half hour at the most, so she still has an hour.

The broken glass tactic takes too long to set up but the upturned nails is quick, they just need scattering. Back to the truck and she pulls the cardboard boxes out and starts back to the grid. Huge drawing pin style tacks with heavy heads and inch long spikes.

Inches from the grid she starts scattering them across the ground, again it won't stop them but it will start to hurt them and open their feet up. Deep cuts that will lacerate the flesh and each step taken after that will make the cut worse until they're limping and weaker. Even if only ten are felled it's still ten less that can hurt whoever they're going after.

With the tacks down the temptation to keep going is too great to resist. The only route is this road and with the building line just metres away it's perfect for more traps to be set.

Standing facing the grid she starts walking backwards, imagining the width of the them and how they will fan out once through the narrower bottle neck. The razor wire would work well if the connecting string was threaded across the road here and the coils set back to the sides of the road to be pulled in.

That garage had fuel pumps, if they could be activated and the petrol pumped out she could do the fire trick again and burn them down. But the ground slopes slightly here so the fuel would run off to gather at one side or drain away. The fumes would still ignite but then in this heat it would soon dry out.

Those gas bottles on the industrial estate were good too, if they could be set down amongst the seats of fire the resulting explosion would also cut them down. Vehicles parked across the road would block their movements and slow them down. Maybe some kind of delayed fuse or something going into the fuel tanks, then drive further on and get more traps set and keep going. Constant chunks taken out of them to wither them down to nothing.

She turns round to start heading back to her vehicle, stopping within two steps to stare up the road at the horde gathered there. For a second she panics, thinking she's got the direction wrong then realises this group are simply moving down to join the horde about to come through.

A whole mass of them, solid lines stretching across the road and lacking the organised coordination of the marching column coming from the other direction. They also lack the restraint and on seeing her they start charging. Paula doesn't know the reason for the change in behaviour, why these are running and the other ones don't but it's enough to get her moving. The jolting fright propels the adrenalin into her legs as she sprints to the vehicle.

The speed of them is staggering, an all-out fast charge and clearly hell bent on getting to her. Into the driver's seat and she twists the key, gunning the engine as she pushes the gear stick into first. The only available junction is up ahead, other than that it's back the way she came, over the nails and live cattle grid. Foot to the floor and the engine roars as she accelerates. They charge towards her, veering over towards the junction as though to cut her off.

Second gear and it's done badly, the vehicle shuddering from the rapid movements of her feet on the pedals. They come on strong and quick, throwing themselves into the path of her vehicle, surging forward with body mass to prevent her getting to the road.

With yards to go the fastest are throwing themselves at the front of the four wheel drive, slamming onto the bonnet and impacting on the sides. Loud bangs and thumps shudder the frame. One leaps high, smashing onto the bonnet and riding up to crash bodily into the windscreen. It clings on, blocking her view, spider web fractures spreading out across the glass.

From calm to all out mayhem within a couple of seconds and she keeps going, unable to see the road ahead but feeling as bodies impact at the wheels and sides. The passenger side window implodes as a head rams through it, the snarling face howling as it tries to wriggle through. Screaming she grabs the rifle and fires, aiming point blank at the head. The rounds spin through the cranium bursting the skull apart. The body slumps but remains wedged in place.

Still with her view blocked she pulls the wheel hard, trying to dislodge the body on the windscreen. The front hits something hard, the sound of screeching metal that breaks and pulls the vehicle to a slow pace then something snaps and it surges forward again. Out of the control with no idea what direction she is going she twists the wheel left and right, catching a glimpse of a brick wall ahead of her.

Stamping hard on the brakes the body flies off to splat against the wall and slide down, inches away from the solid structure she realises she's metres into the junction but veered hard over to the left side.

Reverse selected and she stretches her left arm over the back of the passenger seat, twisting round to watch as she powers backwards. Figures running at the vehicle and slamming into the back, more coming from the sides. The engine whines louder as she builds speed up while trying to get back onto the road proper. The aggression they show is immense, pure unadulterated fury, driven by lustful hunger that sends them surging to their deaths. So many of them, the road fills with figures charging round the corner into the side road.

Heavy on the brake and she grinds the gear into first but her feet and hands are out of synch, the engine stalls with a juddering stop. She pushes the clutch down and twists the ignition key back then forward, the engine ticks then fires. Looking out the driver's window at the shaven headed undead running straight towards her. Head lowered and teeth barred, aiming for the glass and it will smash through to sink its teeth into her face. Time slows and she knows deep within her heart there is no way she can push her foot down to engage the engine to move fast enough to evade the impact from this one solitary animal coming at her. The laws of physics just will not allow it to happen. In that instant she knows it's over. It will smash through the window and be upon her, and even if she does manage to fend him off so many more will engulf the vehicle.

She watches transfixed as it comes, all in split second she wonders what life he had, who he was, what happened to his family? Did he work? What defined this person before he became one of the things? Does he know what is happening? Trapped in the body of a raging monster, screaming to be released, knowing and alert but unable to do anything. So human, so very human but then so animalistic in nature, predatory to the point of being a monster from the worst nightmare imaginable. She even takes in the chipped tooth at the front and the small scar running across its forehead. Inches away and she accepts the inevitable then blinks as it is taken away, simply not there anymore.

Reality hits, the sound of the engine roaring to gather speed, gear meshing and it pulls away. Another one charges in, aiming for the windscreen then it too is just gone, taken away with a flash of something dark. One vaults onto the bonnet and slides up to press its face against the glass, hand pulled back to smash through the already fractured screen. Something drives it forward ramming the head through the glass and driving the body inches into the cabin. A long stick poking out the back of the skull.

Glancing up at a man stood next to a huge blue van, already pulling another arrow into his bow, lifting and firing in one fluid movement and another drops.

Roy takes the one on the bonnet, seeing its arm coming back to hammer the glass in. He knows the impact of the arrow will drive the body forward through the glass but there is no choice so he fires. He doesn't wait to see the impact as he *knows* the outcome the very second the arrow is loosed.

His hand drops, feeling for the fletch of the next arrow and pulls it up, nocks as he lifts, aims and loose. The arrow flies true and straight, the immense power of the compound bow driving the barbed head deep into the skull of one going for the passenger door.

One on the roof, scrabbling to gain purchase. Fletch, nock, lift and loose and it flies off, the carbon fibre arrow slamming deep into the brain. The black four wheel drive seems to take an eternity to gather speed, the engine roars but little power is given to the wheels.

'GET OUT AND RUN,' Roy shouts as he looses another arrow. She seems to hesitate, slamming her fists against the steering wheel. He takes the next one charging at the driver's door.

'RUN,' he shouts again, he doesn't feel panicked or flushed with worry. This is firing arrows and is the most calming thing in the world. His breathing is normal and controlled, his heart rate barely fluttering above normal. Eyes scanning as he grabs the feels the fletch, lifts the arrow into the rest at the same instant as nocking the grooved end into the string, all done as the string is already being pulled back and the bow lifts. The arrow flies, simply going where he wants it to go. Straight and true and taking another one of its feet.

Finally she makes a decision and scans round before wrenching the door open to drop out clutching a rifle. Into a crouch and she aims and fires several times, the loud cracks distinct against the silence only previously broken by the guttural howls of the undead charging forward.

She drops several then leans into the vehicle, grabbing a rucksack and started to run. Roy aims at the one coming up behind her, loosing the arrow to miss her head by inches as it drives into the eye socket of the undead.

She sprints hard, eyes fixed on him as he grabs, nocks, pulls lifts aims and looses, taking the next closest one down.

Roy looses the next one as she reaches the front passenger door, wrenching it open and diving in.

'Cover me,' he says calmly.

The second he hears the rifle crack he drops the bow into the van, slams the side door closed and drops down to run under the passenger side window. Round the front and into the driver's seat. She fires carefully, placing her shots as he engages first gear and pulls away.

The powerful engine complies instantly, turning in a wide arc as he holds the wheel over to the right.

Straightening up he listens to the thumps and bangs as they reach the back of the van, slamming into the sheer sides but with nothing to grasp or hold they simply fall away as he applies speed and creates distance.

The woman stares back out of the window, leaning further and further out as if to keep them in sight for as long as possible.

'Thanks,' she faces forward breathing hard, her face flushed with red cheeks, hair plastered across her forehead and still gripping the black machine gun.

'Paula,' she says with ragged breath.

'Could you do me a favour?' Roy asks keeping his eyes fixed on the road ahead.

'What?' Paula gasps, still with the heat of battle.

'Can you check my back please?' Roy leans forward over the steering wheel.

'Why did they get you?' Paula demands.

'God no!' Roy replies, 'I think I've got a lump there, can you have a look and see if you can see anything.'

'What?'

'My back, my lower back...' using one hand he tugs the bottom of his t shirt up revealing his lower back, 'is there a lump there?'

Still breathing hard with a head spinning from the chaos of the last few minutes she bends over to peer at his perfectly normal back.

'Nothing there.'

'You sure? There must be a lump or something, is the skin raised?'

'No, nothing,' Paula replies then glances out the front, her movements still fast and twitchy.

'What about a rash? Is there a rash?'

She looks again, staring hard at the skin on his back, 'there's nothing, it's clear...just normal.'

'Oh thank god for that,' he breathes a huge sigh of relief, 'you don't know how worried I've been, honestly I really thought there was a lump there, tried feeling myself but you know how it is, twisting round and everything feels weird.'

'Right,' Paula nods still staring with wild eyes.

'Don't suppose you're a doctor by any chance?'

'Eh? No...'

'Oh, nurse? Medically trained? Vet maybe?'

'No,' she shakes her head, 'accountant.'

'Accountant, was it a big firm?'

'Er...quite big why?'

'Did you have a designated first aider?'

'What? Yes...I was...what? Why?...'

'Which course did you do? Was it the one day basic course or the advanced?'

'Is someone hurt?' She asks.

'No why?'

'Why are you asking me then?'

'Just wanted to know,' he replies, 'was it the one day basic then or the advanced?'

'Er, I did two afternoons; someone came in and did a few of us...why?' She grimaces at the memory of all the office men staring at her backside while she bent over to practise mouth to mouth on the doll, then the jokes and comments that followed every time they mentioned chest compressions.

'Oh,' Roy says glumly, 'that one, yeah figures.'

'I...bloody hell,' Paula wipes the sweat from her face and stares about in bewilderment. Grabbing her bag she pulls a bottle of water out to take a long swig then leans back out the window to check behind them, 'er…who are you?' She asks.

'Roy.'

'No I mean who are you? Why were you there? And how the hell did you do that with a bow and arrow? I mean thank you but bloody hell that was amazing.'

'Thanks,' Roy nods.

'So?' Paula prompts after several seconds of silence, 'who are you and why were you there?'

'I'm Roy, have you got a brain injury?'

'What? No why?'

'You keep asking my name. It's Roy.'

'Sorry, I meant…I just meant what were you doing there?'

'You didn't say that, you kept saying who are you.'

'Yes, sorry…just a bit shocked I guess…so *what* were you doing there?'

'Going for the coastal road to find the fort,' he replies happily.

'Oh,' she nods, 'what fort?' This must be a dream. She glances over at the man driving, a bald head with a light layer of very fair stubble on his scalp and chin. He looks clean and handsome in a rugged kind of way, dressed in a tight top that clings to his frame but the way he was firing those arrows, that was unbelievable.

'Have you not heard?' He asks conversationally.

'About what?' She shakes her head.

'The fort,' he repeats, 'they've got doctors and a hospital, shops and a man called Mr Howie that keeps it safe.'

'Really? Where is it?' Paula leans forward staring in shock.

'Somewhere between here and Portsmouth, that's why I was going for the coastal road but then I saw them….then I saw you and well, couldn't just leave you there, thought you might be a doctor or something.'

'Doctor? No…just an accountant, sorry.'

'Not your fault.'

'That makes sense,' Paula mutters, nodding to herself.

'What does?' Roy asks.

'Why they're all going that way…is there a lot of people at this fort?'

'Thousands from what I hear, I just hope they've got a spare bed in the hospital.'

'Why?'

'So I can use it,' he answers as if it's the most obvious thing ever.

'Are you hurt? What's wrong?' Paula switches on, realising how many times he's mentioned doctors now, 'is it your back?'

'What?' Roy asks in alarm, 'you said my back was fine…did you see something? Is there a lump?'

'No! There wasn't anything…but you keep mentioning doctors and you said about your back so I…'

'I knew it, I fucking knew it,' Roy shakes his head.

'Knew what?'

'My back! I knew there was something there, look Paula, I know we only just met but you can tell it to me straight…there was a growth wasn't there.'

'No!' Paula reels.

'Come on, just be honest…I would rather know.'

'There was nothing there, honestly…really nothing there.'

'Check again.'

'Okay,' she shrugs, he leans forward tugging the top up again. Bending over she examines his back closely and without thinking extends a hand to run over his skin making him flinch, 'sorry,' she says on instinct.

'That's okay...what did you feel?'

'Nothing, really there is nothing there, it felt fine. Does it hurt?'

'Oh my god,' Roy wails, 'why would it hurt? You saw something didn't you?'

'What!? No...I'm just asking because you keep mentioning it...'

'Sure?' He asks in a quiet meek voice.

'I'm sure,' she says softly staring across at the strange man.

'Oh fuck...really? Are you sure?'

'Roy, there was nothing there...there *is* nothing there, I promise.'

'Okay,' he nods quickly and takes a deep breath, 'okay.'

'So...' she pauses thinking how to ask him again, 'does it hurt er...anywhere? Do you need a doctor?'

'God yes,' he blurts out, 'my mouth is in pieces and I know I've got lumps growing and tumours...it's been what? Two weeks since I saw a doctor and god knows what's developed since then.'

'Jesus Roy, I'm so sorry,' she says still shocked and struggling to keep up.'

'What for?' He asks quickly.

'Well, you know...that you're having to deal with that while all this is happening.'

'Deal with what?'

'Having Canc...'

'Don't say it!'

'What?'

'Don't say that word...why would you say that? Oh my god do you think I look ill?'

Paula shakes her head again, thinking this must be what swimming through mud must feel like, 'No you don't look ill, you look fine...I mean I never met you before but you look fine now...'

'Then why would you say that?'

She rubs her eyes and forehead, feeling the strain more than ever, 'look,' she snaps, 'are you ill or not?'

'Probably...I do get this weird sensation when I squeeze my thighs together really hard.'

'Right,' she nods, 'I thought you said it was your back?'

'It is, and I get that sensation too, plus my mouth... I must be riddled with it, head to toe and everything infected and diseased and...'

'Riddled with what?' Exasperated she cuts him off, staring across as he watches the road.

'With whatever I've got, probably loads of things...I did a diabetes check but I think the machine was broken and the blood pressure machine too, that was faulty...I mean it said I was fine but well, you can't trust a machine like that can you? You need proper machines with wires and doctors and...

'Roy, are you ill with anything specific?'

'I don't know yet,' he sighs, 'wait and see what the doctors say.'

'Okay,' she say slowly, 'have you been diagnosed with anything?'

'Well no,' he says quietly, 'but that doesn't mean something hasn't developed or started in the last er...thirteen days or...'

'Okay,' she nods again as a dim light starts to come on, 'and your mouth? What's wrong with that?'

'Why did you see something...' He asks quickly.

'No, not at all but you said your mouth was in bits or something like that.'

'Oh yes I did didn't I, well the gums are irritated and well, they just don't feel right.'

'Bleeding?'

'Well no but...'

'Are they swollen?'

'Not swollen but...'

'Do they hurt?'

'Not actually painful but I can just feel them, you know like they're a bit irritated...I keep brushing and using mouthwash but...'

'How often are you brushing?'

'Oh loads, like every hour sometimes...that's why I can't understand why they're so irritated.'

'Brushing every hour? And using mouthwash?'

'Of course, I'm trying to do the best I can and keep the infection at bay but...'

'Roy, maybe the brushing and mouthwash is irritating your gums? Forgive me for being blunt and I know we only just met but...well anyone who brushes that often will have bad gums...'

'I did think of that but...'

'Show me,' she says firmly.

'What?'

'Show me your mouth.'

'Sure? I mean you know...don't want to be weird or anything but...'

'Show me,' she says again, 'pull over for a second.' He brings the van to a gradual stop then holding the foot brake down he faces her and quickly opens his mouth. She leans forward staring as he puts his fingers into the sides of his lips and stretches them wide.

'Hang on,' Paula fidgets for the torch, pulling it out to shine into his mouth, 'teeth are clean, no lumps...nothing swollen or bleeding...gums looks a tiny bit red but that's from being brushed so much...hang on,' she says as he starts to murmur with his mouth wide open, 'she keeps on peering in for several long seconds, making a point of looking into the sides, the roof and under his tongue, 'fine, they look absolutely fine...nothing wrong there at all.'

'But you said they looked red.'

'Not red,' she corrects, 'just a bit pinker where you're brushing so much...honestly Roy there is nothing there.'

He stares at her for a few seconds, deep worry lines etched into the sides of his eyes speak of long periods of anxiety and concern. The dim light grows brighter until it shines down like a football stadium floodlight.

'Honestly, if I saw anything I would tell you,' she says sincerely, 'there was nothing on your back, your mouth is clear...anything else?'

'There's a funny sensation when I squeeze my thighs doc.'

'I'm not a doctor, I'm an accountant.'

'Yeah right, sorry,' he shakes his head.

'What kind of sensation?'

'Like it tingles a bit,' he looks worried sick, really panicky.

'Where?' She asks gently, trying to remember how her GP spoke to her.

'In my er...well my bits,' he mumbles.

'Do they hurt?'

'No,' he shakes his head with such a sorry expression she has to suppress a snort of laughter.

'And it just tingles a bit when you clamp your legs together, like really hard?'

'Yeah,' he nods enthusiastically.

'Like in your testicles yeah? Just a slight tingle that feels a bit weird?'

'Yeah,' he nods harder, clearly hanging off every word she says. Paula adopts a serious expression, hoping she gets this right.

'Roy,' she say slowly.

'Yeah,' his eyebrows go up as he prepares himself for the bad news.

'Everyone gets that, well I mean all men get that…it's your balls being squashed together…that's it…don't clamp your legs together so hard and it won't happen.'

'Really?' He asks in a muted voice suddenly full of hope.

'Oh god yes,' she nods knowingly, 'I know loads of men who said the same thing.'

'Really?' His eyes light up, 'loads of men yeah?'

'Oh yes,' she nods, 'my er…dad….my uncles…boyfriends and cousins and well, loads of them.'

'Oh,' he whispers, 'wow…really?'

'And er…I er…saw a television documentary about it too, one of those doctor programmes, do you watch them?' She asks lightly.

'No I'm banned,' he answers quickly.

'Banned?'

'Yeah my doctors told me I wasn't allowed to watch them.'

That figures she thinks, 'well yeah I saw this programme and it was all about the er...tingling testicles er...phenomenon...'

'Really?' He looks at her in wonder.

'Oh yeah,' she says seriously, 'and that's what it is, apparently,' she continues fully in the swing, 'they get so many men going into GP surgeries about it they commissioned the programme to tell everyone about it.'

'Oh,' he says slowly, nodding with interest, 'yeah that would make sense.'

'But of course if you don't watch them then you wouldn't have seen it.'

'No,' Roy shakes his head.

'So,' she looks at him, 'anything else?'

A hand is thrust under her nose, one finger extended. 'I got a lump,' he says quickly.

'Let me see,' she takes his hand gently and feels along the extended finger, really getting into the swing of it now and she gently opens his hand to feel his other fingers then back to the one he showed her, 'that,' she stares at him and notices the instant worry flood across his face again, 'is a blister.'

'A blister? Oh right yeah I was sharpening the sword for a few hours.'

'Sword?'

'I have a sword.'

'Good,' she replies, 'anything else?' She asks lightly.

'Er...I got this rash on my ankle,' he starts lifting his leg while reaching down to roll his trousers up.

'Heat rash,' she says as soon as the tiny red prickles come into view, 'hot weather, sturdy boots and thick socks…I get the same thing.'

'Anything else?' She asks with patience, seeing the worry start to dissipate from his face.

Shaking his head he looks at her in wonder, like a puppy at its new owner, 'don't think so,' he replies.

'Okay that's good, so I would say,' she speaks slowly, 'that you look to be in perfect health.'

The change in him is palpable, the worry gone instantly and replaced with a big smile and look of complete relief.

'So about this fort?' She prompts as he engages first gear to start pulling away.

'Yeah apparently they've got doctors and a hospital there,' he relays with glee.

'That's good, so you're going there? And I should imagine there must be lots of survivors.'

'Oh the place will be flooded, people always want to group together…which I never quite understand,' Roy says.

'No,' Paula looks at him keenly, 'me neither.'

'I've been quite content living on my own, got my van all rigged up and everything I need…'

'Well I did have until a few minutes ago, but yes I agree with you completely…however there is an almighty army of those things marching towards that fort.'

'What? Really?' Roy glances across at her and starts to slow the van down again, bringing it to another gradual stop and clearly being the type of person who doesn't like driving while distracted.

'Yep, there's a seaside town back that way…'

'I know it,' Roy nods.

'Full of them. And I mean completely full, thousands and thousands. I noticed the village and towns were empty all round here, then I found them all heading into the town, then this morning they're marching out and all coming this way.'

'My town was empty too, I was hunting last night and couldn't find any.'

'Hunting?' Paula asks with sudden interest.

'With my bow,' he nods, 'some people will probably find that weird but I like it...it cuts them down which means less danger.'

'No, I agree, I was doing that in my town too.'

'Oh really? With a bow?' Roy asks hopefully.

'God no, I was setting traps all over the place, used wire and petrol, broken glass...god all sorts of things.'

'And them?' He nods at the rifle then at the pistol on her belt.

'Not really,' she replies, 'they were for defence only.'

'Ah, like my sword and shotguns...I only used the bow for hunting though.'

'You're really good at it, I can't believe those shots you got.'

'Thanks, so you get many? At your town I mean?'

'The whole town,' she says proudly, 'took me long enough but I did it.'

'The whole town you say? Well done,' he nods with genuine admiration, 'er...would you like a cup of tea? I've got lots of herbal ones...camomile and peppermint...'

'Coffee?'

'I have coffee,' he replies.

'I'd love one if that's okay, er...' she glances out the windows, 'is it safe here?'

'Good point,' he checks the mirrors, 'I always like using empty fields myself, preferably with a good line of sight all around.'

'Me too,' Paula smiles, 'I had a different field every night,' she adds as he pulls away.

'Oh I didn't, I had one I used for a few nights and then changed, so you didn't stay in your town then?'

'No,' Paula says quickly, 'went back every day until I got them all.'

'Oh, I went in the day for supplies and the night for hunting.'

'In the night for hunting?' She asks with surprise, 'that's dangerous isn't it.'

'Got night vision glasses,' he explains, 'and if you know how to move and hide, then run and find a new position it's amazing the damage you can do.'

'Wow, and that didn't scare you?' She stares at him again, suddenly thinking of the fear etched into his face when she looked in his mouth and at his finger.

'Not really,' he replies honestly, 'to be honest they don't really bother me that much, I was er...never what you would call a people person so...this looks good, alright with you?' He asks as they broach the entrance to a big field.

'Perfect,' she looks round, 'drive into the middle though so we've got a good view.'

'Okay, yeah so er...the zombies don't bother me so much.'

'Zombies,' she laughs, 'I always called them the *things*, couldn't bring myself to say that word.'

'Well that's what they are,' he comments, bringing the van to a gentle stop and already hopping out.

'I guess so,' Paula replies as he comes round the front and draws the sliding door back, 'oh wow Roy, this is really nice.'

'You like it?' He asks with real pleasure at the compliment, 'I got all those batteries rigged up so I have power, got loads of food and supplies...'

'Is that a Kindle?'

'Yes, all charged up too, downloaded hundreds of books the night it started.'

'Really, that was good thinking...I was trapped in an office with a drunk rapist.'

'Oh god really?' Roy asks with shock.

She hesitates, realising what she just said. She doesn't know this man, he could be as dangerous as Clarke for all she knew. But then he didn't seem dangerous, in fact he seemed completely the opposite and none of the alarm bells were going off, plus he hadn't looked at her chest once yet despite the tight top she was wearing.

'Er...'

'Awful, fucking awful,' he tuts and shakes his head again she glances at him. The way he speaks so calm and mild mannered, polite but yet swearing too. 'I hope he didn't hurt you.'

'Not really,' she shrugs wishing she never mentioned it.

'Do you take milk and sugar? Only got the powdered milk I'm afraid although I do have a book I downloaded on how to milk a cow...so if you see one do shout up and we can get some fresh milk.'

'Okay,' she laughs, pleased at the change of subject, 'doesn't it have to be pasteurised?'

'Oh I wouldn't worry too much about that,' he replies clicking the small travel kettle on. Again she feels confused at a man so worried about any mark on his body yet apparently prepared to drink unfiltered milk fresh from a cow.

She watches as he takes the compound bow he left on the floor and carefully places it on the wall before checking his arrow supply and re-stocking the quiver from a big bag.

Leaning in she glances at the various bows hanging down, then at the bag containing the butts of the sawn off shotguns, the long barrelled one he draws out to rest against the side of the van and then the sword.

'That's the sword then is it?' She asks, 'may I?'

'Please do,' he replies turning his attention back to the drink making.

'Very nice, have you used it much?' She weighs it carefully in her hand, eyeing the length and thickness of the sharpened blade.

'Quite a bit, mainly in the day when they're slow...having said that did you notice the changes in them over the last few days?'

'Definitely, bloody hard work too. In end I had to plan for them being like that all the time.'

'Hmmm, me too,' Roy replies, 'don't know what caused it, I figured it must be the infection inside of them, you know...trying to make them work harder or find more people to eat.'

'Did you know they could talk?'

'Really?' Roy asks in a shocked tone handing her a mug of coffee over, 'no...I can't say as I ever spoke to one, other than to tell it to fuck off or something.'

She glances at him again, at the way he swore so fluently yet the contrast between the politeness and the swearing was almost jarring.

'They do, I met one called Thomas...'

'Gave you his name did he?' Roy remarks, 'well that is strange. Have much to say?'

'Not really,' she replies, 'asked me to go peacefully, said he would get me...that sort of thing, left me a nice note though.'

'A note? You don't say? What did it say?'

'Just telling me to find others of my own kind and lead a peaceful life,' she laughs as he rolls his eyes.

'Well what would he know?' Roy comments drily.

'But,' she say quickly, 'he did hint at something big happening and now of course I know what he meant.'

Roy nods sipping his then reaches in to grab a folding chair to open on the grass a short distance away, he goes to sit down then stands back up and offers Paula the chair. Shaking her head she sits on the edge of the van, 'there are thousands of them, and all heading this way...well I mean that way,' she points back the way they came from, 'and what you said about the fort makes sense, we should warn them.'

'Of course,' Roy replies, 'which makes me wonder why we're sat here drinking tea when we should be doing just that.'

'True,' Paula nods and takes another sip of the coffee, 'although I was trying to get some traps down to slow them up...that's when I got trapped.'

'Traps?' Roy prompts.

'Electrified a cattle grid with car batteries and put some tacks down...that's as far as I got.'

'Good try but it won't stop thousands, the juice will drain with the first few.'

'Oh it was only a stop-gap, you know...just to buy a little time but I didn't realise that town already had a load, didn't check properly which was stupid of me.'

'Yes it was,' Roy replies matter of fact, now a completely different man compared to the nervous wreck a few minutes ago. 'Are they all on foot?'

She nods swallowing her coffee before answering, 'marching, all in perfect time and in perfect rank too.'

He blanches at the news, nodding as though thinking deeply, 'that is worrying.'

'Scary too, seeing them do that I mean, do you have a map?'

'No, sorry...didn't really need one.'

'Mines in my car,' she grimaces, 'how far do you think the fort is?'

'Not sure...maybe thirty miles...could be more.'

'So it will take them sometime to get there, if you're right about the distance.'

'If I'm right,' he concedes, 'but certainly not less than twenty miles anyway.' She notices his steady gaze and the way he moves his head as though constantly listening for sounds. He still hasn't checked her chest out or stared in any weird way. Thirteen days of hell and he seems completely normal, well as normal as any bow and arrow using, sword wielding hypochondriac can be.

'Plan,' she states firmly, 'we get there and warn them, unless we find anything else on the way that they could be after...then come back and start cutting them down. There'll be other villages, towns and places I can get things set up...the further the distance to the fort the more time I will have...Maybe find some supplies and...'

Roy watches her far stare off into the distance as she speaks. He didn't like people. He didn't like any people as a rule, unless they were doctors but the way she spoke to him in the front of the van; well she sounded just like a doctor. She even touched his finger the way a doctor would. He knows she isn't a doctor but she's here and she was kind and understanding. Just the few words from her took the anxiety down to a level he barely felt. It was there and it probably always would be but she had suppressed it the same way a visit to the doctors normally did.

And she hasn't looked at him like a freak, not once. No snide comments or spiteful remarks yet. She seemed confident and sturdy of mind and more than that, she oozed independence with a skill for self-survival, not clinging to the ordinary rules of society but carving her own path. Choosing a different route to everyone else, fighting back for the sake of it and not for the glory. Roy detected the pride in her when she said she'd rid her whole town, not boastful but pride in the sense of doing something that she knew was good.

'We have to get going,' she stands up quickly with a sense of urgency. The few minutes of talking with another human being and drinking coffee have brought her mind back to full alertness and made her realise just how desperate the situation is.

Without thinking she starts packing the van away, her mind whirring as her hands start working automatically. She holds her hand out for his cup, which he hands over without a word and picks her rifle up to carry back to the front.

Loaded up and ready they drive off. Heading to the fort to warn of the zombie army marching their way.

Twenty Three

'He's all clear,' Clarence says as he steps out of the medical tent, 'the wife and daughter have been checked too, they're getting some screens put up so they can just use that tent.'

'Nice one mate, he seems alright.'

'Unflappable, mind you twenty years in a London hospital emergency room will do that.'

'Fair point, what you grinning at?' I ask Maddox as he steps through from the inner gate with a huge grin on his face.

'Have you see this?' He points over his shoulder. We walk over and step through into the fort. Darius and Sierra are marking out the ground for the crews and beyond them stands Agnes, tall and proud with her hands on her hips directing children holding brooms, brushes, mops, buckets and others carrying bright yellow plastic bags and wearing disposable latex gloves to pick bits of body off the ground. Several hoses are already spraying water onto the stained ground as Agnes directs the youths to *get their backs into it*.

'Shit,' I exclaim quietly, 'I didn't mean for her to get the ground cleared.'

'Well she's doing it, and they've all been fed,' Maddox replies.

'Your lot don't mind doing what she says then?' Clarence asks.

'They're shit scared of her,' Maddox laughs.

'At least this heat will dry it out quickly and...'

'Mr Howie,' Blowers interrupts me walking through the gate with Cookey right behind him.

'Alright mate, what's up?'

'We were speaking to some bloke that turned up and he said his town emptied out overnight.'

'Do what?' I ask confused at what he means.

'The zombies,' Cookey adds with an apologetic nod to Clarence, 'he said all the zombies went overnight, just walked off...then we started speaking to someone else...

'Who said the same thing,' Blowers continues, 'different village something like twenty miles away...they kept hearing them every night but not last night, when they got up this morning the whole place was empty.'

'Seriously?' I ask looking at them both.

'Yeah,' Cookey nods emphatically, 'we went down the line asking people and they all saying the same thing...'

'...that's why so many are coming now, cos the things have fucked off so they can get out and do one to here.'

'Howie?' Lani calls from the other side of the gate.

'In here,' I shout back, watching as she steps through with Lenski and Dave.

'Did they tell you?'

'Yeah.'

'We just checked with some more, nearly all of them are saying the same thing, and others saw the lines walking away.'

'Lines?' Maddox queries.

'Lines of the things, walking off together...explains why we're getting so many people here.'

'It does, where they going?' I ask.

'East,' Lenski replies, 'everyone they say the same, the things they go that way,' she motions towards the east.

'Massing,' Clarence rumbles, 'There can't be that many left though.'

'Darren brought loads here and we killed them all, plus all those last night and yesterday,' Cookey says.

'Darren?' Maddox asks.

'Another long story...' I start to say.

'I said this before,' Dave adds flatly, 'Darren brought his from London and picked them up on the way. That Paco and the dog killed high numbers in their town which tells us there are still high numbers within the population zones, the numbers we've killed are nothing compared to the general population.'

'Fuck,' Blowers adds, 'they're gonna be coming for us again.'

'Really, they come here?' Lenski asks.

'No doubt,' I reply, 'they just don't fucking give up do they.'

'I don't feel anything, nothing...if they're all being pulled somewhere then...' Lani looks down at the ground as though thinking hard.

'I not understand,' Lenski says quickly.

'Later,' Maddox cuts in firmly with a nod to his partner, 'we got any idea of distance or location?'

'Nah nothing,' Blowers replies, 'fuckers are just marching off and going east.'

'Right,' every pair of eyes snaps to me, 'Clarence, you take Dave and start showing the crews how to use the assault rifles...'

'What about Lani?' Dave asks.

'What about Lani?' Lenski asks with another look between us.

'Lani got turned yesterday, she was infected...we all saw it but she isn't showing any signs of it now...' I explain rapidly.

'Immune?' Lenski gasps.

'Don't know, not sure...anyway...Get those crews trained to shoot and Maddox, you get a couple of your people to guard the armoury, we get this ground cleared up quickly and those people inside as fast as possible...'

'Wait,' Lenski shakes her head, 'Lani is immune? This is amazing...'

'It is but we've got a lot to do,' I say hurriedly.

'I might be, we don't know anything,' Lani adds.

'Listen,' I snap, we can talk about it later, 'we get the ground cleared and those people inside as soon as humanly possible, Lads make sure the Saxon is fully loaded and ready to go, make sure Nick knows what you've just told me...'

'Why the rush?' Clarence asks.

'We're going after them that's why,' I look at him, then at the others, 'we're not waiting for them to come here, I'm fucking sick of it...we're ending this.'

'This madness,' Lenski replies with a glare, 'we have the big walls and the guns, we wait they come here and we shoot them yes?'

'Not this time,' I shake my head, 'these fuckers can fuck off and get fucked.'

'Well said,' Clarence grumbles.

'I'm in,' Blowers nods, 'about time we fucking had them.'

'Good, we get this place sorted and we go out, we take as much fire power as we can and fucking slaughter them.'

'We got that second GPMG too,' Clarence says.

'Yeah we'll take that.'

'We'll take some crews with us,' Maddox adds.

'Not us mate,' I shake my head at him, 'you got to run this place, we're doing this.'

'Oh not again,' Lani sighs, 'here we go.'

'What?' Lenski asks struggling to keep up.

'Howie picking a fight with some massive horde again and not letting anyone else play.'

'He do this before?'

'Ha, loads of times,' Cookey grins, 'and it's fucking great.'

'I'm coming,' Lani glares at me.

'No fucking way,' I reply with Clarence and the lads all saying the same thing.

'Not happening Lani,' Clarence says.

'You said that last time,' Lani replies, 'and I still went...you...'

'And you agreed that if we took you with us you'd do as I said when I said it,' I snap at her, 'if you're immune then we don't take the fucking risk...'

'And if I'm immune then it doesn't fucking matter if I get bitten does it?' She growls.

'Ooh she's swearing,' Cookey mutters taking a step back.

'Howie's right,' Maddox cuts in, 'it would be stupid to risk you.'

'So me and the dog stay here?' Lani asks pointedly.

'Lani and Meredith are both very good fighters, 'Dave states then stares round with a blank look.

'Leave Lani here and I'll bring some crews,' Maddox says.

'I am coming,' Lani hisses, 'there is no discussion…I am going and that's all there is to it.'

'Don't be so bloody ridiculous,' I snap, 'you are the most important one here now, if anything we should be locking you up or…or…bloody strapping you to a boat in the sea.'

'Try it,' she glares, 'and I'm not the most important one here and we all know it.'

'She's right,' Dave adds.

'Don't fucking start that…' I look between them, 'not that…Lani and the dog…they are the special ones…'

'No,' Dave replies.

'What is this please?' Lenski asks, 'I get the headache and you people are very strange yes?'

'Oh for fuck's sake why do you have to make things so complicated,' I groan, 'Lani you are staying here, the dog too….the rest of us are going out….Maddox it's up to you if you want to come but personally I would rather you stayed here…'

'Maddox he will go with you,' Lenski says with a tone as firm as Lani, 'Maddox he good at the fight and the crew too, show them the guns and they kill many.'

'Fine, but only a few so we can stay light and move fast…everyone get on…we've got a lot to do.'

'I'm coming,' Lani calls out as I walk off. She runs after me and grabs my arm when I don't reply, 'I'm coming too,' she repeats.

'No,' I go to walk off.

'I've had your back since I joined with you and that is not stopping now,' she says in an urgent whisper.

'Lani…'

'No, look what happened last night...remember that? If I was here that wouldn't have happened, you almost died or got turned or...well, that bitch almost had you and what if she's leading this new lot?...I'm coming and despite how angry I am with you I will be standing at your back again, understand?'

'Fucking hell Lani...'

'Don't *fucking hell Lani* me Howie,' she spits, 'this isn't up for discussion...you are the special one amongst us and that means we keep our team together until we find the answer to all this.'

'Lani,' I growl, 'don't fucking start doing a Dave on me...'

'Look at me Howie, look at me...' she steps in closer, 'you will lead and you will win...you have to believe in yourself...no don't interrupt me, look at me Howie...you will lead and you will survive, you will end this...no one else but you can do that, you understand me?'

'STOP!'

'Listen to me,' she speaks soft and urgent, coming in closer, within arm's reach now, 'you will do this, you are strong and you have to believe in yourself.'

'This is fucking stupid...what is it with you and Dave...'

'And Clarence...and Cookey and Blowers and Nick? What Howie? What is it with all of us? What was it with Chris and Tom and everyone else that has fought with you?'

'Just fuck off.'

'Don't ever tell me to fuck off,' she snaps, 'not now and not ever.'

'Sorry, I didn't mean...'

'I will be with you, so will Meredith because this only works *because* of you Howie...don't ask me how I know because I don't know myself...I can just feel it...but don't you ever speak to me like that again.'

'Sorry Lani, I really didn't mean it like that.'

'Swear all you want but don't swear at me.'

'Okay,' I hold my hands up, 'I'm sorry, I really am.'

'Good, agreed then,' she starts walking off.

'No hang on,' I grab her arm this time, pulling her round to face me, 'we haven't agreed anything.'

'Why are you going after them?'

'What?'

'Why are you going after them? As soon as you heard they're massing you had that thing...I saw it...so did the others...why?'

'I already said why, I'm sick of them...it's time to end it.'

'Exactly,' she looks at me, 'you made that decision and even Maddox is up for it...this is the bloke who will stop at nothing to protect his crews...even his bloody girlfriend said he should go with you.'

'So?'

'Oh my god Howie, how can you not see what everyone else sees? You,' she leans forward with an intense, earnest look, 'make people believe in you, you,' she pauses, 'have something so amazing...we all know it, Chris knew it, your sister knew it...'

'Stop Lani,' I plead.

'No, it's time you heard this, we all know it...remember that night in the van when Maddox was going for us?'

'Yes,' I sigh, 'and that was a bloody stupid conversation too.'

'No,' she shakes her head, 'any one of us would have walked out there and then to make sure you lived...why did Marcy go for you then?'

'Fucking hell, I don't know?'

'Yes you do, why, out of all the people she could go for...does she make a beeline for you?'

*...they fear you, we all fear you...there's a power in you that's so dangerous but so good...*Marcy's words from last night flood through my mind, the hairs on the back of my neck stand up as I start to realise just how many times people have said this.

'You know what I mean don't you,' she states.

'No...maybe...I don't know...'

'Yes you do,' she adds softly, 'so I'm coming and I will be right at your back the same as I have been...and this time I will not let you down.'

'You didn't let me down.'

'I did, I should have been there last night but I wasn't...that won't happen again...listen, I don't know what this thing is doing to me or has done to me, but I'm not going to question it too much either...that's your job...mine is to cover your back, the same as Dave...the same as Clarence...You will fix this Howie and we'll all be right with you when you do.'

She walks off leaving me reeling on the spot and it feels like the weight of the world just landed on my shoulders.

Only it didn't did it. The team have made it clear they'll stand with me no matter what the odds. And Lani was right, even Maddox and Lenski were up for it, like my blind enthusiasm is as contagious as the infection.

Maybe this is meant to be then.

Fuck it. Who am I argue.

Twenty Four

The summoning had begun long before Marcy failed to turn Howie and his people. The infection had accounted for the failure and had carefully selected the isolated town to draw all the hosts from the nearby towns and villages. Others that were on the selected route to the fort were gathered and held waiting until the main group passed through.

Tens of thousands drawn from miles around. The knowledge and experience gained from so many failures has propelled the infection to select overwhelming numbers, a huge force that will crush those survivors and allow the examination of Howie to begin.

But something else had happened. A connection has been lost but not through the death of the host. The infection knows each death suffered by each host. This connection had simply faded away.

The body was taken in the same manner as all the others. Every cell was taken over, every organ infected until the heart was stopped and then the body re-started in the perfect state.

There was no sign of anything different. It had the hunger and complied with the orders given by the lead host.

It was hours before the natural defences started making use of the anti-body, but once it did, it swept through and fought back.

Infected cells were purged. Organs under control of the infection were purified.

Infected blood entered the heart but pure blood came. It would not tolerate the foreign body being within this environment.

The infection knew it was being defeated and it fought back, desperately trying to re-infect those cells and organs but they were now shielded and protected.

The brain was the last to go. The final stand made by the infection as it tried to shut the body down and end the purge. But the flood gates were open by this point and there was no escape. Pure blood pumped into the most powerful organic material known on the earth and with it the anti-bodies that defeated the infection. Neural pathways were subjected to bombing missions. Synapses were strafed, centres for control saw invasions that swept the infection aside. Deep tissue was targeted with more precision than the most technologically advanced smart bomb could ever hope for.

The last remaining single solitary cell was surrounded on all sides by a tidal wave of anti-bodies sent to destroy it. This host body not only removed the infection but it then immunised it from ever taking that infection back in.

The infection evolves and learns.

This body evolved and learnt too, and made sure Lani wouldn't be infected again.

Twenty Five

She glances over at Dave, he smiles back, an awkward movement that involves his lips twitching but at least he tries, and she appreciates the trying.

Lani almost forgets she was infected. The day has been relentless, utterly relentless with so much to do and organise that stopping for any period of self-reflection just hasn't been possible. But every time she turns round Dave is there, quietly watching her with those unreadable eyes.

His presence both comforts and chills her and every time she remembers to do so; she fusses Meredith. Just a pat on the head or a quick ear rub. The dog clearly enjoys the attention and looks up at her with big brown eyes and a wag of her tail.

Dave nods each time, understanding that she's constantly testing to see if the infection has become apparent to the dog. Neither of them know if the testing method is reliable but it's all they have.

Stepping into an organising role seemed natural. Lani, like the rest of the team knew what needed to be done so she got on with it.

Nick was brilliant on the GPMG and would stay up there for hours being vigilant. The other two lads were put to one of their best skills by simply talking to people and moving around while all time being as watchful as Nick.

Clarence was just Clarence, getting stuck into whatever needed doing and showing a great skill of seeing what needs to be done and doing it, but also accepting Howie's leadership without question.

As for Howie. He had to keep a step back and see everything. He, along with Maddox, needed to have a full overview of everything that had to be done.

There was also a sense of ownership and responsibility. The fort was theirs so it was only right they got it in order and made sure the new arrivals were coordinated and taken care off.

At the points when she did step back for a second, her mind filled with so many thoughts. Too many for one person to deal with or even hope to understand.

The infection inside her, the loss of so many from the fort, the hurtful thoughts of Howie with Marcy that sent a surge of anger through her, so many people turning up, Lenski and Maddox, being watched by Dave and now a new threat.

News of a massing further down the coast, constant snatches of gossip and whispers of hordes seen in the distance marching off. People waking up to find the undead that had been gathered round their house trapping them inside, were now gone.

And Howie, as soon as he heard of the gathering she saw the change in him. That ruthless demeanour that brought the darkness into his face. She knew as soon as she heard about them massing, that Howie would go after them.

And everything she said to him a few minutes ago was fact. She felt it with every bone in her body. She had *felt* him when he fought, they all did. A power that poured from him and he didn't see how they wilted in front of him, hesitating for the briefest of seconds as though unsure of what he is.

Howie was the one to fix this, if anyone could find a way he would. This wasn't blind devotion or some futile dream of placing the hopes of all the survivors onto one man. This was fact. He had to be supported and that meant she would stay by his side no matter what.

'More,' Lenski says the one word with a nod towards the end of the column. It had been growing at an alarming rate all morning and as the survivors and refugees spoke to each other so they heard and told the stories of the gathering. The new arrivals became restless and concerned, constantly asking when they would be allowed in, why they couldn't go in now and help get it ready. Who was in charge? And the amount of people that have heard of Mr Howie and Dave is staggering. The giant and the lads and even asking Lani if she had met the Chinese girl that runs with them.

Like a folk legend growing before her very eyes and it also made her realise that despite this apocalyptic event, some lines of communication had stayed open. Word of mouth, stories shared along with experiences and horrors.

The fort became an Eden, a beacon of safety and the exploits of Mr Howie and his team became wild with the re-telling. None of them knew that the dark haired man with the brooding eyes that came out every few minutes was the hero they'd all heard so much about. None of them knew the small man flanking Lani was Dave, and none of them knew Lani was bloody Thai and not Chinese.

'Fucking hell that's a big queue,' Roy states, once more showing the conflicting nature of his character as he swears like a trooper while retaining a very polite tone.

'That's a big fort,' Paula replies staring at the huge walls of the building in the distance.

'And that's a big pile of bodies,' Roy nods to the estate. Dragging her eyes away from the now teaming road ahead of the fort, clogged with vehicles, vans, cars and trucks all full to the rafters and people milling about on all sides she looks to the place Roy indicates.

Stacks of corpses, thousands upon thousands of bodies all left to rot. Her now experienced eye takes in the state of decomposition, noting that some are long dead and rotting away after days of being in the sun. Others are fresh with still bright red blood stains on skin and clothing.

'What happened here?' She asks quietly.

'No idea but looks like they got more kills than you and I put together.'

'You're not joking,' Paula comments, 'maybe they ran out of space,' she adds with a glance at the queues stacked up outside the fort.

'Quite possibly,' he replies, 'as long as we can tell them about the zombies and I can see a doctor then...'

'You still want to see a doctor?'

'Oh god yes,' he exclaims, 'I need tests and blood tests and xrays...I wonder if they have an MRI scanner here.'

'I doubt it.'

'You never know, it's got a hospital so they must have equipment.'

'Roy, it's going to be basic field treatment at the most...they won't have equipment like that.'

'I'll fucking get them their equipment if it means I get a proper diagnosis...must be hospitals around here somewhere.'

'I think we might have other priorities first Roy.'

'After that,' he says quickly, 'we'll go and kill your zombies and *then* go and find the hospitals.'

'My zombies?' She asks with a raised eyebrow.

He grins, realising what he just said, 'well, *the* zombies then...not your zombies...'

'You coming with me then?' She asks quietly.

'Course I am, I thought we'd agreed that already.'

'Oh right, okay...'

'I don't have to if you want to do it yourself...but I figured you know...you lost your car and all your gear so we need to get you some new stuff and a new set of wheels so...'

'Yeah, no that's er...thanks Roy...only if you're sure though.'

'Hey listen,' he glances at her, 'the more of those fuckers we kill...the less chance of me getting bitten so yeah, we'll sort them out, get your kit and then go for the MRI scanner.'

'If they don't already have one,' she smiles, 'aren't they really big?'

'Well yes but...'

'And they use loads of power,' she adds.

'Good point,' he nods, 'might need to get them some generators and stuff too then if they don't have enough.'

'You'd really do that? Go to all that trouble to get a scanner so you can get tested.'

'Yes,' he replies seriously.

'Okay,' she nods, 'I'll help.'

'Really?'

'Of course, you 've already helped me once and now with getting me new kit and stuff...and you know...going to kill all my zombies,' he smiles at the phrase, 'so yeah, course I'll help if er...you know...if you want help that is.'

'Look,' Roy points ahead, 'they've got soldiers,' he says at seeing Blowers and Cookey stood at the end of the line and waving them in to stop.

'Hi,' Blowers smiles and nods at Roy through the driver's window.

'Hello,' Cookey greets Paula, both of the lads scanning the people first, checking eyes then looking down for weapons, injuries or anything else that might be nasty.

'Hi, do you have an MRI scanner?' Roy blurts out.

'A what mate?' Blowers steps in closer.

'He said an MRI scanner,' Cookey says.

'What's that then?' Blowers asks.

'One of them things they have in hospitals, you lie down and go in this big tube and it scans your body...'

'Oh yeah I know...why would we have one of them?' Blowers turns back to the man.

'You got doctors here so I wondered if you had a scanner, we'll get one if not.'

'Eh?' Blowers shakes his head, squinting at Roy with a confused look.

'Hey,' Paula leans forward and smiles, 'sorry we we're just having a conversation...forget it...er so this is the fort everyone is talking about?'

'Yep,' Cookey grins, 'we can get you in shortly but you'll have to hang on here for a bit...have you got any weapons...oh yeah you do...that's an MP5 oh you got a pistol too.'

'Got them from a policeman,' Paula explains.

'Nice one,' Cookey grins, 'you got any more in the back?'

'Shotguns, bows and arrows...no rifles or handguns though.'

'Have you been bitten? Scratched? Got broken skin with any risk of the things getting fluid on you?' Blowers starts asking, they both shake their heads, 'had much contact with them?'

'Could say that,' Paula smiles, 'listen have you heard about them gathering and...'

'Yeah everyone is talking about it,' Cookey replies, 'off to the east... have you seen them then?'

'I tracked them to a town, then saw them moving out this morning...they're heading this way now.'

'Fuck...really?' Blowers asks, 'they're already moving...how far away are they?' He looks back to the estate.

'Thirty, maybe forty miles back from us,' Roy answers, 'they're on foot marching so...'

'And you saw them?' Cookey asks seriously.

'Yes, thousands....never seen so many,' Paula replies.

'We got to tell Mr Howie, can you wait here for a minute?' Cookey asks.

'No they should come up with us so the boss doesn't have to walk down here...' Blowers says through the window to Cookey stood the other side.

'Good point,' Cookey grins, 'still a fucktard though,' he adds quickly, 'can you follow us please?'

'Er now?' Paula asks, slightly baffled at the quick insult thrown across them.

'Yeah please, we need to tell them what you said, they'll have questions and...'

'Them? Who is them?' Paula asks, 'and who is this Mr Howie?'

'He's in charge,' Blowers replies, both Paula and Roy switching their gaze from Cookey to Blowers.

'Is the hospital full?' Roy asks stepping out of the van.

'Er...no,' Blowers replies slowly, 'it's er...well it's empty right now.'

'Oh that's good,' Roy nods at the good news and the prospect of having a bed when they see just how serious his condition is, 'so the doctors aren't too busy either then I take it?'

'Well er...you could say that,' Blowers replies with a quick glance at Cookey who shrugs at the sight of the two shotgun butts poking out the top of the rucksack he pulls on.

'We thought it was full up with all these people out here,' Paula remarks as they walk down the side of the waiting vehicles, earning glances from the other survivors at the heavily armed black clad figures walking with the soldiers.

'No, empty at the moment,' Cookey explains, 'we were out yesterday getting fuel and someone left a gate open...the things got in and er...well they got everyone,' he says sticking the agreed account to be given.

'Left a fucking gate open?' Roy asks appalled, 'who leaves a gate open? That's just bloody stupid...how many got turned?'

'Everyone,' Blowers replies.

'Well that was bloody stupid,' Roy tuts, 'so where are they now?'

'Dead,' Blowers gives the one word answer.

'Did you kill them?' Paula asks softly, noticing the incredibly rude way Roy speaks to them.

'Yes,' Blowers says with a hard look on his face.

'Good for you but still a stupid thing to do,' Roy tuts audibly, 'bloody idiots leaving a gate open...'

'They were our friends,' Cookey says quietly.

'So shut the fuck up,' Blowers mutters.

'Well I was just saying,' Roy rolls his eyes as Paula looks at him aghast. She plucks at his sleeve, shaking her head and glaring at him as looks over.

'What?' He mouths.

'Shut up,' she mouths back.

'I'd do as she says mate,' Cookey adds on seeing the exchange.

'Hang on...so the doctors got turned too?' Roy asks with a fresh look of fear as Paula rolls her eyes.

'Everyone,' Blowers replies.

'No doctors?'

'No.'

'We got a nurse now,' Cookey says.

'A nurse? You got a nurse?' Roy starts to sneer then turns to see Paula holding a finger to her lips with a distinctly threatening look on her face.

'Lani,' Blowers calls ahead as they approach the front of the queue, she looks up and quickly takes in the two new arrivals. 'These two just arrived, we need to speak to Mr Howie, they got some information he needs to hear.'

'Okay, wait here...I'll get him.'

'I think we're ready mate,' I say to Maddox as we walk through the fort. The ground is still stained in places but it's been well soaked with disinfectant and almost dry from the incredible heat. The fort looks a different place now with the tents and bodies gone, the blood and gore cleaned away. Agnes gathering all the brooms and cleaning equipment to stack them neatly into a room next to the stores.

He nods as he scans the ground, then over at Darius and Sierra watching the line of youths carrying their supplies in from their vehicles. Tents already going up as the crews work quickly.

'We are,' he replies eventually, satisfied that nothing else needs doing before we can open up.

'Howie and Maddox can you come to the front,' Lani's voice comes through the radio.

'Coming, is it urgent?'

'No you don't need to run.'

'Good, it's too bloody hot for running.'

'What now?' Maddox sighs, 'I'm starting to think we shoulda stayed in our compound.'

'Fuck that mate, you stay here and we'll have it...Get some peace and quiet, you alright?' I shout over to Clarence and Dave walking amongst a group of kids holding assault rifles. The big man gives a thumbs up and I wonder at the slippage in morals as he trains child soldiers to do the work men should be doing.

'Don't worry about them,' Maddox says, picking on my concern, 'don't be fooled by how they look, everyone one of them will kill without hesitating...they ain't like normal kids.'

'They can't be that hard...not all kids from tough estates are like that.'

'They ain't all the kids,' he replies quickly, 'the estate was full of kids...these are the ones that didn't have anything else...no family, no homes...parents on drugs or prison or dead...or just fucked off somewhere else.'

'That bad?'

'Worse,' he stares at me, 'they didn't have nothing before this...what we got now is more of a family than any of them have ever known...they don't play with toys or run about playing fucking kiss chase...they grew up fightin' and stealing' just to survive.'

'Mr Howie,' Lani calls out as we step outside. Two new people, one male and one female. The woman holding a black machine gun with a pistol on her belt, dressed in black combat trousers and a black vest and she looks hard.

The man is dressed similar but in a long sleeve skin tight black wicking top, he looks fit and healthy with a rucksack on his back and the stocks of two sawn off shotguns poking up.

'Hi,' I nod across.

'Mr Howie, this is Paula and Roy, they just arrived,' Lani says.

We shake hands and nod greetings, both of them staring at me with interest and I guess they must be like the others and have heard stupid things.

'This is Maddox, he's in charge here with me,' I make the introduction, sensing Lani was unsure of what to say.

'They're on the move,' Lani says quickly, 'Paula said she saw them, where they were massing and saw them moving out this morning...coming this way.'

'Right,' I nod, 'we need to talk, come inside...Blowers and Cookey, you hold here and don't let anyone in until the crews have unloaded.'

'Got it,' Blowers nods

I turn and lead the group through the inner gate to the front of the medical tent, nodding at a line of youths passing objects to each other.

'You have to get checked before we go in, leave your weapons here...Frank!' I shout out, he comes out and spots the two new people nodding with a quick thumbs up.

'Send 'em in, we're all set.'

'Why do we have to give our weapons up?' Asks Paula,

'Is that the nurse? Are you the nurse?' Roy shouts as Frank disappears.

'I am mate,' Frank shouts out. Roy ditches his rucksack on the ground and without a further glance walks into the tent leaving Paula stood there shaking her head.

'Is he alright?' I ask at the strange behaviour.

'Only met him a little while ago...' she checks to make sure he's gone inside, 'I think he's a hypochondriac, keeps going on about tumours and lumps.'

'Bloody hell, is he stable?'

'Seems so,' she says quietly, 'I got trapped and he saved me with a bow and arrows, he was really far away and firing arrows...getting bloody head shots and they were running flat out.'

'No way,' I look at her with interest.

'Seriously,' she nods, 'never seen anything like it...incredible, as soon as we got away he starts asking me to check his back and finger...but,' she adds firmly, 'he seems fine, hasn't been threatening or anything.'

'Your weapons will be here, no one will touch them. Or you can wait for Roy to come out, up to you,' Lani cuts in.

'No I'll go now, something tells me he'll be a while,' she passes the black machine gun to Lani before pulling the pistol clear of the holster and passing that across too.'

'They're police issue,' Maddox comments, 'are you a police officer?'

'Accountant,' she replies, 'through here?'

'I'll take you,' Lani leads her to the tent.

'What did they say?' Maddox asks Lenski while we wait.

'They say there is town on the coast, it er...it is...'

'Isolated,' Lani provides the word as she walks out.

'Yes they use this word, the town is isolated and the things they go there...now they come here, but the man he say they er...thirty or the forty kilometres away.'

'Miles,' Lani corrects.

'Miles,' Lenski smiles.

'Did they say how many?' Maddox asks.

'Thousands and the woman, she say they all march like in the army...'

Pursing my lips I wait quietly, wishing Nick was here to hand his smokes around, then remembering Blowers and Cookey are only a few metres away and will have some.

'Be right back,' I jog off towards the gate, 'one of you got a smoke?' I ask the two lads stood there.

'Here take my packet,' Cookey offers a full pack over.

'Just one mate or I'll smoke the lot...er...you got a light?'

'Here boss,' Blowers pulls his from a pocket, 'how long we got?'

'Don't know yet, not long though...we're ready to get everyone in but I think we'll be on the road before they all get settled.'

'Can't wait,' Blowers grins.

'Seriously?' I ask him.

'Seriously,' he replies.

'Me too,' Cookey nods.

'I'll keep you updated, you alright out here?'

'No worries,' Blowers nods.

'Could murder a coffee though,' Cookey adds with a grin.

'Leave it with me, I'll get one up to Nick too.'

Going back inside I ask Lenski to ask a youth to ask Agnes to see if she can get some brews on the go. Which is just stupid but we're all still treading on eggshells around each other and not wanting to breach etiquette.

'Mr Howie?' A woman steps out of the medical tent, middle aged and serious looking, 'I'm Frank's wife, er...this lady is all clear, no bites or marks, no broken skin...she seems fine.'

'That's great, thank you very much,' I smile as Paula steps out, noticing as she looks straight to Lani and her weapons before anything else.

'Safe and sound,' Lani hands them over.

'You got a spare one?' Paula nods at my smoke as she pushes the pistol in, 'I lost mine.'

'Ask the lads outside,' I reply feeling a bit guilty.

'You don't look like a smoker,' Lani remarks.

'Only one or two a day, I stopped for years but...stuff it,' she smiles.

'You should stop too,' Lani looks at me.

'Tomorrow,' I reply automatically.

'Really?' She asks.

'Probably not,' I shrug.

'Roy still in there?' Paula asks coming back with a lit cigarette.

'Er...yeah he is,' Lani replies.

'Roy?' Paula calls out.

'Yeah, you alright?' A muffled shout comes from inside the tent.

'You coming?'

'Yeah just getting checked.'

'Roy, we need to get moving.'

'I know...I'm getting checked.'

'What are you getting checked?'

'Er...you know...for bites and things.'

'He hasn't got any bites,' Frank shouts.

'Roy, your back is fine...and your finger...and your mouth,' Paula calls out but with a surprisingly gentle tone.

'Okay,' he replies dully, 'coming.' He appears a minute later looking a bit sheepish, 'sorry, just thought I'd ask.'

'That's okay, did he check them?' He nods back, staring at her like a puppy, 'everything okay?' She asks with what appears to be genuine concern.

'Fine,' he nods.

'Good, we will find some doctors Roy, I promise but we need to tell these people what we've seen.'

'Yep, fucking right,' he nods making us all start at the sudden swear word he throws out.

'Good,' Paula smiles at me.

'Er…right…follow me,' I turn and see Maddox looking at me with strange expression, and quite possibly regretting ever coming here.

In the police office we find Agnes with the women she brought in, the gas stove heating two pans of water with a row of mugs all lined up. Clarence joins us as we pass him by, leaving the youths to grab a drink and a promise not to shoot anyone.

'Need the office do you?' Agnes beams, 'we'll be right out of your way, go on sit down and start your meeting, just pretend we're not here, everyone having coffee? Good cos that's what we're making…did you two have any food?' She glares at Maddox and me with a sudden intense look.

'Er…'

'Don't be erring me,' she tuts, 'I said you should get some food and you promised me…right after your meeting I expect to see you next door in my stores…got it?'

'Yes Nana….er…Agnes,' Maddox says with a brief look of horror as everyone stares at him, 'she reminds me of my grandmother,' he adds to the ensuing silence.

'You can Nana me all you like,' Agnes beams. She organises the brow beaten women into carrying trays of coffee out, leaving a load of freshly brewed mugs on the side, 'after the meeting you two…'she points at both of us.

'We will,' I reply and wait for her to leave before adding 'Nana' quietly.

'Fuck off,' Maddox shakes his head with a grin.

'Nana?' Lenski asks.

'She's just like her,' he shrugs.

We sit down and listen intently as Paula and Roy give their accounts, separately at first as they both explain who they are and how they survived. Then Paula explains how she tracked the zombies to the town and saw them moving out, getting trapped and saved by Roy and the final drive here, noticing the hordes waiting on the coastal road on the way in.

'Tens of thousands?' I clarify when she finishes.

'At least,' she replies, 'I was on the hills above the town and it was completely full...every main road...every street...it was like a festival or something.'

'And marching like that,' Lani adds, 'that's just creepy.'

'Telling me,' Paula replies, 'in perfect timing with you know...perfect space between them.'

'Organised then, must be a strong leader,' I look at Dave.

'Military training too by the sounds of it,' he replies.

'Or the infection has learnt some new tricks,' I add.

'Did you know they can speak?' Paula asks.

'Yes, and they like kissing too apparently,' Lani mutters.

'Kissing?'

'Don't ask,' Lani waves it away, 'but yeah we've met speakers, talkers, biters, growlers, crawlers, gnashers, suckers and complete arseholes along our way.'

'Did you do all those bodies in that area?' Roy asks.

'Yeah that was us,' I reply with a sudden image of Sarah, Chris and everyone else being amongst them, 'the plan was to burn them later but...'

'We've been saying that for days,' Clarence mutters.

'Right, we're going after them...'

'What?' Paula leans forward, 'you're going after them?'

'Yes we are, this isn't going to stop until we finish it...so we finish it,' I add with a shrug.

'Um, forgive me intruding but you're convinced they are coming here then?' Roy asks, 'I mean of course it seems the obvious thing but there couldn't be something else they are after maybe?'

'No, no doubt about it...' I start to reply.

'They want us,' Clarence cuts in, 'or more specifically you,' he turns to me.

'Get off,' I scoff, 'don't you bloody start that shit too.'

'Why you?' Maddox asks.

'Long story.'

'Another one? You haven't told us the first one yet,' he says to me with a fixed look.

'Let's just say that the boss has a special way about him when we're fighting,' Clarence says.

'No let's not just say that, let's just say nothing and get on with it.'

'Cards on the table here,' Maddox snaps, 'we agreed, whether they're coming for you or us...or whoever the fuck...they are coming and that means it's all our fucking business.'

'Good point,' I concede.

'I don't care if you think it's a good point or not, you are holding back on us...if you won't speak in front of these people then they can fuck off and you can tell me straight,' he flares up, his eyes fixed directly on me.

'Hey,' Paula protests.

'The most important thing is that we tackle them and cut them down before they get here...we take as many weapons and as much ammunition as we can carry and destroy them,' I lean in, emphasising my point, 'so who fucking said what to who...whatever has fucking happened before now doesn't fucking matter...what matters is we kill them.'

'Don't fucking tell me what's important to know, I am not a child,' Maddox spits, 'I lead my group and make the decisions for them...that means I want the information before I make the fucking decision.'

'Wow you guys swear a lot, you need to calm down,' Roy tuts, 'have none of heard about blood pressure?'

'Fucking what?' Maddox glares across at him.

'I heard enough of this,' Lenski cuts through with her icy voice, 'we go and kill them yes we do this...this must be done...Maddox you will go and help, I will stay here and run this fort while you are gone yes?'

'Maddox could stay here, the fort will need a strong leader,' I reply.

'Mr Howie I am the strong leader,' she cuts me down, 'I am capable of this...Maddox he is hard like you and if you have so many then you need the hard people. I do not know fighting so I don't do this...but I do what I know so I run this place...these people,' she motions to Paula and Roy, 'they kill many of the things...the woman she kill thousands so you take her and the man too...he kill many...you not go alone to this,' she looks at me, 'you take the people that know the fighting and together you kill them yes?'

Silence descends for a minute as we all stare at each other, Maddox eyeing me warily, Paula and Roy looking between us all.

Instinct tells me to open up and do as Maddox says by laying the cards on the table. Let everyone know what we're dealing with and the risks involved. We don't know Paula or Roy, shit we don't know Maddox really. But we're all that's here and sometimes you just have to go with your gut. So I do and with a nod from Lani and another one from Clarence I spill the beans and tell them everything.

It takes time but something happens during that time. Something I become more aware off as I talk. Paula and Roy opened up and told us who they are and what they've done before coming here. How both of them stayed overnight in country locations before going back into their towns to slowly cull the undead.

Maddox too, he came here and had the strength to realise he needed greater security and that we could offer that.

By sharing, by opening up and telling them everything we know, about Darren and Marcy, about the pheromones and how we think they got inside the fort...then about Meredith and eventually about Lani, by doing that we create a feeling of closeness. Hardened people experienced at survival who haven't just hid or run away but who fought back and clawed something for themselves.

As I finish I can feel the change in the air, the way they nod and listen. The intelligent questions they ask to clarify points and what's more, despite having Meredith and Lani they also understand the need to take them out. That until that is done we will never be safe.

We could be running in the other direction with what we've got and hoping to find a doctor or scientist along the way, but then we'd always be running. They seem intent on destroying us. So we need to destroy them first.

When I finish talking they drop into silence, absorbed in their own thoughts for long seconds. Paula takes a breath and leans forward, the first to break the silence.

'On the way here we passed through another town, the coastal road goes through the town centre...that is a perfect ambush site.'

'We both said it,' Roy agrees.

'Old town with big buildings on both sides, we could bottleneck them...slow them down and start reducing the numbers as we fall back.'

'We've got the two heavy machine guns and enough assault rifles to go round,' Clarence adds, 'and if we get to the party early enough we could get the food and drinks ready.'

'I not understand this,' Lenski cuts in.

'Sorry,' Clarence says, 'I meant we get there early and start getting traps set up.'

'Oh...oh yes like the party with the food and the drink...yes I understand this now.'

'Okay, we go for that town you said about...we set up and get ready...Maddox, how many can you bring?'

'I can bring all of them but that leaves this place unprotected...We'll leave Darius and Sierra here with Lenski and I'll take twenty...'

'Paula, Roy, are you both coming?'

'Yes,' Paula nods quickly, Roy does the same.

'I make that er...twenty nine and a dog against what...tens of thousands...maybe more? Good odds.'

'Fuck it, we'll win,' Clarence and Lani say at the same time, 'besides...we got Dave,' Lani adds.

'True, Dave could stand there with a Swiss army knife and probably hold them back,' I grin over at the poker faced man who just stares back without expression.

'Swiss army knives have folding blades; can I use a different knife?' He asks with a sudden glint in his eye.

'We need to do this now...Lenski, are you okay here if we move out?' I ask.

'Yes,' she answers bluntly.

'Good, get ready then...we go as soon as possible.'

Twenty Six

'This is Clarence in the Saxon, radio check to Paula and Roy.'

'Er yeah hi.'

'Hi Paula, are you receiving me loud and clear?'

'Yep, er...loud and clear...I've always wanted to say that, do I say over and out too?'

'Only if you want, we are receiving you loud and clear also.'

'Roger roger affirmative over and out.'

'Thanks Paula, Saxon to Maddox.'

'Yeah loud and clear.'

'Likewise Maddox, we are the lead vehicle in the Saxon, Paula and Roy in vehicle number two and Maddox you are the follow vehicle. If we get contact on route do not get out of the vehicles as we will be using the big machine gun on the top of our vehicle, copy?'

'What does copy mean?'

'It means do you understand Paula.'

'Oh...er...copy that roger and over and out.'

'We heard you too Clarence.'

'Cheers Maddox.'

'What the fuck are we getting ourselves into?' Clarence mutters as he lowers the radio.

'A great big fucking scrap!' Cookey yells excitedly, 'we're on the road...we're on the road...and we're gonna fuck some zombies up,' he starts singing in a painfully bad tune.

'You're happy,' Lani laughs.

'I am,' he laughs, 'I am I am, you're here and Meredith and Dave has got sharp knives and Clarence has been pumping his arms up and Mr Howie has got his big axe all shiny and sharp and Nick is on the GPMG and you got a big meat cleaver and Blowers is gay.'

'Dick,' Blowers laughs.

'You like dick,' Cookey responds quickly.

'Oh no,' Lani groans, 'not this again...I should have stayed a zombie.'

'Nah,' Cookey says, 'you missed us...didn't you Lani...didn't you Lani...Lani...didn't you Lani...Lani...'

'Yes! Alright...I missed you.'

'Ha, she missed us like Blowers misses cock.'

'Fucking hell,' Clarence mumbles, 'is it too late to stay here?'

'Afraid so,' I laugh, not even out of the flatlands yet and already Cookey is supercharged up.

'We're gonna drive at them and like tell them we got Lani and she's fucking immune so you can all fuck off...and our dog is immune...and Dave has big knives and Clarence will throw cars at you and Mr Howie will do that thing that Mr Howie does when he goes all quiet and they shit themselves and if all that fails we'll send Blowers out with a tub of KY jelly and a big bumper box of condoms so he can bum them to death.'

'Or we could just give you more red bull so you can bore them senseless so they bleed to death from their ears screaming in agony *make him stop...please make him stop,'* Blowers says.

'That's what they say to you when you're bumming them, *please make him stop...my bum hurts...'*

'You have got to stop making gay jokes,' I laugh back, 'how do you know one of us isn't gay and getting offended or hurt?'

'But one of us is,' Cookey laughs.

'Yeah you,' Nick shouts down.

'Not me...ask April...she knows I'm all man, well she did until Dave cut her...'

'I didn't cut her head off,' Dave says flatly.

'Mr Howie isn't coz he fancies Lani, Lani isn't cos she fancies Mr Howie, Clarence isn't... so that leaves Nick and Blowers.'

'Or me,' Dave says.

'Or I could be bisexual,' Lani adds.

Silence for a few seconds, 'I'm not. So stop dreaming you perverts,' she sighs.

'Moving on,' I say after a few more seconds of pointed silence, 'Dave, what do we need to set some big ass traps?'

'Depends.'

'On what?'

'On what traps you want? Sharp, deadly, explosive, to cause injury or death or mutilation.'

'Sharp wouldn't do it, would it?' I ask, 'tens of thousands so we can't just throw sharp sticks at them.'

'Explosives and fire are best options.'

'Should we have brought the fuel tanker then?'

'That's a good idea,' Clarence exclaims.

Twenty Seven

'Clarence to Mr Howie, radio check?'

'Howie to Clarence, loud and clear.'

'Clarence to Paula and Roy, radio check?'

'Roger roger rubber ducky affirmative over and out.'

'Thanks Paula...Clarence to Maddox?'

'Loud and clear...again.'

'Yeah sorry, we forgot the tanker.'

'How can you forget a fuel tanker?'

'Thanks Paula, busy day...Saxon is lead vehicle, Paula and Roy are second, tanker is third and Maddox you are in the follow, Clarence out...oh and Nick...if we get contact don't for fucks sake, shoot at the tanker.'

'I won't.'

'Actually, get Dave on the GPMG.'

'He's worse at blowing things up, look what happened at the refinery.'

'Good point Mr Howie...no one on the GPMG then...just run them over.'

'Roger that.'

'We're on the road...we're on the road...and we're gonna fuck some zombies up...'

'No Cookey, not again,' Lani groans.

'You missed us didn't you Lani...didn't you Lani...Lani...didn't you Lani...Lani...'

'Go up the front, go and sit up the front with the boss,' she urges.

'No,' I shout back, 'Dave's here and we're having a serious discussion.'

'Are we?' He asks.

'We are.'

'Ah, I feel unloved, unwanted...uncared for...'

'We all love you Cookey,' Lani laughs.

'I don't,' Blowers adds.

'You do but not in the right way,' Cookey says suspiciously.

'I love you Cookey,' Nick shouts down.

'Thanks Nick,' Cookey shouts back.

'Me too Cookey,' I call out.

'Thanks boss...April loved me...until Dave cut...'

'I didn't...and if you say it again you'll be making the brews for the next month.'

'He's already making them for the next month isn't he?' Lani asks.

'Then the month after that too...all the months,' Dave says, 'Alex...'

'Yes Dave?'

'Quiet time now Alex.'

'Yes Dave.'

'Thank you.'

'Ha you got Dave'd,' Blowers laughs.

'Dave'd?' Lani asks with a giggle.

'Dave said quiet time,' Cookey says seriously.

'Yeah for you not the rest of us,' Blowers replies.

'That's fine, I shall sit here quietly and dream of my one true love.'

'She was a zombie,' Lani says with pained patience.

'But my zombie,' he sighs theatrically, 'does this mean you can't snog Mr Howie again?'

'Cookey!' Blowers snorts.

'Alex!' Dave turns quickly as Lani bursts out laughing.

'How do you know we sno...kissed anyway?' I shout.

'At the medical tent before we got the dog...we all knew,' Cookey replies.

'Oh...right...'

'No secrets here,' Lani states.

'So?' Cookey prompts.

'Alex!' Dave adopts his warning tone.

'Sorry Dave, I was just asking.'

'Mr Howie kissing Lani is none of our concern,' Dave says primly.

'Sorry Dave.'

'If they choose to kiss then I am sure they will take the appropriate precautions,' Dave continues.

'Eh?' Nick shouts down, 'what like putting condoms on their tongues?'

'Nick!' Dave warns.

'Can we try that?' I laugh.

'You'll be bloody lucky,' Lani says.

'You can get flavoured ones,' Cookey suggests.

'How do you know?' Blowers asks.

'I've seen them.'

'You ever used one?'

'What a flavoured condom? Not really but there was this one time when...'

'Alex,' Dave says again.

'Sorry Dave.'

I zone out to the background chat with a growing sense of déjà vu. How many times have we been here now? Driving in this hot tin can racing to put our lives in danger and face an enemy of overwhelming numbers.

And it is hot. Hotter than I have ever known it. The words *sticky* and *close* don't come into it. Drinking water constantly trying to stay hydrated and my forehead is already tender from constantly wiping the sweat away. Clothes clinging to my body, my feet are baking in the heavy boots and every breath I take is like standing in front of an oven with the door open.

We did agree we wouldn't take anyone else into our team, but the justification is that they're not really in *our* team. They're just going with us to do something that has to be done.

Thoughts about Lani race through my mind, how great it is to have her with us, with me. Like a comfort blanket. Just having her close gives me a sense of security. It's stupid but something about her makes me feel safe, the way she said none of that would have happened last night if she had been there, and the way she has taken control today by stepping forward to organise and get things done.

A feeling like it's fate that took us into that bowling alley that day and found her, that everything after that was pre-ordained and scheduled in a little black book somewhere. We had to fall, to suffer that closeness of death in order for Lani to find out she was immune. That's the other thing, I believe more and more that she is immune. Like an instinct or something, maybe a tangible notion that has buried deep and is now flourishing, demanding to be paid attention. Not a trick. Not another plan or devious intention but that she is genuinely immune. I don't know how I know this, but I know I'm not the only one that feels it.

Our group is close. The bond between us is immense now, we can read each other with a single glance and sense the mood, the feelings, the needs wants and desires of each other.

But then if Lani really is immune, then what the hell are we doing taking her towards possibly the biggest army we've seen yet? Mind you, we've already tried telling her not to come, not that it did any good and with such limited numbers we do need every skilled fighter we've got.

I noticed that Maddox selected the older and bigger youths and I'm sure most of them were the crew chiefs. Clarence told me they were proficient with firing and re-loading the assault rifles and already had a thorough understanding about not pointing the weapons at each other.

Paula already had a police issue single shot machine gun but Dave said it was small calibre pistol size ammunition so she and Roy were both given assault rifles and magazines too.

'The town I was thinking of is just up ahead,' Paula speaks through the radio,

'Okay, we'll keep going for now until we find the front so we know what time and distance we've got...everyone pay attention to the town in case we come back to use it.'

Pushing the radio away I watch ahead as we get into residential roads with big expensive houses on both sides. The road sweeps downhill to a long gentle bend and filters naturally into the High Street with a big dirty multi-level car park marking the transition from residential to town. A huge grey monstrosity built in the seventies with exhaust fume stained walls and one of those twisty access roads that loops round and round, with a ramp giving entry to each level and an open top floor.

The road goes straight through the middle of the town, with huge sprawling hotel buildings on the seaward side and high Victorian shops with apartments above them on the other. Very few side street and the only way out of the main road is through the buildings.

Other than the contrasting shitty multi-level car park, the town looks affluent and well cared for with freshly painted shop fronts and chain brand stores. The usual bodies and debris litter the streets, smashed in windows and cars left abandoned but this would have been a nice place to live.

The main road through is long, a lot longer than I anticipated. After the last solid hotel there is just shore line down to the golden beach and the blue water lapping gently. The other side gives out to pitch and putt play area's and open land with sculpted gardens.

It looks lovely and serene, almost perfect. I say almost perfect because the view is somewhat ruined by the horde sprawled across the road. A thick crowd just stood in the sun obviously waiting for their brethren to sweep through.

'Nick,' I shout up.

'Yes Mr Howie.'

'Clear a path please mate, get as many as possible but don't shoot the bloody tanker.'

'Will do.'

'Saxon to the follow vehicles, we've got a large contact ahead...firing will commence shortly,' Dave relays to the others as I bring the speed down to give Nick more time.

The firing does indeed commence and we watch as the horde gets ripped to pieces, and as soon as the first bodies start to fall they turn and charge with unabated fury. A seething mass of human forms charging across the sun baked road. Nick sweeps the fire across the front, mowing them down with easy strafes.

Bringing the Saxon to a stop we all watch through the windscreen as they continue to surge towards us, the heavy constant thudding sound right above our heads and small movements of Nick's feet as he turns slowly left and right.

Fortunately I judged the distance about right, giving Nick enough time to slaughter them down before they reach us. It's done within minutes as the road becomes thick with mangled bodies lying ruined and destroyed.

'Not exactly a clear path there Nick,' Blowers shouts up as we start driving over the first bodies, the huge heavy wheels squashing them into the road.

'They were running for fuck's sake,' Nick shouts down, 'Dave can I smoke up here please?'

'Yes Nick.'

'Oh that's not fair…' Cookey starts to bleat.

'Open the back doors and have one then,' I shout back.

'Really?' Blowers asks, 'is that alright?'

'It's hot as hell in here mate, might get some air flow too.'

'Nick,' Lani shouts up, 'have you put sun cream on, you'll burn in this heat.'

'I put that factor fifty on you gave me.'

'How long ago?'

'Er…few hours I think.'

'Put some more on then, it burns off.' He drops down as Lani fishes a bottle out of her bag and tells him to sit down so she can rub it into his face and ears.

'Aw is iccle Nick getting his creamy put on,' Cookey jokes.

'I am,' Nick laughs.

'Don't take the piss you two are next.'

'Ah no I don't want any,' Cookey groans.
'Stop being a child and sit down for a minute.'
'Yes Lani.'

Twenty Eight

'What the hell are they doing?' Paula leans forward, closer to the windscreen to watch the back of the Saxon.

'Er, that young lady is putting sun cream on the boys by the looks of it, very sensible,' Roy replies.

'Look at the bodies Roy. It only took them a couple of minutes with one gun...will the van go over them?'

'If I follow their vehicle it should be okay. They're laughing and joking, look at that cheeky one waving at us.'

'Yeah,' Paula waves her hand briefly, 'strange people.'

'Stranger than us?' He asks with a snort of laughter.

'Well, maybe not,' she replies. *Us.* What made him say that? But she sensed the way everyone else in that room responded to them, like a given that they were a unit of their own. Howie's team, Maddox and his team then Paula and Roy. Even when they said how they just met a few hours ago they still assumed that they were one unit.

The strange thing was that Paula didn't mind that assumption. There was something *nice* about being seen as a team. Roy, with his amazing ability with the bow and her ability to plan, prepare and use the ground to cut them down, it was nice and what's more it gave them strength against the larger already established teams.

Paula had watched the people as they spoke during the meeting, how they interacted with each other. Strong men and strong women, all of them with a voice that was both listened to and respected.

Lenski and Lani, despite both being young and extremely attractive women were treated with the same regard as the men, and when Lenski stepped in to end the argument between Maddox and Howie she was deferred to as she obviously knew what she was doing.

What was more amazing was that she even said she wasn't a fighter but she was a strong leader and didn't hesitate to show her confidence at staying to run the fort.

A young Polish female immigrant running one of the last bastions of human society and not one of them balked, blanched, rolled their eyes or made any negative comments.

Howie and Maddox were true leaders, both possessing that intensity that made them easy to watch and although they were young, she found herself hanging of what they said. The electric charge that rippled through the room as they started arguing was tangible to say the least. Maddox was strong and proud, clearly very intelligent too but Howie was the one to watch. He possessed a power that oozed out of his very soul. Quiet and unassuming, polite and joking around and similar to Roy with his polite countenance, but when he flashed that dark look it made everyone sit up and take notice. That, right there was why he was the natural leader.

The incident with Clarke had left a deep distrust for other people, that all men would eventually try and do what he did. If it wasn't offered it would be taken. Without the protection of laws and consequences men would just revert to the Neanderthal pricks they really were. So she had shunned any company other than her own. Roy was different as he was so pre-occupied with his own concerns she doubts he had even contemplated anything of a sexual nature.

The three young lads with Howie had given her a quick appraisal with eyes running over her body but again they didn't linger on her chest or show anything other than youthful charm and respect.

It was those reasons and many, many more that compelled Paula to work with them, that and the prospect of getting an absurdly high number of kills too.

Roy watched the back of the Saxon and the road, carefully negotiating the van to steer over the squashed bodies to avoid getting the wheels stuck.

Howie and Maddox seemed nice, intense but very polite. The young lads were cheeky but funny, despite the way one of them had told him to *shut the fuck up*. But then Roy was used to that, he knew there was something about him that sometimes annoyed other people, and he also knew when his mouth was getting him into trouble but the connection between the voice in his brain yelling at him to shut up, and the words still coming out of his mouth was broken somewhere.

Oh well. The sooner they get this done the sooner they get on and find some doctors. Probing his gums with his tongue and they felt irritated and swollen. Must be something bad. Had to be something bad.

Health anxiety held his focus, not the coming fight or the tens of thousands of zombies marching at them, not Howie or Maddox, not that giant of a man with the bald head or the small one with the eyes of a killer.

Just his mouth. That's what worried him.

Maddox gripped the wheel, staring at the symbols on the back of the fuel tanker, the letters and numbers that were used for the hazardous chemicals recognition.

His team of twenty had been carefully selected, and Howie was right. Most of the crew chiefs had been taken aside and told to choose a number two that would step up as they were all being taken for a mission.

The details were outlined and explained, how a huge army was coming at them and they were going with Howie 's team and two others to cut them down. It was also made clear that none of them were ordered to come, that he wanted volunteers only. Every single one of them stepped forward and together they picked out a few more of the older reliable youths.

They were shown how to use the assault rifles and then each given their own gun with spare magazines which they each held proudly.

Leaving Lenski was hard, and convincing Darius he had to stay behind was even harder. The other youth refusing to listen and demanding to be taken with them. Eventually he reluctantly backed down and agreed to stay behind and get everyone safely inside.

When he thought about it rationally, it seemed completely stupid that they were doing this. Why risk himself and his own people for someone else's fight. But he also knew those tens of thousands wouldn't just stop at the fort, they would have reached the compound and wiped them out too. If they wanted to survive and have a life they had to deal with the threat.

And as much as he mistrusted anyone that wasn't of his own kind from the same background as him, he knew, just knew that Howie was the one to lead them.

Twenty Nine

'Paula to Howie.'

'Yeah go ahead Paula.'

'They can't be that far in front of us now, there's a junction up ahead if we take that we will go onto higher ground and should be able to look down on them.'

'Howie to Paula, got it...yep we see the junction.'

'How far from that town now?' Dave asks.

'Er...just coming up to twenty two miles mate,' I reply.

'Good, that gives us a few hours.'

'You sure it's four miles an hour?' I ask again.

'Definitely, average marching speed to allow the troops to be fresh enough to fight at the end.'

'But these aren't regular troops Dave, they're fucking zombies.'

'They are Mr Howie, but they've also learnt that they get weaker if they are pushed too hard and fast. If the infection has learnt anything it has learnt the balance between moving fast and retaining energy.'

'You're talking like it's a thing mate, like a real er...well entity or something.'

'I think it is.'

'Really?'

'Know your enemy, study them and see who are they, what are their strengths and weaknesses, what advantages can be leveraged.'

'I get that mate but thinking of the infection as an entity with like a conscience or something...I dunno, just seems a bit too much.'

'Not a conscience as that would suggest compassion in the human sense. Not a living entity like you or me but a super organism, like Ants or a beehive, a collective intelligence with a collective consciousness.'

'I find that hard to believe.'

'No offence Mr Howie, but I don't have the restrictions of thought you have. Normal living and the experiences you have had do not apply to me. I kill without compassion or mercy, I do not suffer from moral guilt the way you do, so recognising what this enemy is isn't that hard for me to understand and accept.'

'Maybe.'

'They have evolved.'

'They have,' I agree, 'or changed might be another way of saying it.'

'No, evolved,' he says firmly, 'they learnt to speak and alter the way they do things. The infection can control vast numbers of beings with perfect harmony, which is why Paula is saying they are marching in order. Armies have spent thousands of years learning to do that so the infection is simply taking what we know and using it to its advantage.'

'If you're right then they are getting smarter and stronger.'

'Not they Mr Howie, *it.*'

'So if *it* is getting smarter then we could be in for a bashing today.'

'No.'

'No? Why not? You just said it is getting smarter and stronger.'

'You said that and even if it is getting smarter and stronger we still have the advantage.'

'How? There's what thirty of us against fuck knows how many of them? We probably don't have enough ammunition...'

'We can think individually, that's the one thing *it* cannot do. By keeping a collective conscious and controlling every single one of them it does not allow them to operate as individuals. Soldiers need discipline and training, but the best armies are made up of soldiers that can think and react as they see fit...communist armies have great numbers but just do what they are told and are not allowed to think for themselves, which is great while the General is on the ground, but take him out and they cannot function.

'They attack us with increasing violence and aggression, stronger with more rage but rage makes you unbalanced. Harnessed anger makes you deadly, but uncontrolled rage makes you an idiot. We use that against them. They work as one unit. We use that against them. Even if they split their forces and attack on multiple fronts we can still use their lack of reaction against them. They are predictable. We use that against them. They are many. We use that against them.

'For every strength they have we manipulate and turn it into our advantage. Paula took a whole town out by using the single most powerful strategy ever possessed.'

'Which is?'

'Forward planning and preparation but with an ability to react fluidly.'

'That's more than one,' I reply with a smile.

'And an instinct to use overwhelming violence when appropriate.'

'That's definitely more than one.'

'That Dave,' I say after a few seconds of silence which suggests he has finished speaking, and noticing that the others in the back have all crept forward to listen intently, 'is the most I have ever heard you say.'

'Sorry, did I talk too much?'

'Eh? Oh yeah...fuck me you were going on and on, none of us could get a word in edgeways. In fact, we're always saying the biggest problem with Dave is how much he talks.'

'Don't listen to him Dave,' Lani touches his shoulder affectionately which surprisingly, he doesn't flinch at or show any reaction at all. A few days ago and she could have been judo thrown through the windscreen for even contemplating touching him.

'There,' Nick points across me to my window and a fleeting glimpse in the distance. We've been steadily rising since turning off but the view has been hampered by wooded thickets, houses, farms and buildings. Climbing higher we get a sudden full view as the vista opens up. Sweeping pastures that slope gently down to the shore and the never ending deep blue sea that stretches off to the horizon.

The coastal road is there, a distinct black line that breaks the natural hues of greens and browns that roll down to the golden shore.

Pulling up we clamber out and shield our eyes against the glaring sun beating down on us. Paula and Roy join us first, then Clarence and finally Maddox and his team. All of us standing there in silence staring at the solid mass of figures marching along the road.

Solid, unbroken and never ending. The column stretches back further than the eye can see, disappearing from view as the contour of the land dips and turns through valleys and hills. Thousands upon thousands of figures and despite the distance they move with perfect timing. There is no rippling or undulation of so many people moving in one direction. Just an almost static thing that somehow moves forward without any apparent movement.

We all stare at the front and slowly rotate our heads to take in the miles of bodies filling the road.

'More than the Isle of Wight,' Nick remarks quietly.

'Yep, more than Darren brought too by the looks of it,' I reply equally as quiet.

'Far more,' Clarence adds, 'many, many more.'

'More than all the fights put together, including Salisbury,' Dave adds.

'I wish we had a fighter jet,' Cookey sighs, 'even a Spitfire going up and down that road would do the job.'

'Where we gonna get a Spitfire from?' Blowers asks.

'Fuck knows, museum?' Cookey replies.

'Dave, can you fly a plane?' Nick asks.

'I don't have a licence.'

'Helicopter?'

'No.'

'Submarine?' Cookey asks.

'Alex.'

'Sorry Dave.'

'Even a warship in the sea would finish that lot off,' Cookey sighs again.

'Tanks too,' Roy adds, 'a few of them would do the job.'

'Dave? Can you drive a...'

'No Alex I cannot drive a tank.'

'Er, there are two of us from the army,' Clarence rumbles.

'Sorry, can you drive a tank?' Cookey looks up at him.

'No, but that's not the point.'

'That's a lot of zombies,' I remark casually.

'It is Mr Howie,' Dave replies.

'All coming for us.'

'They are Mr Howie.'

'Whole lot of dirty fucking zombies,' I say slowly as Nick and Cookey start smiling.

'It is Mr Howie.'

'Many...many...dirty...nasty...filthy....zombies...'

'Just say it,' Lani sighs.

'Fuck it,' I laugh.

'We'll win!' The rest of them shout in reply then snigger sheepishly as the others stare at us in horror.

'You've clearly done this several times before then,' Roy remarks with a smile.

'Shit loads mate,' I reply, 'righto, well back to that town then and we best start getting set up...you know what I always say?' I look at Maddox, his team and then across to Paula and Roy, 'I always say that for every strength they have we can manipulate it and turn it to our advantage because we have the single most powerful strategy ever possessed...'

'You didn't bloody say that,' Lani laughs, 'Dave said it...don't listen to him.'

'Forward planning and preparation but with an ability to react fluidly and an instinct to use overwhelming violence when appropriate,' I continue in a patronising *know it all* tone.

'Well remembered,' Dave nods, 'but I said it first.'

'He didn't,' I mutter to the others staring at us like we're slightly freaky, 'can anyone see the end of them yet? No? Shit...that is one big horde.'

'Proper pre planning prevents piss poor performance,' Paula mutters.

'I agree,' Dave responds quickly with intense seriousness.

'Right,' I look round at the small crowd, 'we are a bunch of fucking misfits,' I grin, 'so let's go get ready for a big fight, Paula, your expertise is needed here so have a think what you want to do between here and the town, we'll follow your lead with input from Dave and...' Clarence coughs, '...and Clarence...' I add firmly with a glance up at him.

'I've got some ideas but er...' She hesitates, seemingly suddenly unsure.

'What's up?'

'Well that's a big army...maybe you guys should take the lead, you've er...well you've done this lots of times.'

'So have you,' Roy says quickly.

'I have but...well,' she looks uncomfortable, like caught on the spot.

'Paula, what you said you did in your town we need to do for this lot...just bigger...and quicker...but then it isn't just you this time, you've got almost thirty of us.'

'And a dog,' one of the youths quips with a cheeky grin.

'And a Dave,' Cookey adds, not allowing anyone else to make quips when he's about.

'What's a Dave?' The youth asks with a confused look.

'I'm a Dave...I mean I'm Dave,' Dave says.

They carry on chatting while I zone out staring at the never ending column. Too big and too many. Even if we blew that town apart there would still be a long queue of them coming out the end.

'Dave,' I say quietly.

'I know,' he replies just as quietly.

Turning to stare at him he first looks at them, then at me, 'we got no choice.'

He nods, no expression, nothing said. Just acceptance.

Lani, stood next to me touches my hand with hers, I turn quickly to see her smiling and the feeling is a million times better than Marcy. It's natural and real. A genuine touch from a genuine person that cares. She nods subtly with a glint in her eye.

In the corner of my eye I see Clarence shifting position, stood with legs planted and arms folded across his massive chest. Glancing over and he locks eyes for a second and quickly lifts both eyebrows, then the lads, all three of them with the same glint that Lani and Clarence have.

'Change of plan,' I announce to the group as a feeling like an electric current starts passing through my team. The tension rising with the prospect of battle. 'There is only one way of hoping to get through this...there's too many, simply too many. Even if we blew that town apart there would still be an endless queue of them coming out one side...so,' I take a breath making sure they're all listening, 'Maddox, send someone back to the fort and get more of your crews and anyone who can fire a weapon, take everything from the armoury and get them to that town...'

'Hang on,' Paula waves a hand.

'Sorry no,' I cut her off, 'this road will keep them funnelled until they hit that open land before the High Street, that is where they will spread out so get every available gun at the end of the High Street facing out onto that open land. We'll attack the front now and start cutting them down, that reduces the numbers and buys you time,' I look directly at Paula.

'Me? Buys me time?' She asks with a worried face.

'To get the town rigged, we start now and keep going until we get to that open land...then I want every gun we've got firing into them...then on our signal they get out of there and we'll lead them into the High Street...that road is enclosed with the hotels and high buildings so use that road to set the traps...'

'You are fucking joking aren't you,' she spits with anger, 'this is another joke isn't it?'

'Sorry, not this time,' Lani says softly, 'there's too many Paula.'

'Maddox, you up for this?' I ask.

'Yep,' he says quickly, 'I got over a hundred in my crews...I'll leave twenty there and bring the rest, you do what you can and we'll be ready for you.'

'Good.'

'No, not good...not good at all,' Paula protests.

'It is a good plan,' Roy says with the same unflustered expression.

'Do you know how to make explosive devices?' Dave asks her.

'Er...no...no I don't.'

'They're easy, Maddox you listen in too and I'll tell you what you need...nail bombs are the best for something like this, not just nails but anything small and metallic that will fragment out.'

'Okay,' Paula sighs, 'this is really happening isn't it?'

'It is,' I say firmly, 'seeing them like this has brought the reality home...we're several miles away from them and we can't see the end of the column...there could be more joining them at every junction and side road.'

'But there's seven of you,' she shakes her head in disbelief.

'We got big guns,' Nick says, 'lots of big guns.'

'We'll hold them back as long as we can...' I start to explain.

'They'll probably start charging when we go for them,' Blowers says, 'but that will weaken them for when we get to you...it gives you less time but makes them easier to kill.'

'He's right,' Cookey adds seriously, 'makes a hell of a difference when they're fucked and knackered.'

'Maddox, find a way to block off the side roads on that High Street...we want to keep them funnelled.'

'Got it, leave it with me...like I said, you do what you gotta do here and we'll be ready for you,' he replies confidently and like Roy, he shows no sense of panic or worry.

Nodding at them I look from face to face then back down at the road and all the way along the black snake and still no end in sight.

'We'll go then,' Maddox states, 'see you there and Howie...' I glance over at him, 'we got this yeah?'

'Yeah, yeah of course mate...' And I know he has too, he'll do whatever it takes to get it done.

They file away with Roy offering to drive the fuel tanker if Paula takes his van. Nick taps out some cigarettes and we light up, inhaling the acrid smoke that burns our throats and does nothing but perpetuate the myth that smoking helps anything other than feeding a habit. But we do it anyway.

'Lani...please, will you go with...'

'No!'

'What's that smell?' Cookey sniffs the air, 'urgh Meredith! Right by us too...bloody hell look at the size of it.'

'Christ that stinks...has anyone got a poo bag?' Nick asks putting his hand over his nose.

'Fuck that,' I gasp as Meredith turns round to sniff her own shit then look up at us with pride at the gift she left steaming on the grass.

'Wish I could do that sometimes,' Cookey sighs, 'wouldn't half make life easier wouldn't it.'

'Come on, let's go pick a fight with some zombies,' we stroll back to the Saxon, clambering in an I relent to the requests and flick the air conditioning on for a few minutes.

Might as well be cool on our way to try and stem the flow of the undead army coming to wipe us off the face of the earth.

Thirty

Paula looks between her open notepad on the seat and the tanker in front of her. Following Roy back towards the town and the initial trepidation has already abated. Yes this was different as there were people relying on her and Howie was putting himself into the firing line to buy them time and reduce the numbers.

Dave gave her a quick set of instructions, what ingredients to use and how to make basic nail bombs. Then running through the set up methods. It was far simpler than she could ever imagine. Highly destructive explosive devices made from basic household ingredients. The smoke bombs were interesting, potassium nitrate, powdered sugar and paraffin wax. That was it. No wonder the high school kids found them so easy to make. She floundered when Dave first said potassium nitrate and had a fleeting image of banana's until he said it's one of the main ingredients in tree stump remover, which is also readily available in the DIY store.

The bigger the better Dave said, and as many as possible too. Then how to get a set of wires stretching between them and then running down the street to a waiting car battery, red to positive black to negative then duck.

As the short drive goes on she starts to herself rising to the challenge. That all the previous work had been in preparation for this main event. A whole town just waiting for her to play with.

No time for lists or a written plan. This was head time, plan in the mind and execute with the body.

Getting towards the town she started to pay extra attention to the layout of the road. Howie was right, they were funnelled by a high sea wall on the shore side and high thick bramble hedgerows on the other.

Just before the town she slowed down to take in the sudden expanse of open land, again noting how Howie was right. Driving from this direction it would be natural for the horde to spill out and spread. Not if they were still marching but under attack they would take advantage of the space to try for flanking manoeuvres.

The open land stretched over to the junction of a service road that looped round the back of the stores. That needed to be blocked off and something done to prevent them going that direction. They had to be funnelled through the town.

With the vehicles stopped they meet up at the start of the High Street, Maddox shouting to two youths as they sprint off.

'Where are they going?' Paula asks.

'Get a vehicle and get to the fort like Howie said.'

'Why don't they take your vehicle?'

'Cos we'll need it, they can jack a car within a couple of minutes...watch,' Maddox grins as the two run over to an old Ford, smashing the driver's window with the butt of a rifle, unlocking the doors, climbing in and ducking down to do something to the cowling under the steering wheel. Within a few seconds the engine sputters and fires up, both of them giving Maddox a quick thumbs up as they drive away.

'Wow,' Paula nods genuinely impressed, 'you have got to teach me how to do that.'

'My crew have good skills,' Maddox laughs, 'but they were a bit slow, sorry about that,' he adds for effect. 'We gotta block that junction off...how about we get a load of vehicles jammed in nose to tail, maybe stick some of them bombs in there?'

'Good idea,' Paula flashes him a grin, 'high vehicles though, cars won't do it...we need trucks or vans...can your er...crews is it?'

'Yeah that's what we call them.'

'Can they all drive?'

'You shitting me?' Maddox asks, 'most of them are banned before they old enough to drive for stealing cars...yeah they can drive.'

'Is it okay to leave some here to start getting that done while we go for the DIY store?'

'Whatever you want,' Maddox splays his hands, 'you tell me what you want and I'll get it done.'

'Thanks,' Paula stares at the intense young man, impressed by his deep intelligence, 'okay then...get as many high sided vehicles into that junction as possible...really jammed in as close as possible to block it off...er...can you get them to get the fuel caps opened up too.'

'Listen in,' Maddox turns to call out at his group of waiting youths, 'Mohammed, you take ten and find as many big vans and trucks....get that junction blocked off and get the fuel caps jammed open, you get me?'

'Yep,' the serious Mohammed nods quickly then points to select the youths before walking off towards the junction.

Turning back Maddox stares expectantly at Paula, waiting for the next instruction.

'Right,' Paula says slowly, surprised at the instant response the youths gave, 'er...the rest of us will head to the DIY store then.'

'Do we need to?' Maddox asks, 'tell us what you need and we'll do it, you stay here with Roy and...'

'No,' interjecting she asserts herself quickly.

'All yours,' Maddox splays his hands again, 'shit...MO MO,' Maddox booms a warning as an undead staggers into view from the town running towards the walking youths. A twang next to them and the thing is taken clean off its feet from the arrow driving through its head.

Roy lowers the bow and glances round checking for others. The amiable look on his face is gone, replaced with an expression of complete focus and that same hard stare shared by all of them.

The group turn to stare at the undead on the ground with an arrow stuck in its head, then spin round to stare at Roy. Silence for a few seconds as everyone takes in what just happened. No hesitation, no apparent aiming. He just grabbed an arrow and fired at well over one hundred metres distance and at a running target.

Area scanned and Roy looks first at Maddox, then at Paula, the amiable look back on his face, 'sorry...you were saying?'

'How?' Maddox says slowly...'just...how?'

'Years Maddox...years and years,' Roy smiles.

'SWEET BLOOD, FUCKING SWEET!' One of the youths bellows from across the way before resuming their walk towards the junction.

'Oh and can you find me some fire engines too?' Paula asks suddenly.

Maddox raises an eyebrow for a second, 'fire engines?' he tilts his head back, 'leave it with me.'

'Fire engines?' Roy asks as they walk back to the van.

'Uh huh, something I've been wanting to try for ages, come on...we got to hurry up oh and Roy.'

'Yeah?'

'That was a good shot, well done.'

'Thanks,' he smiles.

Thirty One

I pull over at the side of the road, which earns a quick searching look from Dave as we're still miles from the front of the horde. Having worked our way back down the hill I made sure to drive well away from the undead before getting onto the coastal road.

The grass verge we're on is heavily layered with sand, giving it that exotic almost desert like appearance, and just metres away from the inviting blue waters of the sea too.

'What's up?' Clarence shouts from the back.

'Remember that swim I promised?'

'Fuck yes!' Cookey shouts, 'we going now?'

'Oh nice one boss,' Nick exclaims, 'have we got time?'

'Not long, but yeah we got time for a dip...'

'I'll stay here and keep watch,' Dave says as the rest in the back burst into cheers.

'Sure mate? Come and have a swim?'

'I don't like the water,' he says flatly.

'Up to you mate,' I pop the door open and drop down into the blistering heat and the sun glaring from the sand.

Stripping off we dump our clothes at the front of the vehicle and carrying our rifles we start walking towards the sea, within seconds we're hopping in pain from the hot sand burning our feet.

'Lani? You coming?' I shout back realising she's not with us.

'I'm getting changed,' she yells from the Saxon as Meredith sprints past us, ears flattened low as she powers towards the water, bounding in with a big splash and a bark.

We start jogging, desperate to keep our feet off the burning sand, rifles get ditched a few feet back and we run in. All of us laughing as we wade into the shallow warm water, then further out until we can dive in an let the water soak our parched skin.

The feeling is amazing. The water is warm but distinctly cooler than the super-heated air. I swim out and dive down, using my arms to propel me to the bottom. All other noise is gone, just the underwater sounds of my movement. Opening my eyes and I see a blurry image of the sea bed and just for a second, none of the badness up there exists.

A flash of silver catches my eye as a fish darts away, the sun glinting from the broad side and the strong tail. It hits me that already within the thirteen days of this event, the fish stocks must be recovering already. Cod and white fish harvested and hunted to near extinction so many times and suddenly it's stopped. Whales, sharks...every living creature in the ocean will benefit from our species being culled.

Eventually I break the surface and spin round, spurting the salty water from my mouth and staring back to the shore. What I see surprises me. I was expecting to see the lads going mad at having a few minutes to play, instead we're all doing the same thing. Swimming off for a bit of space to tread water quietly. Blowers dives back down and disappears for a short time before re-surfacing a short distance away. Clarence floats on his back with his arms and legs outstretched and his toes sticking up from the water.

Lani walks sedately from the Saxon to the sea, looking amazing in her black bikini she must have kept from our last swim on the Island. Then the heat of the sand hits her feet and she starts hopping, the muttered curses floating over the near silence of the sea.

She does what we did, ditches the rifle and runs the last few feet to plunge into the water and just as she dives forward I catch a glimpse of the wound on her stomach. A quick reminder of the reality we face.

Dave stands on the Saxon with the sniper rifle, constantly turning as he scans the ground. I sink back and folding my body I let myself sink gently beneath the water, keeping my eyes open to look back up at the rippling sky.

Bliss. Pure silent bliss, encapsulating and almost womb-like. Holding my breath until I feel the urge starting to push in my chest, it gets stronger and stronger as my body uses the available oxygen.

If I took a deep breath now it could all be over. No more suffering. No more pain. No humiliation. No more anything.

The loss of everything hits me suddenly and for a second I cannot bear the pain of losing Sarah and the others. That inner part of me, kept locked and barred bursts open for a second, letting me know of what pain I have still yet to deal with.

Kicking up I break the surface again and draw a big breath, the sea water covering the tears streaming down my face. Snot purging from my nose gets wiped away and I swim away, further out to sea just so they don't see my crying face. Stifling the sobs I try to bite the pain back down, feeling an intense rush of guilt for being here now, enjoying this feeling when my sister will never feel anything again. None of them will. Dead and rotting in those massive piles of bodies stacked up on the estate.

Glancing round and again I realise I'm not the only one feeling this as we're all spread out and facing away from the beach. Even Lani has found a quiet spot and treads water gently. Meredith swims like a shark, a long black object that glides with her chin held up away from the water.

She goes round in circles, seemingly just enjoying the feeling of being suspended, then breaking her pattern she heads towards Nick.

He seems to snap out of whatever dream he is in as she glides by and I see him wiping his eyes then plunging his head under water. When he comes back up he laughs and swims after Meredith. She glances round and swims away with him chasing after her.

Almost as though sensing she is drawing him out to sea she changes direction and heads back towards shore, letting Nick catch up with her. He takes hold of her back end and just gently kicks. Her incredible strength pulling them both through the water.

Cookey spots it and, as with Nick, I catch him wiping his eyes and dunking his face before kicking out to swim after them and once again Meredith breaks the melancholy by drawing them into play.

Lani swims towards me with a graceful breast stroke, her face just barely out of the water as she glides through the millpond.

'How's your stomach?'

'S'okay, hurts a bit...skin starting to itch now.'

'That's good, it's healing.' I watch as she swims closer then eases off to tread water a few feet away.

'This is nice,' she says softly, 'good idea…they needed it.'

'We all do.'

She stares at me for long seconds, her chin dropping and rising out of the water. Clear rivulets stream down her golden skin. She drops her head back to sweep her hair away and faces me with it swept back perfectly black and glistening.

Nothing like Marcy. She's real and complex, difficult but strong. Maybe that bond between us isn't ruined forever.

'What you thinking?' She asks.

'About you.'

'Me?' She smiles, 'why?'

'Cos I want to,' I smile back.

'Not whether I'm infected or not then?'

'Didn't even think of it to be honest.'

'You bloody did,' she giggles, 'you saw me in my bikini and got all fruity.'

'Ah bugger off,' I smile.

'You going all Hugh Grant on me again Howie?'

'I might.'

'Bit late for that don't you think.'

'I'm not sure how to take that comment so I stay silent for a few seconds, 'Lani, I am sorry…'

'It's done,' she says quickly, 'can't take it back can we…so we move forward.'

'Forward?'

'Mr Howie,' she laughs, 'are you fishing to see if I still like you?'

'Do you?'

'Pack it in,' she pushes out to send a wave of water splashing into my face.

'Do you?' I ask again with what I hope is a cheeky grin.

'Not answering,' she splashes me again but this time I'm ready and dive down out of the way, the water is so clear I can see her body seemingly suspended as she makes tiny movements with her arms and legs to stay afloat. Using my arms I dive down under her body and watch she twists round trying to track my movements. Reaching out I brush my fingers against her foot which causes her to yelp out in half panic.

As I start to surface I go close against her body and see the stomach wound just inches in front of my eyes. The skin looks red and sore but so much more healed than it should be. Gently I reach out and touch it, she twitches but then stays still as I run my fingers gently over the damaged skin. Her hand drops to mine, holding it gently as I feel along the puckered skin.

'Looks awful doesn't it, will leave a nasty scar,' she comments as I surface just inches away.

'No,' I shake my head gently, 'it doesn't...so?'

She laughs with delight, 'so what? You still asking that?'

'Yep.'

'Why is it important to know that? It's not like we can do anything is it?'

Shrugging and glance quickly to the shore, watching the horseplay now fully underway with Meredith running back and forth, Dave stood like a sentinel in the distance, 'I still like you,' I say quietly.

'Do you now?' She asks with a small smile.

'Yep, very much.'

'Oh very much is it?'

'Very very much.'

'More than Marcy?'

'Ouch Lani...'

'I'm serious,' she stares at me, reading my face.

'Marcy was...not real,' I shake my head, 'I still don't know how that happened...but...'

'But what?'

'You're real,' I smile again.

'More real than that bitch,' she growls, 'yes Howie,' she adds with a roll of her eyes, 'I still like you very much.'

'How much?' I ask quickly.

'Stop it,' she laughs, a beautiful sound that sends my heart soaring.

'How much?' I urge splashing her lightly.

'Enough to think you were mine,' a flash of seriousness.

'Yours?'

'Mine,' she repeats.

'I like that.'

'Do you?' She asks with genuine surprise.

'Yeah...I do...I wish I could kiss you.'

'Howie, what's got into you...where's the shy blushing boy gone?'

'He's still here...but losing you make me realise...er...well you know...'

'The shy boy comes back,' she giggles, 'but we can't kiss...not until we know...'

'And when we know for sure...that you're immune I mean?'

'Then we can kiss all we like,' she says softly.

'If today goes bad Lani...'

'Don't,' she cuts me off with a warning tone.

'Listen,' I laugh, 'if it goes badly then I will be grabbing you for a big smooch...just as they're coming to chomp our noses off...'

'Smooch?' She laughs again, 'you gonna smooch me?'

'Yeah, a big old fashioned smooching session with one finger stuck up at the zombies like this,' I emulate a wet kiss while showing the finger. She bursts out laughing so loud it makes everyone turn to look.

'I thought we'd go down fighting.'

'Fighting and kissing, we can wave our axes about as we snog.'

'I don't use an axe...'

'Okay picky pants...wave our axes and meat cleavers about then.'

'What about the one finger? How we gonna do that if we're kissing *and* trying to fight.'

'Uh? Good point...sounds complicated...let's just stick to the kissing instead then.'

'Okay,' she carries on laughing, 'I like this side of you.'

'I like *all* the sides of you,' I grin wolfishly which makes her splash water in my face.

'Cheesy...but,' her tone switches to serious, 'what if I am infected? What then?'

'Find a cure,' I reply instantly, 'I won't lose you Lani...we won't lose you...we've lost too many already and it won't happen.'

'And if there is no cure?'

'There will be,' I say firmly, 'you are living proof of that...you might be the cure, something is different with you so that proves it isn't as final as...'

'What if it takes a year to find a cure?'

'Then I'll wait a year.'

'Ten years?'

'I'll wait ten years.'

'Twenty years?'

'Nah, that's too long...you can sod off...oi that went in my mouth,' I spit the salt water out.

'You'll wait all that time to kiss me? Why?'

'Because I kissed you once already and I remember it...so it doesn't matter how long it takes or what I have to do.'

'That was a nice kiss,' she smiles, remembering the stolen few minutes we shared.

'Yeah it was alright...argh,' I hold my breath as she dunks me under, then I pull her down and we start playing, swimming after each other, splashing about as we get closer to the lads and join in with messing about.

But all good things must come to an end and enough time passes for us to be walking out to drip water onto the sand as we gather our rifles and stroll back to the Saxon, getting halfway before we all start hopping and jogging from the hot sand.

Getting dressed the banter is light and easy, all of us smiling and joking as Meredith runs back and forth shaking her coat again and again. Dave drops down to pour water into a bowl which she laps greedily while water drips from her coat to soak instantly into the ground. We drink warm Lucozade and smoke, taking our time as though we can dictate the event that lies ahead of us. Fooling ourselves that we somehow control this environment and choose to do as we please.

Inevitability awaits us. There will much death but no worse than we've seen before and I know one more thing. Once we've killed this lot we'll find the next group and kill them too, and the rest and we won't stop until either we find a cure or the last one falls.

Whichever comes sooner.

Thirty Two

'Is that it?' Roy asks staring down at the supplies stacked on the floor.

'Er,' Paula consults her notebook, again checking the stacked items against the list compiled with Dave, 'yeah,' she nods looking up at him, 'that's it.'

'Shit,' Maddox exclaims, 'you can make bombs from that?'

'Apparently,' Paula replies, 'we got Hydrogen Peroxide...I can't believe how easy that was to find...er...nails and screws for the fragments, then we have...'

'Yeah I can see it,' Maddox cuts her off, 'what's next?'

'Those plastic tubs,' she points to the empty thirty litre plastic buckets piled up to one side, 'will be the casing...we get some cardboard or something and fold it round to create an outer ring in the tubs, then we stack the outer ring with the fragments and the explosive stuff goes in the middle. Then we get the wiring,' she points to the drum holding the looped electrical cable, 'and run it back from tub to tub all the way back to a car battery...when we connect the wires to the battery it goes bang...I hope.'

'How many tubs we got?' Maddox counts them off quickly, 'there's thirty here, we gonna use all of them?'

'Just keep going until we run out of stuff I guess,' Paula shrugs, 'did you get the razor wire?'

'Yeah they're loading it now, you want a hand mixing all this stuff? We doin' it here or what?'

'Dave said the mixture is safe to be carried and won't go off unless an electrical charge is applied or intense heat,' Paula says, biting her bottom lip as she once more flicks through her notebook.

They set to work, mixing household chemicals in the order and amounts as explained by Dave. Each tub has the centre ring pushed in and then the nails and screws stacked in between the inner layer and the casing of the tub.

Maddox watches with interest as Paula makes the first one, stepping back within a few minutes to stare down at the innocuous looking filled bucket.

On reaching twenty of the improvised explosive devices they realise the buckets will run out long before the rest of the materials, so youths are dispatched into the aisles of the DIY store to source more tubs, buckets and anything that can hold nails and chemicals.

Bomb after bomb is made and set aside and with each one Paula is astounded at the ease of the process. Although the ingredients are very specific and the staff would be trained to be alert to anyone purchasing large amounts of them, it is still shocking just how simple it is.

They keep going, stacking the bombs near the ruined front doors and getting the youths to carry them out to the waiting vehicles. Coils of Razor wire already in the vans along with rope and as many bottles of flammable white spirit and paint thinner as they can find.

While Howie and Lani talk quietly in the cooling sea, Paula, Roy, Maddox and his crews sweat with the exertion of mixing, carrying, loading and running back for the next load. When the first vehicle is filled to the brim, Maddox orders two of his crew to take it to the town to leave with Mohammed then bring more vehicles back.

They do as told and by the time they return the store is exhausted of bomb making supplies, with every nail, screw and tub in the place now turned into deadly bombs.

Driving back to the town after a back breaking session of carrying them all out into the blistering sun, Paula drinks quickly from a bottle of water and mops the sweat from her forehead. Roy drives in silence, unfazed by the whole situation and worrying at a new sore spot he thinks he can detect on the inside of his gum.

Reaching the town centre they drive down the High Street, Roy leading the other vehicles driven by Maddox and his youths. A large crowd waits for them at the junction with the side road, a crowd made up of youths armed with assault rifles, shotguns and farm rifles. Knives hanging from belts, bats with nails sticking out the end and all manner of inventive weapons. The youths jostle and joke, excited at the prospect of fighting as they wait for Maddox to give them instructions.

As they draw closer and the view of the junction opens up, Paula notices the vehicles jammed in tight, far more than she would have imagined and more arriving by the minute. Mohammed stood on the top of a big van waving his arms to direct the waiting vans and lorries into place.

'Bloody hell,' Roy mutters at the sight of the two shiny red fire engines parked off to one side.

'How the hell did you get this done so quickly?' Paula shouts to Maddox.

'We don't mess about,' Maddox replies without looking, 'Mo mo,' he shouts over the top of the group. The youth on top of the van turns to wave, 'good job but I want double this amount and get 'em stretched back past the junction.'

Mohammed gives a quick thumbs up before turning to shout more instructions. Maddox, turning to the fire engines asks who got them. Several kids step out from the crowd grinning proudly as Maddox tells them they've done a good job.

'You done well so you get the reward,' he grins as they watch him expectantly, 'they's need emptying so get them hoses working, you get me?'

A look of pure joy spreads over their faces as they turn to sprint towards the fire trucks, others running with them to have the fun of using the powerful hoses. The trucks are started up, spluttering to life noisily as the big diesel engines roar into the quiet air. The youths swarm as they pull the side flaps down to reveal the equipment and dials on show. The end of the hoses get yanked and dragged away towards the beach, the engines increase in pitch as they start to work the pumps talking in excited tones as the older kids work out how to activate the flow of water. The hose stiffens as the right buttons and levers are pressed, the children holding them shouting with delighted joy as they scrabble to release the water flow. When the first one bursts to life, spraying a long jet down onto the sands a dull cheer goes up, quickly followed by hoots of laughter as the two small lads holding the hose get thrown about by the strength of the water coming out. The girl operating the hose at the engine doesn't switch it off but lets the end twist and buck wildly as more kids run down to leap on the animated end, fighting to control it.

The second hose starts spraying, but these youths are braced and ready. Jeering at the first lot as they handle the hose with ease. The two long sprays arching high to spatter down onto the sand like two huge fountains.

Paula and Roy laugh at the sight, smiling broadly at the almost perfect view of children playing and having fun, their young voices shouting insults and jokes but they both notice the way they work together, a strong unit that belies their age and immaturity.

'Where you want them?' Maddox asks, referring to the fire engines, 'you filling them with fuel yeah? I figured you would. One should go by the junction set back with the hose set to spray onto the open land...'

'That's what I was thinking...we just got to work out a way of igniting it from a distance.'

Stepping forward, Roy looks first at the engines and the spray coming from the hoses, then over at the junction, 'fire arrow will do that, let the hoses spray first to soak the ground then I can fire from a distance once everyone has fallen back.'

'Good,' Maddox nods quickly, 'Howie wants everyone here so we can open up when they spread out from the road...we gotta make everyone aware not to shoot the fire trucks.'

'We go forward then,' Paula remarks, 'so we're in front of them...then when we give the signal and start dropping back someone turns the hose on.'

'Howie will be coming from that road,' Maddox points to the coastal carriageway, 'so we make a gap for him to get through then start dropping back in line with his vehicle...yeah then once we're clear we get the hoses spraying juice then Roy ignites it.'

'Hose not hoses,' Paula corrects, 'seeing as we got two we'll use the next one up the road...'

'We could put the second one on the beach,' Roy cuts in, 'the fire engine I mean...put it on the beach with the hose directing out towards the junction...ha! Will be a wall of fucking flames...'

Glancing again at the way the swear words just don't suit him Paula considers the suggestion. The spray from the hoses is great enough to reach across the width of the road.

'If we do that,' Maddox speaks up, 'we need to leave it until they get further in here otherwise they can just hold back till the flames burn out...but that means whoever is switching them on is isolated...how about,' he thinks quickly, his expression focussed, 'the first engine on the junction...the crew on that one run into the back road and round the behind the shops to the side road...the truck on the beach,' he switches his gaze over, 'the crew on that will have to run through the hotels, or down the beach and get back onto the road.'

'Yes, yes I think that will work,' Paula visualises the hoses spraying flames out and the youths scarpering to sprint away, 'then can we get these doors opened up so some of your crews can get to the roofs of those buildings so they can fire down or drop fire bombs...'

'Fire bombs?' Maddox queries, 'you mean Molotov cocktails?'

'Yeah sorry,' Paula grins, 'get them all set up first with rags sticking out then just light the wicks and drop them down.'

'Those bottles are plastic, they won't break like glass,' Roy adds.

'They'll still ignite or burst apart as the liquid explodes,' Paula replies.

'Jagger!' Maddox shouts, watching as a youth breaks free, running towards him, 'see if you can get on those roofs and find a way to work along and come back down further up the street...get the inside doors opened up so you got plenty of escape routes down yeah? We gonna shoot down from up there and drop cocktails.'

'Yeah I got it Mads,' the youth replies, 'where you got the cocktails then?'

'Bottles of white spirit,' Maddox explains.

'They's shit, they ain't as good as whiskey bottles or milk bottles...we tried 'em before innit.'

'Do they flame?' Roy asks.

'Yeah course,' Jagger says, 'but like the flames spread out and don't explode like glass does when it smashes, swear down it still works but...'

'S'all we got Jagger,' Maddox cuts in.

Jagger shrugs and moves off, motioning his crew to follow him.

'Next?' Maddox asks.

'We can't put those bombs in the street,' Roy says, 'they'll go off from the firing.'

'Put them in the shop front then, break the glass windows,' Paula suggests.

'No,' Maddox shakes his head, 'those are big bombs, the glass spreading out will do as much damage as the nails and screws.'

'Okay, so we got the junction here covered...we can put bombs into the cars too?' Roy asks, 'no need to have an ignition on them as the fire will set them off.'

'We'll do that, then we put some bombs into the windows of the first section of the main road between here and the side street...that's where we'll have the first car battery and ignition point.

'Brilliant,' Paula smiles, 'let's get the first section done.'

'Darius, what the fuck you doing here? I said you gotta stay at the fort,' Maddox shouts at seeing the other youth walking through the crowd.'

'Sierra got it, swear down she got it covered...her and Lenski told me to come, what's happening then bro?'

Maddox fills him quickly, Darius nodding as he looks to the sections pointed out by Maddox. Once finished they start working up the High Street. Youths driving the vehicles as Maddox, Darius, Paula and Roy work out where to place the bombs.

They select the best positions, working out which store fronts to use before carrying the tubs inside to attach the wires and spool the cable out to run down to the next one. It takes time to cut and splice the wires with Roy double checking each one is set correctly. Paula worrying that the innocuous looking tubs have been set up wrong and will fail to go off.

The afternoon sun beats down relentlessly into the street as they walk a few metres, pick another store then carry the IED inside to connect with wires before repeating it again.

Roy grabs a battery taken from the parked cars on the junction and carries it to the first side road, getting it set up several metres back from the junction to give the crew some cover. By the time he's done the second section is underway with more tubs stacked into shop fronts and more wires stretching out to the next side street.

Maddox tasks Darius to select a small fast crew that can set the fire engine flame-thrower off then run round to the first side street, set the bombs off and then get round to the second side street for the same again.

Darius breaks away, organising two small teams. He gets the first at the point on the shore where the beach-side fire truck will be positioned and then runs with them down the beach and along the front of the hotels, finding a way through to come out onto the High Street opposite the first side road.

He gets that crew to practise the run several times, and find other routes in case something goes wrong. While they get versed he moves to the other small team and starts the process again. Running from the junction, round the back of the stacked vehicles to find a route into the service road. Mohammed's efforts to block the junction are so good the team has to run further up to find a house, smashing the front and back door in to run through and out the back garden, into the service road and then along the back of the shops to the side road and the waiting car battery where Roy shows them how to connect the wires.

Darius gets them running the route several times, telling them it will be dark with *shit going down everywhere so don't get fucking lost and fuck it up*.

The second section of the High Street is a repeat of the first, with solid hard graft underway. The youths not working on set tasks, busy themselves with dragging items out of the buildings to create obstacles for the horde. Long experienced with having running battles with the police and they know just how to make a long road hard to navigate.

Slowly, they work up the road to the second side street, with Roy getting the second ignition point set up with another car battery. Darius then goes back to the first ignition team and gives them the good news that once they've set the first bombs off they have to go back into the service road and get to the second side road. They take it without complaint and with the boundless energy of the young they start practising that route too.

With the first two sections rigged and ready, Jagger finds Maddox and the other two adults discussing the next set of plans.

'Mad's, we got the roofs done and we got the cocktails up there innit, we got rags and all the shit up good blood, we's can get all the way down to the last building,' he grins proudly.

'Good,' Maddox smiles back, 'now do the same again on the second section...or find another crew to do it.'

'Nah we do it bruv, this be like our thing...'

'On you then Jagger,' Maddox grins, 'and find Darius, he's getting a crew running from the junction to that first side road...there's a fuck load of bombs in them shops so make sure they don't set 'em off until you clear.'

'Got it bruv,' Jagger shouts already sprinting away.

'What we doing here?' Maddox nods to the next section of the High Street, his energy seemingly inexhaustible.

'Razor wire,' Paula replies, 'we get it coiled up at the sides with some rope stretched across the road that we lift up when we go past...they run into the rope and pull the wire in, works a treat.'

'Brutal,' Maddox says, 'remind me never to piss you off lady. We'll make sure Jagger has more cocktails on the roofs to throw down.'

The next project gets underway, with Paula making the children first put the slash-proof gloves taken from the DIY store, before they start handling the rolls of dangerous wire.

'With more batteries we can electrify that wire,' Roy suggests, getting into the swing of things and revealing his love of car batteries, 'like you did with that cattle grid.'

More adolescents are sent back to the junction to find and bring back the batteries as Roy jogs off to get some wire from the electrical cable loom. The razor wire is man-handled into place, coiled in thick loops at the sides of the pavement as thick rope is attached to the ends of the wire and stretched flat across the ground.

'How we gonna get the rope high enough for them to pull along?' Maddox asks, looking down at the ground. 'We can use the litter bins but it'll sag down in the middle.'

'Er...we'll have to try the railings on that side,' Paula points to the front of a hotel building, 'and this side we can use a door handle or something, as long as we just loop properly then it shouldn't tighten up when it gets pulled forward.'

Another round of trial and error begins with the rope being played out while Maddox gets a load of youths to run into it, seeing each time where the rope is falling down or tightening up. Eventually it gets done right and practised several times before both Paula and Maddox are satisfied. Roy gets the batteries put in place and works the cable back to the steel razor wire. Several batteries are connected on both sides to ensure a high voltage is pumped into the metal.

The sun beats a steady track through the sky, starting the descent as it drifts slowly but effortlessly down to give light to another part of the world. Shadows grow longer but the heat remains high as they work the main road metre by metre.

The possibility of the undead swarming along the beach is considered and yet more youths are sent back down the road to block the hotel doors up and make it as *hard as fuck for them to get through.*

The work is grindingly hard and made all the harder by the extreme heat. If society hadn't of fallen the hospitals would be full of heat-stroke victims, the rail-lines would have found another reason to shut down and the tarmac on the roads would be melting from the constant vehicular traffic. Health and Safety reps within factories would be arranging tools down and walk-outs at seeing the mercury in the thermometers rise above the recommended work-place level. The newspapers would be headlining with the record breaking heat that beat the average high temperatures of the Mediterranean resorts. Sales of water would be rocketing as people heeded the advice to stay hydrated. Sun cream flying off shelves as the white pasty northern European skin turned pink and burnt

But society did fall and the event did happen. So they work and they don't complain as one street in a seaside resort of a small town on the south coast of England gets ready to meet the largest gathering of undead yet seen.

Thirty Three

The infection knows the layout of every single road, street and track in the area. From the collective intelligence it knows the coastal road is the most direct route to the fort and it also knows that the movement of such a large body cannot go unnoticed.

Those it seeks will surely be aware of the exodus, and as with before they will surely plan ahead to reduce the numbers and start cutting the host bodies down.

One large body is easy to spot and easy to attack. Two large bodies are less easy to spot and less easy to attack, so the infection starts dividing its forces.

As the front of the horde reach a junction, the infection orders those on the right side of the road to take that junction and those on the left side to keep going. The order is executed with perfect precision as the thick column divides in two. Not a step is missed, not a beat broken but they carry on. As the two branches separate and move further into their respective roads, the infection re-organises the host bodies to move up and retain the same marching pattern. What would take the communist armies of North Korea and China months to arrange as they organise an orchestrated march past of their leaders, so the infection does within an instant of reaching the diverging point.

Two armies with the same objective and marching in the same direction become split as the inland road weaves further from the coast.

The infection then holds the marching section on the coastal road until the next selected junction is reached and again it splits the army to filter off to the right, veering into the next inland road.

Now three armies with the same objective and marching in the same direction and from a birds eye view you would see three thick columns still each possessing thousands of hosts march steadily towards the west.

None of these armies have a leader. There is no Marcy or Randall, no Darren leading them. No Thomas to organise the fight, for the infection has realised the folly of trusting the human mind to understand every risk and counter risk.

The army on the coastal road maintain the average marching pace understood by Dave. The other two increase the pace, commencing a double time sustained march. Chemicals, now far greater understood, are released into the bodies to sustain the expenditure of energy.

More junctions are reached. More sections filter off to march away from the coastal road, and with each one the columns re-adjust to present the same ranking structure on each road. Some of those branches will converge later, some will meet and then separate as further junctions are reached.

The fort is not the objective. There is no set location as the objective. The march is simply a way of drawing him out. He will learn of the march and attack. That is why the columns are split because Howie cannot attack all of them at the same time.

The infection waits. Knowing he will come. Waiting for him to come and willing to sacrifice whatever it takes to get just one bite into Howie.

Thirty Four

'Look at them. Dirty filthy fuckers,' my hands tighten on the steering wheel, 'evil nasty bastards that just don't know when to quit.'

Meredith starts growling, picking up on the foul scent from the thousands of diseased bodies marching towards us. Slowing the speed down they're still a good distance off but even so, they present a solid dark wall that snakes forward.

'Make sure Meredith is tied up, she'll run out if we open the back doors,' Clarence twists round from the front passenger seat to watch Nick attaching a rope to her thick collar.

Bringing the Saxon to a stop I commence a slow manoeuvre to turn round and present the back of the vehicle to them. With Meredith tied on the back doors are opened and Dave climbs up to take the first stint on the GPMG.

After discussing the tactics it was agreed to just use the one machine gun fired by Dave until either something changes or the situation develops.

'Dave, you got a lot of ammunition for the sniper rifle?' Blowers calls up.

'Yes, help yourself, ten shots each at a time, the most headshots for each round gets a prize.'

'A prize? Seriously?' Cookey is on his feet already, almost jumping up and down on the spot with excitement.

'Ladies first,' Blowers nods respectfully to Lani as Clarence and I exchange a quick glance. This might be the time we notice something different if she hesitates or shows any discomfort at killing the infected.

'Why thank you,' Lani says politely. Keeping the Saxon stationary we wait for the horde to get a bit closer before we open fire.

'Hang on,' Nick calls out, 'how we gonna know what shots we get...Dave'll be getting headshots too.'

'Good point, Dave you'll have to hang fire until we've done the first round,' I call out.

'Roger that, standing by...someone pass me the binoculars and I'll count the shots...remember what I taught you, breathe steady and squeeze the trigger.'

'I'll keep at a steady five miles an hour so we're just ahead of them,' I say. Lani settles down on the back of the Saxon, lying prone with her shoulder against the butt of the rifle as she takes aim and gets prepared. With the doors open, Meredith stares fixed but seems to understand we're not in immediate danger as she doesn't growl or bark, but just lifts her upper lip every few seconds.

'Ready?' I call out, 'moving forward now.'

With the horde getting closer by the second I gently press down on the pedal to ease the vehicle forward, once satisfied that we're held at roughly the same pace they're marching at I give the all clear and twist round to watch.

The first shot is taken within a couple of seconds of twisting round, no hesitation, no apparent leniency.

'Shoulder,' Dave calls down, 'breathe Lani.'

'Okay,' she calls back, settles for a second then takes the next shot, 'got it!' She cries out.

'One,' Dave calls down.

'Nice Lani,' Nick says quietly.

She takes her shots, cursing when she clips a shoulder or arm, and getting a round of "oooh's" when she gets a throat.

'Six, not bad Lani...' Dave calls down as she stands up and hands the rifle to Blowers.

'It's a lot harder than it looks,' she says, 'just the slight motion of the vehicle is enough to make it sway.'

'Big distance though,' Clarence says climbing from the front to watch Blowers take his go.

'Ready?' Dave calls down.

'I am,' Blowers replies.

'All yours Simon.'

The first shot rings out, a head shot that Dave reports down getting a round of cheers and a comment of a lucky first shot from Cookey in response.

'Six,' Dave counts the total score.

'Same as me Blowers,' Lani pats his shoulder.

'Fucking watch this,' Cookey boasts, 'this is gonna be a straight ten. He lies down, grasping the rifle to snuggle in close. He goes quiet as he focusses on the scope, getting the movement of the vehicle in synch with the march of the undead.

'All yours Alex...head shot... well done.'

'Ha,' Cookey mutters, waits a few seconds and takes the next shot, and the next... the first five shots are clear head shots.

He takes the sixth shot while I try and keep the vehicle steady, twisting to watch the road then back to Cookey.

'Head shot,' Dave announces.

'Six in a row,' Nick calls out, 'well done mate...keep going.'

Cookey stays silent, picking his next target before pausing to get the sway then squeezing the trigger, a loud retort and another one drops down to be trampled from view.

'Head shot,' Dave says in the same flat tone.

'Seven! He's in the lead,' Nick says.

'Go on Cookey,' Clarence urges, completely swept up in the competition.

'Miss, shoulder,' Dave calls down to a round of groans. The next two are close but Dave reports neither can be counted as head shots and Cookey stands up with a broad grin, both pleased with his score and annoyed at himself for missing the last ones.

'Nick,' he hands the rifle over, 'good luck mate.'

We all flinch as the GPMG bursts to life with a quick strafe, turning to see a row of heads explode along the front rank, the visible pink puff as Dave scores an instant ten.

'Dave,' Lani chastises him.

'Sorry,' he calls down, 'I fancied a quick go,' which amazes me that Dave would do something like that and I can imagine the small wry grin on his face as he listens to the moans and groans coming up.

Nick settles in and takes a full minute to get ready. Dave tells him he's good to go and the first shot rings out, instantly blowing a skull apart as Dave shouts *good shot.*

Nick works quicker than the others, his hand to eye co-ordination faster than the other three as he picks the target, adjusts for the motion and fires. Scoring eight solid head shots in a row much to Cookey's annoyance, the ninth clips an ear which Dave allows as it counts as part of the head, again much to the annoyance of Cookey who says if he'd known that rule he would have shot all their fucking ears off, which earns him a quick reprimand from Dave for unruly conduct in a competition.

The tenth is a straight miss, Nick standing up to glare at Cookey, 'you're fucking whining put me off.'

'Clarence, you having a go?' Nick offers him the rifle which he takes with a grin and waits for the others to move so he can squeeze his big bulk onto the floor.

He scores a straight nine in a row, with solid shots dropping them quickly. The tenth shot rings out and another body drops down as Dave reports it was throat and not head.

'Boss? Your turn, let me drive for a minute,' Clarence says as he pulls himself up. We swap over and wait while Clarence gets the Saxon moving at a steady pace again.

'Straight ten Mr Howie,' Lani winks as I move past her.

'Be lucky to get one, I'm crap at this,' I grin back but take my place at the rear, settling down to pull the rifle in and relax my position before I look through the scope.

The magnified faces of the undead swim into view and I take a few seconds to watch as they march in perfect timing. As I scan for a target I wonder why they're letting us just take pot shots like this. They've got tens of thousands but we've still just taken almost fifty down, not counting the quick burst from Dave.

Their heads are held steady too, not lolling or rolling about. They look composed. The faces aren't showing that hungry look but are set and focussed. Eyes forward with mean looks and there's no doubt we're being watched by many pairs of eyes.

Feet swing and plant in perfect synchronisation. Arms swing to maintain momentum. I pick a big ugly male in the front and breathe out slowly as I gauge the sway and motion of the vehicle.

The first shot takes his head off, one second he is there, walking along and the next his head is gone as the ones closest to him get sprayed with bits of brain and gore. They don't flinch but keep moving.

The next one is a female, old and wrinkly with lank grey hair hanging down and a ragged wound festering in her neck. Her head is taken off with another clear shot.

Third one down and another head shot, watching the pink explosion as the body flies back into the one marching behind it.

Four and another clear shot. Five then six. Number seven is a teenage male, all gangly arms and legs, not a child but not yet a man and he never will be now as I remove his head for him.

Seven clear shots. Eight is another woman and I can start to feel a prickling sensation coming up my spine. I take the shot and drop her, Dave shouting down that it's another clear shot.

Nine and I pause as the hairs on the back of my neck stand up, a sense that all is not as it seems. This road makes them easy targets. Far too easy. If they're evolving and getting smarter then why pick the one road we can use to cut them down.

'Nine,' Dave shouts as I take the shot.

Too easy. This is too easy. They're smarter than this. Well *they aren't* but *it* is. The infection sent Marcy in, and it worked so well too. If not for Dave again we'd all be turned by now.

'Something wrong boss?' Clarence asks as I hesitate, sweeping the scope across the rank but with no idea what I'm looking for.

'This isn't right.'

'What isn't?' Lani asks with concern.

'This,' I lift to my knees and stare back at them with my naked eye, 'Clarence...stop the vehicle mate.'

He brings it to a stop within a few feet as we gather to stare out the back, the rest of them flicking between me and the oncoming horde.

'Make ready to fire, all of you...Dave, be ready if they start running, Clarence too.'

'Say the word,' Clarence replies, 'what you got boss?'

'Not sure...something,' my voice trails off as I watch them coming. Step by step and each one bringing them closer to our position.

I pass the sniper rifle to one of the lads and take up an assault rifle, racking the bolt back and making ready before lifting it up to aim. The others do the same, following my cue to rack and aim.

'What's up?' Lani asks in the quietness of the vehicle.

'This isn't right,' I murmur again.

'What isn't?' She presses.

'I don't know...something...' the sniper rifles was blowing them away, then the quick strafe by Dave with the GPMG, but it's nothing we haven't seen or done many times before. As we dropped one so another moved up to fill the space. But they've done that before too.

The expression on their faces. That's what bothers me. They're not showing the signs of aggression but just look focussed, they don't look to be growling or making noises, just marching with their heads fixed upright.

'They're getting very close Mr Howie,' Nick mutters.

'I know mate, just hang on a second,' I keep watching them. Watching them looking at us. Just a short distance away now, close enough to pick out individual details on their faces.

They come to a stop. Not a shot is fired and no one moves. They don't stamp their feet down like an army would, they just stop and stand still in that perfect positioning.

'What's going on?' Cookey whispers.

I don't answer but keep watching. Why have they stopped? They should be swarming us now, charging forward to try their luck. Doing something. Running past us even but they don't, they just stand there.

Meredith growls, the deep throaty rumble filling the Saxon. Clarence revs the engine slightly and Blowers shifts position, his boots creaking on the metallic floor.

They don't show expression nor reaction, but neither does Dave and Lani is also very poker faced, and over the last few days I have become adept at reading both of them, sensing their moods and what they're thinking. And right now I get the overwhelming impression this horde is suddenly unsure of what to do. No, not that, unsure of what we're doing is more like it.

The sense of being watched sounds stupid as there are thousands and thousands of them stretching back over a long distance, but only those at the front can see us and it's from them I get that creeping sensation of being watched. Not by them, but by what's inside them. Assessed and evaluated, waiting to see what we do next.

I lift the rifle and take aim again, they show no reaction so I lower it down without taking a shot and still they wait.

Arms hanging limp at sides, bodies upright and poised. Heads fixed with eyes staring forward. No lips pulled back, no teeth bared and no howls or guttural groans.

Think Howie. You're missing something here.

'Dave, can you see the end?'

'No.'

'Boss, what we doing?' Clarence asks again.

I step forward to the edge of the Saxon and look out, taking a deep breath before I shout, 'what do you want?'

Nothing and I feel suddenly stupid for throwing a dumb question at a giant horde of unthinking undead. Only they aren't *unthinking.* Something is controlling them, something is making them march in perfect timing and that same something is making them stop and wait there.

It was that something the question was directed at. But how can it answer. I don't even know what *it* is. Like a conscious entity or a living thing with a mind. The idea of it is fleeting and hard to fix in my mind but I sense I'm on the right track.

'HOWIE,' thousands of voices boom out saying my name. Not shouted or screamed, just spoken. Male, female, high and low pitched but the word was clear and again I feel the hairs on the back of my neck prickle.

'I'm here,' I shout back, 'I'm Howie.'

'Fuck me,' Blowers mutters and I can feel the tension ramping up inside the vehicle. They don't respond and I have to think hard to convince myself I didn't imagine them saying my name.

'I said I'm HERE!' My voice starts to shout and ends up bellowing the last word as I feel that pinch of anger starting to gnaw away.

'This is sooo fucking creepy...can we just shoot them please,' Cookey asks.

'Lani, do you feel anything?' Dave calls down.

'Nothing, apart from being creeped out like Cookey and wanting to blow them apart,' she answers in a half whisper.

'Mr Howie, there's another column working along a road inland from here,' Dave says softly, dropping his head for second so his voice comes down and not out.

'They've divided their forces,' Clarence says, 'they knew we'd come for them on this road...we just walked into a trap.'

'Is that it?' I murmur, 'I SAID IS THAT IT? YOU TRYING TO TRAP US?' I shout as the anger builds up.

It watches the vehicle and the people within. It recognises all of them now. It knows the small one that is so deadly. It knows the giant and the laughing young men. It knows the girl was a host but now is not. It knows the dog is the one that took so many hosts down.

More than that, it knows Howie.

It recognises his voice as he shouts. It watches through many eyes and listens through many ears and it holds the hosts steady.

It studies and learns. Trying to understand why he is different, for even from this distance the infection can feel a chemical change within the hosts. Subtle yet definite. Fear grows in the hosts from this man and the infection does not know why.

So it waits. The divided forces are coming now as they start to flank and move closer, then it hears Howie shouting again, asking if it is trying to trap them.

The infection doesn't answer. It can answer and has done so simply as an attempt to unnerve Howie. Knowing from the collective intelligence that thousands of voices saying his name will cause a reaction.

'Dave.'

'Yes Mr Howie.'

'You ready?'

'Yes Mr Howie.'

'All yours,' I stick one finger up as he opens fire, withering the front ranks within seconds as they burst apart from the heavy calibre rounds slamming through them.

'MOVE,' I shout as they burst to life, gripping a handrail as Clarence accelerates away from the now charging horde. Dave's precise aim keeps them back and once again we watch utterly mesmerised as he strafes left to right getting perfect head shots. His mind must be able to compute the tiny variables in height, making constant adjustments up and down and he doesn't keep hold of the trigger either, but presses and releases perfectly in time with the strafing.

'They've stopped running,' Nick shouts, I spin round to see them back at the orderly march. Figures constantly moving forward to take the place of those cut down.

'Ahead on the right,' Dave shouts down, 'junction…they must be on that road.'

'Take the junction,' I say to Clarence as he starts dropping the speed off to negotiate the bend. He still takes it fast, causing us to either hang on tight or go flying across the inside. Once out of the junction he pushes he foot down, holding the big vehicle in the centre of the road.

'Contact ahead,' Dave shouts after a minute of tense driving. With his height advantage it takes until we've cleared the next bend to see the horde coming at us, already charging flat out and Dave doesn't wait for the order but starts firing the second he gets a clear line.

Clarence drops the speed, bringing the Saxon down to a stop before selecting reverse and starting to move backwards, buying time for Dave to fire into them before they swarm us.

'MR HOWIE,' Dave roars over the firing, 'CLIMB UP AND SEE.' I clamber over into the passenger seat and open the door, using the step to lever myself up onto the roof. The noise of the gun is deafening and I can feel the air ripping apart inches from my face as Dave continues to fire. I get up top and watch as he strafes to the left at the spot I was blocking on my way up.

On my feet and I stare out, the horde ahead of us is still charging and this close I can see their faces are now twisted with aggression. Bodies sprawling across the ground and the light coloured surface of the road runs thick with blood.

To the left, in the distance must be another lane or road, another column snaking along just visible as a dark mass drifting amongst the green and brown hues.

Spinning round I look off to the right in the direction of the coastal road, the first horde will be running now, trying to get us boxed in.

'OKAY,' I shout and drop down the back to climb into the rear, 'another one off to the left, they must have been using the junctions to peel off.' 'Clarence, turn round and face the other way.'

'Will do, narrow road so it might take a minute.'

'Get ready to fire out the back, DAVE?'

'Yes?'

'We're turning round, be ready to fire to the front and we'll take the rear, they'll be coming in from the coastal road.'

'Roger,' he commences firing again as Clarence starts the fifteen point turn, shunting forward until the front of the vehicle is making a big hole in the hedge, then backing up while turning the wheel the other way. The narrow road makes it difficult but it also reduces the width of the attacking horde, making it easier for Dave to hold them off.

'They're coming from the coastal road,' Dave bellows.

'Clarence we're side on, we need to get turned...'

'I'm bloody trying.'

'Everyone out now, form a line across the road...DAVE...pick a side and we'll take the other.'

'Take the left side,' he shouts.

'Nick, get the second GPMG, Clarence hold still while we get out.' He stops with the front buried in a hedge while we jump out the back and sprint a few feet down the road. Nick drops down behind the GPMG, pushing the tripod stand out while making ready. The rest of us place magazines on the ground ready for quick changes. Meredith going nuts in the back of the vehicle at being restrained and unable to join us.

'I fucking love this job!' Cookey shouts as he takes aim at the bend in the road ahead of us.

'Come on....I am fucking itching to use this,' Nick adds, his hand ready on the trigger guard.

'NOW,' We open up as they charge into view and at the point of seeing us they really do charge. Full on sprinting with legs pumping high and arms working to drive them on, the sight is amazing; the elderly and fat running like Olympic sprinters, they've even got their hands stretched out to prevent drag.

Two heavy machine guns and four assault rifles make a hell of a racket as this quiet leafy lane is turned into a war zone. They change tack, swerving left to right as they run. Shots start getting missed as they duck and weave. Some of them getting dangerously close before they're shot down.

'GET IN,' the loudspeaker booms out as we start a fighting retreat, waiting for Nick to stand up and move backwards, his whole body vibrating from the power of the weapon.

'Dave...SWITCH,' I scream out as he twists round to take our lot now to his front while we put the fire down to the rear of the vehicle.

One by one we get inside, Nick holding them off, then we cover him as he pushes the GPMG in then jumps up.

'COMING ACROSS THE FIELD,' Dave roars down.

'DAVE, MAKE A PATH...CLARENCE GET US OUT OF HERE...'

'HANG ON,' the big man shouts, giving us a second to find something to grip before he floors it. The engine screams with fury as it gathers speed, Dave firing straight ahead to make a gap.

'HOLD US,' Blowers shouts as he takes a stand next to me, hands grip our belts to hold us steady so we can release our grip and fire out the back. Only two of us but nearly every shot takes one down. The hedgerow starts blurring as we gather speed, Clarence shouting a warning a second before the front impacts straight into the horde.

The vehicle lifts, bouncing up on the fallen corpses to slam back down. As we power deep into them we start to see them from the rear doors. Realising they have a way into the vehicle and a message must pass between them as they surge for the back doors as we get deeper.

'MOVE,' Nick shouts, we both step aside as he walks forward holding Meredith on her lead. He braces as she reaches the edge. Her strong jaws and lightning speed preventing any of them from getting into the back. They lunge and dive but she moves deftly from side to side, white teeth flashing against the black of her fur. Blood spraying as she grips, shakes and lets go.

One dog holds the back clear, Cookey and Lani gripping Nick by his belt to stop him falling as he holds the lead.

'BRACE,' Clarence roars, I spin round just in time to catch a glimpse of a solid mass of undead lying in the middle of the road. More diving in to create a wall of bodies that quickly forms higher than the vehicle, more running in behind to make it thicker, denser. The speed of them is sickening, the way they sacrifice tells me the infection is driving these undead, watching us and learning how to react.

The front of the Saxon ploughs into the wall, more undead throw themselves at the pile. We start to lift as the front wheels find purchase on the human forms and as we lift I see them flinging themselves into the middle between the tyres, trying to ground us.

The motion rocks us violently and all we can do is hold on. Nick stumbles, barely held by Cookey and Lani at the same time as Meredith lunges forward, ripping the lead from his hand. She stumbles and loses grip, falling out the back as we scream, but there is nothing we can do but hold on tight.

The front lifts higher as the vehicle tries to climb the sudden hill of bodies. Their constant motion makes us slide left and right, the wheels spinning in the air as they lift and fall back down. A glimpse of Meredith as she fights at the back, spinning and leaping and still keeping them away from us.

A solid charge from the rear as we're getting bogged in. A mass of them surging forward towards the open doors. Meredith on her own and about to be engulfed. Dave still firing to the front and sides, trying to clear them away. Clarence jerking the wheel hard to the left, then to the right as he powers on and off, using the weight of the vehicle to slowly squash them down so the wheel can find grip.

Flat on my back now, one hand gripping on to stop from falling down and out the back doors and I see them charging in closer and closer. The Saxon bucks and bounces, slamming my back against the floor. The others hanging on for dear life. Meredith is all that stands between that charging horde and the back of the vehicle. She's alone, defending us and fighting desperately but every second sees her getting swamped.

With a roar I twist round and see my axe handle sticking out between the seats. As the Saxon bucks up I use the motion to dive forward and grip the shaft. My hand closes round it, pulling the beautiful double bladed weapon into me.

Then I let go and let gravity slide me down the long floor of the van to land on the road with my axe already up and swinging. I pile into the solid mass, scything wide and letting the razor sharp edge whisper through necks, faces and skulls.

I've learnt to use the axe now and make use of the length of the shaft, swinging it wide and gripping the end before I slide one hand up to hold it like a battering ram, pummelling at the same time as chopping them down.

The Saxon roars behind me, Meredith snarls and leaps as she tears throats out. Then she's at my side, a dark shape that stands her ground as we stare out in defiance at our common enemy. Her lips pull back showing the rows of deadly blood stained teeth. Her eyes are alive with the glory of battle, standing with her pack as we face them down.

They charge again and so we do. Just me and the dog hacking them to bits. She senses my movements and works to protect my sides as I swipe out. Together we hold them off, bodies dropping, limbs severed to fall with an unheard thump onto the ground. Glancing back I see the Saxon almost upright with the front high in the air. The rear wheels drive into the bodies, churning them up and spraying bloody gore like mud puddles. Like a beast it rocks and bounces as Clarence refuses to give in. He knows the limits of the vehicle and pushes it harder. Dave spins round, unable to fire forward so he shoots over my head deep into the ranks coming at us.

With Meredith savaging them, my axe chopping and Dave firing we clear the space. Meredith doesn't try to run forward but stays next to me.

A loud thump and the Saxon reaches the apex of the bodies, tilting over as the front drops quickly. The weight of the vehicle condenses the bodies, forcing them into the ground and the front wheels drop to find purchase and grip like hell to drag the back end free.

'NOW,' Dave shouts. I grab the dog's collar and start running for the back. She gets the idea and bounds ahead of me, her agile body using the corpses as stepping stones to leap up into the rear of the Saxon as it drops back down.

I'm not so agile and slip, slide, trip and curse my way over them. I throw my axe in and go to jump but slip down to land amongst the bloody cadavers, one hand plunging into a chest cavity and I can feel the warm gooey insides squelching between my fingers.

Back up and I keep going, hands reach out and grab my arms heaving me into the back where I land on my back grinning like an idiot at Lani standing over me with a face like thunder.

'What the hell?' She shouts, 'you happy now?'

'Yeah,' I laugh, 'much better.'

Bouncing back down the hill of bodies and Dave spins to start firing at the front again as Clarence picks the speed up to use the solid metal front as a battering ram.

Suddenly they break apart and dive to the sides giving us an empty road which he makes full use off to accelerate us out of danger.

'Round one to us you fuckers,' Cookey stands near the back doors showing them a finger, 'hear that? Round one to us.'

Clarence gets us out of the lane back onto the coastal road, slowing down a little once we're fully clear with a good distance from them.

'Good girl,' I laugh as Meredith sticks her nose in my face, licking my ears and neck as her tail wags excitedly. I ruffle her neck and stroke her head and she drops down to rest her front paws on my chest.

'We fucked 'em off didn't we girl…yes we did…yes we did!' She barks high pitched with the speed of her tail threatening to spin away any second.

'She's a good girl!' Nick drops down to rub her back and with two of us giving her a good fuss she gets even more excited with a look of pure bliss on her face and bloodied chops.

'That was bloody good thinking Nick, well done mate.'

'Cheers boss,' he replies quietly.

'Fuck that,' Cookey exclaims, 'that was fucking awesome…can we go back and go over them again…'

'We only just made it that time,' Clarence rumbles, 'did you see that tactic? That was incredible.'

'Pull up a minute mate,' I shout out, waiting for the vehicle to come to a stop before I push the dog off and slide out the back. Grabbing water bottles I start sluicing the gore from my arms and hands as Nick starts washing Meredith's face and paws.

'You alright Mr Howie?' Dave drops down from the top, then down onto the road, taking a bottle to swig from.

'Yes mate, what was that?' I ask, still flushed from fighting.

'That's what I was just saying,' Clarence walks round, 'they were trying to ground the vehicle...clever fuckers.'

'Almost did it too,' I reply, 'good driving though, you got us clear.'

'Only just, for a second I thought we we're gonna be stuck up there.'

'Why did they pull back?' Lani asks, 'they just stopped and let us out.'

'Cos they lost,' I shrug, 'like Cookey said, round one to us.'

'You think so?' She asks, 'what so...like they were losing too many so they dropped back? That's smart,' she shakes her head, 'too smart.'

'Evolving,' Dave says.

'We need to get to that town, they don't know the hordes have split,' I say quickly.

'Come here,' Lani grabs a bottle to pour on my hands, using her own to wash the bits of gore off. Then grabbing a pack of anti-bacterial wipes she starts on my face, roughly swiping at my skin as I yelp and try to duck, 'stay still, you're covered in it,' she smiles, 'and what was that?'

'What?' I ask innocently.

'That?' She asks, 'charging out on your own.'

'I wasn't on my own, Meredith was there.'

She grins and softens the swipes, rubbing more gently as she works to clear the gunk from my cheeks then my neck, 'well, just tell me next time so I can go with you,' she adds softly.

'Will do,' I grin as we lock eyes for a second until Clarence coughs pointedly.

'The hordes?' He prompts.

'Eh? Right yeah...the town...let's go, it's getting dark already.'

'You can have your car back,' he grins ruefully, 'I think that's put me off driving for life.'

Thirty Five

'Maddox, it's Jagger bruv, they coming down that road.'

'Yeah Jagger it's Maddox, you on the roof?'

'Yeah bruv, I can just see 'em.'

'Is Howie at the front?'

'Nah bruv, I swear down I can't see him.'

'Did you hear that?' Maddox asks Paula stood next to him, the sudden look of worry on her face tells him she did hear it.

'Look for muzzle flashes,' Roy speaks up, 'can he see muzzle flashes?'

'Jagger you see any muzzle flashes bro?'

'No Mads, don't see nuffin', just them.'

'We'd hear the guns if they were firing,' Paula says, 'it's so quiet we'd hear them a mile off.'

'Summin gone wrong then,' Darius adds, 'he should be at the front shouldn't he?'

'POSITIONS,' Maddox shouts, 'they's comin but Jagger can't see Howie or his vehicle, we stick to the plan you get me?'

'Mads, there's two loads coming, one on the road and the other coming into that open land where the kids play park is.'

'That's okay,' Paula says quickly, 'they have to converge at this point.'

'Unless they work round the back or try and come in from the sides,' Roy says, 'or worse they go right round and come in from the other end...it's too dark here, we need to give them something to aim for...'

'Make some noise,' Maddox shouts, 'COME ON YOU FUCKERS,' he roars into the air, waving his arms to get everyone else to join in. The youths need no further persuasion as they give voice, screaming abuse and insults in a cacophony of noise.

'Mads, 'they's comin' quicker now bruv...both of 'em are running.'

'ENOUGH,' Maddox shouts, the shouting drops out plunging them into silence save for the increasing noise of feet drumming across the ground. 'The vehicle ain't coming so listen for my voice...' Maddox shouts. The crews for the fire trucks were prepped to set them off once the Saxon had passed and was into the main street.

'Where are they?' Paula mutters with concern.

'Fuck 'em,' Maddox growls, 'we worry about us right now...here they come...'

'Oh my,' Roy says mildly as the moonlight illuminates the dark shapes emerging from the shadows. Silent figures running towards them, their features becoming more apparent as they get closer. The drumming of feet slapping against the road getting louder with every second.

'WAIT...' Maddox shouts, watching them come he knows they are too far off. The gathered group all stare as the front of the horde reaches the open land and, as predicted, make immediate use of not being funnelled by spreading out. They keep order and maintain the same pace, almost slowing down to give themselves time to spread across.

The column from the coastal road comes first, quickly joined by the spreading darkness of the second group coming across from the park. Silent and eerie, like shadows growing out of nothing. The blend of black and greys of the night make it hard to see clearly, so they merge and form, drift and grow.

'WAIT,' Maddox shouts again. The temptation to fire now is strong but most of shots would be wasted, going too high or low. The youths can all shoot but none of them are trained or experienced enough to judge great distance and adjust accordingly.

'WAIT,' Maddox watches the closest lad and the way his fingers grip the trigger, using him as a guide for the rest. 'NOT YET,' Maddox shouts again, the boy flexes his hand, quickly stretching the fingers out in a subconscious effort to alleviate the sudden build-up of tension.

The youths are hardened and even before the outbreak they were toughened against the ordeals of hard living in a tough place. But even the bravest find the sight of the awful dark figures emerging from the gloom frightening. Like something from the worst nightmare, monsters that gather and come forward. Silent and gruesome. They all expected to see the Saxon working a fighting retreat as it fired into the masses. They were ready to gather at the sides and join Howie and his crew as they cut the monsters down. But the Saxon isn't coming and without it they suddenly feel very alone, very young and very outnumbered.

'WE IS GONNA FUCK 'EM UP,' Maddox booms, 'THIS IS GONNA BE HARD BUT WE...WILL....FUCK...THEM....UP!

'COME ON...TELL 'EM...TELL THEM FUCK'S WHO WE ARE...' Maddox screams as loud as possible, sensing the ripples of fear running through his crews. Giving them a release of that nervous energy by screaming defiantly. They respond and again start shouting, the noise builds as they push their fear into their voices. Boys and girls yelling and screaming.

The merging hordes respond, and almost as though they detect the lightness of tone of the youths they give back with deep adult tones, bass filled and resonant. Deep and evil, showing they are strong and many. Two jeering sides that scream at one another across a once calm expanse of open land of a pretty seaside town.

Maddox, knowing they won't hear him give the order to fire, lifts his assault rifle and pauses for a few seconds, waiting that excruciating extra bit of time to make sure they are well within range of all the guns.

With a hard grin, eyes glinting in the darkness he squeezes the trigger. The rifle booms louder than all the shouting and every gun is lifted, every hand grips and squeezes and the air is split apart by bright muzzle flashes all across the front of the line they form. The noise is incredible and unlike anything any of them have heard. A solid boom of guns being fired and the first volley slams into the front ranks dropping scores of undead.

'KEEP FIRING,' Maddox booms and presses the trigger again. His assault rifle is kept on single shot, indicative of his character by giving him complete control over every single shot fired instead of holding the trigger down and hoping for the best.

Guns fire, assault rifles crack, shotguns boom and rifles retort. After the first solid volley the firing becomes erratic, still sustained and constant but the different weapons fire at different rates.

The charging figures are cut down in their droves but still they push forward, as though sensing the young bodies just metres away. They charge with utter determination and at first they go head on, running flat out into the guns.

Then they start swerving, turning the solid mass into a writhing undulating twisting sea of figures that bob, duck and weave. Some of the youths become confused, and instead of just firing into the central mass they try and track individual targets. The firing becomes slower, the four elders stood in the middle of the front row realise the danger.

'FALL BACK,' Maddox roars, 'FALL BACK...FALL BACK...' The order takes several precious seconds and both Maddox and Darius start grabbing to pull the children back.

Some turn and fire as they fall back which just about holds the front of the horde off for that vital few seconds but they are getting dangerously close.

'NOW...FIRE THE TRUCKS NOW...FIRE THE TRUCKS...' Maddox screams with all his worth. For a second nothing happens and they all fear the crews have been wiped out in the darkness.

Then the hose in the junction starts spraying pungent fuel high into the air, the powerful spray is directed up to rain down and soak the ground. The second hose on the beachside starts up with a second jet that just meets the first one in mid-air above the heads of the charging horde.

Roy pauses and draws the arrow prepared with a white spirit soaked rag tied onto the point, pulling back he nods at Maddox who applies a flame, igniting the end. Roy lifts and looses, the arrow soaring high to plummet down in a bright arc to plunge into the roaring jets of fuel.

The fuel ignites and the air comes alive as the darkness is banished by huge flames that give light to the whole area.

The effect is far greater than any of them could have hoped for. Paula grins with delight as the area becomes impassable. The undead still try and push through, flaming bodies bursting from the flames staggering towards the junction but they drop within seconds.

Even from their position the heat and the smell hits them hard. The stench of chemical fire, diesel and burning flesh fills the air. The group drop back further into the junction, backing away from the awesome spectacle of two giant flame throwers.

The end of the first hose starts to melt from the intense heat, the metal fitting simply unable to withstand the high temperature. It distorts and softens, slowly turning to liquid and dropping away. Without the metal end the material of the hose burns quickly, opening up to spray fuel from tiny crevices that ignite. Those smaller flames burn more material away which bursts the hose apart in a long fireball that shoots down the length right back to the truck. The flames shoot inside the internal working of the pump. Inch by inch the liquid ignites within the vehicle until that first tiny flame reaches the tank.

The resulting explosion is fantastic. A majestic screeching of metal bursting apart and flames that mushroom up into the air. Whole swathes of undead are eviscerated as the pressure wave removes them from existence.

Scorching hot metal fragments embed into soft fleshy bodies in one direction, and in the other they bury deep into the surrounding vehicles. With the fuel caps all opened the fumes from the petrol contained within the many vehicles starts to ignite. The vans and lorries closest to the fire truck go first. Exploding with less force than the fire truck but still with enough power to render the area just a sea of death and destruction.

Swarms of undead, already trying to clamber over the vehicles to outflank the survivors are taken away from this planet and put back into the most basic form of carbon.

Fuel tank after fuel tank goes up. Then the home-made bombs within the tubs, stuffed into the vehicles go up too. Boom after boom fills the air. The nails and screws burst out destroying more swathes of undead.

The second fire truck goes up in the same manner as the first. Exploding into a bright fireball that scorches the air. The burning fragments burst through the windows of the neighbouring hotel, starting small fires in the old wood furniture and exposed wooden floors.

Youths duck and drop back as the sight and noise threatens to overwhelm their senses. The human mind simply unable to compute the constant explosions going off in such quick succession.

Paula stares with wonder, never imagining it would be this effective. She catches sight of bodies still trying to get through the flames. But less now, almost as though they are probing and sacrificing just ones and twos to find a way through the fire.

As spectacular as the exploding fire trucks are, the flip side is all the fuel is burnt off in one go, the hoses gone and the middle ground is now without solid sheets of flames. Sporadic burning sections as the grass stays aflame or bodies smoulder with thick smoke coming from them.

They charge again. A trickle of a few that find a way through the flames. More follow and within a few seconds the mass of them is coming once more towards the youths.

They don't wait for the order this time but start firing as they work their way back along the street. Maddox imagining the crews racing through the streets to get to the second position.

The undead reach the front of the High Street and find a rain of plastic bottles dropping down onto their heads. Plastic bottles filled with highly flammable white spirit, stuffed with long burning rags. The trails of light look almost pretty and serene as they drop from the top of the buildings. They land and splatter the contents out, igniting from the burning rag and creating more fire that flames up.

More bottles come down amongst them as a cheer erupts from the youths fighting on the ground. Jagger had timed it perfectly, getting some of crew throwing the cocktails and others firing weapons down.

Now with two sides attacking them the horde suffer greater losses but still they surge in with ruthless determination to get at the youths.

Maddox pulls them back slowly, resisting the temptation to work back faster in order to get more of them into the street. Paula and Roy both fire assault rifles, using single shot like Maddox to pick their targets.

Shotguns spray hundreds of pellets that wither and drop the zombies. Rifles send good solid rounds through chest cavities and skulls. Assault rifles blow heads away or strike multiple rounds into legs which drop the things to crawl and get trampled.

The flames from the cocktails bathe the street in an orange glow that flickers and dances in reflection from the fronts of the buildings. Thick black smoke now billows from that first hotel set aflame from the fire truck.

A pause in the firing above as Jagger moves his crew to the next roof and starts again with more cocktails prepped and waiting. Light trails falling gracefully from the sky to land amongst the ranks.

Still they push in, a never ending supply of host bodies that refuse to yield to the constant bombardment.

Back the youths go, forced step by step by the ever advancing horde. They reach the first side street. Roy running down to check the team is ready to press the wires to the battery.

They hold position as Jagger throws the last of his cocktails before getting his crew down from the top of the last building.

With the horde now pushing so close Maddox worries they won't be able to set the bombs off for fear of being pushed back. At the last second Jagger and his team burst out with guns up and firing into the front ranks as they run down to the disappear inside the next building after the side street.

'MOVE BACK,' Maddox yells, on command they all move quickly down the street, 'NOW,' Maddox adds.

Roy relays the order, having positioned himself that bit closer to the crew waiting with the battery.

Red wires are pressed to positive, black to negative. An electrical current is sent into the wires that surges along the ground and round the corner into the High Street. The surge of current goes underfoot of the horde and down further to the first plastic tub sat in the darkness of a shop display window. The current reaches the chemicals. The chemicals react as intended and burst the tub apart.

The sound of the explosion is dulled by the solid dense ranks of the undead but the effect is highly visible as an arm of flame shoots out, sending scorching hot nails and screws across the whole width of the pavement. They go down like dominoes, blown apart and creating a sudden gap.

The current reaches the second bomb, then the third and all the way down. Pop after pop. Boom after boom and with each one a whole section of the street is taken out.

The explosions create many crawlers who buck and writhe, still determined to keep going but they also do create a whole empty section of destroyed bodies. The bombs send fire, nails and screws out to all sides, which in turn causes more fires to break out within the stores that were placed in.

With the first section of the High Street wiped out the following horde surge in, a relentless wave that pushes to take the place of the first.

Firing starts again as the weapons come to life. Bodies dropping down as the slaughter goes on.

Paula prepped the area with help from Roy. But now Maddox runs the fighting, like a general of old he watches every youth and senses the speed changes as the undead pick their game up to push harder than before.

'MOVE,' he starts grabbing children to force them away.

The action is repeated as the group drops back, drawing the horde in closer and closer. Once past the junction, Jagger commences his second barrage from above. More flaming cocktails sent down to land amongst the ranks. More firing which keeps dropping body after body.

They howl and roar and refuse to stop, instead they drive on harder and faster as their already dead bodies are pumped with strong chemicals, turning them into nothing more than wild animals.

Reaching the second junction they again hold and wait for Jagger to come down. He just makes it as the undead scream with unabated fury to charge in.

Roy doesn't wait for Maddox, he can see the charge is seconds away from getting to them so he gives the order to the breathless team waiting at the second ignition point.

Again they apply the wires and again the current ripples along the wires to the first charge. Again it goes off and again the street is cleared.

Youths cheer and roar, faces covered with grime and soot, blackened from the fires and debris, ears ringing from the constant firing of weapons within the enclosed environment. Young shoulder ache from the recoil of the weapons. Paula grimaces at the sight as the undead are once more destroyed in vast numbers.

The first section of the High Street is now well aflame on both sides. The fire eating into the old buildings. It does nothing to hamper the rate of charging but only serves to choke the air and give them more light.

Into the third section and the battery ignition crew run back to the front of the coiled razor wire. Roy running with them to make sure the connections are intact and applied properly.

They wait for the main group to drop back and apply the charge, electrifying the razor wire. As the last of the kids go by the specialist team moves across to lift the rope in the practised method. Roy now sticking with them with his heavily armed body bouncing with weapons. An assault rifle held by a strap. His compound bow looped over his shoulder, his backpack with the two sawn-offs poking up and the sword hilt sticking out.

Still he doesn't panic and even takes the time to wink and smile at the teenage boys and girls as they set the next trap. Panic doesn't bother him. Panic of this nature never bothers him. But that gum does feel a bit sore and inflamed though, his tongue probes down between his teeth and his cheek.

While the youths work he quickly pulls a small bottle from his pocket and swigs at the contents, holding the Corsodyl in his mouth as he makes sure the rope is set right.

They run back as he spits the contents out, feeling the pleasant tingle from the familiar taste of the mouthwash.

The youths start firing as soon as the rope team are out of the way. The oncoming horde now flat out as they keep the potential hosts in sight. Growling with hunger, driven by adrenalin and testosterone, fuelled by rage and fury.

'HERE,' Jagger yells, his crew pull a couple of boxes of prepared cocktails out from a shop front, 'WE MADE

THIS INNIT, WANT SOME?' He grins like a maniac as small hands grab bottles and start igniting the rags before sending them high into the air.

They drop back firing weapons and throwing bottles of flammable liquid. The street soon fills up again as the front ranks reach the rope and drive it forward, pulling the wire out and into the ranks. The electrified wire bites at the first few, making them rigid as current courses through them.

All the down the street, zombies are rooted to the spot, electrocuted by the rows of batteries pulsing voltage through the wire. The wire not only burns and contracts the muscles but bites deep into legs, opening arteries and removing fingers.

Blood sprays out to soak the road. The wire pulls in further, tangling the upright and falling bodies. With the section now a tangled mess the group stand their ground and fire relentless volleys, withering them in great numbers.

'MADDOX,' a girl runs in, grabbing at his arm while pointing behind them up the street. The leader spins round to see the front of another horde coming in from behind them. The moonlight just catching the first couple of ranks as they emerge from the gloom.

Casting about he searches for an escape but there simply isn't one; the High Street is chocked full of writhing undead. There are no side streets here.

The first alternative comes to mind and he screams the order again and again, 'CAR PARK...GO NOW...CAR PARK...' He repeats it as Darius and Paula realise the trap and start pushing the youths towards the sloping vehicle ramp.

The first children get to the ramp and lay fire down at the oncoming zombies, cutting them down to buy time for the rest to get into the entrance. With all of them inside Maddox gets them climbing the ramp to the first tight corner, holding them there and ready for the first to appear at the bottom.

'Jagger, Mo Mo,' Maddox shouts as the two older trusted lads push forward. 'Get to the top and find a way out of here.'

They nod without reply and set off, both of the fit lads racing up the ramp.

'FIRE,' Roy shouts as they reach the bottom of the ramp. A withering volley destroys the initial charge. The ramp just being wide enough for two vehicles and it makes them funnel into a tight space easy to defend.

However, with the constant rate of firing the ammunition will deplete and run out then it will be down to fighting old school. The youths are fast and tough but against a seemingly never ending stronger opponent they will lose eventually.

Slowly they start working up the ramp as the undead push further into the entrance. Solid walls of zombies that trample and crush those already cut down. Streams of blood start pouring down the slope creating another minor obstacle as the attackers start to slip and slide.

'Where the hell is Howie?' Paula snaps.

'Fuck him,' Maddox replies, 'like I said, we're on our own now.'

Thirty Six

'MAGAZINE,' Dave shouts from the top.

'Now? Really? Shit,' I curse as the heavy machine gun ceases firing at the huge horde charging towards us.

'They're coming from the rear too,' Dave says as calmly as if he was talking about the weather.

'Get that second gun going out the back.'

'Already doing it,' Clarence grunts hefting the heavy weapon in place as Nick and Lani get the rear doors open. Even in the dark there is enough moonlight to see the oncoming mass of figures running towards us.

We didn't get more than a mile before another column charged out of a junction in front of us. Dave reacting with his lightning speed to start cutting them down and we held ground instead of risking getting caught out with the last trick they pulled trying to ground the Saxon.

But now the rear lot have caught up, they must have been running flat out since we got away knowing that this new section would be blocking our route. Clever bastards. One round each then for now.

'Oh and that lot that were coming across that field back there,' Dave calls down again, 'they're coming across this field now.'

'What? Seriously? Wankers...'

'Attacking three sides, nice,' Clarence adds as he gets comfy behind the weapon.

'Dave, can you see them in that field?' I shout up.

'Er...yes Mr Howie, I just said I could.'

'Yeah alright, stupid question...is the ground flat?'

'I don't know...it's night and I can't see the ground.'

Ask a question and get an answer, 'right,' I say firmly, first twisting round to look at the rear horde, then back out the front at that horde, then at the high thick hedge on the bank above us to the right. The sea is on the left with the tide in, so there's only a thin sliver of beach left and I wouldn't risk the weight of this vehicle on the sand anyway. 'Fuck it...close those doors and hang on tight.'

The doors slam shut and I catch a glimpse of Clarence half turning back with a worried look on his face, 'Dave, you braced?'

'I am Mr Howie.'

'Ha, have some of this,' I mutter, engaging the gear box and slamming my foot down. The engine roars defiantly as it surges forward directly towards the oncoming figures sprinting at us. Gathering speed I hold the course steady going through the gears to get some decent speed up.

'We won't get through them?' Clarence shouts.

'HOLD ON TIGHT,' I scream, seconds away from impacting with the front runners and I turn the wheel sharply to the right, veering off the road and up the high bank. The front wheels leave the earth as we reach the top and crash through the thick bramble hedge, landing with a heavy thump and loud cheers coming from the lads and Lani.

I push the vehicle on, getting deeper into the field at the same time as staring across to the new lot quickly changing course to start running across the grass. A big grin stretches across my face at the sight of them. A big long line all stretched out into the darkness and as one they change direction, an almost comical movement.

Grabbing the handset for the loudspeaker and I flick the switch, activating the system, 'DIDN'T EXPECT THAT DID YOU?' My amplified voice booms across the meadow, 'COME ON FUCKERS....YOU HUNGRY?'

'They're coming through the gap we just made in the hedge,' Dave shouts down.

'Well fucking shoot them then,' I shout back.

'Can we open these doors now or are we going over any more fucking jumps?' Clarence calls out.

'Er...not at the moment mate...can't really see anything though.'

'Mr Howie,' Nick calls out politely, 'we've got headlights.'

'Oh yeah, shit I forgot,' fumbling for the switch I find it and flick them onto full beam, the British army might have lots of things wrong with it, but they put bloody powerful lights in their vehicles; these lights could probably be seen from space they're so bright.

Which gives me another idea so I start to slow down, giving Clarence and the others a chance to get the doors open. Both heavy guns start firing at the same time, Dave aiming into the field and Clarence going for the ones coming through the hedge.

Cookey gets to the front, reaching over the seat to pull the handset free, 'May I?' He shouts, his words hardly heard over the sound of both guns going for it. I get the gist and nod with a grin.

'ZOMBIES....' He drawls in a long slow voice that booms round the field, 'ZOMBIESSSS RUN ZOMBIESSS...ARE WE GOING TOO FAST? WE'LL STOP FOR YOU.'

I slow down to a dead crawl, just inching along as we watch them start to weave and stagger, Clarence holds off firing for a few seconds, then Dave stops…silence descends as we hold still and quiet, waiting for them to catch up.

'COME ON,' Cookey urges, 'WE'RE HERE WAITING…AND WE'RE TASTY TOO… WHO IS GOING TO GET A FEAST FIRST? WILL IT BE THE HORDE FROM THE FIELD OR THE HORDE FROM THE ROAD? SO CLOSE BUT THE FIELD HORDE ARE CLOSING FAST…OH NO…THE ROAD HORDE ARE GAINING NOW…RUNNING FLAT OUT BUT NO…THE FIELD HORDE HAVE THE ADVANTAGE…COME ON BOYS AND GIRLS…WE'VE GOT SOME LOVELY MEATY BRAINS IN HERE…WELL SOME OF HAVE, MAYBE NOT BLOWERS…get ready,' he whispers to me.

'On it,' I reply with a grin.

'COME ON…RUN MY ZOMBIES…SO CLOSE…SO CLOSE NOW…CAN YOU TASTE IT? I BET YOU CAN TASTE US? OOOHHH SO CLOSE,' he taps my shoulder, 'SO CLOSE…COME ON….YOU CAN DO IT…OH NO…IT'S TOO LATE!'

I pull away as both guns open up again. Swathes of undead being slaughtered after an all-out sprint across the field. Glancing up I see Cookey in fits of laughter and behind him the others giggling hard at the sight.

'OKAY OKAY,' Cookey continues, 'SORRY WE SHOULDN'T HAVE DONE THAT, UNSPORTING BEHAVIOUR ON THE FIELD…WE'LL GIVE YOU ANOTHER CHANCE…'

Both guns cease at once as I bring the speed down, amazed that Dave is willing to play along with something so stupid and infantile while we're slowly getting surrounded, but with them all here attacking us at least they're not going for the town.

'RIGHT WE'RE HOLDING STILL THIS TIME...COME ON YOU CAN DO IT...GET THEM KNEES UP...YOU CAN'T BE VERY HUNGRY IF THAT'S ALL YOU DO...OH THAT'S BETTER...BOTH TEAMS ARE MERGING NOW AS THEY ENTER THE FINAL STRAIGHT...ARMS PUMPING AWAY...OH WE'VE GOT A FRONT RUNNER...THE ONE IN THE RED TOP...COME ON MATE YOU CAN DO IT...COR LOOK AT HIM GO FOR IT...THAT'S THE WAY TO DO IT...ALMOST HERE...ALMOST...LAST BIT NOW....YES...YES..' Cookey shouts in an increasingly excited tone, 'YES...YES...BUT NO...SORRY!'

Again I pull away and both guns open up as the front runner in the red top gets just metres away, his face almost as red as his eyes.

This time I drive on, gaining a decent distance as I complete a wide turn, switching the headlights on to dim before we get back facing them. Holding steady at a low speed I drive towards the front, waiting with my fingers on the light switch. The field is packed with them now, hundreds and hundreds already charging after us and more pouring through the gap in the hedge. With fifty metres to go I flick the switch onto full beam and laugh as the front runners are blinded. Even in their pumped up undead testosterone driven bodies they flinch and veer away from the powerful lights. Veering left and right and tripping over each other as the whole front section are blinded at the same instant.

Pushing my foot down I drive straight into them, letting the hard solid front of the Saxon plough through their ranks. Dave firing from the top and as soon as we break through Clarence opens up from the back.

With both guns going they are cut to pieces. Body after body being ripped away by the large calibre bullets ripping through them. They respond quickly though and the more I drive through the field, changing direction to draw them on the more they remind me of those underwater documentaries about the huge schools of fish being hunted by sharks. Hundreds of thousands of individual fish all moving as one giant organism. Changing direction instantly, diving deeper or going towards the surface. Smooth and precise and mesmerising. These are the same, changing, twisting, weaving and all the time running after us.

Whatever the thing is that controls them has a tight grip to control them so precisely. But the field is big and we make use of the length and the width. Pulling them behind us in long strung out lines that we can cut down with ease and the body count mounts with every second. The field becomes thick with a carpet of corpses that causes them to trip and fall every time we change direction.

Then they switch on and withdraw, a sudden reaction that sees every single one of them turning to run towards the coastal road and again the action is clearly done to prevent such huge losses being racked up.

We pull up in a far corner and stare out in silence, wondering what to do. Nick and the lads take the chance to light up, taking quick hurried drags and blowing the smoke out the back doors.

'We going after them?' Clarence asks as he feeds a fresh belt of ammunition into the GPMG.

'We could go cross country to the town,' Nick suggests, 'lure them after us like we planned.'

'That's a good idea,' Lani adds, 'stick by the road until we're clear then get back down.'

'Righto,' I reply cheerfully, 'we better get back I guess, they'll be wondering where we are...I bet they're all stood there at the junction tapping their feet and tutting away while we're fucking about in a field.'

Thirty Seven

'Move! Move out the fucking way…' Mohammed runs in front of the car driven by Jagger, shouting to get the crews to move aside. The large four wheel drive had been left untouched on the first level of the car park and was a prize too good to ignore.

Window smashed, door opened, cowling ripped off and wires pressed to start the engine. Fuel cap prised open and a long rag dipped into the tank then pulled out to hang down against the body of the vehicle.

'Maddox…you got a light bruv?' Mohammed shouts as they reach the front. Spinning round Maddox takes the sight in within a split second, grinning broadly as he runs over.

Jagger gets half out of the driver's seat, one foot still in the vehicle pressed on the foot brake. The second it flames Jagger releases his foot and youths push the vehicle down the steep ramp.

They release release and drop back, all of them turning to run further away, knowing the vehicle will get jammed at the first bend.

Paula and Roy run with them, heaving themselves up the ramp as they hear the vehicle smash into the side wall, screeching metal against concrete then silence as they all get round the next bend and pause to listen.

Weapons are up and aimed as the horde take advantage of the momentary ceasefire to surge up the ramp, flooding over and round the vehicle. The rag burns quickly, the flames eating up like a short fuse to drop down into the fuel tank.

The fuel ignites. The pressure inside the tank expands so rapidly is disintegrates the structure of the vehicle surrounding the tank.

A huge fireball bursts out, sending scorching hot twisting metal fragments deep into the undead.

In the enclosed space the noise is immense; deep, long and echoing. The stench of burning fuel and chemicals wafts up.

'You two,' Maddox points to Jagger and Mohammed, 'I told you to find a way out,' he barks, 'good work and all that shit but get us the fuck out of here...you,' he switches his pointing finger to two more kids, 'do what they just done and get more cars down here.'

Everyone else gets ready, aiming weapons at the bend. Roy hands his assault rifle and magazines to a youth armed with a single shot rifle. After seeing the new method of the zombies weaving and swerving he knows it's only a matter of time before a few of them get through, and that would cause carnage.

So he draws his bow, quickly testing the string and rolling his shoulders. From his pack he pulls out the night vision goggles. The inside of the car park is dark and the bulky goggles help cut down his other senses, giving him a sense of being isolated and detached.

He pulls them on, adjusting the strap and staring down the now bright green ramp, the flames from the burning vehicle giving enough light source to make the vision clear. The only thing that bothers him is the large amount of people now staring at him. They make him feel uncomfortable which he doesn't like.

However he also knows that as soon as the first zombies appears they will be facing down there, and not at him.

From his pocket he draws a pack of sugar free chewing gum and pops one of the little white squares into his mouth. Humming quietly as he reaches back to grasp an arrow, bringing it over head to apply the groove to the string and bring it onto the arrow rest in one smooth movement. He gives a few small practise pulls and with each tug he feels the calming sensation spreading through him.

The assault rifle is good, very powerful and all that but without constant training he doesn't have the precision of aiming and taking down a moving target.

These youths have enough firepower to cut them down on mass, so now he will focus on the ones that threaten to break through.

'Roy! I said are you alright?' Paula's voice breaks through his focus. He nods curtly before turning to face her. Staring at her face bathed in green.

'Have you got your torch?' He asks.

'Yeah why?' She replies.

'Just check my mouth, my gum doesn't feel right.'

'Now Roy?' She asks gently, 'we're kinda busy.'

'Yeah I know but it just feels weird.'

'Okay, open up.'

Roy closes his eyes and open his mouth, looking slightly up to prevent the torch glaring into the night vision goggles. He flinches slightly when Paula's fingers touch his chin gently to move his head left, right then up and down.

'It's fine, it looks fine Roy, your gums are pink and healthy...no lumps...no growths or cuts...nope it's all clear,' she speaks in a calm voice, again adopting the tone of her own doctor.

'Thank you...er...sorry I just er...you know.'

'Don't worry,' she touches his shoulder, 'anytime Roy, really...'

'They're coming!' Someone yells. Roy steps away, switching immediately back to the task at hand.

Bow slightly lowered, arrow nocked and he watches as they appear, charging into view at the bend. Guns open up and fire into them, cutting the bodies down. Left hand on the bow frame, right hand holding the end of the arrow. Watching it all with a feeling of being detached, not here, not part of it.

Bodies get slaughtered and slammed away. Slowly the solid mass start gaining ground and Roy watches with curious interest as the front ranks start weaving left to right but with no set pattern.

If the youths focussed on just firing into the masses they would do well, but they get caught up with trying to track targets and missing. The rounds still strike but they hit more arms, legs and bodies which don't kill them.

Several break free, charging in that weaving fashion. Roy looses on instinct. The arrow driving deep into the skull of the one at the front. As the body slams into the wall and starts to slide down, Roy is already nocking the next arrow, pulling it back to hold ready. Another one getting in front, he looses and strikes solid straight through the eye socket.

A feeling of clam inside him. Heart rate barely above normal and between shots he chews the gum slowly, enjoying the taste and sensation.

Habit of hand and without conscious thought the next arrow is grasped, nocked and ready. His eyes scanning the bend, not really paying any notice to the death taking place, not realising the solid wall of noise coming from the many weapons firing repeatedly so close to him.

All he watches for are the ones that break free and start making ground. Those are his. Those are his targets. Just like back in the ranges when he was alone and could fire again and again, running between the targets until his legs ached and his hand was cramping.

Loose and the arrow flies true and straight; the power of the missile taking the zombie clean off its feet.

'BACK,' Maddox roars.

Roy goes with them, his movement slow and steady, his feet sliding over the ground behind him to be sure he won't trip.

'CAR COMING DOWN,' Paula shouts, he steps to the outside wall to keep a full view of the road ahead.

The sound of an engine reaches his ears, youths shouting and talking but he blots it out, focussing on the solitary figures that weave and dance in front of him.

'NOW,' Maddox shouts. Roy watches as the vehicle rolls past him then gently jogs back with the others, reaching the first level of the car park. The car bogs down amongst the zombies this time and doesn't make it to the wall. The effect is still the same and it goes bang just like the first one did.

The ramp flattens out as they reach the first level but they press on, sticking to the curvature to start up the incline to the next level.

The zombies appear within a few seconds, a relentless surge that just keeps coming. Detached and distant, Roy detects that there are not so many weapons firing now. Some of the youths must be running out. Only a few less but given time and they'll all be running out.

He looses the next arrow and holds his position, somewhere in the back of mind he wonders if there is a way out of here? He hasn't spent a great deal of time in multi-level car parks but generally speaking you drive up, park and walk down the stairs to the ground level. Those stairs will be no good as the ground will be thick with the zombies.

They are trapped with nowhere to go but up, but that thought is somewhere in the back of his mind and still his heart rate doesn't increase.

Paula senses the same thing. Watching some of the youths holding their now inert weapons. Shotguns and rifles mainly as they still have plenty of assault rifle magazines but those will soon deplete from the constant sustained firing.

Roy's abilities are stunning and far beyond anything imaginable, and for a fleeting moment it makes her wonder just how many people there were in the world that have simply incredible skills and abilities but shunned any form of limelight.

That thought is banished as quickly as it comes, replaced with a sinking feeling that Howie isn't coming. Something has gone wrong. Clearly very wrong.

Thirty Eight

'Why does it feel that this is going wrong? I shout back at yet another column making themselves known ahead of us.

'The road is clear,' Dave shouts down. Still in the fields and we've been battering our way through the hedges and crossing the rough ground but coming towards a lane we see another dark mass waiting for us. Standing silent and ready for us to pop through the hedge right into the middle of them.

They've got smart. Very bloody smart. Every lane and road seems to have another thick column. Tens of thousands of undead, possibly more and they've split into solid chunks intent on slowing us down while the others charge in from all directions. It's almost as if they know our primary weapon is the GPMG which cannot hold off multiple points of attack, and every time we get them into a position where we can cut them down in huge numbers, they simply withdraw and re-group.

As we change course on the field and aim for the road Dave shouts down that they're moving off, also heading towards the road. I thought we just needed a straight run into town but now there is a growing sensation that we've been outwitted and kept occupied. The time we've taken to get out of each little skirmish has meant they could have easily reached the town by now, and I can only hope they've got the defences up and aren't relying on us.

'BRACE,' I shout, not through worry of impacting with the hedge as we've gone through enough of them with barely a tremble. What concerns me is the steep bank down to the road and the impact as we drop quickly, the front wheels taking the brunt but still sending a violent rattling bone jarring jolt through the vehicle.

Once straight I accelerate hard, determined to get past that junction before they burst out. Normally we wouldn't worry and just plough through but after trying to ground us, I'm now trying to avoid going through any more than a few at a time.

Dave fires as soon as they show, his aiming as true now as ever before and once again I find myself worrying needlessly. The bodies fly off, spinning and crashing as we sweep by, Dave twisting round to fire deep into the junction and take whole rows of them out.

Fixed with concentration I keep eyes forward, the headlights on full to give us the best view possible. Within a few minutes we're hitting the outskirts of town and seeing the orange glow of fire. The burning buildings illuminate the area and as we come out of the coastal road into the patch of open land before the town we see the signs of intense battle.

Bodies everywhere, some clearly shot down and others in varying states between burn to a crisp and smouldering away with oily fumes coming off them. Even from inside the vehicle the air is rancid; chemicals mixed with burning rubber, oil, fuel and of course that stench of foul meat being cooked.

Slowing down and the lads crowd towards the front, staring out the window at the scene laid out in front of us. Vehicles packed into the junction to seal it off, smouldering with just the metal frames left to melt into the road.

'GUN SHOTS AHEAD,' Dave calls down, 'Assault rifles and shotguns.' As the road straightens into the High Street we see the back of the horde ahead of us.

Some of the shops are blown apart with clear signs of explosions which must be from the bombs Dave told them to plant. The ground is absolutely covered in corpses with the zombies standing and walking on them as they push forward. There must be thousands of them, all crammed in deep and thick and facing away from us.

Maddox must have retreated up the High Street, setting traps off as he went. God knows where they are now but if Dave can hear gun shots they must be relatively close. But the fact we can't see them means this horde is by far the biggest yet.

Glancing round I can see some of the vehicles have burnt out which indicates this battle has been going on for some time. They've slaughtered many of the undead but with so many left and surging forward they can't have long left before they get overwhelmed.

Stopping at the start of the High Street I select reverse and pull back as far as I can until there is a decent distance between us but still close enough to fire effectively, then I manoeuvre until we're facing away so the back is towards the horde.

I don't even need to give the instruction now as they get the back doors open and drop down to form a line across the back with Clarence in the middle with the second GPMG. Magazines get put down in front of the kneeling lads. I stay close to the driver's side and make ready.

'They're gonna charge as soon as we start firing,' I say while stacking my magazines on the ground, 'and it won't be long before they come from behind us.'

'I'll keep watch,' Dave calls down.

'We'll stay here as long as possible...try and get as many down as possible and draw them towards us, as soon as they come from behind us we'll drive off and try to lure them away.'

'Sounds good,' Clarence replies in an absent minded tone, fiddling with the ammunition belt, 'bet it goes bloody wrong though.'

'Really? You think?' I add in a softly sarcastic voice.

'Nah,' Lani cuts in, 'it never goes wrong...'

'We ready?' A chorus of soft replies which shows how tired we're all starting to feel. Sweating continuously and now surrounded by so many foul stenches and bodies. Not a happy place and not a happy time. This place looks like the very worst image of hell and it's about to get nastier.

'Dave? You ready?'

'Yes Mr Howie.'

'Righto, best get on with it then...' My finger squeezes the trigger, sending the first shot bursting out the end to spin through the air and into the first skull, and hopefully out of that skull and into another one...but it's dark so I can't see, and within a split second of my shot going out everyone else opens up, filling the air with noise, more heat and more smells.

The two heavy machine guns give their dull staccato thuds, accompanied by the slightly lighter but faster sounding noise of the assault rifles. From our combined fire power nearly the whole of the rear rank goes down within a couple of seconds. Then we're firing into the second and third ranks.

They react quickly, whipping round and as one, in that same synchronised motion, they start the charge. A deep rear section that breaks away to come at us.

There's only seven of us but our rate of fire is enough to pummel them with ease. Dave and Clarence, both so experienced on the big guns do deadly work with Clarence bellowing up that he'll do the right side if Dave does the left. With the big guns having a far smaller area to focus on, and the rest of us firing our rifles they go down in huge numbers.

Rows of dominoes falling again and again. None of them get more than seven or eight steps towards us before being felled by a spinning round. Heads erupt, skulls explode, intestines get shot out, limbs shorn off. Blood sprays, gore flies and the corpses mount up. Every single one of those we kill represents a human life. A person who had hopes and dreams and was no different to us. Luck is the only thing that separates us, and it could so easily have been us in that horde and a few of them flinging super-hot bullets into our faces instead.

A dull roar that grows into a rage filled howl lifts from them. Trapped and unable to do anything other than try to get at us. We're behind you and far enough way to fuck you up. I just hope that whatever mess Maddox and his lot are in, they can hear our guns and take some comfort that we're close.

'MAGAZINE,' Cookey shouts, ejecting one to ram another home, he racks the bolt back and commences firing again. His young face normally so jovial now consumed with utter focus as those hard eyes glare at the things he destroys.

'ATTACK FROM THE REAR,' Dave's drill sergeant voice.

'CAN YOU HOLD THEM OFF?' I shout back.

'YES,' he replies in that tone that implies utter confidence, fact, no doubt. He can hold hundreds off with one gun.

Dave twists round to open up on that lot while Clarence goes back to strafing across the width of the street. When his belt feeds runs out we have a few seconds of mild panic as we try to suppress the charge with just five rifles but glancing down I can see the big man moves quickly with long practised movements that get the next belt fed in.

The impact of the bigger gun opening up is clear as the charge is put down, but it does mean they got a lot closer and if anything happens to that gun, or it runs out, well, that will be the time to do one and leg it.

'TIME TO GO,' Dave roars out and it's enough to get us moving. Clarence covers the others as I run down to get in the driver's seat, chucking my rifle into the middle between the seats.

'GO,' Lani shouts after a brief pause while Clarence ceases firing to get up into the back, once in he starts up again, getting a few more shots in while I start pulling away.

With the junction jammed up and the coastal road now thick with incoming undead the only option is to aim for the open land and hope for the best. The powerful headlights sweep across the ground, picking out the children's play area and the streaming figures running through it. We bear left and aim beyond the junction, going round the packed in burnt out cars and a much larger molten lump at the centre of the scorched remains of the fire. Dave continues up top, now aiming at the High Street until the end drops from view then switching to the others coming from the other direction.

Paula and Maddox have blocked the junction too well as it seals us into the area. Sweeping round in a wide circle and the only two ways out are the High Street and the coastal road, unless we can find a way through the play park. Driving closer and I batter through the low fence, getting into the once manicured grounds.

We get through the park okay and then onto a novelty pitch and putt area with ornamental windmills, toadstools and model churches. All of which get mown down or battered aside as I swerve and weave to avoid the thick masses flinging themselves at us. The vehicle takes an almighty battering, bouncing and jolting as it lifts and drops, destroying everything in its path. Aiming for the far end and then veering towards the left I try to guess where the back of that junction will be, trying to batter a way through to get behind it and work through the side streets to the far end of town.

With the constant firing filling the vehicle, the smell of cordite and gun oil, the oppressive heat that sucks all the moisture away it is bloody hard work. The headlights are great but using them means I can only see what they're pointing at as they ruin my natural night vision. Hard going with many twists and turns, avoiding the larger obstacles. Lani comes to the front, pressing a bottle of sweet syrupy energy drink to my lips. I end up wearing most of it due to the jolts and bounces but some gets into my parched mouth.

She grabs a water bottle to soak a cloth, using it to wipe the back of my neck and forehead. The effect is lovely, so cooling and refreshing and with her gentle hands it lifts my mood.

In the end I aim for a house in the far corner, some kind of grace and favour park keepers cottage lovingly maintained by hard working people. We ruin it anyway, well the grounds and in particular the front garden. Battering through the fence to churn up the nice grass, drive over the pretty flowers bed and smash through the fence on the other side.

They think that's bad, but we're just one vehicle and we're being chased by fucking hundreds of hungry buggers that will pour through and ruin *all* of the flower beds, still, the ones we shoot down will rot away slowly and maybe give some nourishment to the soil.

Onto a road in front of the park keepers house and the going is suddenly smooth and easy. Clarence shouting that it's okay as he has at least one unbroken rib left to go.

Clever bastards have come over the vehicles in the jammed up junction and are now coming at us from that direction.

Making use of someone else's driveway I turn round, miscalculating my speed of approach and shunting into the back of a little hatchback that slams forward into the front of the house, ploughing through the porch and embedding in the frame of the front door.

Reversing out and we get back to facing the other way, Dave twisting his aim to shoot the buggers down that were running up behind us.

I charge on, ploughing the front of the Saxon into the running bodies which splatter and bounce off. Blood and goo splashes over the windscreen making me use the washer and wipers to smear it over the thick glass. Thumps and bangs join the sound of two guns firing. One clever zombie tries to leap high over the front, sailing gracefully through the air before being flown backwards by the rounds of the GPMG splitting him apart.

We pass the park keepers ruined front garden and break out to an empty road ahead of us, now with a thick stream pouring after our vehicle that both Dave and Clarence take great delight in shooting down.

With Lani now at the front helping me navigate the route while I try to avoid destroying everything in sight we get into the side streets and start working along adjacent to the town. Using the now massive fires of the High Street to guide us along. Both weapons stop firing within seconds of each other with Clarence shouting they've stopped running.

Now the pressure is on, knowing they'll either be heading back to the town to bolster those forces trying to take Maddox or maybe even finding a more direct route to cut us off. The silence is blissful, even just for a few minutes and the lads take full advantage to grab drinks and Nick shouting for Lani not to look while he pisses out the back door.

Both Dave and Clarence change magazines, feeding fresh belts in and although I know we got good supplies from the navy ship they won't last forever and the sheer numbers being sent against us is staggering. Relentless and utterly determined, and it wouldn't be so bad if they stayed behind us as we could cut them down with ease. But by dropping back and reserving their resources it means we know they will wait to attack on mass again. One or two points of attack we can handle, but multiple points and that's when we have problems.

'Did you see that?' Lani asks quickly as we sweep past the entrance to a side street.

'No, what was it?'

'They were running down it towards us, whole street was thick with them.'

'Nice.'

'They really don't like us do they?' Cookey calls out.

'Who is smoking?' Dave shouts down, 'Nick is that you?'

'I'm at the back!' Nick replies in a half apologetic and half defensive tone.

'I am too Dave,' Blowers adds.

'I said they could have one,' Clarence calls up, 'give 'em a break.'

'Have they got the empty shell casings out...'

'Yes Dave they have,' Clarence snaps, 'it's hot as hell and we're on our chin straps so ease up.'

'We are not on our chin straps,' Dave replies pointedly, 'we have hours to go yet so...'

'Dave,' Clarence growls with a low warning grumble.

'Yes Clarence?' Dave replies but with a very rare edge to his voice.

'Can someone pass me a drink please,' Lani calls out diplomatically. As Cookey walks up she motions something with her hands, pointing at me then at something else. A flame is ignited and I glance across to see Lani lighting a cigarette before passing it over to me with a wink.

Grinning I take it and lean towards the open window, knowing Dave will be tutting and shaking his head above us.

I inhale like a schoolboy hiding from the teachers in a second of a shared secret, grinning and trying not to laugh while Lani waves the smoke away. After a few drags I tap the ash and smile at the thought of Lani lighting one up for me, as well as wiping my face with a damp cloth. Jesus. She lit the cigarette, it was in her mouth. I stare down at the end as my heart thunders in my chest.

'Shit,' she gasps, 'put it out.'

The red end swirls into the night but the damage is done. We have shared. Whatever is in her system and on her lips is now in me. She looks utterly horrified, with wide eyes full of tears and one hand covering her mouth.

'Oh Howie...oh my god Howie.'

My hand finds hers and grips tight, I don't know what to say except it's done now. There was no malice or evil doing here. 'It's okay,' I whisper back, 'Lani, look at me...it's okay.'

Bringing the vehicle to a quick stop I start to clamber out of the seat, 'Blowers, you drive. Nick, take over from Dave I need him down here.'

They react instantly and without question. Clarence staring at me with a puzzled expression. Blowers takes over, jumping into the seat and pulling away within a few seconds. Dave slides down and steps to face me as Nick climbs up top.

'Lani lit a cigarette for me, I put it in my mouth without thinking...' I draw my pistol and hand it to Dave who just looks at it for a few seconds, 'Dave, take it...when I turn you'll have to do me.'

'What?' Cookey asks appalled, his voice trembling.

'It was my fault...I didn't think,' Lani cries, shaking from head to toe she looks wretched and mortified.

'No,' shaking my head firmly. Clarence just stares at me with utter shock etched onto his face, like everyone has just come to an end.

'What the fuck?' Blowers twists round, glancing back between me and the road. Even Nick drops back down, unable to stay up the top. All of them look more frightened than I have ever seen them. All apart from Dave who just stares at me with funny look on his face.

The rear doors slam shut as Clarence seals us in. Meredith staring up at us all with interest, wondering what's going on.

'Mr Howie...' Nick says softly, 'maybe she didn't lick her lips or...maybe it didn't pass...'

'Nick it's done mate...'

'No,' Cookey shakes his head defiantly, 'no Mr Howie, no...not you...'

'Oh god,' Lani bleats, 'oh my fucking god...what have I done...'

'Not like this,' Cookey keeps going, he slumps down onto a seat staring up with a slack expression of shock, 'not like this Mr Howie...' shaking his head he repeats it over and over.

'Listen in,' I speak fast and firm, 'don't any of you blame Lani for this...not ever...you understand?' I glare round getting nods from them all, 'Blowers, did you hear me?'

'Yes,' he replies, his voice muted and weak.

'Good, this has happened and we've got to deal with it the same as anything else...'

'Oh god no,' Lani weeps, tears streaming down her face. Clarence stretches one hand out to steady her trembling form.

'When it happens, let Dave take me outside...just me and him...got it?' Not waiting for a reply I keep going, 'you keep going, help Maddox and the others and do what we set out to do...find doctors for Lani and Meredith...and kill as many of them as possible...'

'I can't....I didn't think...I just didn't think, you looked so hot and tired so I washed your face and gave you a drink and...and...I got Cookey to give me a cigarette for you...'

'It's my fault...I should have lit it,' Cookey joins in.

'No,' I cut them off, 'it doesn't matter...none of this is anyone's fault but those fucking things out there...stay together and keep going, listen to Dave and Clarence and do what they say okay?'

'Howie no,' Lani cries harder, the tears streaming down her cheeks.

'Boss,' Clarence shakes his head, his voice so low I can barely hear him. He looks awful, white as a sheet with his big hands shaking.

'Blowers, speed up and find us somewhere to pull over.'

'Okay,' he whimpers soft and scared and I feel the surge of the vehicle accelerating.

So many things I want to say, so many things I want to tell them but the words don't come. The speed of it all, the shock just sends me numb, 'lads, you've done me proud okay...'

'Stop,' Cookey sobs, 'don't...please...'

'Cookey, you're going to be okay...all of you are going to be okay. Stay together and keep going...'

'Mr Howie,' Dave interjects staring at his watch.

'Yes mate,' I sigh, staring at the man who has saved my life more times than I can count.

'It's been well over three minutes, do you have any pain?'

'No.'

'No sensations anywhere?'

'Er...' I pause, dipping my head while I focus on my own body. I feel tired, hot, very bloody hot and my heart is going like the clappers but other than that...I don't feel anything, 'no...nothing.'

'Then you're fine,' he says firmly, 'it would have taken by now.' He looks up, his face as devoid of expression as ever.

'Do what?'

'I said you're fine,' he repeats, 'it's almost four minutes now...it never takes that long.'

'Shit...oh....' I stare round at the faces staring wide eyed and suddenly I feel like a complete dick, 'oh...right...'

'YES!' Cookey's on his feet grabbing me while shouting with joy. Laughing more out of embarrassment I give him a quick hug.

'Sorry about that...er...' Cookey steps back and I find a big grinning bear coming at me.

'Don't ever do that again,' he rumbles giving me another hug, 'shit...'

'Sorry,' I laugh again, the tension crumbling away, glancing at Dave who tells us all it's now five minutes.

'Howie, I'm so sorry,' Lani says softly. Reaching out I pull her in for a hug, wrapping my arms round her body and smelling the sweet fragrance of her hair.

'Don't worry,' I whisper, 'if I was going to turn I'd want it to be you,' I joke.

'Don't,' she snaps, 'don't say that.'

'Er...are we pulling over or not?' Blowers shouts back.

'Yes please Simon,' Dave replies, 'Mr Howie is driving.'

We all freeze as Meredith starts growling low and deep, her upper lip curling back to show her long white teeth. My heart, just easing off from the first fright has gone straight back up to full on hammering again. Everyone stares at me, the vehicle filling with her throaty growl. Holding my breath I wait for the leap and her teeth to clamp round my throat.

'Is that the dog?' Blowers calls out, 'we just passed a side road with fucking loads of them...how does she know they're outside? That dog is amazing.'

Swallowing I finally exhale and take a few deep breaths, Clarence chuckling softly and Cookey sinking down onto the seat whimpering to himself.

Nick goes back up to the top and within a few seconds we can smell cigarette smoke coming down.

'Here's clear,' Blowers brings the vehicle to a stop, jumping out as I wait for him to pass, 'I'm glad you're okay boss,' he gives me a quick grin, reaching out to shake my hand.

'Fuck! Me too,' I mutter in reply, patting him on the shoulder.

Driving on I keep taking deep breaths, my mind working like a demon as I try to understand if that means anything, if it means Lani isn't infected, or there simply wasn't enough on the cigarette end to get into my system. It could be still working into my system now, driving into my cells to start the process. But then Dave was weird, the way he stared at my pistol before taking it and he was so quick to say I was fine.

The rear doors get opened up again as Dave shouts up to Nick, asking if he's finished that smoke and to come back down. They swap over and I hear low murmurs from the lads as they talk quietly, then Clarence's deep rumble. They all looked terrified which worries me. They have to be able to keep going if anything should happen to me.

'You okay?' Lani asks quietly, leaning over from her position in the front with me.

'Fine,' I grin back, 'that probably means you're not infected,' I keep my voice loud enough for the others to hear.

'We were just saying that,' Nick shouts up, 'that's got be a good sign.'

'Definitely,' I reply.

'Still shouldn't have happened,' Lani says.

'You can probably snog again,' Cookey laughs.

'Mr Howie, up ahead we can go left and get back into the town I think,' Dave calls down, switching our minds back to the job at hand.

I take the junction onto a wide road and work down, recognising the route within a short time as the road that leads to the multi-level car park.

'Shots ahead,' Dave calls down again, 'can't see anything yet, they're muffled...must be inside somewhere.'

As the town comes into view we see exactly where they must be from the monumental horde surging into the bottom of the multi-level car park. The street is packed and dense from figures straining to get inside. Bodies stacked back far down the road and more streaming towards them, glowing and bathed from the flames shooting out from the windows of the burning buildings on both sides. A scene of utter devastation but if Dave can hear shots then they must be alive.

'I'll turn round,' I shout out, giving Clarence a chance to get ready to fire out the back doors again.

Once turned I start reversing, taking the Saxon closer and closer to the horde, and the closer we get the more of them we see. They're straining and pushing, physically driving each other into the opening ramp of the car park. With the back facing them I can just make out the muffled gun shots coming from inside and what looks like thick black smoke coming out from the open sides.

'Muzzle flashes,' Dave shouts, 'second level.'

'How many levels are there?' I ask.

'Three,' Clarence shouts, 'top one is open air by the looks of it, they'll be trapped...they must be holding them on the ramps...'

'But getting driven up if they're on the second level,' Lani adds.

'Start firing whenever you want,' I prompt as both guns stay silent. The prompt works and both of them come to life, booming into the air and instantly ripping into the densely packed ranks.

Blowers and Nick kneel either side of Clarence and join in, firing their assault rifles on single shot. Lani opens the passenger door and jumps down with her rifle, bringing it to aim and firing within a second of landing.

That just leaves me and Cookey sat there twiddling our thumbs, with a quick nod he jumps over the passenger seat and gets out behind Lani to start firing.

Left on my own and I feel all left out. So I clamber down and join in with the fun. All of our guns now firing and we shred them to bits.

Sustained and constant firing, a deafening and glorious noise that will hopefully tell Maddox and Paula we're outside and doing what we can.

The horde don't react like I thought they would. I figured they would separate and start charging at us, but instead our attack seems to motivate them to get inside the car park. A definite fresh surge ripples through them as they push harder with more disappearing from view.

Realising we could be making it harder for Maddox but there is little we can do other than keep going and with seven automatic weapons going, we're ripping them to bits.

Changing magazine I glance round to see movement further up the street, figures emerging from the shadows as they charge down towards us. Cursing at how they're moving so quickly and getting us trapped I shout for Dave to turn round.

Lani and Cookey spin about too and we at the front start directing our fire at the new lot, leaving Clarence and the other two at the back.

'They're charging,' Clarence roars. Looking back and they've timed it perfectly. Waiting for the fresh horde to attack from the other side before sending huge numbers from the High Street towards us.

Now it's frantic. We cannot lose ground either way. Leaving here will be abandoning Maddox and everyone else to certain death and there are still so many of them left, and more arriving with every passing minute.

We can't leave Maddox. That just cannot happen. They're trapped and getting overwhelmed and if we stay here we'll get bogged down and never be able to help them. Other than Maddox, Paula and Roy they are just kids. Fucking hard little buggers but kids nonetheless.

Do something. Do what they are not expecting. Take the fight to them and do it harder than ever before.

'GET IN,' I bellow across to Lani and Cookey, pausing while they get into the passenger door, Cookey diving straight over the seat to give Lani room.

Back inside I slam my door and twist round, 'CLOSE THE BACK AND BRACE.' They respond instantly, Clarence ceasing firing as the two lads ditch their rifles to the side and lean out to slam the doors closed.

I'm already moving off, pushing my foot down to gain speed as I aim straight for the middle of them. Strung out like they are and I had already noticed they wouldn't be able to try the grounding trick so I let the Saxon get some kills for a change and roar with pleasure as the beast slams them aside, ploughing through as we crumple, squash and pulverise every figure that's stupid enough to get in the way.

Using a side street I complete the turnaround quickly, reversing out to drive back down the road and get the ones we missed the first time. The lads crowd to the front cheering as we slam into them again and again. Dave continues firing, rotating round to fire towards the front and then the rear as we sweep down the road.

The car park comes back into view. A solid mass of writhing pushing undead still trying to force their way inside. The section that broke away for the charge had already dropped back to re-join the main horde. On seeing us they charge again, about turning smartly and instantly at the run.

'Hold on tight,' I growl, gripping the wheel I keep the speed decent and aim for the middle. The front of the Saxon meets the charge with brutal efficiency and we feel the bumps, bangs and thuds as the bodies bounce off. Some try to jump high to gain the top but Dave has already switched back to firing at the front and he rips them out of the air.

Still going and I veer slightly towards the entrance of the car park, coming in at an angle so the passenger side will be facing the ramp.

Lani grips the dashboard as I show no signs of slowing down, pushing on towards that wall of undead bodies.

They seem to realise what the plan is at the last second, hundreds turning as one to come at us but it's too late. I drive the front of the Saxon deep into the middle, taking a whole swathe of them away from the entrance. The engine roars as it finds increasing resistance from the bodies squashing with a concertina effect. Driving my foot down and the Saxon responds, driving us further and further into the crowd as we batter them down. Dave firing on sustained and he takes many more out at the sides.

Coming to a sudden stop I select reverse and quickly back up, feeling the jolt as we bounce over bodies. I spin the wheel and push the back end into the middle of the street and aim the front of the vehicle towards the ramp. Back into gear and I floor the pedal again, not giving them chance to react.

They do react and they do it far quicker than ever before, bodies lunging down between the wheels as they try to create a high wall and prevent us moving off. But we still have that little bit of surprise and momentum so we surge over and through them, getting onto the ramp and increasing the speed as we go.

Those undead already on the ramp try to throw themselves at us too but we've got the winning hand for now and we push on, slamming them away, running them down and still Dave fires, shooting down the back of the ramp to get anything the vehicle has missed. Rounds ricochet inside the concrete enclosure, pinging off the walls and ground to bounce off the armoured panels of the vehicle.

'DAVE FIRE AT THE FRONT,' Clarence booms as we get to the first level and find the entrance to the ramp up to the second level clogged thick. Dave pauses, turns and commences firing again within a second or two. Bodies get cut down as I push the front of the Saxon into them, using the weight and power in addition to the GPMG to force a path through.

'LADS, BACK DOORS,' Clarence dives down to his second gun, the rear doors get opened and again the air is filled with the thunderous roar of multiple weapons firing. Meredith barking like mad, desperate to be released from the lead so she can charge out and attack them.

Second level and still they're thick and heading towards the last ramp to the top level. Lani grabs the loudspeaker handset, pressing the button down before shouting, 'MADDOX...WE'RE COMING...HOLD YOUR FIRE...' She repeats it several times as we batter and shoot the undead out of the way.

The powerful headlights illuminate twisted faces full of hate and fury, blood encrusted skin, lips pulled back and red bloodshot eyes everywhere. Gruesome and intensely frightening but the adrenalin is up now and at least we did something they didn't expect, and took out a whole shit load of them at the same time.

We might now be just as trapped as they are but fuck it, we can fight together and show those dirty diseased bastards that we stand as one.

The Saxon bursts out onto the top level, into the open air and the sight of a thick line of children holding guns high and cheering at the tops of their voices. Maddox and Paula in the centre and now looking very relieved, Roy off to one side wearing a big pair of goggles.

'You took your time,' Maddox grins with a shake of his head.

'We're here though...there are fucking thousands of them coming...the whole street is full.'

'You got ammo?' He asks quickly.

'Plenty for now, Blowers, get the magazines out to hand round...listen in,' I shout across at everyone, 'we've got enough fire power to keep them back for now so take the chance for a drink and a quick rest, we've got loads of water in the back.'

'I'll do it,' Lani shouts running to the back with Cookey, as Blowers appears with Nick handing out new magazines to the youths with assault rifles.

The armoury has been stripped bare by the looks of it and all the guns we got from the refinery are now up here, and well used too judging by the thick carpet of shell casings on the ground.

The youths look haggard and drawn. Paula drinking from a bottle of water as Roy stands quietly to one side keeping an open line of sight to the ramp.

'You okay?' I call out to her, knowing we've got a few seconds before they run from the bottom to the top.

'Very glad to see you,' she smiles grimly, 'but there's no way down other than the way up.'

'S'alright,' I grin, 'let them come to us for a bit, we got enough guns for a while.'

'But you said there's thousands...how long will the ammunition last?'

'Probably not long enough,' I reply quickly, taking the offered smoke from Nick.

'So,' Maddox scratches his head, 'what you doing here then? We're all trapped now.'

'We are mate, but we stand together...that's how it is.'

'Very dramatic,' Lani scoffs as she walks past with a crate of water bottles, 'just need some theme music to go with that line.'

'Paula,' Dave calls out, 'you did well with the town, good work...' he adds racking the bolt back and taking aim at the ramp.

'Thanks,' she nods.

'Any losses?' I ask Maddox softly.

'Nah,' shaking his head, 'one of them cut his finger open on the razor wire and another tripped over but that was it.'

'Seriously? No losses? That's very good mate.'

'INCOMING,' Clarence shouts from the back of the Saxon.

'Shit that was quick, they must have legged it flat out up those ramps,' I say to Maddox as we both run to the back. Dave opens up from the top, filling the roof space with the beat of the GPMG.

For a few minutes it looks like he will be able to hold them on his own as they come out in a steady trickle, but those are obviously just the fitter ones who could get up the ramps quickly.

The rest surge up as one. Presenting a solid writhing mass of undead surging up the ramp to spill out onto the flat concourse. Like a super organism, a huge snake of one form that just pours onto the roof in a never ending wave. Every foot of space between that top ramp and going all the way to the ground must be filled with undead coming up.

Clarence and the lads open fire. The surge is so powerful, so sustained that even with all our guns firing we only just hold them back. Bodies that take multiple rounds to the chest and stomach keep pushing on. Innards and guts spill out but still they charge in. The ones we cut down are trampled and booted aside. Undead work to shift them, not allowing the fallen to hamper their progress.

'MO MO, Look over the wall, how many in the street?' Maddox shouts as he changes magazine. Youths come forward to join us, firing whatever weapons they've got as the surge is just too strong to hold back.

'Whole fucking street is packed,' Mohammed shouts as he runs back.

'STAIRS,' Roy yells. I spin round to see the double doors leading to the stair well bursting open spewing another solid massed horde that surge out. Roy fires his bow, slamming an arrow into the front centre. Guns turn to fire at them, reducing the fire power we have to hold the ones coming from the ramp.

The air is filled with solid gunfire. Children shouting at each other and undead howling like crazy, a vicious roar coming from them as they give voice, sensing they are so close to taking us.

'MAGAZINE,' Dave bellows and for the few seconds it takes for him to feed a fresh belt in we're watching them slowly encroach. The body count is mammoth with so many being killed but still they come on.

Every single one of us fires and fires, empty magazines being thrown aside as we scrabble with hurried hands to get new ones in. Blowers running back to the Saxon to dump fresh cases of full magazines down. Maddox gets youths running them to the groups firing. Relentless and utterly despairing as we can all see just how determined they are.

Then they stop and there are no more undead surging out from the ramp. I spin round to see the same at the stairs. Silence descends as we all stare at each other, looking about to see what's going on.

Mohammed runs to the wall and climbs up, taking care to look down at the High Street without falling off, 'still fucking packed,' he shouts.

'Are they still coming in?' I call out.

'Yep,' he answers.

'They're doing something,' Clarence growls, 'this is going to be a big push so get ready...'

'Blowers, get the axes and hand weapons out and ready, tie Meredith to the end so we can unhook her quickly,' I shout the instruction as he jumps back into the vehicle, passing the axes out and Lani's meat cleaver.

'You all got hand weapons?' I shout to the rest of the group.

'Only knives and shit,' Maddox replies.

'If it comes to it then you take the stairs and we'll hold the ramp...get the youngest into the vehicle and if you see a chance to drive down then take it.'

'Me? You want me to drive down?'

'If you get the chance yes mate, take the youngest and go.'

He nods, scanning his crews as he mentally picks out the ones to be protected, they all look away, not one of them wanting to be taken away from their mates.

Groans come from the ramp and the sound of movement and things being dragged, something flies out of the dark opening to land with a thump on the ground just feet in front of us. The item rolls and comes to rest. The head of an adult male, the face contorted with the lips still pulled back and the red eyes showing. We all stare at it in confusion, then another one comes flying out, then another and within seconds the air between us and the ramp is thick with body parts being thrown out. Torn off limbs and heads starts slamming down amongst us. Sickening and gruesome with blood and bits of flesh spinning off. Several of the youths are hit by the grotesque lumps of meat. A heart lands inches away from my boot, intestines and organs, hands, arms and legs all launched out.

The filthy dirty evil fuckers are ripping the corpses up and using them to batter us. Infected blood and flesh starts coating out clothes and the throws get harder, sailing higher to drip down and land on us.

'GO BACK,' I shout, running for the Saxon to pull it out of range of their missiles. Clarence keeps the rest in order, stepping back until we're free from the barrage.

Laughter floats out from the ramp as I run back to the line. A single solitary laugh that echoes and rolls round the roof space. High pitched and maniacal, others join in slowly at first but building as more and more of the undead start laughing. Loud and sustained and it grows to hysterical all out laughing, the kind of laughing you associate with mentally ill people. More body parts fly out, landing in wet thumps on the ground, legs and arms with bloodied stumps.

The youths look round aghast at the sight and sound. Disconcerting to hear such a maniacal human sound while they tear up their own kind to throw the bits at us. Inhuman and evil, showing us exactly what they are and it sends shivers of fear rippling through the group.

At the top of a shitty grey multi-level car park in some unknown town, surrounded and trapped with thousands of diseased undead. Fires raging down the street, smoke billowing along and clogging our lungs. The heat is still unbearable and sweat pours from our blackened faces. Shell casings lie amongst the chunks of body.

Tears start streaming down the faces of the young. My lads look appalled and horrified at the sight and the laughter grows in intensity. Every undead gives voice, all down the ramps, the stairs and on the street.

Maddox walks into the middle of the group near us and speaks quietly to one of the girls. She looks young and frightened but nods back and follows him towards me.

'How do you make the loudspeaker work?' He mutters. I take him over and show him the controls for the handset. Nodding he gets the girl to climb into the passenger seat and carries on talking to her in low earnest tones. She cries with hot tears that spill down her cheeks but she nods and takes the handset, holding it close to her mouth. Closing her eyes she takes a few deep breaths and seems to almost fade away, like her body is here but her mind is elsewhere.

With her hand pressed on the button the air is filled with the sound of her breathing, a soft noise that does nothing to help the situation. Maddox steps away and glares with complete defiance towards the ramp and the noise of laughter coming out.

Children's heads start being flung out. The faces of the young and innocent sailing through the air to land and roll towards us. Teeth get knocked out of the detached heads, noses broken and the white spinal column sticking out the end. Sobs break out and someone vomits.

Our energy and more importantly, our will to fight is being eroded by the psychological warfare being waged against us.

A long quavering tone fills the air from the speakers as the girl starts singing into the handset, a soft trembling voice that grows in volume and strength until it fills our ears with perfect harmony.

Amazing Grace from a pure strong gospel voice, the long notes quavering perfectly. Every head snaps to the Saxon as the girl squeezes her eyes closed and sings. She gains in strength and confidence as her amplified voice rolls around the roof-top.

They get louder but so does she. They are course and hysterical. She is pure and human, full of love and warmth. Voice soaring and carrying the chilling notes in glorious harmony.

The laughter goes up a few notches but the thousands of voices they have cannot, and will not ever defeat that one girl singing her heart into that handset of an old battered British army APC loudspeaker.

Bodies stiffen and stand taller, the hairs on the back of my neck prickle and stand out. Chills run up and down my spine and for a second I close my eyes and let that sweet voice transport me somewhere else.

Hope is given to all of us. Those that know the words join in and give voice. Clarence looks defiant, his eyes fixed and his jaw set. The lads stare with those hardened eyes at the opening to the ramp. Lani tilts her head back and lifts her top lip. Paula just stares fixed, Maddox looks at his youths and nods.

The girl sings and fills the air with beautiful music made just by her. The undead try and get louder, they try and compete but we win. We have the girl with a pure voice and love in her heart and for that they will always be wanting.

Reaching the end of the song she starts again from the beginning, louder and more powerful this time. The notes longer and stronger, almost as though she knows that sound produced by her will lift our spirits higher than anything else can at this moment.

Movement from the ramp and the laughter ceases as the missiles end. A dragging noise comes and we watch with expectant defiance as the girl makes our chests swell with pride. Adrenalin begins to pump but more than that; a sense of honour, of humanity. That we chose this fight and we chose to do this.

A solid wall comes into view. Dead bodies all prone and being presented to us as a hard compacted wall. The undead carrying their fallen brethren in front of them as a shield. Dave starts firing but even the large calibre bullets have little effect, ploughing into the thick bodied corpses that must be two or three bodies thick. How there are being held is beyond me, but they are. The living dead hiding behind the true dead as they inch forward, pushing the heavy wall in front of them.

Rifles start firing, guns opening up but all we do is send rounds into the dense material of human corpses, maybe a few get through to the pushers on the other side but not enough.

'CEASE FIRE,' I bellow, the order repeated as the guns die off, 'CLARENCE WITH ME...EVERYONE ELSE STAY HERE BUT DO NOT FIRE....DAVE BE READY...'

'On it,' he shouts down.

Ditching my rifle I grab my axe as Clarence hefts his, 'Nick, release the dog.'

He jumps up, unhooking the lead and holding the huge straining animal by her collar. We start towards the corpse wall, walking at first then jogging that builds up in pace as the fury within me is unleashed.

'NOW NICK,' Meredith bounds from the back of the Saxon, her legs opening up as she sprints forward with an ever increasing growl that grows into a snarl as she leaps high. The whole wall shudders from her impact alone. Then Clarence and I are there, axes swinging as we roar and hack away. Clarence destroys so many with his strength. Meredith grabs limbs and drags them, twisting and ragging the bodies.

I go berserk and hack away, slamming the axe deep into the bodies again and again. Within seconds the lads are joining us, unable to restrain themselves to stand and watch. Our axes fly and dig into the corpses. Maddox runs in, Clarence hands him his axe and goes to work with bare hands. Grabbing bodies to heave them out and launch them back over the wall.

Roaring with anger the giant demolishes them one at a time. Throwing adult sized cadavers like they are rubbish bags, sailing them over the top to land and crush those on the other side. We focus on the middle, clawing and hacking. Arms get coated with gore and the wall starts to erode as they push on with relentless energy.

Two sides growling and fighting. We rip the middle out, opening up a hole through which we can see just a solid press stretching back into the darkness. Undead pushing and straining as they try to march towards us, driving that wall on.

'MOVE NOW,' I shout, we burst away left and right, 'DAVE...'

The gun opens up, aiming directly for the hole we created in the middle. The rounds whip through and start taking out the undead on the other side while we start working at the edges. Clarence gets another hole created and shouts for the GPMG to be brought to him. Children run down carrying the heavy weapon between them.

Bodies get shoved into the gaps from the other side but Clarence just rips them out again before grasping the big gun, shoving the barrel through the wall and opening up. Strafing left and right. The pressure against the wall starts to slacken as the bullets tear them apart.

'MORE GUNS,' I shout, rifles get brought down and we copy the big man, shoving the barrels through the gaps to fire into the ranks beyond.

'PULL BACK,' Dave orders. We comply instantly, all of us pulling our guns out to start running back to our line. The wall collapses as we run, bodies falling down as they go back to full on straight charging but this time they're closer, having gained a few metres from the wall.

We get back and the line opens up, every single weapon firing on full. Meredith pulled away by Nick and she goes back into the Saxon to resume her poised standing. Glancing over and the second team at the stairs are fighting just as desperate as we are.

Slaughtering hundreds of them again and again but they are endless. Arrows flick out and take out weaving runners that break free from the front but slowly they gain ground. Just inches at a time and they have to work to clear the bodies out of the way.

Cookey jumps into the back of the Saxon, running to the front and within a few seconds the opening bars of *Missy Elliott We Run This* booms out. As with the girl the uplifting strong beat gives us a fresh surge of energy. It makes them angrier and they surge harder but we cut them down.

'LAST MAGAZINE,' Dave shouts.

'ME TOO,' Clarence adds.

'DAVE, GET DOWN HERE...SAVE IT,' I shout up. He nods and jumps up and onto the roof of the vehicle. I grab an assault rifle and throw it up, catching it one handed he lifts aims and starts firing.

Clarence starts on his last magazine. Dave ends his first, knocks it out and slams another home, single shot firing and no doubt getting a head shot with each bullet.

'WE'RE RUNNING OUT,' Blowers shouts, ramming another one into his rifle.

'MY TEAM IN THE MIDDLE WITH ME...MADDOX GET YOUR YOUNGEST IN THE VEHICLE...' He bursts away, grabbing reluctant children and forcing them into the back of the Saxon. Paula stands with us, firing her rifle with determination.

'You're going with them,' I shout.

'Staying,' she shouts back.

'Nope, we're going hand to hand in a minute...can you do that?'

'Watch me,' she growls.

Roy comes into our group, firing arrow after arrow with an incredible speed. Robotic and fluid and they sail off with utter precision.

'MADDOX, SEAL THE DOORS AND GET A DRIVER INSIDE IT.'

'DONE,' he shouts as he runs back and starts firing again.

'ALMOST OUT,' Clarence directs his fire into the middle, driving them back but they just surge and push on.

'IS THE DOG OUT?'

'WITH ME BOSS,' Nick shouts.

'DONE,' Clarence stands up, grabbing an assault rifle he starts firing that but without the GPMG going they gain ground quicker now.

'WE READY?' I roar out, 'LANI...'

'Right behind you...' she growls.

'THIS IS IT...WE'RE GOING IN...AND WE DO NOT YIELD...HERE ME? WE DO NOT YIELD.'

'NEVER,' they scream back.

'Dave?'

'Yes Mr Howie.'

'You ready Dave?'

'Yes Mr Howie.'

'HAVE IT....' Casting my now empty rifle down I take my axe up, roaring as the rifles are dumped and weapons drawn. Roy rips his mask off and drops his rucksack, pulling his sword out with a look of utter violence etched onto his face.

The clatter of weapons as they fall to the ground, knives, axes, blades, sticks and chains get pulled out. We scream with terror and fear and rage and then we charge.

Oh we charge.

Adults and children who refuse to give in. Maddox proud and strong with a long bladed knife in hand. Dave going low with his arms out behind him, knives reversed. Meredith streaks as she is finally allowed to attack them.

Lani right with me. Clarence striding on with Nick at his side. Blowers and Cookey together as always.

Oh we charge.

Dave leaps higher than I have ever seen him go, his arms stretch out and he turns in mid-air to face back towards us and as he drops down I see a huge grin on his face. He plummets deep within their ranks and sets to doing what Dave does best.

Meredith goes low and drives in between legs as though working to get near Dave. The two of them explode out and start attacking from within as the rest of us hit the line.

Axe out and swinging, taking heads off as we all drive deep to create more damage. The flush of real battle surges and powers us on. The music set on loop and it blasts out as we fight and hack. Youths driving blades into eye sockets and dancing around them. Maddox fights like a demon, stabbing and pushing them aside with his strong arms. Paula uses a big commando style knife, stabbing with utter fury.

Roy swings the sword with glorious energy, driving them back as he slashes and lunges, showing what an amazing weapon the sword is in the right hands.

Blowers and Cookey fight with that brutal efficiency they've learnt so well. Always at each other's sides and despite the constant abuse they give, neither of them will allow anything to happen to the other.

Lani ducks and weaves, as graceful as a ballet dancer. The meat cleaver slices and whispers across throats.

Me? I hack and chop and slice and just batter them down and slowly, ever so slowly I start to feel that sensation coming over me but they too seem to sense it and the intensity explodes as they rush forward towards me. Every undead focusses on me, all of them coming my way. Then they start swirling, not individually but on mass. Like a giant Catherine wheel made up of ranks of undead. Some lines go one direction and other thick lines go against them.

Confusion all around and I start to get swallowed up, getting swirled and pulled further into the ranks by the ever revolving lines. My axe flies left and right, forward and back as I cleave them down but they pay no heed and just keep rotating round and round, literally drawing me into their ranks.

I hear my name being called by many different voices but they get further and further away. My feet run to keep up with the pace, desperate not to trip and go down. I yell for Dave, Lani, Clarence and I slash and hack but deeper and deeper into their ranks I go.

The ground drops away and I'm at the top of the vehicle ramp. They're driving me down into the murky, gloomy depths. I try to hold back and stand my ground but it's impossible and no matter what I do I get sucked down the ramp.

Dark here and only the tiniest sliver of moonlight gets through. The heat and stench are unbearable. So many rancid decomposing bodies all pumping heat out. My space gets smaller and I lash out round and round trying to drive them back.

Fury and rage spill out of me as I get carried down. I refuse to go any further and focus on those on the ramp above me, not letting them get close enough to push me down.

They surge in harder and faster, low growls and the flash of red eyes picked out by the moonlight. Desperate and sweating so much, alone and isolated getting sucked further down and away from my team.

Against the wall now, pushed hard, battered by bodies slamming against me. Buffeted left and right and trying to swipe out at anything I get the axe into.

The side of the wall is rough and I get rammed into it again and again.

Hands start grabbing at me and in the dark I can't see who or where from but I twist and buck, kicking out as my axe swings and digs deep into flesh.

Something hits the back of my legs and I go down, landing on my back to cycle my legs up and around. Kicking out and still waving the axe but the space gets increasingly smaller as the hot fetid bodies push into me.

One above me bearing down. Just blackness now, pitch black and I'm screaming in utter desperation trying to batter it away. It gets heavier as it pushes down on me. My axe blade bites into the stomach ripping it open then something grasps the shaft and yanks it away, snatching it from my hands.

Without a weapon I heave and push at the heavy body plunging down onto me, imagining the mouth open and the drool ready for the bite. My hands claw at the stomach, feeling the edges of the ragged wound. Gripping and tearing the flesh open and it doesn't matter that I'm surrounded by hundreds, possibly thousands of them. This one will not get me, just this one is all that matters right now so I push my fingers deeper into the hole and grope at the warm sticky entrails within the stomach cavity.

My fingers grasp and twist, pulling wet things out but still it comes down at me. Intestines get yanked out and I fight harder, both pushing him back and trying to rip his insides out with my naked hands.

So hot I can hardly breath, sensations all over me as bodies buffet and feet slam into my sides. One of them trips and lands on the one on me, the weight is too much and they crash down crushing my chest. Twisting and shaking as they try and break free, my hands out of the stomach and groping for the creatures neck. I feel the jaw line and the spiky stubble then move my fingers up to the eye sockets, it thrashes and tries to bite down but I push my thumbs into the eyes, feeling the pressure build up until they pop and spray hot liquid over my face.

I get a hand down to his stomach wound and find another hand is already pushed into it. Our fingers grip and slide against each other as we fight and struggle. The undead gnashing his teeth so I drive my forehead up to head-butt its nose, feeling the crack as the bone breaks and a shooting pain from the impact.

Blood pours down and soaks my face. I twist and shake, desperate to avoid the blood going into my mouth. The hand in the stomach rips free and I feel bony hard fingers searching for my mouth. Teeth clench and I growl with increasing panic as the digits push to open my mouth.

Sharp nails scratch against my teeth but I keep my mouth clamped shut, pain flares from my jaw and my mouth opens as an involuntary reaction. Fingers get inside, prising my jaw open further. I bite down and feel my teeth sinking into flesh and bone. Hot liquid bursts into my mouth to drip down my throat.

Then something else is pushed in. Something hot and beating and spraying blood. The heart ripped from the first undead is shoved into my mouth, still warm and the beats die off as the final bit of energy is expended.

Bloody tissue, thick and firm, hot and sticky with metallic arterial blood pumping into my throat.

Drowning I try and swallow it down and keep fighting but my vision starts to go. Unable to breath from the weight on my chest and the heart jammed into my mouth. Tears pour down my face and I reach out to feel a throat, gripping and squeezing with every last ounce of strength I have.

My grip fails, hand dropping weak from lack of oxygen. No pain now, my body is shutting down to try and keep the brain alive. But it's too late. I've ingested so much blood and infected gore that within a few minutes I'll be one of them, waiting for the whisper of Dave's knife against my throat.

I think of the lads smiling and laughing in the back of the Saxon. I think of Tucker and Jamie and Curtis. Blowers and Cookey so close to each other, Nick so clever and eager to help. I think of Clarence and how he chose to come with us and be part of our team. We were special. We were something unique for we didn't run or hide. We all knew the risks and here I am, succumbing to the greatest risk of all.

I think of Lani so beautiful and graceful and my heart soars one final time as I think of that kiss we had. Images race through my mind, Marcy and Sergeant Hopewell, Ted and others from the fort. Big Chris grinning with his white teeth stark against his black beard. Sarah, my sister, taken so horribly and I see her smiling face, my parents too, grinning and laughing as we sat round the table having Sunday dinner.

Then I think of Dave. That special man that saved me so many times. We've killed so many of them, but none of it would have been done without Dave. The way he stuck by me through thick and thin, always by my side. He will be heartbroken at this, that he didn't protect me but he will go on. He will give that protection to the lads and with Paula, Roy and Maddox they will live and succeed.

A final fleeting thought enters my head as I slip away. That there are so many undead streaming past me towards the roof that this could be it, maybe they won't survive and even Dave will be taken out.

Darkness descends. Final and infinite darkness takes me and I am no more.

Thirty Nine

'MR HOWIE?' Dave roars, the loudest he has ever roared but there is no response, just the intense sounds of fighting from all around. This shouldn't be happening. Mr Howie is the one to fix this. That is fact. Dave knows this. Since he first saw Howie fight back in Boroughfare, then the way he led them in Salisbury, Dave knew Mr Howie was the one to make this better. It was intrinsic and undoubted. Dave had to protect Mr Howie so Mr Howie could fix it.

But for first time in his life he left a nagging sensation of doubt. That he got it wrong. That Mr Howie is being pulled away from him to a place that Dave, despite his amazing talent for killing, simply cannot get to.

For every undead that he kills, more surge in front of him. He fights harder and faster than ever before. Utter sheer brutality at lightning speed as his hands flick and dance, cutting throat after throat open.

He weaves and swerves, ducks low and leaps high. Gradually he gets deeper but still they push in and prevent him. The swirling patterns they make are confusing but Dave knows Mr Howie has been taken to the ramp. He doesn't question how he knows this, just that he does. Mr Howie is in *that* direction, so *that* direction is the one Dave takes.

A growing feeling of dread builds in his stomach, a tiny knot of fear that blossoms and spreads through his entire body. Dave doesn't feel fear so the feeling is intense and electrifying. It scares him which just makes him faster and harder, that maybe the faster he goes he can escape the truth that is battering into his head. That Mr Howie is gone, he has been taken.

Dave is scared, fearful and above all else he feels a burning rage. Inhaling long he starts to roar, the drill sergeant voice growing louder by the second.

'I AM DAVE,' he bellows, his voice carrying far and wide. He reverts to the tactics taught to him, scare the enemy, make them fear you. 'I AM DAVE...I WILL KILL...'

Pushing on he fights and kills, just a blur of arms that spin, 'I DESTROY... I KILL...I AM DAVE...' But still they drive into him and block his path.

Dave is expert at killing and in the long battles they've had together, he knows the undead fear Mr Howie. They wilt from him and show tiny reactions that they don't do to anyone else. Dave can kill more than any man alive but they don't fear him, they fear Mr Howie. But Mr Howie has been taken. Mr Howie is alone and isolated. Mr Howie trusted Dave and Dave has failed.

'I....KILL...I....DESTROY....' The voice floats clear and deep. Mr Howie showed him respect and kindness. Mr Howie offered genuine friendship. Mr Howie sacrificed himself that day at the motorway service station and no one has ever done those things for Dave. In the services he was just a deniable asset, a machine that was deployed against the enemy. He didn't have friends and he did what was asked. But Mr Howie chose to fight alongside him. Mr Howie chose to have Dave as a friend. He chose to take Dave with him that night in the supermarket.

He was the one. He was going to fix this. What went wrong? It failed because Dave failed. Mr Howie is now dying a slow painful death because Dave didn't do the one thing he was meant to do.

Pain inside his heart, sorrow in his soul. A feeling of emptiness grips his gut. Tears brim in his eyes and spill down his cheeks but still he fights on. Because that is all he knows to do.

Clarence casts about, being a head higher than most he saw Howie being sucked into the ranks and bellowed after him. Fighting to try and save him but they were too strong and the swirling motions made them too difficult to fight through. Those near the front got strung out and separated, youths got taken down and trampled. Others fought their way free to stand apart from the mass an stare in horror at what was happening.

Clarence tried again and again to get into them but their motion and constant movement made him confused and lost. Slamming his axe round and round he cleared space but Howie was gone from view. The same sickening feeling spreads in his stomach, the same pain in his heart that Dave feels. Howie is gone.

Howie wasn't an army officer, he was just a supermarket manager but he was the greatest leader Clarence had ever followed. His ability was immense and something about him drew all these survivors to fight *with* him and *for* him.

Now he is gone. Taken and alone. Fighting for himself just to survive but without all of them with him, he cannot hope to live.

It's lost. Everything is lost.

Tears stream down the lad's faces, utter fury erupts from them as they plunge in again and again. Fighting without mercy but they cannot make ground. They cannot get into the masses to go after Mr Howie. Blowers screams with frustration, Cookey grits his teeth and Nick fights with wild abandon. Mr Howie saved them that day in Salisbury. He didn't have to do anything but he fought through that huge horde and then led them to take the Saxon. That man led them day after day and they followed him because of who he was, because of the way he spoke and the sheer passion he projected. They, along with Dave and Clarence, sense his loss. They sense the increasing distance between them.

The boss is being taken away to be killed alone, and there is nothing they can do. They fight and attack, getting many kills but not enough and they feel the growing sense of hopelessness spreading inside.

Lani doesn't fight. She doesn't attack or try to cut them down. Instead she senses they want Howie so she pushes through them. They don't go for her but do the job they are told to do and swirl and move and create confusion.

Lani goes with it, pushing and squeezing through gaps as she searches for Howie. She knows she cannot fight them off and doesn't care for anything other than being with him. Just to hold his hand while they both get taken. To give him that same comfort he gave her every night, holding her tight as they cried. She knows he is special but to her is special in so many different ways.

So polite, so unassuming but that ferocious passion that comes into him. That drive to win through and defeat such massively superior numbers. Even tonight they could have just driven far away and never had to fight again, but Howie knew those children were up here so he attacked just so he could stand with them.

Howie took that Saxon and drove it into the masses, then fought his way up to the top for nothing more than to give hope. He attacked that wall of bodies as he saw a task that needed to be done so he went at it.

The pain he felt at last night with Marcy was obvious. It was etched into every line in his face. He was heartbroken at what happened, even though he didn't have any control over it he took the responsibility without complaint.

Lani doesn't know how or why she isn't infected now but she does know it has something to do with Howie.

She knew she loved him. She loved him dearly and would give her life for him to live another day, another hour, another minute. That's why she pushes on, just to hold his hand that one last time, so he can feel the warmth of someone that loves him when he goes down, so she can tell him how thankful they all are that he was there, but it's too late.

Howie is gone. She feels it but pushes on, her heart fracturing into a thousand pieces but she pushes on. She will get to Howie and if he's dead then she will die too. If he's turned she will kill him then die too.

Forty

The infection has Howie. It sent wave after wave at them but finally, now after thirteen days it has the special one.

The patterns it created worked perfectly and drew Howie away from the others. It wanted him isolated and alone and in the end an opportunity arose for the purest source of the infection to be passed. Straight from the still beating heart into his mouth, so the blood can drip down his throat and be ingested directly.

It has Howie.

The objective is complete.

Those special few across the world can now be understood and the power they have can be used to take more hosts.

The infection will survive and it will succeed.

The Undead Day Thirteen

Forty One

The infection was in the finger severed by Howie's mouth. The infection was in the juices of the eyeball that burst and dropped into Howie's mouth. The infection was in the heart that pumped thick arterial blood into Howie's mouth.

The infection did what it has always done and attacked the cells. Entering the blood stream it was carried round the body in seconds. Attacking every cell within his form. Organs were attacked. Nerves were attacked. Veins and skin cells were attacked.

The blood pumped the infection into the brain and that too was attacked.

Of all the battles that Howie has been in since the event happened; none of them are as one sided as the battle taking place inside his own body.

The infection drives on and within minutes it is in every part of his body. And within minutes it has turned not a single cell.

Instead, Howie's body takes the natural anti-body it has and produces more of it. It produces lots of it.

Then those anti-bodies go into the bloodstream and remove the infection. The battle is one sided as the anti-bodies are far, far stronger than the infection. It is eradicated and removed. It ceases to be.

Howie's heart pumps the pure blood and kills the infection. In turn, the infection senses the loss taking place and tries to counter-act by mutating and burying deep within tissues. But the anti-bodies are ruthless and seek them out.

The infection now knows why Howie is feared.

He cannot be turned.
He is immune.

18463980R00315

Printed in Great Britain
by Amazon